Confessions of a Fellow
'Einstein in Flamingo...

"addictive—the surreal journey of a likeable eccentric that gets more colorful with every chapter. It has everything, zero fields, aliens, mystery, witchery—Magic was in the air at the Maui shore where the author wove the fates of his enigmatic characters."

  Ashen Venema – Author
  Course of Mirrors

"very, very clever; worth the read on cleverness alone."

  K.C. Hart – Author
  A Summer Rose

"a treasure. Is this guy nuts or is something really going on here? Each character has a story worth telling. Yet it is the wacky stream-of-consciousness ramblings of the narration that puts *Einstein in Flamingoland* over the top."

  PD Allen – Author
  Murderer's Sky

"riveting stuff, extraordinarily moving, beautifully written."

  D. A. Seaby – Author
  Badd

"a wonderfully gentle human journey."

  Monique Grbec – Author
  The Male Influence

"beautifully humorous. Inevitably, parallels will be drawn with this and 'The Hitchhiker's Guide to the Galaxy', but it is much more than that."

  Nicholas Boving – Author
  The Warlock

Einstein in Flamingoland is a novel, by definition a work of fiction. Other than those well-known individuals referred to for purposes incidental to the telling of the tale, names, characters, and events are products of my imagination. Any resemblance to persons, living or dead, in this or any other universe is purely coincidental. This disclaimer is necessary to keep the lawyers at bay and could be a true statement.

g. brinner

https://brinnerart@earthlink.net   www.brinnerart.com

Cover design and graphics by George Brinner

Thank you to Georgette Kaapo'okalani Baldwin and to Timothy Brinner

Paintings by George Brinner – brinnerart.com

The Beach at Keawakapu Oil on Canvas 48"x60"

Canyon Wall II Oil on Canvas 48"x60"

Einstein in Flamingoland

Einstein in Flamingoland

Confessions of a Fellow Traveler

A Novel by

George Brinner

1

Sergeant Tom

They tossed me in a cell with an old redneck jailbird from north of Payson on my first day in Arizona's Winslow Prison. Flat on his back in the top bunk, he didn't bother to look down when the door clanged closed behind me. An hour passed before he acknowledged my presence.

"They're shipping me down to Perryville in the morning," he said. A smoker's rasp underscored his country drawl.

Disoriented and having no idea what he was talking about, I made no reply.

He turned on his side and peered down at me, now prone on the bunk below him.

"You know, in 'eighty-one, I was on the first busload of convicts into Perryville. It was all shiny and new then," he said.

As he droned on, I closed my eyes in the hope that he might disappear and this nightmare end.

"Now, ten years later, here they go hauling me back down there," he said. "It's hotter than blue blazes in that hell-hole too, I can tell you that—it sure don't seem like I'm makin' a whole lot of progress."

"Judging from what you've told me so far, no, it doesn't seem that you are," I said.

I think in jest, the old jailbird bristled some and said he was making a statement, not asking for my opinion. He said my opinion wasn't worth a hill of beans to him and that I should consider keeping it to myself in the future.

"What's your name, son?" He asked, watching intently as I stood and leaned against the cell bars.

"Gille—Gille Barker."

The old man bugged his bloodshot eyes in mock dismay.

"Jill, you say; never met a *man* named Jill," he said. "Your folks must have been a little twisted." He choked on a snorted chortle.

Not wanting to sound disagreeable, I said, "I never asked where they came up with the name and they never told. One thing though–it's spelled G-i-l-l-e, not J-i-l-l, like you might suppose— French I think."

"Well, you *do* realize most of us in here ain't too culturally inclined," the old man said. "I sure wish I could be around long enough to hear you explain that French connection to the boys in the yard—you're liable to get some mixed reviews.

"Safe to say some of 'em won't take too kindly to a spelling bee either, so you might want to take that into consideration."

He snorted another chortle and lobbed a tobacco chaw from his jaw into a rusty old coffee can, inches from my toes.

"What kind of time you look'n at, Gille?"

"Three years."

I was plenty scared now, and he knew it.

"You should be all right, son; just stay with the Caucasians and——"

He paused in mid-sentence and strip-searched me with his eyes, an experience only slightly less humiliating than the real thing I endured two hours before.

"You are a white boy, aren't you?" he finally asked.

"Uh huh."

"Well then, like I was saying, stay close to your own kind. Blacks and beaners might be considered good company where you're from, but this is your world now. Best you don't make eye contact either, at least not until you get the hang of things. And, whatever you do, don't cut in on any kind of line."

He fell back on his bunk and was soon asleep.

2

Although his 'blacks and beaners' reference was disagreeable, it did make sense behavior familiar to me may not be viewed in a favorable light by everyone behind these prison walls. Weighing the options and considering the gravity of my situation, I decided to take his advice on all counts. A few months later I heard the old jailbird dropped dead in the Perryville yard. I never had a chance to thank him.

**

Surviving Winslow prison is no longer a concern of mine as I walk down this stark white corridor with Sergeant Tom Haynes close by my side. The Sergeant fiddles with buttons on his walky-talky, barking reports of our progress to guards in the prison tower. The monotonous clap of his leather-soled shoes bounces off the concrete floor and echoes down the corridor. Harsh fluorescent light turns our flesh ghostly gray.

We approach a massive steel door. An actor in a play of his own design, Sergeant Haynes holds the walky-talky against his lips and feigns a whisper.

"Opening corridor gate one."

The salt and pepper hairs of the Sergeant's walrus mustache rustle with each breath, a breath textured, moist and pungent, like the smell of rotting fish that garnered him his Tommy Tuna moniker among the inmates. His incessant popping of cinnamon Tic-Tacs has scant influence on the unpleasant aroma of a bluefin in decay.

Crackles and screeches from the walky-talky fall into a static calm.

Ron, my old friend from planet Zargon in the galaxy of Dargo that is hundreds of millions of light years but only a short wormhole away, glides along just paces ahead. He looks back. He nods and transmits a smile before passing through the prison's steel door with the ease of a hot knife through jello.

Ron visited me seven times while I was stuck in a cage on Winslow's high desert plateau. He stayed over on occasion, lounging on the empty bunk in my cell, jabbering through the night about this and that in his telepathic way. He was carefree as

3

a weekend vacationer at one of the elite resorts of Wailea on the island of Maui, my home before the State of Arizona saw fit to make me a felon worthy of spending endless days in the company of petty thieves, drug dealers, psychopaths of every stripe, and my fellow victims of circumstance.

**

Sergeant Tom and I stand quietly in front of the prison exit door. A high-pitched garbled voice from his walky-talky breaks the silence.

"Copy that, Sergeant. Opening gate one."

"Ten-four," Sergeant Tom replies.

He clips the walky-talky to his breast pocket and pulls out a double ring of keys bolted to his belt on a retractable spool. He unlocks a metal box mounted to the wall and pushes a red button that begins flashing like a traffic stoplight. A deafening beeping echoes down the corridor as the exit door grinds open on its slider tracks. The spooler snaps the Sergeant's keys back against his belt like jangling trinkets on a yo-yo's yo.

I grip my bag in front of me, my duffle loaded with the few odds and ends I have collected during the last nine hundred fourteen days, and step over a bright red line painted across the threshold.

"Good luck, Gille." Sergeant Tom shakes my hand with both of his. He smiles, revealing teeth that show the nicotine stains of a two pack a day man double-timing his way toward the undertaker's metal slab.

"Why thank you, Sergeant," I say.

But I know Tommy Tuna's wish of 'good luck' has no chance of bringing me any such thing. Luck has nothing more to do with the future than the past, or the present for that matter–it has no meaning in the reality of things.

I have known this truth since Ron, my friend from Zargon, dropped many of life's secrets on me while explaining the workings of the Zargonian evolutionary game–the initial purpose for human existence on this planet. That was soon after our first

4

encounter more than thirty years ago, two nights before my eighth Christmas, in nineteen hundred and sixty-two.

**

I raise my hand above my shoulder and wave a casual Hawaiian shaka of farewell toward Sergeant Tom Haynes as I walk away from the prison for the first and last time. I don't look back. Making that sign of friendship toward my captor after these hundreds of days under his lock and key must seem strange to him, as it would to me if I weren't aware that my programming calls for a polite manner and a civil disposition.

The door grinds back across the slider track and slams shut against its metal casing. I have heard that sound, muffled by prison walls, hundreds of times before while sitting on a bench in the exercise yard, or sipping a cup of coffee in the cafeteria, or lying on my back in my cell divining the secrets of time as it fluttered by. It is the sound of a prisoner's return to the real world– a swindler turned back on his prey–a mugger on the loose once more–a new dawn for those of us not criminally inclined. Yes, I know the sound well.

My time to walk out that door had finally come. Now I rejoin those of you on the other side. I scan across the horizon. Zargon Ron has disappeared for now.

I find myself thinking of Sergeant Tom Haynes, a captive of his own fate. As I consider the mindset that must be in place for a man like the Sergeant to spend thirty years of ten-hour days in voluntary confinement behind Winslow's prison walls, a conversation we once had comes to mind.

**

It was on one of the more tolerable days at Winslow Prison, after I had been locked away for the better part of a year that seemed like ten. I was sitting on the gray hard-pan and gravel of the prison yard, my back against a concrete pillar, my thoughts lost somewhere between the chain-link fence, fifteen-feet high, topped with coiled razor-wire that surrounded me and framed puffs of clouds floating free across the cerulean sky.

5

Sergeant Tom strolled down the fence-line and stopped next to me.

He patted the sweat from his brow with a handkerchief and scanned the horizon, and, for that moment, we might have been kindred spirits with thoughts somehow intertwined.

"Nice day, a hot one though," Tommy said.

"Yes sir. It sure is that."

I stood and dusted the dirt from the back of my pants.

"How long you been doing this, Sergeant?" I asked.

"Doing what? Oh, you mean how long have I been a prison guard?"

I nodded.

"A little over twenty-seven years now—only three to go. Think of that, Gille," said Sergeant Tom, "you'll be out of here before I am."

His crooked smile betrayed the irony of his condition.

I told the Sergeant it didn't seem as though he was looking forward to his retirement, and he said that might be so. What was he going to do on the 'outside'? What job was he qualified to do in the *real* world?

"Who the hell's going to hire an old prison guard?" he said.

Tommy had the same fears as those of a lifer up for parole after spending most of his days locked behind prison walls. Life without his peculiar prison in it was going to be a scary thing for Sergeant Haynes. Turn a thief or drug dealer back on the streets and he can always find a liquor store to stick up or someone willing to pay for a gram or two, but what can the future hold for an old prison guard?

Greeter positions at Walmart are in short supply.

Behind the walls of Winslow Prison Tommy was 'Sergeant Haynes', a position that gave him at least the semblance of self-respect most can only seek.

Those days would be gone.

"Gene over at the Standard station said he might have a job for me pumping gas," said Sergeant Tom. "If that doesn't work

out, I could probably bag groceries part-time at the Safeway. There's not much more I can hope for."
**

As dire as his situation seemed to him that day, I knew Tommy's fate will be far more grim than he suspected.

You see, there are times that I'm transported as an observer to the site of future events in other people's lives as well as my own.

I've been blessed or damned with this ability since that first meeting with Zargon Ron thirty some years ago. At that time Ron told me I would learn to embrace my new powers of 'selective omniscience', as he called it— 'it's a gift', he said. But, because of this 'gift', I often, and without warning, find myself hurled through spacetime to places I don't want to go.

My travels are into the past as well as the future and even alternate realities of present spacetime. You might say I am omniscient, all-knowing, for those moments, but these events are random, unexpected, and beyond my control. There is nothing 'selective', as I had been led to believe, about the process unless it is from the Zargonian point of view.

Whatever you want to call it, what I see is often disconcerting, as it was when I saw three years into Sergeant Tom's future while he stood there next to me in the prison yard.

Sergeant Tom, Billy Jean, and Polaris

My venture into Sergeant Tom's future began on the day before the new year of nineteen ninety-three, two months after his retirement dinner where Warden Jacobs handed the Sergeant a silver-plated watch before escorting him to the prison's exit door.
**

An orange sun sits on the dusty horizon as Tom pulls his old Ford pickup into Winslow's Kentucky Fried Chicken takeout lane. He would have chosen the Safeway across the road; it was half the price, but Kentucky Fried had always been his wife, Billy Jean's, favorite, and her favorite is what he wants on this night.

7

Sarah Bale hands Tom his box of fried chicken parts through the Colonel's pick-up window. He has known Sarah since she was no more than six or seven and her daddy began to bring her along on his Saturday afternoon outings at Bucky's Billiards Parlor.

"Happy new year, Sarah," Tom says, "and tell your daddy I said hello."

"I sure will, and you have a great new year too, Mister Haynes."

**

Tom plops the box of Kentucky Fried on his living room coffee table. He grabs the last can of Blue-Ribbon beer from his refrigerator. He clicks the television on and a head babbling news materializes on the screen. He sits on the sofa, pops the top on his beer, and opens the Colonel's cardboard box to reveal a tub of mashed potatoes and two chicken legs, extra crispy.

I ordered original recipe. Couldn't they get it right this one time?

Tom stirs the mashed potatoes with a Colonel's plastic fork. He stares blankly past the reporter affecting his concern for a dozen or so dead bodies scattered across a burning field that appear to be at his back but are a world away from his green-screen's fabricated reality.

The talking head cuts to commercial. Tom sips from his can of beer, and a blue-eyed woman with sparkling teeth tells him he will be in good hands if he buys insurance from Allstate.

Sergeant Tom walks across the living room to the entry closet and puts on his old uniform jacket, adjusting it just so in the hallway mirror. From a shoebox on the closet shelf, he takes his loaded S&W Model 10 revolver and stuffs it in his pants pocket. He walks out the back door to the patio deck he built sixteen years ago for his beautiful bride, Billy Jean.

Not more than a month after Tom hammered the last nail into that patio deck, Billy Jean found a lump the size of a popcorn seed below the nipple of her breast– probably nothing. Billy Jean died in his arms in the early days of that spring. They were sitting on the same wooden bench swing he is sitting on now.

Tom rests his heels against the deck floor and rocks the swing. He swivels his head back in search of the Big Dipper in the clear northern Arizona sky, the way he had on his last night with Billy Jean when she asked him to point it out for her again, the way she had asked him many times before.

"I miss you, sweetheart," Tommy says to the Big Dipper and Polaris as they speed away in the ever-expanding Universe.

**

All my trip into the future of Tom Haynes came to me in moments. I didn't tell the Sergeant what I was seeing as we stood there near the fence-line of the prison yard. Warning him of his fate would have been pointless. I was aware there was no way to change the course of things. He wouldn't have believed me anyway.

It all fell back to what Zargon Ron said to me soon after we first met— "My advice is that you tell no one of our conversations," Ron said. "Ridicule is the only reward you will receive from people with no memory of a similar experience if you suggest you've had contact with alien beings."

Ron wasn't kidding about that. With only one disastrous exception, when I was very young and new to the game, I have followed Ron's advice. My lips have remained sealed.

"Oh, I wouldn't worry too much Sergeant," is what I did say that day in the yard when Tom Haynes voiced his concern about what retirement might bring. "Something always turns up, you know."

Sergeant Tom folded his arms in front of him and stood there for a moment gazing up at those puffs of clouds floating free above Winslow State Prison. He turned and slowly walked away.

"Take care of yourself, Gille," he said.

"You too, Sergeant—you too."

**

Back on my trip into Sergeant Tom's future, wind whistles through the patio bench swing chains.

9

The Sergeant shudders.

With no sign of recognition, he stares at the revolver in his hand that has been his since before he became a guard at Winslow Prison.

The nearly full moon glistens against the gun barrel.

In my all-seeing, but impotent, state, I can only watch Sergeant Tom stick the end of that barrel under his chin and squeeze the trigger. I am witness to that moment of doubt that flickers in a man's eyes when he realizes he has reached a point of no return. Powder explodes as the hammer strikes down. It's the first shot Tommy Tuna has ever fired at a living thing.

Bull's-eye.

2

Lightfoot

For the first time in nine hundred and fifty-four days no wall or barbed wire separates me from you. But I'm still in Winslow, Arizona, and would be hard pressed to tell this side of the wall from the other if not for the simultaneous feelings of relief and anxiety that accompany my return to freedom.

The sky disappears in a bone-chilling Winslow winter zephyr that blows clouds of powdered clay across the high desert plateau. I lean into the wind. A gust struggles to wrest my duffel from my grasp.

Holding my free arm up to shield my eyes, I push on, lumbering up the steep entry-road grade toward the last guard station between the prison confines and the 'real' world. Outside the station, a taxi should be waiting to take me the few miles to Winslow's La Posada Hotel, where I plan to spend my precious first nights as a free man.

**

The wind subsides as I approach the guard station. I take note of an old four-door Chevy Impala flattop sedan parked to the side. It appears someone is in the process of turning this sixty's classic into a homage to the more questionable tastes of its time.

There's chrome everywhere and huge whitewall tires on fancy wire rims. Dueling antennae slant back at sixty-degree angles from each rear fender. Recently painted, the hood and flattop sparkle like metallic blueberries, even though covered with a dusty glaze. Since the rest of the Chevy's body is primer gray and under repair, I can only imagine what the owner has in mind.

When I reach the gate a guard waves me through without question. Other than a prison wagon, the blueberry Chevrolet is the only car there. Seeing that I'm looking his way, a lanky young man propped against the Chevy's front fender stands and adjusts the brim of his well-seasoned Stetson off his brow.

"You Mister Barker?" he says.

I nod. "Yes, I'm Gille Barker."

"Nice to meet you, sir," he says. "I'm Jeff–Jeff Lightfoot, your driver." He shakes my hand. "Here, let me take that."

He pulls my treasured leather duffel, my sole companion in travels from Maui to Mykonos and so many stops between, from my grip. He tosses it on top of rust-spotted tools and oily car parts scattered across the car trunk's grungy floor. He fastens a bungee that had been dangling from the back pocket of his jeans to the trunk's latch, loops it around the back bumper, and pulls the lid closed. He opens the back driver-side door.

"Here you go, Mister Barker", he says, motioning for me to get in. He doesn't wait for me to take my seat before climbing behind the wheel.

As I'm sliding onto the seat, Lightfoot hits the gas. The car lurches in reverse. The door slams closed as I reach to pull it shut. I'm pitched forward. My forehead bangs against the beaded trim on the front seat as the two-ton classic careens fins first toward the highway a hundred yards behind.

Bone white gravel and dust fly from the tires and pepper two guards leaning against the exit gate portico. Their arms remain folded across their bellies. Their heads swivel only slightly as we speed away. I can feel the slow-burn in their eyes through the silver plating of their aviator glasses.

Jeff spins the steering wheel hard left, and the Chevy beast sways into a ninety-degree turn onto the highway. He slams on the brakes as he steps on the clutch and throws the stick-shift arm hanging from the steering column into first gear. He plunges the gas pedal toward the floor.

Prone on the nose of the blueberry hood is a bare-breasted chrome goddess with angel's wings spread wide. As the Chevy squats low on its rear tires, the chrome lady rises and points north toward a bank of dark clouds hanging on the horizon above Winslow town. Matching black plumes of burned rubber float up behind the Chevy's rear tires and meld into the leaden gray sky.

Lightfoot reaches for the nub of the Marlboro cigarette clinched between his teeth with the coolness of James Dean in a couple of movies he managed to make before accidentally bumping himself off.

Sparks fly as the cigarette paper sticks to Lightfoot's lip and his fingers slip down across the fire. The cigarette, flaming ashes hanging from its tip, falls between his legs. With smoke curling up from his crotch, Lightfoot thrusts himself up from the seat, his right foot driving the gas pedal to the floor.

"Jesus Christ!" he says.

The engine screams for Lightfoot to shift gears before it blows into so many pieces of metal rubble. He scrambles for the cigarette butt and quickly flicks it out the window. His foot slips off the clutch pedal as he grinds into third gear. I lean back in my seat and look to my sides—there is no seat belt.

"My sister's brat kid cut all the buckles off the straps with one of those box cutter knives."

I look up and see Lightfoot's crooked smile looking back at me in the rear-view mirror.

"I stuck what was left of the straps down that crack in the seat," he says. "You can dig them out and tie yourself in if you want. I never really saw much use for the things myself."

"Yes, they can be a nuisance," I say while anxiously attempting to tie the straps together across my lap.

"How long are you staying at the Posada, Mister Barker?" Lightfoot asks. He adjusts his mirror to better view me while awaiting my reply.

I answer quickly, hoping to encourage his focus on the highway ahead rather than my mirrored image.

"I'm not sure," I say.

Visions of me crashing through the front window and flipping end over end when Lightfoot smashes his taxi head-long into the John Deere tractor rapidly closing on us from the north reel through my mind.

Splat! I look out the side window in time to see my head explode against one of the creosote telephone poles rushing by at rapidly increasing speeds. My body slowly slides down the pole and collapses at its base in a pile of jumbled parts like Ray Bolger's scarecrow after a run-in with the wicked witch. Music crescendos—Judy Garland and the Tin Man skip by on a yellow brick road.

"Not more than a few days though," I say.

My head snaps around to watch through the rear window as the John Deere whisks by in a bright green and yellow blur. The Cowardly Lion hangs from the back of the tractor's seat by one front paw. Wind blows his mane over his shoulders and into his eyes. He smiles and acknowledges me with a boy-scout three-claw salute before the tractor fades into a distant swirl of dust and sage.

"Well, if you need a driver or help finding something special in this neck of the woods, I'm your man," says Lightfoot. He winks at me in the rear-view mirror and reaches back to hand me his 'business card', a piece of white construction paper cut to size with his name and a phone number printed neatly in black ink on one side.

"I can find about anything you want found around these parts, and I know Flagstaff better than the back of my hand—you know what I mean?" He shows me the back of his hand.

**

I'm certain I know what he means, and yes, I do need a driver, but not for what Lightfoot has in mind. If I plan to legally cross an Arizona state line, I will need a ride to Flagstaff for my parole office appointment in eight days, and before I return home to Maui, I should take a trip to Scottsdale. Despite my gallery director's best efforts there, painting sales have taken a harder hit than expected during my stay in Winslow prison.

I could handle all of that on my own if my driver's license hadn't expired seven months ago while I was out skidding on my knees across the prison yard baseball diamond's center field of rock shards, clay, and stones in a fortuitously vain attempt to retrieve a pop-up off the bat of our cell block's only known serial killer.

Crownose Crocket was his unlikely name. Crownose was doing life without parole for throttling his neighbor, a preacher's wife, with her own clothesline cord. At his sentencing Crownose made it clear that, although he found her snooty attitude annoying, he had no real quarrel with the woman. He offered no apology.

**

Sticking Lightfoot's card in my jacket pocket with one hand, I brace against the door with the other as he makes a sharp right turn up the steep drive into La Posada's parking lot. He skids the car to a stop at the front entry stirring up a cloud of dust that powders a row of out-of-state rental cars and Ford pickups sporting Arizona plates with racked shotguns across their back windows.

My bag from the trunk already in his hand, Lightfoot unlatches the passenger door.

"Here we go, Mister Barker," he says.

**

I had been to La Posada before, but not as a free man, and never at the front door. I had helped program the computers in La Posada's cellar offices on a convict work release program arranged by the new liberal-leaning hotel owners, who, although beautiful people, suffered in the belief there was more good than evil in the worst of human beings — understanding and a show of respect would put any strayed soul back on the right track. They had most certainly never met a Crownose Crocket.

The hoteliers came from Southern California to this wide spot on a high desert road and turned a once treasured relic of a railroad waystation, only days from the wrecker's ball, into a first-class hotel. They did that in a town with little going for it other than faded memories of the glory days of Route 66 and an anthem by the Eagles and Jackson Browne that made Winslow a symbol of last resort for a generation of dreamers and disenchanted souls.

I had even sampled a mesquite-grilled hamburger smothered in goat cheese with Kula onions and sweet pickles and fresh-sliced red tomato from the kitchen of La Posada's world-class chef. His wife, Patricia, a computer illiterate then, smuggled the burger to my desk as a reward for allowing her to drain what little knowledge I had of the workings of a computer from my brain into her own.

Having not been there, you could not know how good that hamburger was to me after nearly a year of generically bland prison chow made more so by the necessity for mediocrity in the effort to please every special interest group on the planet. There were Blacks, Whites, Mexicans, and American Indians on my cell block. There were twin brothers from the Philippines. There was a snake worshiper. There were Christians, Jews, Muslims, and plenty of atheists to go around.

All of them, even the atheists, had their own champion insisting there be nothing on the prison menu that might risk offending their charges. The prison kitchen couldn't put out a decent meal even if the powers-that-be had been so inclined.

But, though I had been treated to that most wonderful of ground meat treats in the bowels of La Posada, I had never seen the elegantly carved front entry doors, or anything else a guest might have seen, unless they had accidentally stumbled across our cellar entrance in the back of the hotel next to the garbage man's slop barrels of left over elk medallions in cherry sauce, wild turkey pâté, churl lamb, and black bean soup awaiting his rounds.

**

That garbage man, as Jeff Lightfoot would soon inform me, is his cousin, Luke.

Luke has picked up those containers every other day since La Posada reopened its doors three years ago. A farmer, Luke slops the gourmet scraps scraped from the Turquoise Dining room's sated patron's plates into a pair of wooden troughs, each twenty feet long, for the dining pleasure of his hundred squealing pigs. The pigs are more than happy to line up on cue for their daily sampling of Arizona's finest regional fare.

"Let me tell you, those are some happy pigs," Jeff would soon tell me. "At least they're happy till Cousin Luke turns them into pork chops and slabs of bacon and pickled pig's feet. Best damned bacon you ever tasted, I can tell you that, Mister Barker. No need to take my word for it though—you can sample some when they recycle those porkers back through the kitchen with your scrambled eggs in the morning."

Jeff thought that was funny. I had to smile.

**

As we approach, the massive double entry doors to La Posada silently swing open.

"This is for sure one beautiful place. Don't you think so, Mister Barker?" Lightfoot says.

We cross the front entry corridor on large random-shaped flagstone slabs surrounded by stucco walls in shades of pastel green, Indian orange, and pearl. Rising to a peak of thirty feet, the creamy white ceiling is trimmed with rustic wooden beams and elaborate chandeliers of silver, painted metal, and precious desert stones.

Large, Bosch-like paintings of wonderfully eccentric characters and unexpected places in tinted cadmiums and shimmering shades of gray adorn the walls. It is beautiful all right.

"Yes, Mister Lightfoot, it certainly is," I say.

A young Indian woman, her jet-black hair in a single braid that hangs to her lower back, watches our approach from behind the high counter at the registration desk. She smiles to greet us. Deep dimples crease her cheeks. Anna Towahongva is her name, and she is as stunningly beautiful as any artist's portrayal.

**

Undeterred by harsh winters and crippling summer droughts, Anna's Hopi ancestors endured for hundreds of years on these northern Arizona mesas. Despite their grim reality, Anna's father and his father and his father before him fired beautiful pieces of clay that told stories of their Maker's love for the earth and the sky and the eagles that glide on the wind. They voiced praise for the spirits who had seen fit to provide for their survival, and they did survive, and in their way flourish on this high desert plateau.

All of that was before the white man came to town. These days, unless you go to one of the reservation casinos, a Hopi Indian is about as hard to find in Arizona as a pure-blooded Hawaiian in Waikiki.

**

"Good morning," Anna says. Her face is the color of light chocolate cream. Her gaze stops for only a moment on Jeff Lightfoot before moving to me. She nods and her smile widens, as if in recognition of a long-lost friend. Anna glances at her watch. It is a quarter past noon.

"Or, good afternoon, I should say." The coal black pupils of her eyes sparkle with rubies and sapphires in light filtered through a stained-glass dining room window, thirty feet away.

Without taking his eyes from Anna, Lightfoot gives a slight tip of his head toward me.

"This is Mister Barker," he says to Anna. "I think you're expecting him."

Lightfoot drops my duffel to the floor with a thud. A cloud of Chevrolet trunk dust rises from the bag ever so slightly before falling to the freshly polished flagstone floor.

I reach across the counter to shake Anna's hand.

"Good afternoon, Anna," I say.

"Welcome to the La Posada, Mister Barker," she replies.

Anna knows who I am. She knows the state saw fit to release me from prison this morning after almost three years behind bars. She knows I am a somewhat famous artist from the island paradise of Maui, three thousand miles and an ocean away from the Arizona home where her Hopi Indian tribe was left to the inhospitable dust bowl north of Winslow town.

She knows how I came to be a jailbird. She knows the cop who plowed his squad car into the rear of the Oldsmobile I was driving the night of my arrest was full of vodka. She knows it was fortunate I fired my incompetent attorney and took it on myself to point out to the court the cop was intoxicated at the time of the crash that took his and his partner's lives.

When I think about how close I came to a lifetime behind bars cold sweat collects on my brow. It is collecting there right now, even though I know that scenario just wasn't meant to be.

In this small town where most of the population owes its paycheck to the human incarceration game, it is not surprising that Anna, or anyone else living in Winslow, would know these things about me. My story was already circulating through Winslow's gossip mills before the bus dropped me, cuffed and shackled, at the prison's front gate.

But now, since Anna and I have met, she knows something about me the other citizens of Winslow do not. Anna knows I am one of the few earthlings allowed by our creators from planet Zargon to retain conscious knowledge of the Zargonian evolutionary game, the true reason for life on this planet.

It takes one to know one.

3

The Einstein Room

"We have you in the Einstein suite, Mister Barker," Anna says, handing me a key taken from one of dozens of wooden cubicles on the wall behind her. She points to an open line near the center of the page in a leather journal on the counter. "Sign there, sir," she says, "and we'll have you on your way."

I scribble my name across the line.

Lightfoot smiles. "Been a while since anyone called you 'sir', huh, Mister Barker," he says.

"A while, yes," I say, addressing my reply to Anna, "and I would much prefer 'Gille' to 'Sir', if you don't mind, Anna."

"Gille it is then," Anna says, reaching across the counter to shake my hand again as if we were now meeting for the first time.

I stand there, as if spellbound by the softness of her touch, her hand held in mine.

Lightfoot grabs my duffel by the strap and throws it on his shoulder.

"Okay," he says, breaking my moment, "follow me, Mister Barker."

**

Jeff leads me across the lobby and up the stairs to the second floor.

He opens the door to the Einstein suite, walks across the room, and tosses my bag onto the foot of the old-fashioned canopy bed. He pushes the bathroom door open wide.

"I think you're going to like this." Lightfoot flips the bathroom light on. "This Jacuzzi is killer, a double—bet you haven't seen many of those, huh, Mister Barker."

I had *never* seen a bathroom with a Jacuzzi of any kind. I could barely remember taking a shower without the feeling at least one of my fellow convicts was surveilling my every move. Lounging in the warm swirling waters of my own private Jacuzzi is a far distance from that picture.

"No, Jeff," I say. "I believe this is the first I've seen."

"Yeah, this is a killer room all right." Lightfoot sits on the edge of the bed and bounces. "Nice and firm," he says. He flashes a sly grin. "Queen size too—gives you plenty of room, in case you need it, if you know what I mean."

"I believe I do," I say.

"There's a great Jacuzzi in the Howard Hughes room but the bed is a little soft for my liking," Lightfoot says. "Now, if you're looking for extra firm, you might give the Bob Hope or Charlie Lindbergh a try."

My cab driver's personal knowledge of La Posada's accommodations has no discernable bounds.

Lightfoot pops up from the bed and walks to the window. He pulls back the opaque window drape. "It's still blowing, but kind of a nice day out there," he says.

"Yes, it is," I say, with no conviction. Ominous black clouds are working their way toward Winslow from the north-west. A winter storm is brewing.

"Uh-huh." Lightfoot's thoughts are wandering as he walks toward the door and plops down on an antique-looking lounge chair.

"But the bed in the Carole Lombard room is my favorite," he says. He leans forward and continues, speaking in a confidential sort of way.

"I've been told, by reliable sources, Carole split the sheets in there one morning with Gene Autry and Tom Mix before coffee and croissants. A threesome back in those days, Mister Barker—

can you imagine that? Of course, that's only a rumor and wouldn't have been on the mattress that's in there today anyway."

"I would assume the sheets have also been changed," I say.

The wit of my repartee rates no notice by Lightfoot.

"I was told they rode horses the five miles out to the reservation afterward and were back in time for happy-hour at the Martini Lounge," Jeff says. "I asked my grandfather if he remembered anyone like that and he said he *did* recall three folks who fit the general description coming to the reservation back in those days, but he couldn't say it was them for sure. I ran across a picture of Gene Autry a couple of months later and showed it to grandpa. He said the guy sure looked familiar all right, but he couldn't say it was him he saw."

"There's always that possibility," I say.

"Could be so. Anyway, like I said, Carole's room has the best bed now, but there's no Jacuzzi. I guess a woman like that wouldn't need one."

"Really? And why not?" I say.

"Just seems to me there would have been plenty of Jacuzzis available for the likes of a Carole Lombard."

"Well, I can't argue with that, Mister Lightfoot," I say.

I do not ask Lightfoot how he knows these things or who his 'reliable source' might be when it came to the goings on of Carole Lombard. It has become apparent Jeff should be asked questions only by those with an abundance of time on their hands.

"Can I help you with anything else before I go?" Jeff says, as I edge him toward the door.

"No, Jeff." I hand him a five-dollar bill. "Really, thank you. All I want is rest. I haven't had a good night's sleep in four days."

Lightfoot's eyes light up. "I have just the thing," he says. He digs into his pocket and pulls out a silver pillbox. He takes three red capsules from the box and hands them to me. "There you go," he says.

"What are these?"

"Take one tonight—one should do the trick. You'll feel like a new man in the morning, guaranteed. You can trust me on that, Mister Barker."

I wonder what he means when he says, 'you can trust me on that,' —were there other matters likely to bring his trust to question?

"Maybe I will give one a try—how much are they?"

"No charge for you, Mister Barker."

What does he mean, 'no charge for me'? Is Lightfoot in the habit of charging for pills? Is he some sort of drug dealer, a dope peddler, the Winslow candy man?

"Thank you, Jeff," I say. I open the door.

"Well, thank you, Mister Barker," Lightfoot says, as he takes a slight step backward into the hall. "You have my number—just give me a jangle."

"All right, Jeff. I'll keep you in mind," I say. He is still hanging onto the knob as I push the door closed.

**

Relief washes through me as I latch the deadbolt. Alone at last, I listen to the quiet, waiting for the incessant chatter of convicted felons that ricochets through cell bars and off the concrete walls of every prison — the hubbub of a madhouse — the din of a cuckoo's nest. I instinctively brace for one of the sudden bursts of rage that erupt like clockwork in Winslow prison, the hollow sounds of forced laughter from across a corridor, the boisterous threats of bodily harm, the string of expletives from a tortured soul, the occasional bone-chilling scream from a victim of threats fulfilled. For the first time in two and a half years, there is only the wonder of silence.

Relief is the right word. Hollywood, the movies made there, would have you believe only two things are on the mind of a convict when he is first released from prison—find a seedy bar, drag up a stool, toss down a couple of shots of whiskey, and then get laid by the first bar fly of his gender preference that happens to darken the barroom door.

But that is not the reality of it, at least not mine. I feel only fatigue, the fatigue I imagine a soldier must feel after months of combat he had thought might never end. Whiskey and getting laid by a stranger are the farthest things from my mind.

I pull the heavy drapes closed and climb into bed. Within moments the unfamiliar silence takes on a weight all its own. My mind races. Too tired to sleep, I switch on the bedside lamp and sit on the edge of the bed, aimlessly thumbing through pages of La Posada brochures and tourist pamphlets from the nightstand drawer. A pamphlet points out that I am indeed in the Einstein suite, named, of course, after Albert Einstein, the world's most famous physicist, the man who reshaped our understanding of the cosmos with his concepts of the nature of space and time.

According to this pamphlet, Albert was a guest at La Posada during this railroad hotel's golden age, as was F.D.R., Charles Lindbergh, Will Rogers, Harry S. Truman, and a host of other world leaders and celebrity types of their day. The new hoteliers named La Posada's suites after those famous guests like so many sandwiches on the menu of a Phoenix fast food restaurant I once visited.

I turn the light off and slip down until I am flat on the bed.

Rejecting sleep, my mind races back to the day I ordered that fast food restaurant's 'Roy Rogers Combo', a greasy hamburger topped with bacon and a slab of cold cheese on a bun smothered in mayonnaise accompanied by a side of soggy fries. After spending the night on my knees puking into our toilet, my partner at the time took the opportunity to suggest a better choice might have been the Dale Evans tuna salad and a bag of chips.

I turn the light on and prop my head up against a pillow.

It is forty-five minutes past noon according to the bedside clock. I close my eyes. My mind jumps from Will Rogers' twirling lasso to giant slabs of sizzling bacon and on to the crippled F.D.R wheeling his clunky chair across the grassy lawns of Saratoga. I make mental notes to search the Shirley Temple suite for a stashed bottle of grenadine and the Howard Hughes for errant toenails—I reach under the covers to casually inspect my own.

My thoughts are disturbingly unfunny when I am sleep deprived.

**

I switch off the light. I lower myself onto my back and stare up into the dark. My eyes close. My mind races past Roy Rogers and Dale Evans and Trigger to Charlie Lindbergh on his solo flight from New York to Paris.

Charlie, strapped to a wicker chair, is skimming across the Atlantic waves at ninety miles per hour in the bare-bones cockpit of his Spirit of Saint Louis. A foggy mist coats his goggles with sprays of instant ice while he fights the demons of suspended consciousness. Charlie searches for land through his periscope and sees the coast of Ireland on the distant horizon. His fuel is low. Will landfall come too late for Charlie?

A hamburger the size of a cocktail table with onions and lettuce and a sweet pickle as big as a cucumber appears, suspended in space below the canopy of my bed. My eyes snap open in time to save Charlie from crashing into a giant tomato floating by on the Irish sea.

I turn on the bedside lamp and walk to the bathroom for a glass of water before crawling back into bed. Lightfoot's capsules sit on the nightstand. Are they harmless sleeping pills? If I take one of those capsules, will a pack of purple jackals come visit me as I sleep, tear my heart from my chest and have it for breakfast? Not likely.

I pop two in my mouth and swallow. I plump my pillow, pull the bed covers over my shoulders, and curl up on my side.

**

Though I surmise it is only late afternoon when I.am awakened, the room is dark except for light filtering through a crack under the hallway door. I sit up and lean against a stack of pillows in fresh silk cases propped against my bed's Cherrywood headboard. There is a figure at the foot of my bed sitting in a big, overstuffed lounge chair. The sliver of light from the hallway silhouettes the figure's rounded shoulders and bushy hair. I blink and rub my eyes, but the figure does not disappear.

"Who's there?" I ask.

"Good evening, Gille."

I know that voice.

I turn on the bedside lamp. My jaw drops.

"Mister Einstein?" I say.

He.is Einstein all right. There is no mistaking the man I see. And I now know he, as am I, is one of that chosen few, the earthlings who retain awareness of the Zargonian evolutionary games, the sole reason for life's turbulent existence on our planet. And, of course, he knows that about me.

**

"Yes Gille, I am Einstein, as if you didn't know," Einstein says.

He pushes off his chair's wide arms to a standing position, stretches his legs, and shuffles across the carpet to the bedroom window.

Einstein parts the drapes. He gazes up toward the cloudless sky at earth's full moon, lost in thoughts of what might have been. What if he had been less self-absorbed, less selfish in his search for confirmation of those theories presented to him by alien beings from the planet Zargon in the galaxy of Dargo, so close yet so far away?

Jesus. How could I have given up my only daughter to a fate I did not know? And Mileva. "They didn't deserve—"

"Did you say something, sir?" My question cuts Einstein short in mid musing.

"No. No, I was just thinking; just looking at the moon, Gille, just looking at the moon."

Einstein's brown wing-tips are scuffed with wear. His baggy, gray pants, cuffed short of his shoe tops, reveal sockless ankles nearly as white as my silk bed linens. His left arm rests across his stomach. He absently strokes one bushy gray sideburn. His famous profile appears, ghost-like, perfectly framed in the reflection from a windowpane. His thoughts are far away as he continues to gaze past the stars and into the total darkness of space

26

to unseen stars in this galaxy and this universe and then on to another and another.

I turn toward the man who is, arguably, the greatest of all earth's theorists and sit up, feet dangling over the side of the bed. I yawn and rub sleep from my eyes.

"What are you doing here, Mister Einstein?" I ask.

Einstein reels around to look at me, throws his hands, palms up, out in front of his chest, and shrugs his shoulders.

"Hey, this *is* the Einstein Suite, you know." He does a double take toward the door like a comedian timing his exit punchline. "What —you want I should leave?" he says.

"Of course not, Mister Einstein."

Einstein shuffles back across the room. He plops down on the dark velvet chair at the end of my bed where he first appeared to me. He rests his palms on the chair's wide arms. His body relaxes and melds into the deep chair cushions.

"Albert—please call me Albert, if you don't mind," he says.

"Well then, Albert," I say, "may I ask you a question?"

"Why yes, Gille, of course. Fire away."

**
The exact question I asked that triggered his response escapes me now, but Albert tells me he had occasional fits of remorse about taking all the credit for the E=mc² business.

"I had been stuck for months–so close. It was like my brain had been drained. There was no more water in the well," he says.

"Lucky for me, Mileva was one smart gal. If she hadn't found the key to that simple thing that had eluded me, I might never have found the answer—no telling how long she had been holding that little gem in her pocket," he mutters, seemingly with a sense of new-found suspicion.

"Don't be so hard on yourself, sir. You needed rest, you know, some time off to recharge the old battery," I say. "The solution would have come to you in time."

"Maybe so, Gille, but that's not the point is it."

Einstein looks away. Lost again in his thoughts of Mileva and Lieserl and their time together in Zurich a hundred years and more past now. He slowly twirls his unruly mustache between his thumb and fore-finger.

Einstein leans forward. He motions for me to move closer so that I can better hear what he is about to say.

"I've never told anyone of this, Gille," Einstein says, "not even Gödel, and I told him almost everything. The little guy could bleed a turnip, I swear."

Albert's eyes cloud as, in a vision, he and his old friend Gödel, clad in his favorite woolen long-coat, walk down a Princeton sidewalk on another winter day, Einstein's wide-brimmed hat pulled low over the tops of his ears, the cuffs of Gödel's pants nearly scraping the concrete as he shuffles along.

"Gödel was a mousy looking fellow wasn't he," Einstein says.

"I really couldn't say."

"The question was rhetorical, Gille—of course he was, but I loved him just the same."

Einstein turns his head slightly askew and arches a brow. He moves in close, his considerable nose almost touching mine, as he searches my eyes for any sign that revealing his private thoughts to me had not been a lapse in judgement.

"I hope you understand the importance of our conversation remaining in this room," he says.

"Oh, you can count on that, Albert," I say. "Your secrets are safe with me."

4

Dinner at La Posada

My eyes blink open. I click the bedside lamp on to check the time—it is six-thirty p.m. I fall back against my pillow and crook my arm across my eyes against the light.

It is eight when I wake again. I sit up and scan the room. There is no Einstein. Could our conversation have been imagined—only a dream?

The chair where Einstein was sitting is still at the foot of my bed. It's obvious the chair was moved from next to a floor lamp by the window—the chair's footprints remain pressed into the carpet there.

I climb from bed and walk to the window. The window is tightly closed, the lock fastened. I go to the door and twist the doorknob—it does not budge. The deadbolt is in place.

"Albert?" I listen for an answer.

I walk to the bathroom, push back the shower curtain, and turn the hot water to full force. I splash my face with cold water from the sink. When steam wisps over the top of the shower curtain, I drop my boxers and enter the stall. Before stepping under the nozzle, I adjust the water slightly to avoid a scald. I lather my body with a surprisingly refreshing liquid soap, 'compliments of your host and the staff of La Posada.'

I am fascinated by the patterns of freshly scented soapsuds as they curl toward the drain. It is nice to shower without the feeling prying eyes lurk just beyond my peripheral view. I could stay here for hours but get out when I notice my fingertips are shriveled like the skin on dried prunes.

Within moments I'm shaved and dressed and on my way to La Posada's Turquoise Room for this free man's first dinner.

**

While waiting to be seated, I survey the room. Though barely quarter till nine on Friday, there are only nine people in the large dining room. Maybe the hour is late by Winslow standards.

A hush in the air is broken only by the shutter of the kitchen door and the tinkle of crystal. Four couples are scattered at tables around the room. A beautiful woman with long auburn hair sits alone by a window in the far corner, a cup of steaming something cradled in her hands. Her gaze is fixed out the window toward the old red-brick rail station across the hotel veranda. The curl to her lip, the cut of her cheek—something is familiar about the look of this woman.

My fragile concentration is broken by the approach of Anna Towahongva.

"Good evening, Gille," Anna says. "One for dinner?"

"Yes, please," I say. "How about there?"

I point toward a booth against the back wall, not far from the lady with the auburn hair.

Followed by a young waitress, Anna leads me to my table. They wait patiently while I slide across the u-shaped banquette seat to its center so that my back is against the wall. Anna hands me a menu and fills my stemmed glass with iced water while introducing my waitress.

"This is Gwen," Anna says, indicating the girl who had been following her to my table. "She will be your server tonight."

Gwen wishes me a good evening. She addresses me as Mister Barker and I tell her my name is Gille, not Mister Barker. Gwen smiles and a mouth full of silver braces glisten in the warm light of a chandelier.

Looking at her watch, Gwen informs me she has fifteen minutes to get my order to the kitchen–that the kitchen closes at nine.

I tell Gwen I will only need a moment. She asks if I would like something from the bar and I tell her a cold bottle of beer would be highly prized.

**

Though certain of what I want, I open the menu and curiously peruse its listings while waiting for Gwen's return; Wild Turkey Pâté with Cherries and Hazelnuts, Churro Lamb, Honey Glazed Duckling with Braised Leeks and Sausage Dressing, Exotic Mushroom and Walnut Pâté, Wasabi Ice Cream—the selection is surreal in the eyes of this ex-jailbird. I read on.

Fish flown in fresh this morning from Ninilchik, Alaska.

Is that even possible?

I don't think so.

When Gwen returns with my beer from the bar, she has a basket brimming with fresh hot breads and whipped butter that she sets in the middle of the table.

"May I take your order now, sir?" she asks.

"Though these breads look delicious Gwen," I say, "I'm not really interested in a full dinner. I was looking forward to one of your famous beef burgers with goat cheese, but I don't see it on the menu."

"Oh, no problem sir, and you're welcome to the breads anyway. My sister-in-law bakes them fresh every morning—the pumpernickel is to die for."

"I'll give the pumpernickel a try then. Thank you, Gwen."

"Anything else, sir?"

"A glass of Cabernet with my sandwich would be nice."

**

For months, every portion of soupy navy beans ladled on my plate at the prison mess hall had brought visions of a Turquoise Room hamburger to mind.

In a dream that re-ran almost nightly in my cell, I spread Dijon across a toasted bun and piled crisp Romaine lettuce on a fresh-ground patty of Turquoise Room beef smothered in melted goat cheese covered with sautéed sweet onions from the Kula mountainside on the island of Maui, my home in the middle of the

31

Pacific, only to have the dream end as I picked up the sandwich for that first taste.

Yes, it is true—in more than two years, I was never allowed that first bite. Now, how could I forsake the culmination of that overdue experience for a plate of Wild Turkey Pâté?

**

I am down to the last of my Turquoise Room burger that has been almost everything I had hoped for when I look up. The auburn-haired lady is standing squarely in front of my table, somehow transported there without my seeing. She is slender and tall and towers above me in a simple black dress that only accents the beauty of her emerald eyes.

Emerald eyes—Jesus, I do know her!

"Could I have your autograph, Mister Barker?" she says.

"Belinda?"

I barely believe it could be her. I spring from my seat and reach out to touch her hand, knocking my glass of Cabernet crashing to the Flagstone floor.

Gwen and a busboy are quick to the scene with towels and a mop.

I apologize to Gwen for the mess. I wipe the few splashes of wine from the booth seat with my napkin while Gwen and her helper sop wine and shards of crystal from the floor.

Motioning toward the booth, I ask Belinda to join me.

She sits and takes my hand in hers as I slide onto the bench seat beside her.

"It's so good to see you, Gille," she says, ignoring my unease. "I must say, it is remarkable how little you've changed since that night we met at Claire's." She touches my hair. "Of course, you didn't have all this gray, but you *were* a boy then."

I nod. Yes, that is true – I was a boy then.

**

The last time I saw Belinda was nearly twenty years ago. It was soon after her sister Jodi, my fiancée, disappeared from their family's Illinois country estate. Jodi had been killed and buried

32

under the dark clay floor of the deserted railroad depot storage room in Mason City, but neither of us knew that then.

So, what has brought Belinda to Winslow, Arizona now? Why were we destined to meet again after so many years, and why in this remote desert town? There are so many questions I have for Belinda.

As had been the case many times before, lack of self-defense in conversation with this beautiful woman takes control as my mind rushes scrambled signals to my facility for speech.

"Could I buy you a drink?" I manage to say.

**

Three couples sit at cocktail tables sipping after-dinner cordials in La Posada's Martini Lounge. Heads turn as Belinda and I walk through the entry door. I had witnessed this reaction to Belinda sightings before. The allure, the mesmerizing witchery of her presence—whatever you want to call it, her sister Jodi had it too. Her mother Elenore had it in spades.

I pull a stool back from the empty six-stool bar for Belinda and stand next to her. The bartender pushes through the saloon doors from a storage room with a half-dozen bottles of liquor loaded in her arms. Her right shoulder appears painfully disjointed by the load.

"Evening folks, what can I get you tonight?" she says.

Belinda asks for a white Russian on the rocks.

"I'll have a vodka and water with a splash of cranberry in a bucket glass, please," I say, pleasantly surprised by the number of words I had strung together.

"Will this do?" The bartender holds a squat, wide-mouthed glass out in front of me and I see her hand for the first time.

She has only four fingers, one opposing the other three in the way of my own thumb. All appear to be of equal length, thin, and half again longer than *most* people would expect to see. But I am not surprised—this is not the first time I've seen hands like these.

The bartender's fingers are of the same design as those of my alien friend and self-appointed mentor, Zargon Ron. The similarity cannot be denied. What is going on here?

Still holding the glass in front of her, the bartender snaps my train of thought. "Mister Barker? The glass? Will this do?"

"Oh, yes. Of course," I say.

**

I was eight in nineteen sixty-two, thirty some years ago now, when Zargon Ron first appeared outside my bedroom window. I watched quietly when he cupped those strange hands of his to his forehead and peered in at me through the slight opening between the slats of my Venetian blinds. I felt no sense of alarm, nor did I when he passed through my bedroom wall, squatted on the foot of my bed like a Buda, and spoke to me for that first time.

Looking back, the only thing that seems strange to me is that I remember little of that conversation. I do remember asking the Zargonian how it was that he could walk through a solid wall and not just fall through the floor? He mumbled something about a zero-point field and sub-quantum behavior of matter and energy that was naturally beyond my understanding then, and despite university level inquiries since, remains so today.

**

I notice a slight limp as the bartender with alien hands totters to her mixing station. When she turns to make our drinks, I realize carrying the load of bottles was not what caused her shoulder to appear deformed. A goiter the size of a small cantaloupe is perched on the top of her right shoulder like an extra neck-less head bulging under her blouse. A card pinned to her lapel tells me Rhonda is her name.

My mind races back in time. I had seen a goiter like Rhonda's and those same hands on a sultry young bartender in a dive-bar I patronized during my misspent youth. If the two were standing in front of me now, I doubt I could tell them apart. Coincidence would not explain this, even if there were such a thing.

Rhonda sets our drinks on the bar in front of us.

"Thank you, Rhonda," I say.

"Thank you, Mister Barker," she says.

She knows my name. How could that be? She could have heard Belinda call me Gille when we ordered, but there had been

34

no mention of a Barker—Mister, or any other kind. Perhaps the hotel staff is kept so well informed as to know these things about their guests, but that seems unlikely.

"Anything else for you folks?" Rhonda asks.

"That'll do for now," I say.

Nat King Cole comes into the room through the overhead speakers with a song about stardust and lonely nights.

Belinda clicks her glass against mine. "Cheers," she says.

"Yes, of course. Cheers," I reply.

5

A Night at the Martini Lounge

It is ten-thirty and six degrees above freezing when Donkey
Dabbs pulls his old Harley into the La Posada parking lot. His
friend, Buster Dale, passed out since their late-night journey
began fifty miles ago in Flagstaff, bounces across the cobblestone
drive in an ancient side-car next to Donkey.

Donkey and Buster are hard core drug abusers, inveterate
pub-crawlers, and petty thieves. They set out for Winslow tonight
because they had been pitched out of Banger's Pub, Flagstaff's
bar of last resort.

Unaware of their arrival, Belinda and I are ordering our
second cocktails as Donkey and Buster stagger toward La
Posada's front door.

**

Jeff Lightfoot strolls into the Martini Lounge. I acknowledge
him with a tip of my glass.

"Evening, Mister Barker—how's things," Jeff says. He drags
a stool up next to mine.

"Could I buy you a drink?" I say.

"You sure could," Lightfoot says to me before turning his
attention toward the bartender.

"I just took an ear-bending from Hank Toumala all the way
from Prescott. If that doesn't call for a drink, I don't know what
does—right, Rhonda?"

"Maybe you should be more selective about the company you keep," Rhonda says. She flashes a smile at Jeff over her hump while pulling a mug of beer from a spigot on the backbar.

"You're a hard woman, Rhonda, but I still love you," says Lightfoot.

"Keystone and a Jack, I suppose?" Rhonda says, spinning two coasters, one by one, onto the bar in front of Lightfoot.

"Damn, girl," Lightfoot says. "I believe you're getting the hang of this—you might have a future in the bar business after all."

"Lucky for me you don't have any idea what you're talking about," Rhonda says.

"I get the idea you might be a regular around here," I say to Lightfoot.

"He can't stay away from me," Rhonda chimes in.

"Never mind that," Lightfoot says, "are you going to introduce me to your friend, Mister Barker?"

"Oh, excuse me. Belinda, this is Jeff Lightfoot. Jeff gave me a ride to Winslow this afternoon."

Belinda salutes Lightfoot with her glass. "I thank you for that, Mister Lightfoot," she says.

Jeff smiles. "No reason for that, mam. I *am* a cab driver, you know."

"Well, thanks to you anyway, Mister Lightfoot."

**

Rhonda plops Lightfoot's beer down on one of his coasters and a shot glass on the other. She pours whiskey from a bottle of Jack into the shot glass from a foot above and twists off the whiskey neat, just over the line. Rhonda is a pro, whether she likes it or not.

"There you go, big boy," she says to Jeff.

"Thank you, dear," Jeff replies.

"And thank you for the whiskey, Mister Barker." Lightfoot says, clicking his shot glass against Belinda's and then mine. "Here's to your stay at La Posada," he says. "I would add one of those witty Indian proverbs to my toast, but none come to mind."

Jeff leans his head back, tosses the shot of Jack Daniel's between his lips, and swallows. "Oh yeah," he says, "don't take any wooden nickels."

He sets the empty shot glass on the bar and motions Rhonda for another.

Jeff seems edgy. He downs his second shot of Jack. He picks his bottle of beer up from the bar and stands between me and Belinda, his arms draped across the backs of our bar stools. He leans in close and nods toward two gangster-looking types sitting at the table behind us.

"Excuse me while I have a chat with these gentlemen," Lightfoot says.

The younger of the two men has long black hair slicked straight back to the top of his shirt collar. He is slouched in his chair, seemingly only interested in the ice cubes he is swirling in his glass with the tip of his finger.

I guess the other man to be forty-three or four, probably ten years older than his partner.

"Have a seat, Lightfoot," he says.

He sends a chair skidding back from the table with a kick and motions for Jeff to sit.

"Sure thing, Gene," Lightfoot says to the man. "How're you doing, Richard?" he says to the other man. Jeff offers his hand, but there are no takers.

Gene–that voice—I glance over my shoulder for a second look. I know this man but cannot place from where. His googly eyes narrow from behind black-rimmed Buddy Holly glasses. As our eyes meet, the faintest of smiles flickers across his lips. He nods, seemingly in recognition.

It comes to me as I turn away. Bobby Rivera—this Gene guy looks like my old friend, Bobby Rivera. Granted, memory plays games and Gene is about a generation older than Bobby was the last time I saw him, but the resemblance is uncanny.

I tell Belinda that this Gene reminds me of an old college classmate from my art institute days in Chicago.

38

"Even his voice is the same," I say, "and those Buddy Holly glasses with lenses that magnify his googly eyes to the size of ping-pong balls—I never saw anyone but Holly and my friend Bobby wear glasses like those."

I turn discreetly to have another look at the man Lightfoot called Gene.

"I would swear that guy is Bobby Rivera if I didn't know better," I say to Belinda.

"Well, Gille, you were surprised to find me here, but here I am. Maybe this is just a night for reunions," Belinda says.

I glance back over my shoulder for another look at the man.

"Anything is possible," says Belinda

"Well, I know that is a popular position to take," I say, "but Bobby Rivera hanged himself in a Mexican jail fourteen years ago. I helped carry him to his grave. I shoveled a scoop of dirt on his coffin. I'm reasonably certain that man over there can't be Bobby Rivera."

"Now that's just spooky," says Belinda.

I swirl the ice in my own nearly empty glass as I contemplate this Gene guy's face until his eyes meet mine again. This time a chill courses down my spine.

"Should we have another?" I ask Belinda.

"If you insist, Mister Barker," she says.

**

Two obviously intoxicated men stagger across the La Posada lobby toward the Martini Lounge. One stumbles across the bar entry threshold and falls forward, ripping a knee of his Levi jeans. He topples forward and cracks his head against the bar's brass rail, a foot or so from the leg of my stool. A lump the size of a chicken egg pops up on his forehead.

"He hah–damn Buster, that was a good one," snorts his sidekick, who begins an intent search of his pockets with both hands. He paws through some change and tosses a quarter high into the air that rolls to a stop inches from Buster's nose on the barroom floor.

"There you go," he says, "bet you that there quarter you can't do that again. He hah."

Buster fumbles in an unsuccessful effort to pick up the coin. Unsteady, he staggers to his feet. He dabs at blood seeping from his scraped knee with the dirty bandanna that had been tied around his head.

"Shut the fuck up, Donkey," says Buster to his still braying friend.

"He hah," says the Donk. He takes Buster by the arm and leads him toward the empty bar stools. "Come on, Buster, I'll get us a couple of whiskeys."

Donk's laugh *does* sound like a donkey's bray. Like me, I suppose others in the bar now assume that is how this fool came by his name.

"Hey beautiful," Donkey calls out to Rhonda, "how's about a couple of Buds here." He pounds the end of a fresh pack of unfiltered Camels on the bar top, strips the cellophane, and fumbles an attempt to tear the foil from the end of his pack.

"Sorry boys," Rhonda says to Buster and Donkey, "I can't serve you tonight."

"You gotta' be kidding." Holding on to the edge of the bar, Donkey totters back on his heels and gives Rhonda the best side-eye he can muster.

"Why the fuck not?" the Donkey says.

"Because you've had too many already? That works for me," Rhonda says.

Buster looks up. He sees Rhonda for the first time.

"Jesus, woman, what the hell's that thing you got growing alongside your head there?"

Buster reels around toward Donkey. "What the hell, Donk," he says, "I thought we was going out drinking, not to some damn freak show."

"Great, ain't it? He hah," says the Donkey.

Buster reaches in his pocket and pulls out a knife. With considerable concentration, he unfurls the five-inch pocket-knife blade. Holding on to the bar rail with one hand, he slices wildly at the air with gestures meant to be menacing. He closes one eye and sights down the knife blade at Rhonda. "Here—let me carve that thing off there for you, sweetie," he says. "You can thank me later."

"He hah," says the Donk.

Lightfoot jumps up from his chair, grabs a handful of Buster's hair, and slams his already damaged forehead against the top of the bar. He twists Buster's fingers against the back of his hand and the knife clatters to the floor.

The yowling Buster crumples back to his knees.

"Sorry, friend—here, let me help you," Jeff says.

He yanks Buster to his feet and shoves him stumbling out of the Martini Lounge into the lobby. While Buster struggles to gain his footing, Jeff grabs Donkey and then drags and shoves them both across the lobby and out the front door.

Once outside, Jeff pushes Donkey aside, breaks across the parking lot, and races down old Route 66. He runs through downtown Winslow, cuts back across Main Street and up the railroad grade. He crosses the tracks and slides down the other side of the grade into a field of scrub brush and tumbleweeds. Gasping, his lungs burning, Jeff squats with his back braced against the upright floorboards of a discarded railroad handcar lying on its side in the brush.

The sky is clear. Jeff sees the outline of Winslow State Prison and the gases floating up from the prison's giant smokestacks, three miles away. And beyond is the blackness of the winter storm gathering on the horizon.

**

Lightfoot had run halfway across the parking lot before Gene realized he had slipped away.

"Damn it Richard! That son-of-a-bitch took off," Gene says.

"What?"

"Lightfoot—he's gone."

Gene jumps from his chair. Richard grabs his glass and gulps the last of his cocktail. He draws a pistol from his shoulder holster as he and Gene run across the lobby and out the front entry double doors. The sudden rumble of the old Harley startles Gene as Donkey and Buster race by and out the parking lot exit. After confirming that Lightfoot's car has not left the lot, Gene and Richard search La Posada's grounds, but only briefly, in the coming blizzard's mind-numbingly cold winds.

**

The buzz of muted conversation goes silent when Gene and Richard return to the Martini Lounge. The hum of the bar cooler motor fills the void. Rhonda, seemingly unperturbed, stands at the service station drying a hurricane glass with a bar towel. Gene glares at me. I look away. He and Richard sit at a table by the fireplace near the far side of the room. They warm their hands close to the flames.

Now calm, as if nothing has happened, Gene asks Rhonda for a Drambuie, "a double, please."

"Make that two," Richard says.

Rhonda delivers their drinks.

"There you go," she says, "that'll be twelve dollars."

"You don't charge enough for that stuff," Gene says.

He peels a twenty from his money clip and motions for her to keep the change.

It seems strange that, having just chased after Lightfoot, Gene now shows no concern for his whereabouts. But what I do not know is that, before he and Richard came into the Martini Lounge the first time, they had found Jeff's Chevy in the parking lot and planted a tracker behind his front bumper. Jeff is not going anywhere in that car without them knowing.

**

"I'm not so crazy about guns in bars," Belinda says to me.

"Maybe it's time we leave," I say.

In no hurry, we stroll across the lobby. Belinda wraps her arm through mine.

"I love you, Gille. I've always loved you—you know that, don't you, Gille?" Belinda says, and my ego allows me to believe that is so.

"Yes, I do," I say, "and I love you too."

42

More than once my unintended glibness in these affairs has led me to voice that heedless reply. But I believe it may be true this time. And I had always loved her, I suppose, but had loved her sister more. I don't know—maybe not. Anyway, though I must admit limited understanding of the subject, I think that odds are I love Belinda now.

6

The Gazebo

Belinda and I cross the lobby and climb the few stairs to La Posada's grand ballroom, now dark and deserted, lit only by flames in a fireplace against a distant wall. We sit close on a cushy leather divan in front of the great gray-stone fireplace. Embers spark from the fire onto the open hearth.

An expressionistic painting, maybe six feet wide and five feet tall, of three nuns in black habit with craggy crimson faces and long pointy fingers gnarled with age hangs above the fireplace mantle. Their mien suggests an occult conspiracy. They are nuns from the dark side, their toothy smiles sinister, their eyes menacing and demonic in the firelight. The flames cast tones of gold and orange dancing across our faces. Deep blue shadows reach out toward the darkest corners of the room.

My eyes are drawn past Belinda by a motion that is Einstein watching from the shadows, rocking ever so slightly in a ladder-back chair. On the wall behind him is a painting, a painting much larger than the nuns from hell, maybe six feet tall and twenty feet from side to side, of famous accidental and intentional victims of suicide in party hats with spinners and paper horns and hands full of confetti at the ready.

Hemingway is in animated conversation with Marilyn Monroe. With a Mona Lisa smile, Mark Rothko watches us side-eyed from across the room as Virginia Woolf whispers in Van Gogh's good ear near a bowl of red punch. A puffy Elvis is resplendent in sparkling cape and blue suede shoes. There are dozens of these forlorn travelers in distracted conversations sitting among long party tables, stuck in the purgatory of the painting's eternal warp of time.

**

"Is that you, Albert?" I say.

Einstein raises his hand. He nods to acknowledge that, yes, it is him I see.

Belinda's eyes have followed mine to the ladderback rocking chair, but she sees no one. "Was someone there?" she asks me.

"I thought a man I talked to earlier today was sitting in that chair over there," I say, nodding toward the rocker in the shadows. "My mind may be going a little haywire."

"Why do you say that?" Belinda asks.

"Well, for starters, the man is Albert Einstein and the last time I saw him he was in my hotel room."

Belinda looks at me quizzically, but not at all with the skepticism I thought my confession would derive.

"In your room? You're telling me Albert Einstein was in your hotel room – today? *The* Albert Einstein?" she says.

"Yes, that's the one," I say.

"Oh my God!" Belinda's quizzical look has turned to one of expectation; she is anxious as a child awaiting a promised bedtime story. "Go on Gille," she says, "please go on."

"Oh, it was nothing, probably a dream, but it did seem real," I say.

"Don't try to back out on me now, Mister Barker. Give it up – and spare no detail," says Belinda.

"Okay, if you promise to hold your tongue until I'm through."

"I promise – not a peep."

**

I tell Belinda of waking to the sight of Albert Einstein sitting in the overstuffed chair at the foot of my bed.

"There was no mistaking that face, of course," I say.

Belinda cuts me off with a motion of her hand. This is not at all what she wants to hear. Belinda wants details.

45

"What color are Einstein's eyes?" she asks

"Maybe brown."

"What was he wearing?"

"A dark gray suit and a white shirt, open at the collar, that I remember. And one of those sweater-vest things buttoned up the front—had a hand-knitted look to it, but I couldn't say for sure. I wasn't really paying attention to what he was wearing, you know."

"I understand. Was he the old Einstein?"

"Gray hair and all that?"

Belinda nods—yes, that's what she wants to know.

"Yes, his hair was gray, but he seemed to be in good shape for an older man. Now, may I continue?"

"Excuse me. Please do."

"I know I said it was probably a dream, but I don't believe that," I say. "He was there, Belinda. Einstein was there, right there, in my room. He was sitting in a chair at the foot of the bed when I first saw him. It was almost like we were old friends. We talked a while and then, I don't know why, he walked to the window and looked up at the sky, just like anyone might do, but not really the same. You know what I mean?"

"I think I do," Belinda says.

"It's hard to explain, but watching Albert Einstein standing at that window, looking up into that darkness, I could feel his regrets, Belinda: I could feel the man's pain. I don't know. Maybe it *was* a dream, but it was real to me."

**

Belinda turns her gaze into the fire.

"My father knew about dreams," she says.

"He knew about dreams? What does that mean?"

"In the middle of the night, when I was ten or so, I woke crying—I couldn't stop crying. Father came to my room and sat on the edge of my bed. I reached out to him and he held me. 'What is it, Belinda?' he asked. "What's troubling my girl?" he asked me.

"You know, I was always 'my girl', or 'sweetheart', or 'honey' to Daddy—I never heard him say my name. Doesn't that seem strange to you, Gille?"

46

That seems *very* strange to me.

"Not really," I say.

"I told Daddy I had a terrible dream, and that, in the dream, Mother buried him in our rose garden. I could only look down on the dream, not a part of what I could see. I could only watch while Mother rolled Daddy into a shallow grave. Then, in the dream, Mother took an old spade from the garage and covered Daddy with dirt, one shovel-load and then another, while I sat screaming from the shadows, unseen, unheard."

"How awful."

"Yes, it was. The dirt slid in slowed time from the shovel onto Daddy, and Daddy raised his head upright in his grave for a moment, his chest caked with black clay, and he looked toward me, now knowing, now seeing I was there. He smiled toward me and he said 'goodbye sweetheart' but I couldn't *hear* his voice, and then he lay back down, and no matter how I strained, I couldn't see him anymore. And Mother scooped a final spade of dirt on Daddy and packed the dirt down with the back of her shovel. I screamed for Mother to stop but she did not hear. I wasn't there to her."

"What a terrible dream," I say.

"That is exactly what Daddy said. He said the dream was terrible all right, and for what it was worth he didn't much care for the idea of being buried in the rose garden, although that was probably as good as any other place to be."

"He said that?"

"Yes, he did. Well, the tears just rolled down my cheeks. Then Daddy stood up from my bed and said, 'but, as you can see, I'm simply fine.' His saying so did not help though. I could not stop crying. He sat back down on the bed and rocked me in his arms for the longest time. Then he said that he had something special to tell me about dreams."

Belinda squeezes my hand.

"It's all right, Belinda," I say.

"I can't tell it the way Daddy told me. I now know his story was about parallel universes and time travel, things I hadn't even heard of before. Daddy was always keen on those sorts of things, spacetime and all, but he didn't get into any of that then. I wouldn't have understood one bit of it anyway."

Belinda picks up her purse and nervously fumbles through the lipsticks and makeup and keys inside. She doesn't find whatever she was looking for and sets the purse back on the floor.

"I was so young," Belinda says. "I just didn't understand what he was saying. But much later I learned he believed that what we call dreams are in fact our minds taking flights to alternate realities."

"So, he believed there are other dimensions, other worlds?"

"Oh yes, many more. And, in those other dimensions of time and space, he believed there to be alternate universes, each with planets not unlike our own. He believed that another of each of us living on earth exist on any number of those planets in those alternate universes."

"You mean like clones?"

"I don't pretend to know what he meant."

"Okay. Was there anything else?"

"Well, Daddy said although most dreams take place in other dimensions of our own past or present space in time, many dreams transport us to our spacetime in one of those alternate universes."

"No trips to the future?" I ask.

"You know, that's what I asked Daddy, and he said that was the perfect question because those 'into the future' dreams were the point of what he was telling me.

"Travel to the future in our universe isn't possible, Daddy said, because the future isn't yet a reality in our three-dimensional world, and since that is true, and he was sitting there holding me, my dream of him being buried alive could only have been a view into another dimension or of his counterpart in one of those other universes and was nothing for me to worry about."

"So, did you sleep then?"

"I did."

Belinda pulls a tissue from her purse and dabs tears from her eyes. I hold her against me.

"Daddy lied to me," she whispers through her tears.

"What?"

"I believe I can travel to the future here on earth in my dreams; Daddy lied. Six months after that awful dream, he *was* gone, just disappeared. The next morning, two men came to the house and poured a cement slab in the middle of the rose garden."

I see where this is going, but I ask the question anyway. "And—?"

"And then, no sooner than the cement had dried, that wonderful furniture maker—I can't remember his name."

"Beidenharn; Henry, I think."

"Yes, that's it. Mister Beidenharn came to build that gazebo on top of the cement slab for Mother. You know the gazebo, don't you, Gille?"

"Yes, I know it."

"Oh, right, of course you do. I remember you and Jodi spending the night out there when it was new. I couldn't bring myself to step foot in it then."

"So, you think your father is buried under the gazebo?"

Belinda shakes her head. Yes, she thinks Daddy is planted in the rose garden under Mister Beidenharn's magnificent gazebo.

"But you never told anyone?" I say.

"What purpose would it have served? Daddy was gone; that was all I really knew. I certainly could not say anything to Mother. What was I going to do, call the police? What if they believed I could visit the future and while on a trip there I saw Mother plant Daddy in the garden six months before it happened? It's not likely, but what if they *did* believe me?"

"You mean what if they believed you to have the power to transport yourself into the future and they tore down that masterpiece of a gazebo and busted up the cement slab and dug up dear old Dad?" (Of course Belinda wasn't aware that, to my mind, this was not an outrageous possibility.)

"Exactly—or what if he wasn't there? God, it would have been the most awful thing either way. I would rather think Daddy is alive and sitting on a beach somewhere watching sunsets."

We sit in the silence of the deserted ballroom. I glance back toward the chair where I had seen Albert—he isn't there. Fireplace logs settle. Sparks crackle from the fire.

"Gille?"

"Yes?"

"I would like you to take me to your room now."

**

In the middle of the night, I awake to Belinda's voice.

"Gille," she says, nudging me gently from behind. "Gille. What is that?" she asks, pressing her warm, naked body against mine.

"What is what?" Still half sleeping, I lean on my elbow and pull the nightstand clock closer to see the dial. It is four in the morning.

"Listen." Belinda pulls herself tight against me now. "Do you hear it?"

I hear something—perhaps a branch scraping a windowpane.

"It's the wind," I say. "Pay it no mind."

"Gille, please."

"All right, I'll take a look," I say.

I pull back the covers and turn toward the window. My bare feet hit the cold floor. "Damn, it's freezing out here. Keep that spot warm, mam — I won't be a minute."

"Sure thing, mister," Belinda says.

Closer to the window, I see the end of a bamboo fishing pole with a teaspoon strapped to its point slapping against the glass. I unlock the latch, raise the window, and peer down. Jeff Lightfoot stands two stories below, jiggering the bamboo pole.

"Lightfoot, what the hell are you doing?"

Jeff holds his finger across his lips. "I need your help, Mister Barker," he whispers out loud.

Belinda throws a cover across her shoulders and comes up behind me. She presses against my back and wraps her arms and the blanket around me. Her bare breasts are firm and warm. Her fresh mint breath drifts across my shoulder. Cupping my hand to

50

my mouth, I exhale and breath in through my nose. Where did she find that mint and how do I get one?

"Come back in four or five hours, Lightfoot," I say, "and when you do, try knocking on the door."

"I won't be able to do that, Mister Barker."

Belinda whispers into my ear.

"He sounds like a fairly desperate man, Marshal Dillon," she drawls, "maybe you should strap up and go see what's on the pilgrim's mind."

She wraps her hand around the shaft of *this* desperate man's rising pecker.

**

Oh, Lightfoot is desperate all right. I do not know what he did to get on the bad side of his friends in the bar, but I have a suspicion whatever he wants from me has something to do with them. I know they have guns and are less than happy with Lightfoot. I see no upside to inserting myself into the situation.

"Isn't this your hometown, Lightfoot?" I say. "There must be someone who can help you, maybe a relative, an old school chum—you know, someone who has known you more than a couple of hours and gives a damn."

"Please, Mister Barker. I'm in a real bind—had to hike a mile down those damn tracks to get here." Jeff points toward the railroad tracks that run by only twenty yards behind La Posada's garden gate.

Apparently overestimating my interpretive powers, Belinda gently tightens and releases her hold on my now fully erect member in an attempt to urge me to Lightfoot's aid.

**

"Give me a minute," I whisper toward Lightfoot, "and stay out of sight until I get down there."

"You can count on that, Mister Barker."

Belinda turns me toward her and kisses me. "You really are my hero, Gille Barker," she says.

I feel no obligation to chance altering Belinda's opinion of me by pointing out the fact that I want nothing to do with being a hero, and that applies in spades when any risk to my wellbeing is involved.

"This shouldn't take long," I say to Belinda.

I splash my face with warm water. I throw on my clothes and push my arms into the sleeves of my jacket, a jacket made to break the chill of an early fall day, not as protection against a blizzard like the one in its early stages outside.

"Take this with you." Belinda hands me a clumsy looking thing about half the size of a shoe box. It's a cell phone, something that had barely existed before I was hauled off to Winslow Prison. I have never held one before.

"Call me," she says.

I stuff the thing in my pocket. I will figure out how to use it later.

"Here." I pull back the bed covers and motion for Belinda to lie down. I pull the covers up around her bare shoulders. I bend down and kiss her lips.

"Be careful out there," she says.

"Not to worry. I'll be back before you can say Jackie Robinson."

"Say what?"

"Never mind," I say.

7

The Traffic Stop

I walk across the deserted La Posada lobby and out the veranda door to the garden gate.

I call out Lightfoot's name. "Lightfoot?" I say.

"Over here, Mister Barker, over here" comes the faintest reply from the direction of La Posada's old brick railroad station.

Unsure of my footing in the dark, I creep toward the voice down the narrow cobbled path through the fallow gardens. With no sign of Lightfoot, I'm standing under the slight light of a single shaded bulb that hangs above the door to the tiny station when Lightfoot grabs my arm and pulls me into the shadows.

"Thanks for coming, Mister Barker," he says, "you're a life saver."

"Well, I certainly hope it's nothing that serious," I say.

I suffer a twinge of anxiety when Lightfoot makes no reply.

The winter breeze stiffens. I push my hands into my pockets and rock on my sneakers, waiting for Lightfoot to say *anything*.

"Get with it, Lightfoot," I finally say, "I have better things to do than stand out here freezing my ass off."

"I need your help, Mister Barker."

"Damn it, Jeff, get to the point."

"If you could just help me get my car, I—"

I turn to walk away, and Lightfoot grabs my arm again.

"Please, Mister Barker," he says, "please hear me out, sir."

I look at my watch. "You have two minutes. I'd get started if I were you," I say.

For reasons unclear to me, Lightfoot begins rambling on about his thirty-nine-year-old cousin, Luke, the pig farmer. For fifteen years, he says, Luke has been picking up the gourmet scraps scraped from the plates of La Posada's sated diners and slopping his happy hogs with samplings of Arizona's finest regional fare.

"You've seen the menu, huh, Mister Barker. Luke's pigs eat pretty high on the hog, I'd say."

"It would seem so," I say. "Get on with it, man."

"Yes sir," Lightfoot says, but in what seems to be an avoidance of whatever the issue is at hand, he continues with his pig-farmer cousin's life story.

He tells me Cousin Luke, who, 'by the way', has never had a driver's license, drives his old slop-barrel-laden flat-bed truck on the twelve-mile round trip down to La Posada's Turquoise Room and back to his pig farm every other day.

"Those slop barrel runs are the only driving Luke does. The hotel pays him cash and he gets the hog slop free. Now that's a sweet deal, wouldn't you say, Mister Barker?"

"Sounds like a sweet deal all right. You're boring me to death, Lightfoot."

"Sorry, Mister Barker, but that's what put me in this mess. I think you need to know that to understand my problem.

"Anyway, Luke doesn't trust the Winslow Bank to keep his account particulars to themselves— especially with that Rebecca Thomas being the head teller. Seems Luke and Rebecca had a thing a few years back and Luke doesn't trust her for sour apples."

What the hell is Lightfoot talking about?

"One minute," I say. "You have one more minute, Lightfoot."

"No problem, Mister Barker," Lightfoot says, "No problem.

"So, since Cousin Luke doesn't have a driver's license and doesn't trust the Winslow bank to keep his business off the gossip page, he has me haul his deposits over to Flagstaff.

"It's like clockwork, Mister Barker. On the third Friday of every month, I pick up a bank bag from Luke out at the pig farm, drive to Flagstaff, and drop off his deposit at the Wells Fargo Bank there. The last trip I made was yesterday."

"Am I supposed to care where the hell Cousin Luke keeps his money?" I ask.

"Well, like I said, that's how this mess started," Jeff says, "I had to begin somewhere, you know."

"Yeah, yeah, just rush it along every chance you get," I say.

"After I made that last deposit, I picked up some books for Aunt Wanda, like she asked, and stuck them in Luke's briefcase. It was lunch time when I left the bookstore, so I decided to grab a sandwich at the Denny's across the street. That's the first time I saw them."

"Them?" I ask.

"The same guys that were at the bar tonight, Mister Barker — they sat down next to me at that Denny's counter."

Lightfoot fumbles with his lighter, striking it again and again in a futile attempt to light another cigarette. His jaws clinch, first one side and then the other. He is lying—maybe not about seeing the two men at Denny's, but definitely about it being the *first* time their paths had crossed.

**

I think sensing my doubt, Lightfoot sheepishly looks away and jams the hand holding the lighter into his pocket, nervously continuing to pop the lid open and closed.

"Richard, the one with the slicked-back hair and the dimple in his chin, reminded me of that actor — you know the one I mean, Mister Barker?"

"John Travolta," I say. The resemblance was obvious.

"Yeah, that's the guy. He asked me to pass the sugar."

"What the hell, Lightfoot! I don't give a damn about the sugar *or* John Travolta's freaking dimple. I'm freezing." I tap the face of my watch. "Let's wrap this up," I say.

"Not much more to it," Lightfoot says. "I grabbed what I thought was Luke's briefcase from under the counter when I left Denny's and drove straight to the pig farm. Luke wasn't home, so

I put the case in the kitchen closet, just like I always do when he's not home."

I am skeptical. "You didn't open the briefcase?"

"Hell no–wasn't any reason to. Aunt Wanda's books were the only things other than an empty cash bag in it, as far as I knew, and none of that interested me. I just put the briefcase in the closet, grabbed a beer, and split, just like always. I thought all was well till I saw those two sitting in the bar tonight.

"Even then I didn't realize I had picked up the wrong briefcase until that Gene guy asked me what the hell I did with his bag. I have a problem, Mister Barker,"

My skepticism is on the rise. For one thing, I heard Jeff call Gene and Richard by name when he sat at their table in the Martini Lounge. How would he know their names if he only saw them the one time in Denny's coffee shop and the only conversation was a request to pass the sugar?

"As I recall, your Denny's pals have guns," I say. "I don't know a lot about these things, but I would say you have a *serious* problem."

"I have to get out of town, Mister Barker. I need my car."

"You need to get that Gene fella's briefcase back to him, that's what you need."

"Yeah, I know, but I can't get the briefcase without my car."

"I get the feeling you're not telling me the whole story, Lightfoot," I say. "I can't help you if you're not straight with me."

Lightfoot averts his attention to the toes of his shoes. He thrusts his hands deep into his pockets and rocks on his heels, almost losing his balance. He is a piteous sight.

"I did know who they were before I saw them at Denny's," Lightfoot finally confesses. He says that, although he had never met the men, he knew them by reputation. He knew 'Gene' was Gene Cardenas, a well-known drug dealer in Flagstaff, and that 'Richard' was Richard Gleason, equally infamous as Gene's psychotic 'handyman'.

"I'm sorry, Mister Barker," Lightfoot says, "I should have told you, but I was afraid you wouldn't help me if you knew."

He was right about that. Of course, this is when I should turn and bolt for the Einstein room and the bed kept warm by Miss Belinda Jones.

"Do you have a plan?" I ask, at the same time hoping that he does not.

Lightfoot's face brightens. What a pretender this Indian can be.

"You bet," he says, "and it's a good one too, Mister Barker."

Lightfoot has a plan all right. Since Gene and Richard are, 'without doubt' he says, still searching Winslow for him, he wants me to sneak into the parking lot, get his car, and drive it to the railroad crossing on the prison road, about a mile away. He will meet me there.

"Don't they know what your car looks like?" I ask.

"How could they?"

"Maybe they asked someone. Everybody in this one-horse town must know your car—did that possibility even come close to entering your mind? Jesus, how do you think they tracked you to here?"

"Well, there's one thing for sure—they do know who *I* am, Mister Barker. If I go wandering around the parking lot, they'll nab me for sure. But they wouldn't think anything of it if *you* walked up to a car—my car for instance, got in, and drove away. They don't know you. Why would they think anything of that?"

What makes Lightfoot think they would not be suspicious of me? They saw him talking to me in the Martini Lounge only hours ago.

"And what about a driver's license," I say, "I don't have one, you know."

"It's only a mile or two, Mister Barker," says Lightfoot. "What could possibly go wrong?"

I must be out of my mind. I take the keys from Jeff's hand. I look around the corner of the railroad station. The coast seems clear.

"You better be there when I get to that railroad crossing, Lightfoot. I won't be waiting for you."

"Thank you, Mister Barker."

"Gille, damn it, my name is Gille."

"Yes sir."

I hurry off toward the parking lot.

**

Should I seek the shadows, stealthily wending from car to car? Why bother—if Gene Cardenas is watching Lightfoot's Chevrolet, my goose is cooked no matter the stealth of my wending. And there is another problem with that approach. Only fifteen or twenty cars dot the parking lot. Cardenas may not know which car is Lightfoot's but seeing me dodging from car to car in the nearly empty lot would likely wet his suspicions.

I set out on my quest, my legs less willing with each stride. I take my time. Do I appear nonchalant? My heart is pounding. I want one of Lightfoot's cigarettes. It takes only a minute that seems like ten to reach Lightfoot's car. I fumble through the dozen keys on his chain. None look like a car key.

Why didn't he tell me which key? Why didn't I ask?

I try half-a-dozen keys before pulling on the latch handle in frustration. The door screeches open. The sound echoes back at me loud as a fire alarm from the garden wall.

I get in and let the door hang open while I search for the ignition key. The Chevrolet's dome light unexpectedly flickers and then shines bright, a traitorous beacon announcing my presence.

My fifth key choice slides into the ignition. Eyes closed, I turn the switch, fully expecting a bomb planted under the floorboard to shower the parking lot with my body parts.

The starter grinds–the engine sputters.

The starter grinds again and the engine springs to life. I ease off the clutch and the Chevy rolls out the drive onto old Route 66.

**

In the Lindbergh Room, just four doors down the hall from Belinda, Gene Cardenas is napping. Richard, barely awake in a chair near the window, sees the blip of Jeff's Chevy creeping out

58

the drive on the monitor for the tracking device they had attached to the Chevy's frame. He shakes Gene's shoulder.

"He's moving, Boss. He's moving."

Cardenas bolts upright. Richard grabs the monitor. Belinda is awakened by their hurried footsteps as they pass her door and trundle down the steps to the lobby.

Cardenas slides behind the wheel of his Jaguar. As Richard runs toward the door, Gene thrusts his hand out the window in front of him.

"What, Boss?"

"The keys, Richard, give me the damn keys."

After handing Gene the keys, a puzzled Richard stands frozen next to the driver's door. In the three years he had worked for Gene, he had never seen him drive.

"Richard, what the hell are you doing?" Gene asks him.

"I'm not sure."

"Get in the freaking car, Richard," Cardenas says.

**

There is no sign of Lightfoot when I pull the Chevy onto the railroad crossing where he said he would be. I drive across the tracks and slow to a crawl on the gravel apron of the road. Lightfoot, gasping for breath, pops up from the grade behind the rails. I scoot over to the passenger seat and Jeff climbs in. He grinds the Chevy into first gear, smashes the accelerator pedal to the floor, and launches us down the narrow blacktop road.

"Thanks, Mister Barker, I owe you one. I wasn't sure you'd show up," Jeff says.

What reason did he have for saying that? I could have been offended by such a remark if I cared.

"Now to get that damned briefcase back to those guys," Lightfoot says. "You up for a little ride, Mister Barker?"

Was Lightfoot being honest with me? Indians do not lie, do they? Or is that Eskimos. Are Eskimos Indians? Anyway, what business is this of mine? My only goal is to get back to the La Posada and Belinda Jones, isn't it?

"Go," I say.

What else *could* I say? I am a writer of sorts, unhealthily inquisitive by nature and cursed with the need to know, and this is a mystery, isn't it? Besides, Lightfoot cannot risk a run-in with Gene and Richard by taking me back to the hotel and I wouldn't make it halfway in this weather if I tried to walk there.

The roadside power lines sway on the edges of the headlight's high beams. Sleet and snow pelt the windshield. No, I am not going to end up alongside the tracks frozen stiff as one more board among the railroad ties and tumble weeds—not tonight. Not if I can help it, that is.

**

Cardenas barrels down the steep La Posada parking lot exit and bounces the car onto old Route 66. Sparks fly as the Jaguar's front bumper strikes the road.

Corporal Paul Mendoza, the only police officer on night shift in this sleepy town, is just rounding the corner as the Jaguar races across the eastbound lanes. Mendoza clicks on his siren. Cardenas runs a red light and skids around the corner onto old westbound 66 with Corporal Mendoza closing from a block behind.

"We have company, Boss." Richard pulls the pistol from his shoulder holster and checks the clip.

Cardenas, with Mendoza's flashing lights bright in his rear-view mirror; pulls the Jaguar to the side of the road.

"Put that thing away, Richard," Gene says.

Mendoza pulls in behind Cardenas. He radios the Winslow station.

"Got a reckless stop westbound 66 and Prison Road, Myrtle—Arizona tag 287 ZRG."

"Roger that, Paul. How's the weather out there?"

"Gettin' nasty; looks like we might be in for a blow."

"10–4 that," says Myrtle.

The patrol car's flashing lights turn the white sleet to an eerie red background for the silhouette of Mendoza as he approaches the Jaguar.

On Mendoza's instruction, Gene cracks his window and hands over his license and registration.

Richard has his pistol under his right thigh, cradled in his hand.

Mendoza walks back to his patrol car and relays Gene's information to the station. There is nothing of interest on Cardenas in Arizona, and no record of his drug-dealing Miami days pops up on Myrtle's screen. Cardenas had stayed clean there by lining the pockets of Miami's finest.

Corporal Mendoza pecks on Gene's window. "Mister Cardenas?"

Gene cracks the window again. "Yes, officer?"

"Did you know your driver's license is expired?"

"I had no idea," Gene says, and that was true.

"Please step out of the car, Mister Cardenas," Mendoza says.

An approaching state police car slows and pulls off the highway across from Mendoza just as Richard is pulling his pistol from under his thigh. Gene grabs Richard's forearm and forces it back down. The state police turn on their flashing lights and watch Mendoza and Gene from the comfort of their squad car.

"Out of the car, Mister Cardenas," Mendoza says.

Cardenas, indicating the blizzard conditions outside with a motion of his hand, asks Officer Mendoza if that is necessary.

"Out of the car, sir," Mendoza replies.

Gene zips his unlined Ferragamo jacket up around his neck and steps out into the deep freeze. The wind swirls up his sleeves.

Corporal Mendoza shines his flashlight into Gene's eyes, inspecting his pupils as they constrict in the glare. He had planned to run Cardenas through the DUI routine, but his own fingers are growing numb.

"Does your friend drive?" Mendoza asks Cardenas.

"He does."

Mendoza asks to see Richard's license. He shines his flashlight on Richard's license and then on his face. Richard would blow Mendoza's brains into the drainage ditch for that if the two state cops were not sitting across the road.

Mendoza hands Richard's license back to him. "Are you all right to drive tonight, Mister Gleason?" he asks.

"Sure am," Richard says.

With Richard now behind the wheel, Gene escapes Mendoza with only a warning, but not without consequence; the monitor's blip of Lightfoot's Chevrolet has disappeared.

8

Pig's Feet

Sleet peppers our windshield hard now as we cruise down Arizona Route 87, a narrow strip of black top that winds south from Winslow through the Mogollon Rim Mountains to the Verde River.

It is past four a.m. when Lightfoot turns onto the rutted dirt lane blanketed with ice-crusted snow that connects Cousin Luke's pig farm to Route 87. The Chevy slips and slides down the steep quarter-mile grade to Luke's ramshackle farmhouse surrounded by out-buildings, junk cars, and aged farm implements in various stages of decay.

Unpainted wood fencing and pig wallows and slop troughs and scrap-wood pig shelters flank the house. I hear the babel of a hundred squealing pigs fifty yards before we reach the front gate, even though there is not a pig in sight. It's obvious pigs know enough to stay in the pig shed during a northern Arizona storm.

Jeff stops the Chevy at the front gate of the fence line, twenty yards from the house.

"Doesn't look like Luke is home," he says. "I'll check the door." Jeff pulls his jacket over his head and runs through the drifting snow to the front porch. He bangs at the door with the side of his fist and calls out his cousin's name.

"Luke?" Lightfoot says. "Luke—you in there, Luke?"

Jeff drags a key from under an old wash bucket full of dirt and grubby work boots sitting next to the porch steps. He opens the door and motions for me to join him.

I crack the window and let him know I'm fine with waiting in the car.

I roll up the window and turn the heater on high. A blast of warm air surges across my feet and up my pant legs. I drag Belinda's phone from my pocket. I push buttons until a light comes on and call Belinda. She answers on the first ring.

"Hello? —Gille?" she says.

I start to answer, but Belinda cuts me short.

"Where are you? Will you be back soon?"

I recount the Lightfoot's tale to Belinda, his trip to Flagstaff with Cousin Luke's deposit and the supposed briefcase mix-up. I tell her we are getting the briefcase from Luke's house now.

"I should be back to the La Posada in an hour or so," I say.

In my peripheral view, Lightfoot is wading through snow drifts toward the car.

He pecks on the window. He says the briefcase isn't where he left it and that he could use my help searching for it. Motioning for me to follow, he runs back toward the house.

**

Having heard Lightfoot, Belinda asks me, "Do you believe him, Babe?"

Uh-oh. When did I become 'Babe'? I never liked those names, those generic terms of endearment – 'Babe', 'Sweetheart', 'Honey', 'Boo' and on and on. Now I have become a 'Babe'. There must be thirty or forty million 'Babes' in America alone.

"I'm sorry, I didn't catch that," I say.

"Do you believe him? What do you really know about this Lightfoot anyway? Not much, I would guess."

"I know he's a cab driver and a hustler, and right now I wish I had never met the guy—that's about all I know for certain. But I have a feeling he is telling the truth about this briefcase thing; you know what I mean?"

"Oh yeah, I know what you mean," Belinda says.

Her cynicism does not escape me.

"I'm serious," I say. "I don't think the guy's smart enough to make this stuff up."

"You might have a point there, but as a writer of fiction, dear, and please don't take this in a derogatory way, you know it doesn't take a genius to twist the truth. The hard part for Lightfoot will be keeping his story straight."

"Yes, I know."

"My train to L.A. leaves in three hours. Is there a chance you'll be back before then?"

"I should be," I say.

Holding the phone to my ear, I listen to the silence from Belinda's end of the line.

**

I hear the pigs in the barn, gossiping, as pigs are want to do. What is all the squealing about?

It's five minutes past feeding time. Where is my Churro Lamb? Who has my honey-glazed duckling? Why isn't that handsome Luke slopping my trough? I could eat a horse about now. Oink.

Maybe the pigs are discussing their diets and how they might quit making such pigs of themselves and postpone the inevitable trip to the slaughterhouse of the fattest of their lot—make a competition of it until they are all successful victims of pig anorexia, and Luke shoots the worthless skinny pigs in their heads and piles their corpses high behind the troughs where they had previously taken great pleasure in eating their daily fill of gourmet La Posada table scraps. And then Luke would slosh gasoline on their lifeless bodies and set the rebellious pigs on fire.

Flames from the gas and pig-stuffing would shoot eighty feet into the night sky and be visible by anyone who might be looking toward Cousin Luke's pig farm from Winslow town, five miles to the north—evidence of yet another idea judged good by vote of a committee gone awry.

Maybe the pigs do not understand a single pig's squeal. Maybe the squealing means absolutely nothing, not even to another pig, other than '*I'm hungry*' or '*something is chasing me—I have to get out of here.*'

Maybe the pigs are in the same pickle as the thousands of their human neighbors locked away from the real world behind the bars of Winslow Prison until many of them come to think of their cells as home and just can't give a pickled-pig's-foot if they ever get out of those cages. At least the pigs can observe the goings on around their open-air pens while gobbling down La Posada's gourmet fare before a refreshing wallow in the mud, or a little sexual intercourse down behind the barn.

Maybe Luke's pigs don't have it so bad after all. I believe it is most likely the pigs don't give a big rat's ass one way or the other, and, of course, that is just as good for the pigs anyway.

**

Belinda interrupts my pig musings with a thought of her own.

"Gille–I think I love you," she says, I think I always have."

She thinks she loves me? She thinks she always has? She said the same thing last night, didn't she? Twenty years seems like a long time to keep that tidbit of information under wraps. I guess it is better to find out now than never, but the repetition could prove annoying.

"And I love you," I say. I hate it when I make that reply but at least this time around, as I said before, it might be true.

"I should have dragged you back to bed instead of sending you out to help Lightfoot," Belinda says. "I just found you—I can't lose you again."

Although her voice betrays nothing of the kind, I imagine a lone tear falling from the corner of Belinda's eye.

"Believe me," I say, "I feel the same."

There I go with another of my easy-way-out replies, but I do believe, for the most part, I am being sincere.

"When will I see you if you're not back before I leave?" Belinda asks.

I tell her I plan to stay at La Posada until I am allowed to cross the Arizona border and then I'll be on my way back to Maui.

"When will that be?"

"My appointment is in ten days. I should get my release then," I say.

"May I go with you?"

"If you want—I suppose they have a waiting room."

"Are you being dense on purpose, Mister Barker?" Belinda says. "I sure as hell don't want to sit in a parole office waiting room. To Maui—when you go back to Maui, may I go with you?"

Though it is not true, I chuckle before making my reply, hoping to indicate I'm not a complete nit-wit, and was aware of what she meant all along.

"Of course," I say, "I would like nothing more. I was just working up the nerve to ask."

Although it is the first time the thought has entered my mind, I believe it is true. Yes, I think I would have asked.

"Do you have a pen?"

"I have a pen. What sort of writer would be without a pen? Give me a second," I say.

Fumbling through Jeff's glove box, I find an old ballpoint pen. I hold it next to the heater fan and then scribble the warmed nib across my palm until ink flows.

"Got it—fire away," I say.

I pull my sleeve up and scribble Belinda's phone number across my forearm.

"If you don't make it back before I leave, please call me tonight," Belinda says. "I'll be home by six, seven at the latest."

"Will do. I should go help Jeff take Luke's place apart now," I say.

"Be careful, Gille. I love you."

To which I come back again with my standard lame reply.

"I love you too, sweetheart," I say.

**

By the time I walk in, Jeff has ransacked the kitchen; cabinets stand open, pantry and closet doors are ajar.

"Jeff?" I call out.

"Up here."

The temperature drops as I climb the narrow stairs to the second floor. The upstairs is heated by what little warm air that rises from below through small open grates cut in the floors of each room. Trails of powdery snow drift through cracks around weathered windowsills.

I find Lightfoot rummaging through closets in what I assume is Luke's bedroom. He points down the hall toward a second bedroom and asks me to search there. I turn the room upside down, carefully replacing things where they were as I go

**

The porch screen door squeaks open and slams shut. I go down the stairs to the kitchen and peer out into the dark. Jeff is fighting through knee-high snow drifts to get back to the house.

"What were you doing out there?" I ask.

Lightfoot stomps snow from his shoes onto the kitchen's faded linoleum print floor. He flicks on the switch to a flashlight and shines the beam in my eyes.

"I went to get this from the car. Come on," he says, "we don't have much time."

I look up from the flashlight at Lightfoot. His eyes refuse to meet mine. His flashlight story stinks. A battery lantern, far better than his flashlight from the car, is sitting on the kitchen counter. I know he saw it there, but I do not question him now.

After briefly rummaging through a last storage room in the basement, Lightfoot drops onto a chair at the kitchen table. He opens the refrigerator and a scrap pad held to the door by a magnetic pencil drops to the floor. He picks up the pencil and pad and sets them on the kitchen table.

"How about a beer?" Jeff says.

He pulls two cans of Keystone from the refrigerator stocked with a couple of cases of the stuff along with odds and ends of indeterminable identity wrapped in butcher paper and tin foil.

"I don't think so," I say.

Jeff pops the top on one of the beer cans. He asks me the time. It's five-thirty I say. He picks up the pencil on the table and absentmindedly doodles shapes and body parts and names on the scratch paper between sips of Luke's beer.

Waynette—circles and squares and then a woman with a big ski-slope nose in profile view — Thibodaux — Louisiana — Thibodaux, Louisiana — Boudreaux — Waynette Boudreaux — a stick man with a stick penis and scraggly-haired sack of balls — Thibodaux.

Twirling the pencil between his fingers, Jeff surveys his handywork. He tips his head back and swallows the last of his beer. He underlines the words 'Waynette Boudreaux' and 'Thibodaux, Louisiana'. He throws the empty beer can in a trash bag next to the sink.

The snow has paused for now. Dawn brings a line of orange light across the horizon of the still dark and stormy sky. Jeff walks over to an old wall-mounted phone in the hallway.

"I think I'll give Aunt Wanda a call," he says. "Maybe she knows where Luke is."

Jeff dials the phone. He leans against the wall in a curious way that leads me to believe he is holding the phone's cradle down and only pretending to call.

"No answer," Lightfoot says, and at that moment the glare of headlights shines through the kitchen window. An old Ford pick-up, its bed full of clanging barrels, is bouncing down Luke's snow-covered dirt lane.

"No wonder she didn't answer," Jeff says. He walks outside and stands at the fence-line gate.

Aunt Wanda slides the pickup to a stop on the ice just short of Lightfoot. She rolls her window down a crack.

"Jeff. What the hell are you doing here?" she shouts.

"I'm looking for Luke—don't happen to know where he might be, do you?"

"I happen to know exactly where he *might* be," Aunt Wanda says. "Out of the blue, Luke and your Uncle John decided it was time to go hunt some damn deer. What the hell do you think I'm doing here at daybreak? Somebody's gotta slop those damn pigs. God damned Indians, I swear."

"So, where did they go?"

"Well, I guess I don't know exactly, but I do have a general idea. I heard them talking about that place down by Pine. You should know more about that than I do."

"They say when they might be back?"

"Hell no. Probably three or four days would be my guess."

"Pull her on up." Jeff motions for Wanda to back the pickup next to the fence line. He helps his Aunt pour La Posada's gourmet fare from the barrels into the slop troughs.

"Did you happen to see Luke before he and Uncle John left?"

"Sure did. How the hell do you think I came into possession of this truck and all these beautiful damn slop barrels?"

"Did Luke have a briefcase?"

"You mean that big old doctor's bag of his? I didn't see it. Could have been in the duffle he had slung over his shoulder, I suppose. That's the only bag I saw. I remember it because the thing looked so heavy, I asked him, 'what the hell you got in that damned bag, son?'"

"And what did he say?"

"He said it weren't none of my business, but for my information, it was full of long-johns and socks and about a case of beer."

Wanda jumps in the pickup and slams the door. She rubs her hands together between her legs, soaking up warm air the heater is pumping onto the floorboards.

Lightfoot ties the barrels back in place on the pickup and Aunt Wanda slips and slides the truck back up the icy grade until she disappears over the crest of the hill.

**

It is ten till six when Lightfoot coaxes the Chevy back up Luke's lane and onto the blacktop road. What is Jeff's plan? I ask him what he thinks Cousin Luke is up to.

"Luke's not the problem, it's Uncle John I'm worried about," Jeff says. "My guess is Luke opened the briefcase and found something other than Aunt Wanda's books. Whatever is in there must have been one hell of a surprise to him. Knowing Luke, his

70

first call would have been to me, and when I didn't answer he high-tailed it over to Uncle John's. Unlike me, if Uncle John found something worth keeping in that bag, there's only one rule he would consider."

"What rule would that be?" I ask.

"Now, that's just obvious, ain't it? Finders-keepers, of course. You know, it's not necessary to be a white man for that rule to apply."

"I see. So, you don't think they're hunting down by Pine?"

"Hell no," Jeff says, "Pine would be the last place to look. If what is in that bag is worth anything, Uncle John is out peddling it to the highest bidder. My guess is they are headed for New Orleans as we speak. Uncle John has 'friends' down there who deal in that sort of thing.

"I knew we were in trouble the minute Aunt Wanda pulled up with those barrels in the truck," Jeff says. "No way would she be slopping Luke's pigs while he and Uncle John went on a pub crawl, especially this time of year. I'll bet a dollar to your donut my aunt knows where they really are and exactly what's in that bag."

**

Yes, keeping a tall tale straight on a second telling is the hard part, and I am paying close attention to Lightfoot's story lines.

When Jeff said his best guess was the missing case is on its way to Louisiana he was telling the truth if details and time were not taken into consideration, but I didn't know that then.

My situation is of more immediate concern to me than Lightfoot's briefcase problem. I am in trouble. I do not dare go back to La Posada for fear Gene Cardenas and his fellow sociopath will be lying in wait. I'm certain that, by now, they are aware I've been stupid enough to get myself involved in this mess.

**

Jeff pushes the accelerator pedal toward the floor. The Chevy lurches into passing gear, tires spinning on the snow-packed blacktop. I look up and see a freight train dragging a hundred and more cars toward the rail crossing a half mile ahead that separates us from Winslow town.

The Chevy's engine whines and the pistons clatter in their cylinders. The speedometer arrow gyrates to a hundred and six and back down to sixty as the tires search, then find, and then search again for traction on the icy blacktop road. Hail stones the size of Chinese checkers marbles begin their rat-a-tat-tatting off the windshield. We might just make it. No, we won't.

"Stop!" I scream.

'Stop!' had already run through Jeff's mind. He is pumping the brakes and the Chevy's tires are trying, against all odds, to find traction. The car slides crabwise across the ice toward a roadside concrete culvert. Jeff fights for control and the Chevy rights itself for a moment before spinning around and sliding backward past the culvert. The rear wheels grab in the loose gravel apron of the blacktop.

I'm slammed against the passenger door, and, for the first time, I see Einstein sitting in the back seat, his arms twined across his belly. He is looking out the side window with no more care than a man surveying the landscape on a leisurely Sunday drive.

"What the hell are you doing here?" I blurt out at Albert.

He pays me no mind.

The train's lead engine passing by my window on the other side of the crossing gate is the last thing I see before closing my eyes in preparation for impact. The clatter of road-apron gravel ricocheting off the Chevy's undercarriage and the distress-filled warning of the train's whistle fill my consciousness as we slide to a stop a foot short of the flashing red crossing lights.

Tires churn gravel and then spin sidewise across patches of ice-covered blacktop as Jeff jockeys the Chevy into position in front of the crossing gate. The first of the train's cars roll by. I look at my watch to see what the hour was when I dodged the grim reaper this time, an old habit first applied after flipping my father's Ford Fairlane end over end through twenty rows of a cornfield in mid-summer of nineteen eighty-two.

It's four minutes past six.

**

"Sure you won't have one of these Keystones, Mister Barker?" Lightfoot holds a can from the six-pack 'borrowed' from Cousin Luke's refrigerator out in front of me. "Looks like we're going to be here for a spell."

"I think I'll pass. I'm not much of a beer drinker before breakfast."

"Well, it *is* after dinner, but you have to draw a line *somewhere*, I suppose," Jeff says.

"And Jeff?"

"Yes?"

"It's Gille; please call me Gille."

Lightfoot lifts his can of Keystone in salute.

"You got it, Kimosabe," he says.

9

The Railroad Crossing

The blizzard's blinding snow now flies sideways across the highway. The train's cast-iron wheels click and clack against old metal rails. The Chevy heater fan whirs on high.

"How about a little music, Mister Barker?" Lightfoot says.

"Sure, why not."

Jeff spins the dial. Bob Dylan is croaking a ballad about an answer blowing in the wind.

I call Belinda—there is no answer. Chances are she is having morning coffee in the Turquoise room while awaiting the Amtrak to LA.

Maybe she is thinking of me. I'm tired. I rest my head against the seat-back and close my eyes.

"Your friend—what's her name again?" Lightfoot asks.

"Belinda, Belinda Jones" I say, neither opening my eyes nor showing interest in further conversation.

"Belinda," Jeff says. "Now that's one nice lady, and beautiful too."

"She's very nice," I say.

"Known her long?"

"Yes, I have," I say.

**

I first met Belinda in Mason City, Illinois when a sudden storm brought her to pick up her sister Jodi after a Saturday afternoon matinee at the Arlee, the movie theater in my

74

"Saint something or other – a Catholic church – that I do remember," Jeff says. "And I remember it was on Bourbon Street in Thibodaux, same name as the Bourbon Street in New Orleans. Don't suppose there are any churches on *that* Bourbon Street, huh, Mister Barker."

"Rent might be a little steep there for the true believer crowd," I say.

"Well, it must be dirt cheap in Thibodaux. I didn't count them, but I'd bet there are at least a dozen churches on Thibodaux's Bourbon Street."

**

I am of the opinion the church to tavern ratio of any town is the surest measure of its disposition. I would not say here that one is better than the other, but be you pious of nature, or inclined toward a life of deceit and foolery, or would prefer to just mix it up a little, you might want to take the church to tavern ratio into consideration before planting your roots. If you are a natural born hell raiser, one church to every ten taverns in a town would be a favorable indicator for you. On the other hand, those who feel they hold the moral high ground are likely to find a ratio favoring the church crowd by a substantial margin more to their liking.

Experience is the basis for this opinion of mine. I grew up in Mason City, as you know, an Illinois farm town of two thousand souls then, and probably now, living the idyllic life of relative isolation among thousands of acres of soybeans, wheat, and corn.

For as long as anyone could remember, there had been seven churches and seven taverns in my hometown. Most of the citizenry were pleased with this finely-tuned standoff, and for decades harmony prevailed between the forces of good and evil.

All of that changed when Al Cranwell, who would soon become a great pal of mine, opened his tavern on the edge of town. Even though the village elders insisted Al build his roadhouse a quarter mile outside the city limits, the relentless forces of evil soon prevailed and things went to hell in a hand basket. The balance can indeed be precarious.

**

"And you wouldn't believe what the preacher's name was." Lightfoot says. "Take a guess, Mister Barker."

"Jimmy Swaggart?"

"Jack Nicholson, same as that actor, and that preacher was a dead ringer for psycho-Jack in 'The Shining' — you see that movie, Mister Barker?"

"The name rings a bell."

"I bet. Psycho writer? Yeah, I bet that *does* ring a bell, huh, Mister Barker? Ding-Dong. Anyway, that Preacher Jack had the same crazed look as Nicholson, and all dressed up in that priest garb, white collar and all—that was just too weird. You know what I mean?"

"'Too weird', yes, I know what that means."

"— been six years now, maybe five, since I was in Thibodeaux last." Tipping his Keystone to his lips, Lightfoot drains the last drops from the can

He fiddles with the radio, aimlessly twisting the dial from station to station.

"And?" I finally say.

"And what?"

"And, is that the end of your story?"

"I don't think so. Let me see now, where was I?"

"Preacher Jack. Six years ago, maybe five."

"Oh yeah, well shoot, I haven't even told you why my fiancée gave me the brush."

"Please, spare no details," I say, remembering only too late that Lightfoot does not recognize sarcasm.

And so, he begins.

**

"I guess I should start with Johnny Ray," Lightfoot says.

"Waynette, had two brothers, and the older one, a few years older than me I'd guess, made it clear from the start he had no use for Indians, especially Arizona Indians. He was a big old boy, a red-neck hard ass and his name was Johnny Ray. I tried to keep my distance from Johnny Ray."

"I get the feeling things aren't going to go well between you and Johnny Ray," I say.

"Yeah, well, a couple of days before the wedding, Johnny Ray, all smiles and harmony at the family dinner table, told me it was customary in Thibodaux to throw a bachelor party for the groom the night before a wedding. He said he and some of my soon-to-be relatives would like to throw one of those parties for me.

"Uh oh."

"That was my first thought too, but with Waynette's family there at the table, I didn't want to seem like a dick by turning down my future brother-in-law's offer. I told Johnny Ray I was familiar with the bachelor party concept and that it would be my pleasure to be the guest of honor for their Thibodaux version. 'All right then,' Johnny Ray said. 'I'll pick you up at seven.' And so, he did."

"A man of his word," I say.

"That he was. He picked me up at seven on the dot and drove what seemed like forever before he turned down a winding muddy road, not much wider than his pickup truck.

"It was pitch dark. All I could see was the outline of swamp grass on either side of the road in the truck's high beams. We must have gone two or three miles before I heard the faint sound of fiddles playing drift into the truck on that muggy swamp air.

"The fiddles grew strong and clear now as Johnny Ray drove another quarter mile or so to a clearing, maybe half the size of a football field. And smack in the middle of that clearing, at the end of the road, was a big parking lot stacked full of cars and pickups and an old barn someone had stuck a porch on the front of. And above the roof on that porch there was a neon sign flashing 'SWAMP DADDY'S ROADHOUSE'—let me tell you, I was sure happy to see that place."

"You had no idea where he was taking you?"

"Hell no. Johnny Ray hadn't opened his yap since I climbed into his truck. I was beginning to wonder what was up though, scared shitless to tell the truth. Like I said, Johnny Ray hadn't exactly kept it a secret he was none too happy about the prospect of having an Indian for a brother-in-law, so you can bet it was a relief to see Swamp Daddy's neon sign show up out there in the middle of nowhere.

"Must have been two or three hundred folks in Swamp Daddy's, and they were all drinking from shot glasses or beer bottles, with not a cocktail glass in sight. There were dancers wall-to-wall, and a fist fight broke out over by the pool tables just as we walked through the door."

"Sounds like quite the place," I say.

"Yes sir, it was. We must have been there for two or three hours. I was about as drunk as anybody by the time I hopped in the bed of Johnny Ray's pickup with a half dozen of my rowdy soon-to-be relatives for a trip to another shack of a saloon. I don't remember the name of that place, or even if it had one.

"The Buckwheat Zydeco Band was in full swing when we walked into that place, but I didn't know who they were. They were just a bunch of kids to me then—man, those boys could play."

"They still can," I say.

"Yeah, anyway, by the time Johnny Ray told me Thibodaux rules forbid us to call off the party before daybreak, it was already past two and partying until sunup seemed like no problem to me.

"Everyone was so friendly. A kid I'd guess to be about twenty claimed he would be my second cousin after Waynette and I tied the knot. Then he said he was his own brother's uncle–said it just like that, even though we had never met before and I hadn't asked. He told me how that was possible, but I don't recall the details. I *do* remember thinking that was a peculiar thing for him to be telling a stranger though."

Jeff pauses for another sip of Keystone, *'The beer that's always smooth, even when you're not.'*

"I had downed at least my share of Keystone and Jack by the time another future cousin sidled up to me. Darrel, that was his name. He was kind of a funny looking guy—no hair and ears all pointy on top, like elf ears. He walked with a strut, like a flashy runway model only not so flashy, you know, and he cocked his wrists a little more than most guys do. He was a strange one, for sure.

"Then, out of nowhere, two girls showed up and sat down with me and this Darrel. Looking back now, they were dressed a little whorish, but I thought nothing of it at the time, and, besides, they seemed to know Darrel and were getting better looking by the minute—you know how that goes."

I nod. Yes, I know how that goes.

"We just danced and drank and threw down a few shooters there toward the end — we talked, you know, nothing out of the ordinary. Then, with no kind of warning, the girl who had sort of paired off with me said she thought I was about the finest looking piece of ass she had been privileged to see lately.

"I remember now—Janice was her name.

"Anyway, this Janice said she had never fucked an American Indian and wanted to know if I'd mind helping her remedy that oversight in the interest of changing a bad string of luck that had been following her around for a month or two. She said she tried out one of those Indians from Bombay a while back with no satisfactory consequence."

**

Jeff pauses to pop the top on another can of beer.

The warning wail of the train's horn sounds at a distant crossing as it moves slowly away toward Albuquerque and Kansas City and on to the city of Chicago, the town Jodi and I had called our home before she was murdered and buried under an abandon GM&O railroad depot storage room dirt floor. In this moment that strikes me as a coincidence even though I know there is no such thing.

The train slows to a stop with at least fifty cars yet to pass the crossing.

Jeff holds a can of Keystone in front of me. "Sure you won't have a beer, Gille?" he says.

My surprise at Jeff finally addressing me by my first name must have affected my reasoning.

"Thank you, Jeff," I say, "I never really cared for that 'never-before-breakfast' rule anyway." I take the beer and settle in for the rest of Lightfoot's Thibodaux tale.

**

According to Jeff, Darrel bought a couple of six packs at last call and they loaded the city girls in Darrel's 'fancy-assed' convertible.

"You should have seen the gravel fly when that fool stomped on the gas, Gille. I thought he was going to kill all of us before we could get out of the parking lot."

Sipping beers and smoking buds, the wind whipping through the two whores' starched hair, they flew through the bayous that crowded the narrow strip of blacktop. Darrel turned onto a rutted dirt road, barely a trail, that angled off to the west and wended its way to a small clearing at the edge of a swampy lake. He parked next to a rickety looking catwalk with an old wooden rowboat tied to a mooring post there.

Darrel, and what he was now referring to as his girlfriend, took the rowboat out onto the lake. Lightfoot said he watched for the moment it took the boat to disappear into a stand of moss-covered Oak trees not far away.

**

"So anyway, with her so hell-bent on changing her luck, me and this Janice girl are giving it all we got in the back seat of Darrel's convertible, top down of course, when a pickup truck slides to a stop next to us. It's Waynette, you know, my fiancée, and her two brothers."

"Damn."

"Yeah, that's what I say now, but then I didn't even notice they were there until Johnny Ray turned a spotlight on me. My red ass bouncing up and down in the beam of that spotlight—now that is a sight I'm embarrassed to even think about *anybody* seeing, let alone Waynette."

"That's a tragic story, for sure," I say.

"You got that right. Johnny Ray and his little brother, who's about the size of a Winnebago, jumped out of Johnny Ray's pick up and grabbed me by the legs. I saw them coming from over my shoulder, but there was nothing I could do about it with my pants in a bunch down around my ankles. Besides, those boys were huge, and I was still ass up and hard as a rock, you know."

"Enough said. I'm getting a disturbing picture."

"Well, things went downhill from there. First, they grabbed my pant legs and skinned them the rest of the way off, skivvies and all. Then they dragged me out across the window trim and plopped me down on my belly in the mud. The fronts of my legs were all scraped to hell by that metal thing on the door where the window goes down. I tell you, I was bleeding like one of Cousin Luke's stuck pigs.

"When I tried to get up, they kicked me around a bit, and that's when Johnny Ray made it clear to me that 'no damn Arizona Indian is going to marry my sister, not while I'm alive.' That's what he said, only his language wasn't so polite, you know.

"I was still kind of in a daze when they picked me up from the mud and slammed me against the side of Johnny Ray's pickup. I think that was what cracked a couple of ribs."

Lightfoot pauses to raise his shirt and point out the ribs in question.

"Johnny Ray told me to get my Indian-ass dressed. I glanced through the window of the pickup. Waynette was just sitting there with her hands in her lap. Her head was turned down. I couldn't see her face very well. I tried to talk to her, but she wanted none of that. I could hear her sob though when Johnny Ray knocked me to the ground with a slap to the ear. I couldn't hear anything but the ringing in my head for an hour after that."

"God damn, Jeff, you're lucky they didn't kill you."

"Oh, they would have if Waynette hadn't been there—I'm sure of it."

**

Johnny Ray stuffed Waynette's engagement ring down Lightfoot's throat and clamped his mouth shut until he swallowed before he and his brother tossed him in the back of their pickup. They hauled Jeff to the Thibodaux bus station that was not a bus station at all, but an old wooden bench out front of a Texaco gas station where a bus stopped most mornings around seven and picked up anyone in the vicinity with a ticket or cash in hand.

"Bloody and covered with mud, my head still ringing, I lay flat out on the bus-stop bench for hours before a bus pulled in.

"A sorry sight I was. Stink—man, did I stink, and I hurt all over.

"A mother covered her baby daughter's eyes as I hobbled my sorry ass onto that Greyhound bus. A bum dressed in rags slid to the middle of his seat so there would be no room for me to sit there.

"I limped down the aisle to a wooden bench-seat at the back of the bus. When a passenger sitting on a cushioned seat toward the front of the bus got off at the first stop, I went for his seat, you know, and a snaggle-toothed woman in one of those paisley-flowered feed-bag dresses got right up in my face.

"An ugly tow-headed kid with greasy black hair was cradled in her arms—the kid had to be at least two years old and big for his age at that. She leaned the back of the kids head right up against my chest, him sucking away on her tit, while she reminded me the back of the bus was reserved for black folks and Indians and I was to go back there where I belonged."

"What did you do?"

"Hey, I'm not stupid. I held my tongue. I was in no hurry to get another redneck ass whipping. Hell, in my condition that feed-bag woman could have taken me down."

"I'd say you made an excellent decision, Mister Lightfoot. Congratulations on recognizing your limitations."

"Uh-huh, but I had some fun with those folks. Any time I caught one of them sneaking a peak my way, I turned on an old crazy-Indian gaze my granddad taught me when I was a kid, grabbed an imaginary head by its hair, scalped that head with my imaginary tomahawk, and tossed the imaginary head to the floor. Grandpa used to freak out tourist kids with that move on the reservation. He thought it was funny as hell."

"I think that's probably one of those things you just have to be there to appreciate," I say.

"Yeah, well the bus driver didn't appreciate *my* interpretation one bit. He stopped the bus and waddled back to my seat. He leaned in, his nose to mine, and yelled in my face. I almost threw up from the stench of corn-nuts and coffee.

"'One more outburst and your ass is going off this bus. Do you understand me, Chief Shitbird?' That is exactly what he said. Do you believe that?"

"Now, that is no way to address an Indian brave," I say.

"To tell you the truth though, Gille, he reminded me of that Jackie Gleason character—you know the one, the bus driver guy, the way the veins on his neck popped out when he threw one of his hissy-fits?"

"Ralph Kramden."

"Yeah, Ralph Kramden, that's the one. Now that was one funny guy. It was like Ralph Kramden was threatening to kick my ass. My bust-up ribs hurt so bad from holding back a laugh that tears rolled down my cheeks. I told him I was sorry, and that it wouldn't happen again. Those tears must have made old Ralph feel guilty. He just turned around, waddled back to his seat, and never looked in the rearview mirror the rest of the trip."

**

About the engagement ring Johnny Ray stuffed down Lightfoot's throat—Jeff told me the ring meandered through his intestines and plopped into a Winslow McDonald's toilet bowl two days later— 'stuck to the side of a turd the size of a Chiquita banana', he said. He said he flushed the toilet before thinking but happened to catch a glint of the diamond's sparkle as it clung to the side of a giant pointy-ended turd swirling toward the drain.

Seeing that sparkle, Jeff plunged his hand down into the water and grabbed that spinning turd just as it was reaching the point of no return, and he yanked the handful of shit up from the stool with his diamond ring intact. He said that he keeps the ring in a bedside table drawer and that, on occasion, wears it on his pinky finger.

**

Jeff relieves himself behind the car. He unhooks the bungee on the trunk and reaches inside. When he gets back behind the wheel, he has three more Keystones in his hands. "Almost forgot about these." He holds a can out in front of me. "Ice cold."

"No thanks," I say. "So, where does this story go from here?"

"That's about it," Jeff says, "end of story"

He sips on his beer. Again, the train's horn sounds its forlorn distant howl. Freight cars struggle to inch forward as gravity grinds their wheels against the rails.

"Waynette Boudreaux, that was my fiancée's name. I told you that, didn't I?"

"I believe you did," I say.

"The girl sure could cook, and nice to look at too, but what I couldn't get out of my head was that 'like mother, like daughter' thing. It did worry me some that Waynette's momma was looney tunes. I guess lust wins out over common sense, right, Gille?"

"Roulette is a sucker's game, but there are plenty of players," I say.

**

The Burlington Northern and Santa Fe's twin locomotives continue to snake away in the distance, dragging two hundred cars laden with showroom-bound Cadillacs and Chevrolets. Container cars loaded with every kind of freight, bound for Sears, and Walmart, and Costco pop the rails as they continue their way east to Albuquerque and on to Memphis and Chicago's south side.

The crossing lights illuminate our faces like red strobes flashing in the last hour before the desert dawn. We lean back against our headrests and listen to the rickety-clack of the train's wheels rolling across the loose joints of the rails.

Einstein taps me on the shoulder with the tip of his pipe. "Do you have a match?" he asks.

"Albert—I thought you had gone."

"Gone to where."

"I don't know. Wherever it is you people go. Anyplace you want, I suppose." I dig through my pockets. "No, I don't have a match."

We sit in silence watching the train rumble by.

Albert taps me on the shoulder again. "Trains are fascinating, aren't they, Gille," he says.

"They are," I say.

"I love trains; I always have," says Albert. "When I was a boy, I sometimes sat for hours on the long bench that ran across the back of the platform outside Munich station. I especially enjoyed watching the passenger trains. I would rest my elbows on my knees and steady my head with my hands on either side of my eyes, like horse blinders, so all I could see was that part of a train directly in front of me as it rumbled by.

"Holding a steady gaze, it was impossible for me to tell if the train's cars were passing by the station platform or if the bench had broken free and I was the one in motion, riding that bench down the platform at break-neck speeds until the last car passed from my limited view. Then, like magic, the bench returned to its original position on the station platform where I waited for the next train to come. You know, Gille, it's all relative."

"I had a feeling you were building up to something like that. I *do* think I know what you are talking about though. I've watched rows of corn and soybeans rush by while riding trains through the open farmlands of Illinois, and my mind would sometimes become confused about what was moving and what was not."

"Exactly," says Einstein.

"Something else I noticed."

"Yes?"

"When a train comes into their view, cattle standing along the right-of-way stop whatever it is cattle do and press against the barbed wire as if they are suddenly in a catatonic state that only allows them to stare at the cars rumbling by. Do you suppose they experience that same feeling you did as a boy at Munich station? Do you think they might be trying to hold their balance as they skid across the pasture at break-neck speed?"

"Now that's something I hadn't considered, Gille," Einstein says, shrugging his shoulders. "Your guess is as good as mine."

**

I'm startled awake by the pop of the top on another can of Keystone beer. The marketing geniuses at the famous Coors Brewery came up with Keystone. They must have had Jeff Lightfoot in mind when they coined the slogan for the Keystone brand printed on every can, and this, as I have said before, is it.

'Keystone–Always Smooth, Even When You're Not'.

An unopened beer sits in a Walmart cup holder on the console between me and Lightfoot alongside his big metal spool of dozens of keys—car keys, skeleton keys, house keys, safe deposit keys, keys to gates, and padlocks, and freezers, and drawers. What need would a part-time cab driver have for all those keys in a place like Winslow, Arizona?

Lightfoot points at the beer. "Help yourself, Mister Barker," he says.

"No thanks," I say. I lean back and close my eyes, not wishing to spur further conversation.

"You know, I think I really loved Waynette," Jeff says. "Funny how those things happen, right, Mister Barker."

"What things?" I ask, resigned to my fate.

"Oh, you know what I mean."

"Can't say that I do."

"My cousin, Danny, lives a little south of Thibodaux. He had been coaching football down there at Nicholls State for four years or so when I decided to pay him a visit. That's how I came to meet Waynette Boudreaux. She worked at Nicholls State then.

"When I caught up to Danny, Waynette was sitting at a table with him in the school cafeteria. He introduced me to her, and that's all there was to it, I was hooked. Funny how lives can get all tangled up by chance, huh?"

"Yes, it is," I say, even though I know 'chance' had nothing to do with his meeting Waynette in that cafeteria in that space of time. It was part of the plan, the natural way of things—Jeff could not have avoided that meeting if he had tried.

Lightfoot takes another sip of beer. He turns the radio up slightly and taps his finger against the steering wheel to the beat of the last few bars of Dylan's *Ninety Miles an Hour Down a Dead-End Street*. He turns the radio down to a whisper at the song's end.

"What's your thought on that kind of thing, Gille?" Lightfoot asks.

"What? Dylan? He wrote some of my favorite songs; not much of a singer though," I say.

"No, not Dylan. What do you think about things happening that way—the way I met Waynette?"

"I'm not sure what you're asking."

"Well, with no purpose in mind, I drove fifteen-hundred miles, through deserts and into the bayous of Louisiana, and what did I find? My soul-mate, that's what. No way in hell would I have crossed paths with Waynette Boudreaux if I hadn't taken that trip. Now, doesn't that seem strange to you, Mister Barker; like it was somehow meant to be?"

"About as strange as me sitting here in this old flattop Chevy, thousands of miles from home, at the break of dawn, in a blizzard with a Hopi Indian fresh off a reservation north of Winslow, Arizona I didn't even know existed a day ago," I say.

Lightfoot smiles. "Yeah, you got it, Mister Barker; that's exactly what I'm talking about," he says. "Sometimes I think everything that happens is just part of a master plan. How about that, Mister Barker? What do you think about that?"

"Bingo! Congratulations, Jeff. Even if it was by accident, I think you hit the nail right on its head."

"You can be a real pain in the ass, Mister Barker."

"Be that as it may, the question here is not what do I think, it's what do I know."

Okay then, what is it that you *do* know?"

**

Of course, what I know is that Lightfoot, like all life on this planet, is a pawn in the ongoing Zargonian evolutionary games. That much at least had been made clear to me years ago by my friend, Ron, from planet Zargon in the galaxy of Dargo, millions of light years but only a short wormhole away.

Unaware, as are most of us, Lightfoot is hard-wired to believes he makes decisions in the moment, that his choices are spontaneous affairs. Quite the opposite is true. In fact, his meeting with Waynette Boudreaux was on his program from the beginning. Free will resides in the imagination. There are exceptions, but the chance any of those exceptions apply in that, or any other, instance is slim to none.

Those few free will exceptions are the result of an element of chance added early on to the evolutionary games for the amusement of our Zargonian masters. The chance free will has a part in any decision is less likely than hitting a Las Vegas slot machine's jackpot.

With that in mind, though choices Jeff makes seem to be his own, odds are he has no control in any matter. Chance barely rates as a concept in Jeff's life, or yours, or even mine.

So, you see, I know the answer to Jeff's question, but am I going to tell him these things? Or, am I going to follow the advice given to me by Zargon Ron when I was a child—when he made it clear to me I would be one of the few on this planet chosen to retain memory of contact with our alien creators from Zargon. You may have memory of that conversation, but here is a part of it again for your review.

"Yes, Gille," Zargon Ron said to the then eight year old me in his confidential and telepathic way, "you are now aware of things of which few other earthlings can even imagine but let me give you a word of advice."

"Yes?" I said.

"Guard these secrets well, my friend," said Zargon Ron. Sharing this conversation with those who have no memory of alien encounters is seldom well received. If you must, it is best you speak of these things only with those few you are certain share your knowledge."

"Okay, Ron," I said. "That makes sense to me."

**

"I can't claim to *know* the answer, Jeff," I say, feigning a lack of knowledge when it comes to the mysteries of chance, "but my guess is your meeting Ms. Waynette Boudreaux was the luck of the draw."

"Yeah, I guess," Lightfoot says, "but it still seems strange to me."

We sit quietly, lost in our own separate thoughts of things past and roads all of us delude ourselves into believing might have been taken.

"Where is this Waynette Boudreaux now?" I ask.

"I talk to Danny every now and then. He doesn't know much about Waynette since she quit working at Nicholls State, but he thought she was living with her mother on the home place down by Thibodaux; he wasn't sure.

"Danny said he heard old Johnny Ray was dead — got shot or killed in a car wreck, he couldn't remember which; doesn't really matter—dead is dead. That was a couple of years ago."

"And where is Thibodaux?" I ask.

"Not far from New Orleans, sixty miles, a little south and west of there, I think," says Jeff. "Only been there twice myself."

"Uh huh. So, what's the story with the mother?"

"The old woman had cancer; that's what the doctor told her. But Mrs. Boudreaux wasn't believing a word of it. She told the doctor to leave her some morphine and not bother coming back till she called him for more of the same."

"Why?"

"Why what?"

"Why didn't Waynette's mother think she had cancer?"

Lightfoot takes the pack of cigarettes from the cup holder console. He offers me one.

"No thanks. You know I don't smoke."

"I've been trying to give the damn things up myself," Jeff says. "I was up to about two packs a day but have it down some now. I only smoke when I'm drinking these days."

Jeff sticks a cigarette between his lips and sets the pack back on the console.

"You'll get a kick out of this one, Mister Barker. But it is the God's truth, I swear."

There he goes with that swearing to the truth again.

"Hold on a minute," Jeff says.

He steps out into the cold and puffs on his cigarette a few times before dropping the butt to the snow-covered blacktop and stepping back into the car.

"Voodoo." Jeff looks at me side-eyed. "That's why the old woman didn't think the cancer was her problem."

"Voodoo, you say."

"I kid you not. For years, the Boudreaux clan had an old Quadroon housekeeper they treated like family. Then things started to go missing and Hillary knew the woman had to be stealing the stuff; there wasn't anyone else around. I guess that went on for a while before Hillary confronted her and all hell broke loose. Anyway, Hillary was certain the old woman put a curse on her on the way out the back door."

"Do you believe that?" I say.

"Hell, I don't know voodoo from Scooby-Doo," Jeff says, "but I know that's what the old woman believed, and for sure something took her down to a ninety-pound bag of bones in no time. Hell, that's been a while now, more than five years. She's probably long gone."

We sit in silence watching the last of the train's cars rumble by.

"That was the pluckiest old woman I've ever met," Jeff says. "Her eyes were coal black and sunk deep in the hollows above her cheeks like she was one of those zombies in a Hollywood movie." He shakes his head. "Gave me the heebie-jeebies, those dead eyes of hers. Spooky as hell, I'm telling you."

"Heebie-jeebies, you say. Hmm."

"You think there's any truth in that stuff?" Lightfoot asks.

"What stuff?

"You know–voodoo, zombies, black magic–all of those things."

"That's a strange question for you to be asking, you being a Hopi Indian and all."

"Now, what's that supposed to mean?"

I tell Jeff, he, as a member of a tribe of Native Americans who still have a medicine man shaking the dust from dried pig skins on anyone suffering a fever, or a heart attack, or a shotgun blast to the belly while summoning the spirits of earth, wind, and fire to cure the ailment, should have no problem believing in the power of the voodoo curse of a Haitian Quadroon from the Louisiana bayou.

Not to mention the hundreds of years his tribe had spent pounding on drums, dancing around campfires in a hallucinogenic haze, and yelping at the moon to hasten a spring drizzle.

"And war paint. And witch doctors. What the hell is that all about, Mister Lightfoot, if that really is your name?" I say.

Jeff shakes his head and smiles.

"You're a funny guy, Mister Barker," he says.

"Yeah, so I've been told."

**

"I'd sure like to just talk to Waynette again though," Jeff says. "Who knows, maybe we could get back together. I guess she wouldn't have hung around Thibodaux for long once the old lady was gone. There's not much in Thibodaux for a girl like Waynette."

"There's only one certain way to find out, my friend."

"Now, how would that be?"

"Go down to Thibodaux and see for yourself."

"You mean now?"

"Why not now? We need that briefcase before we show our faces around Winslow again, and like you said, odds are it's on its way to Louisiana as we speak. It seems Thibodaux is on the way to wherever it is we need to be."

The engineer sounds his warning horn some two hundred freight cars away as the caboose rolls past in front of us and the red crossing lights go dark. Lightfoot revs the engine. He flicks the headlights on high beam. The motor races as he slowly lifts his foot from the clutch pedal and the old transmission slips into first gear.

The two-lane ribbon of blacktop road is hidden under a sheet of ice and snow. The skies have cleared. Dots of light from thousands of stars come to view after century-long journeys from all number of light years away. And the light from just one of those stars, a star forty times the size of our sun, sits inches above the horizon, still visible in the early morning sky, like a distant lighthouse beacon for we fellow travelers on caravan to bayou country and Thibodaux, Louisiana, down by the Gulf of Mexico.

10

Sam's Shell

Lightfoot points through the windshield toward a cluster of lights twinkling low on the eastern horizon. "That's Lafayette, right over there," he says. "We should be in Thibodaux for breakfast — country-fried sausage and eggs and a big old scoop of grits — two hours, tops. You like grits, Mister Barker?"

"Not particularly."

"Oh, I suppose you're more of a beignets kind of guy."

"Well, yes, I guess I am."

"To tell the truth, grits aren't on my favorites list either, not since I met a Koasati Indian chief's old widow last time I was down here — turned out she was my aunt a couple of times removed.

"Anyway, she makes the best fry-bread, better than any damn French donut, that's for sure. Hold the grits — give me a slice of auntie's fry-bread with *my* sausage and eggs. Maybe I can talk her into giving you a sampling, you being my good friend and all. How does that sound, Mister Barker?"

"Sounds delicious. I had hoped our friendship would have a reward someday."

"Very funny, Mister Barker, very funny. But I guarantee you'll be thumbing your nose at those fancy-assed beignets once you taste auntie's fry-bread."

**

It is fourteen hundred miles from Winslow to Thibodaux through desert and scrub on ribbons of road monotonous enough to hypnotize the most resistant. We had made only four stops since Lightfoot pulled his Chevy onto interstate 40, thirteen hundred miles ago.

A Texaco station outside of Albuquerque for snacks and gas was stop one. We didn't pull off the highway again until the gas gauge pegged on empty. We were in the middle of the nowhere that is about halfway between Amarillo and Memphis, Texas when, in desperation, we took an offramp in hope of finding a gas station, even though it appeared none was there.

**

With relief, I point across the overpass. "Over there, Jeff," I say.

Barely visible in dusk's muted light, a small clapboard building sits in a grove of pine trees. A single hooded bulb clamped to the gutter of the weathered shake roof shines intermittently on a faded yellow sign with crudely painted red letters scrawled across its surface: this is SAM'S SHELL — GAS AND BAIT are sold here.

And there are two ancient gas pumps in front of the station with shiny new seashell-shaped glass globes on top. Jeff pulls off the exit ramp road onto the concrete path that circles under the portico connecting the gas pump island to the building.

The station appears deserted. Chirping crickets, gone silent at our approach, resume their conversation.

"Doesn't look promising," Jeff says.

I step out of the Chevy and stretch. I peer through a window into the station, lit only by a half moon's light. The room is small, barely large enough for the cash register counter and rack of chips that I see.

Strands of multi-colored beads hang to the floor from a rod across the top of an open doorway to a back room that, judging from the shape of the building, I guess to be about the size of a two-car garage. I notice a sliver of light from under a closed door across from the cash register and tell Jeff what I see.

"Hello?" Jeff raps on the warped screen door that slaps against the doorjamb.

Jeff hits the screen door frame with the heel of his fist. "Hello — anyone in there?" he says.

An unexpected raspy reply comes through the station door.

"HOLD YOUR HORSES, for Christ's sake," the voice says.

"Thank you, sir," Jeff replies before walking around the side of the station.

I sit on a wooden bench close by the front door and lean against the wall next to an old soda machine. A white metal sign nailed to the wall beside the machine says I can get an ice-cold soda for 25 cents. I put a quarter in the coin slot and pull out a bottle of Orange Crush. I open the soda and clouds of ice crystals float to the top—ice-cold, as advertised.

I hear the flush of a toilet and the stretch of a spring as the flimsy plywood door across from the cash register opens and then slams closed. Light from inside floods through the station window.

A man wearing bibbed coveralls walks out the door. He is five feet six or so and built like a wine barrel, his arms bulging from the short sleeves of his tee-shirt. His wide face, ruddy-red cheeks, and white beard give him the look of a buffed-out Santa. He drops a crumpled six-month-old Playboy magazine, still open to Ms. June's centerfold, on the bench and sits next to me.

"A man can't even take a dump and catch up on his reading these days without somebody bangin' on the door. Might as well move the damn station out on the highway for all the privacy I get here. What the hell is that all about anyway? Heh, heh." His eyes twinkle. "What can I do for you boys? Need gas, I suppose."

"Yes sir," I say.

Crickets stop their chirping to listen to the crunch of pinecones underfoot as Jeff walks back from the side of the building adjusting the zipper on his fly.

"Didn't think we were going to make it," Jeff says. "I've run that old Chevy out of gas often enough to know when that gauge means business. Another mile or two and we'd have been on foot with our thumbs out for sure."

"Well, you probably would have ended up here just the same. This is the only gas station for forty miles any direction you go from here — course you could have stopped most anyplace along the highway instead of pissing in my back yard. Heh, heh."

"Sorry about that, sir; I didn't realize the emergency until I got out of the car," Jeff says.

"Don't let it worry you, son. I was just having some fun with you, heh, heh. As to you coasting in here on fumes — happens all the time," Sam says. "I wouldn't get any business at all off that highway if fools didn't drive till their tanks were near dry before looking for a station. No offense meant, by the way. Heh, heh."

"None taken," I say.

Jeff sees the sodas-for-sale sign tacked to the wall. He feels inside the pockets of his jeans, first leaning to one side and then the other, squeezing his hands down to the bottom seams in an exaggerated effort to show his pockets are empty.

I hold out a palm full of coins. "Help yourself," I say.

**

Sam reaches inside the station door and flips a switch. The Shell gas pump globes light up bright yellow.

"Regular or super?"

"We'll go for the super," Jeff says. "Fill her up, please."

Sam pushes a lever down on the side of the pump and inserts the hose nozzle into the Chevy tank. He pulls the hose trigger back and locks it open.

"I hear our gang of nitwit politicians down in Austin is going to outlaw these trigger locks," Sam says. "Seems a few months back some moron pumping gas lit himself up over by Houston.

"Of course, those statehouse boys blame his incineration on the equipment rather than him being a dumb ass. What kind of fool thinks it is a good idea to light a cigarette while he's pumping gas? The politicians don't even consider the fact the guy was breaking a law they already had on the books. Oh well, I suppose they'll be messing with these old pumps of mine while they're at it — seems they just can't keep their noses out of a man's business."

Sam grabs a squeegee from a barrel of water and scrubs it across the windshield. He polishes the window dry with crumpled pages from the Amarillo Globe-News and tosses the pages in an old trash barrel. "Check the oil?" he says.

"No need – just stick a couple of quarts in there," Jeff says.

I reach for my money clip. "What's the damage?"

"Looks like twenty-four-fifty counting the oil. Guess you boys were running on fumes for sure."

"There you go." I hand Sam two twenties.

"Come on in while I get your change," he says.

Sam pulls an old beat-up tackle box out from under the counter. "Twenty-four-fifty; let me see now." Sam's brow wrinkles as he concentrates on fishing a ten and a five-dollar bill from the tackle box full of bills crumpled into a hodgepodge of mixed denominations. He takes a fifty-cent piece from his coverall's breast pocket. Apparently, the cash register is only a ploy to keep the tax man at bay.

"Thank you, sir," he says, handing me my change.

"Name's Gille," I reply. Hesitantly, I offer Sam my hand and am pleasantly surprised when he doesn't put it in a crippling vice grip. I nod toward Lightfoot. "And that's Jeff," I say.

"I'm Sam, Sam Gillette, same as those razor blades. Suppose you already figured the Sam part out from the sign."

"Sam would have been my first guess," I say.

"Heh heh," Sam says.

**

Sam follows Jeff and me back to the Chevy. He nods toward the license plate. "From Arizona, I see."

"I'm from Winslow," Jeff says.

"Do tell. I went through there once back in '70 — might have been '71," Sam says. "Sarah Blane, a lady friend of mine; talked me into the trip while we were doing some busy work out behind the barn — said she wanted to see the Grand Canyon and wanted to spend the night with me up at that Grand Canyon Lodge.

"I asked her what the hell made her think of the Grand Canyon right in the middle of what we were doing, and she said she saw a picture of the Lodge sitting on the Canyon's rim in one of those travel magazines while at the hairdresser's that afternoon and that was probably why it came to mind. Can you imagine?"

99

Sam's mind drifts from now to thoughts of Sarah Blane

"You were saying?" I ask.

Eyes glazed, Sam looks at me as though we had not yet met.

I ask him again. "About the time you went through Winslow—you were saying?"

"Oh, yes, Winslow. Came to find out later the wind was gusting ninety to a hundred and more that day, blowing tumbleweeds and anything else that wasn't tied down across the highway. Never saw anything like it before or since, and I'm from Texas, so that's saying something.

"Dirt blowin' so thick I couldn't see past the hood ornament on my car—stopped me right there in my tracks. Couldn't tell if I was on the road or not–most likely not. All we could do was sit there and hope none of those fools still trying to drive in that stuff would kill us in the bargain."

"Scary as hell, I bet," says Jeff.

"That's for sure, son," Sam says. "Not only that, flying grit beat up my Buick so bad I had to have the thing repainted. It still wasn't all that good — looked like somebody peppered it with buckshot when the light hit it right." Sam shakes his head. "That cost me six hundred bucks for nothin'."

"I've been in plenty of Winslow windstorms," Jeff says, "but only a couple of those really bad ones."

"Well, son, nasty weather ain't the point. If you would stop interrupting, I could finish my story," Sam says.

Jeff plops down on the picnic bench and leans back against the station wall next to me. "I'm all ears," he says.

"Must have been stuck there three hours, maybe more," Sam says, "and, when the dirt finally quit flying, we could see this pile of twenty, might have been thirty, cars and pickups smashed together like an old, squeezed accordion not fifty yards in front of us — people lying along the side of the road like scattered cordwood. The wind had been howling so, we hadn't heard a thing until the distant wail of ambulance and firetruck sirens announced that they would soon be on the scene."

"You know, I wasn't around, but I sure heard about that," says Jeff, "most people killed in one of those Arizona storms ever, so I was told."

"I don't doubt that, son," says Sam. "If you don't mind me asking, where are you boys heading?"

"Louisiana. Thibodaux, Louisiana," Jeff says. "I don't know where after that."

"I'll be damn," Sam says. "Thibodaux is my hometown, for Christ's sake — born and raised there."

I tell Sam, no, Jeff was not kidding. We are indeed Thibodaux bound. I hop in, close the door, and lower my window as Jeff starts the car.

"Now that takes the cake," Sam says, leaning down toward my open window. "I grew up down on Bayou Lafourche; spent many a weekend pub-crawling across Thibodaux in my youth. You boys get a chance, drop by Tuffy's Tavern and tell Tuffy Sam Gillette said hello."

"We will certainly look Tuffy up when we get there," I say.

"Speaking of cake," Sam says, "my birthday was yesterday, fifty-fifth one so far. Don't you boys worry though–I have at least another thirty in me, heh, heh. Anyway, Mrs. Baldwin from over by Memphis baked me an angel-food cake and a peach pie. I have cake and pie coming out the yin-yang." Sam rolls his eyes up toward his brow. "And I have homemade ice cream too. How about you boys join me for some before you hit the road? Now that's the best offer you're going to get for at least seven hundred miles."

Jeff shuts down the Chevy. "Homemade ice cream is an offer I can't refuse," he says.

**

We follow Sam into the station, past the counter, and through the hanging beads strung across the doorway to the back of the station that is Sam's home. Everything is new and tidy-clean. Custom wood cabinets line the back kitchen wall. A window above the sink looks out on a dozen acres of fenced land. Two rows of trees the size of those in orchards of apples or oranges stand bare-armed. A concrete walkway between the trees curves gently down a hill to the first barn I have ever seen with either a picture window or a sky light, and this one has both.

"Are you an artist, Sam?" I ask.

"Oh, I suppose I have my moments," Sam says, "why do you ask?"

"The picture window and the sky light–your barn looks like it could be an artist's studio."

"Hadn't really thought about it," Sam says. He shows no interest in continuing along this line of conversation.

"Let's have some of this pie, shall we?" he says. "Have a seat while I get the ice cream.

"Homemade ice cream isn't usually that good after it sits overnight you know. Don't get me wrong–I would gladly take week-old homemade over the freshest store-bought kind. I have no idea what Irene does to it, but her ice cream tastes like fresh churned for days."

Van Gogh-yellow orchids in a cut-glass vase sit on an island bar next to Mrs. Baldwin's peach pie. The pie crust is a lattice design, a technique I had seen many times, but nothing to compare. The aroma of pie popped fresh from the oven still fills the room.

Sam sets a half-gallon of ice cream on the counter.

"Okay boys, dig in," he says. "Let's see if we can finish this off tonight."

Three helpings of ice cream and pie later, Jeff is in full recline and sound asleep on Sam's recliner chair.

"Well, thank you, Sam," I say. "Please tell Ms. Baldwin I said she makes the best peach pie."

"I sure will," Sam says. "She'll prize the opinion highly when I tell her it came from such a noted artist and peach pie connoisseur. Now, could I interest you in a glass of wine?"

"I'd like that," I say, now curious as to how Sam had come to know I am an artist of note, or any other kind.

**

Sam pulls the cork from a bottle of Cabernet and gives us each a liberal pour.

"A friend of mine over in Napa makes this stuff, the best Cabernet I've found, and free is a good price too. I like it cold– some folks don't, I know."

"Cold is fine by me."

"My friend surprises me with a bottle now and then," Sam says. "The last time I visited the vineyard we must have spent half our time out by 'the pool house', they call it, sampling wines; Cabernets, Chardonnays, and I don't know what else. Now that's the good life — I felt like I was the Duke of Something or Other for three or four days there."

We lift our glasses in a toast to Irene Baldwin and Thibodaux, and Sam's old friends, Sarah and Tuffy, and then to homemade peach pie a-la-mode and those folks who know how to make a fine Cabernet over in the Napa Valley.

"And to you, Mister Barker," Sam says, clicking the edge of his glass against mine.

**

"Gille," I say, "please call me Gille, Sam.

"Why certainly. Gille it is." We toast to that. Sam pours more wine. "Isn't this the best stuff you ever tasted?"

I nod in agreement. "It might be. It seems to improve with each tip of the glass, but I'm no wine expert."

"Well neither am I, but I say it is," Sam says. "Why anyone would buy the French swill at four times the price is beyond me."

With that, I must agree. Suddenly it dawns on me that, although there has been no mention of it, Sam had called me by my last name. How does he know who I am?

"Sam, you called me Mister Barker."

"Well, you are Gille Barker, aren't you?"

"That's true, but how did you know?"

Sam looks hard at me for a long moment, as if considering whether I am worthy of his trust. He pushes his stool under the counter. He grabs a third wine glass and another bottle of cabernet from the ice bucket and opens the door to the tree-lined path that leads down to the barn.

"Come with me, Gille," he says, "I have something you should see."

**

The night sky is clear between the bare branches of the two dozen orchard trees that line either side of Sam's walkway. Our breaths steam in the chill winter air, but I feel a Cabernet's warm inner glow. The barn sits low against a tree grove at the far end of the walkway, lending the scene an unearthly, apparitional air. That too could be the Cabernet.

An unmistakable figure sits in the center of an old wooden porch swing hanging from a metal frame next to Sam's fallow garden at a far corner of the lawn. The figure, slumped forward, looks to be sleeping.

"Albert?" I call out. "Is that you Albert?"

Einstein's head pops up from his chest. His animated wave seems to indicate he has been awaiting my arrival for some time. I wave back.

"Albert?" Sam looks in the direction of the garden. "Is someone there?" He questions me.

The now empty swing rocks ever so slightly.

"I thought I saw a friend sitting on your garden swing," I say. "Do you suppose I've been over-poured?"

We sip our wines and smile, continuing our stroll toward the barn.

"This is a wonderful walking path, Sam," I say, breaking our silence.

"Hand mixed every bit of concrete and hauled it from around front of the station," Sam says, "nine hundred and forty-two wheelbarrows of the stuff.

"Might have been more. Irene's husband Keller came by one day and rolled a few around while I went to town for car parts. I was keeping track of the loads on an old blackboard you might have seen hanging out by the soda machine. I don't think Keller marked his trips on there, but nine hundred and forty-two is what ended up on the board."

"No wonder you have Popeye arms."

"Heh, heh. Well, that was a long time ago; I'm not so sure I would be up for it now.

"And the trees," Sam says, "you notice anything special about the trees?"

From his manner, it is apparent Sam is proud of something about the trees that line the path. I feel it is only polite that I act as though I give a damn about his trees.

With some fanfare, I study the tree lines with first one eye closed and then the other.

"At first glance I thought they were all the same kind of tree," I say, "but looking more closely now, I see that about half have trunks like apple trees while the others have trunks that separate into small trunks from close to the ground. And the trees with trunks like apple trees still have a few red berries on their limbs while the others are bare."

"That's good, Gille. Anything else?"

"No, that's about it." I rock back on my heels and take another sip of wine.

Sam points toward the station and says, "See those trees up by the house?"

"Yes."

"The first four on each side of the walk are Hawthorns. They have a single trunk, like an apple tree, as you said. In the spring, they're covered with small white blooms. It smells like a funeral parlor out here when they're in bloom"

"Is that a good thing?"

"Heh, heh," Sam says, obviously none too impressed by my inquiry.

"Anyway," he continues, "you can smell them all the way out to the interstate. The next three trees on each side are Mexican Redbuds. Their limbs are covered with bright purple flowers that time of year. The next three are Hawthorns again, and after those three Hawthorns, I planted two more of the Redbuds and then again two Hawthorns. Finally, as I came to the end of the path, I planted a single Redbud, another Hawthorn and then the last tree, the one next to the barn, is a Redbud."

I look down toward the barn and back at the station.

"You don't get it, do you?" Sam says.

He is right; I don't get it. What is to get?

105

Because nothing else comes to mind, I say, "I think it must be beautiful in the spring when all the trees are in bloom."

"That it is, but that's not all. Think about it, Gille."

I study the tree lines again. "I don't know, Sam. Could it be the way they're spaced evenly and in perfect rows?"

"That's part of it too, but there is more."

"Go on," I say, "I know you're dying to tell me."

"Okay. Imagine this. Anyone who steps from the house onto my back walkway in the Spring finds they are in a canopy of white and purple blooms that stretches all the way to the barn. It's a beautiful sight, but the fun part is that I skewed the perspective.

"Looking down the walkway through the canopy, the number of trees with blossoms of the same color standing next to each other diminishes in the distance and gives the illusion that the barn is nearly twice as far away as it really is; maybe a hundred yards instead of fifty. And from the barn, looking back up the path, it appears to be no more than half the distance back to the station."

**

Now, halfway down the path, I look toward the station and the trees blossom with millions of white and purple blooms and some of those blooms break free to float lazily to the ground in front of me. The intoxicating odor of the Hawthorns fills the air. I look down the path through the canopy of blossoms and the barn recedes, as if by magic. I look across the lawn's winter cover of dormant grass to the still fallow garden. The bare branches of a distant stand of Oaks sit in wait of the first breath of Spring.

"This is really something isn't it Gille."

I turn toward the voice and there is Einstein standing at my side.

"Albert! I thought I saw you. What are you doing here?" I ask him.

"I was sitting in my room growing bored when, out of nowhere, it came to me — Gille is on a trip to Louisiana and I wouldn't mind seeing that part of the country one more time before it disappears into the Gulf of Mexico, why not tag along?"

He takes my glass and swallows what was to be my last sip.

"That *is* good, isn't it," he says.

106

"You've been in the car all the way from Winslow?"

"*Most* of the way."

"But I haven't seen you, not since we left the railroad crossing."

"I thought you understood, Gille," Albert says. Didn't your Zargon friend explain how this works?"

**

Einstein's question was a good one. Zargon Ron's candor had been questionable to me since his first visit back in nineteen sixty-two. It had come to my attention on several occasions over the years that in explaining the creation of, and purpose for, life on planet Earth to me, Ron left sizeable holes in the fabric of things.

For instance, he pretended to be shocked when, a few years after we first met, I asked him about God — if his Zargonian pals were responsible for creating life on Earth, where did God fit into the picture? That was what I asked him then.

"What's this about a God," he said, "there is no God in this equation–God had nothing to do with it."

He got all huffy about it, like, who was *I* to question *him*? So, then I asked Ron, well, if no God was involved in any of this, who created him and his Zargonian pals?

"Did you boys just materialize out of thin air?" I asked him. He had no reply.

**

"I have no idea what you're talking about, Albert," I say.

"Well then, let me be the one to explain."

"Before you get in to all that —" Sam hands Einstein the extra wine glass he had brought along and pours each of us four fingers of Napa Valley's finest. "I wouldn't mind hearing this myself," he says.

For some reason I am not taken aback by Sam's awareness of Einstein's presence or that, since he brought an extra glass, he must have known Albert was in the back yard all along.

"You two know each other?" I ask.

"Don't think we ever met," Sam says, "but everyone knows Einstein, don't they?"

107

"You are aware Albert died some time ago, aren't you?" I say to Sam.

"What's that got to do with the price of green peas?" Sam says.

"Thank you for the Cabernet, Sam." Einstein interrupts. "I do enjoy a good glass of wine,"

"There's more where that came from, my friend," Sam says.

"That's good to know," Einstein replies. "Now, where was I before you gentlemen interrupted me?

"Oh yes, regarding your inquiry, Gille, there are two things to remember. I go where I want to go and can only be seen when I want to be seen. And it just so happens those are my favorite things about being released into the full reality of spacetime."

"You're getting a little ahead of me there, Albert," I say.

"Yeah, I'm confused myself," Sam says, not appearing to be concerned by any confusion, his eyes slightly glazed.

Einstein polishes off the last of his wine. The bottle gulps as Sam refreshes his glass.

"I think I can make this clear to you two," Albert says. "Kurt and I argued about this for years — we still do."

"Who's Kurt?" Sam asks.

"My friend Gödel, Kurt Gödel."

Sam looks at me and shrugs his shoulders. Neither of us have a clue who this Gödel might be.

"This could be more difficult to explain than I thought," Albert says. "Let's not worry about Kurt right now."

"That suits me just fine," Sam says.

"All right then, so this is how it is," Einstein says. "The main thing to remember is that time and space are one and the same. Everything that happens at any single moment takes up that place in space for eternity. That moment is always out there–as is this moment in our multi-dimensional universe. And what we refer to as the future is here too, another slice in spacetime."

Sam refills my now empty glass. I feel a wave of understanding. I *see* the slices of spacetime as we three amble from one slice to the next in our stroll through now into now and on to the next now in silence under the canopy of the Hawthorn and Mexican Redbud's white and purple blooms.

**

At the end of the path a simple metal clock mounted loft-high on the weathered wooden planks of the barn comes into view. It is a simple round clock like those on many kitchen walls, but this clock is four feet in diameter and has the mischievous face of the cartoon character, Elmer Fudd, the shotgun toting archenemy of Looney Tunes' Bugs Bunny, painted on its dial.

Red-gloved index fingers at the ends of Elmer's arms are the clock's hands. As we approach the barn, both the hour and minute hands extend directly above Elmer's head. The clock tolls midnight as Sam unlocks two big brass-plated padlocks and the heavy barn door creaks open.

Albert at my side, I gaze into the barn's blackness. Sam reaches inside and flips a half-dozen switches before backing away into the garden. Six banks of track lamps fill the room with a blinding white light. My irises dial down from the dark to view the interior's pure whiteness. I am stunned by what I see.

The room is large, how large I cannot say. The stark white floor and walls are as if one, endless, wrapped in a gauze-like haze with no real place of reference in the space of things. A dark-wood banquet table, twenty, thirty, maybe fifty feet long and ten feet wide, legs elegantly carved with swirling vines and clusters of wooden grapes, floats, seemingly suspended, in the whiteness.

Seated at the table on a massive high-back armchair with wine-red velvet trimmings is my long dead fiancée, Jodi Jones, as young and beautiful as the day I last saw her so many years ago. And next to Jodi is her sister, Belinda, who had professed her love for me and me for her only yesterday. Belinda's head is bowed, eyes downcast in consideration of unfamiliar hands, but her hands, that rest one on top the other on her lap.

To the right of Belinda are two handsome boys, eleven and thirteen, in black formal attire. They are my sons, not yet born. A girl, an angel-child with cobalt eyes and light silken hair, stands beside the younger of my sons holding his hand in hers.

My mother and father, both passed from this life now, stand next to the girl, facing me, smiling, their arms intertwined. And seated next to my father is his father, my grandfather, and to his left is my dear friend, Ruth, my grandfather's second wife, her rust-red hair brilliant in the white light, and standing to the side behind my grandfather is his first wife Jane, my father's mother, who slipped from life in this Universe while still young, as she is now. And sitting on the high-backed chair in front of my mother is her mother, Winifred, teacher of all children and protector of my youth.

Barely visible at the far end of the room, Zargon Ron is seated on a regal velvet throne with Anna Towahongva at his side.

The table is set with hand-painted china and elegant sterling of the same design as the silverware in Sam's gas station. Neatly spaced across the table's length are two dozen red candles. They flicker in gold candelabras, their flames burning through the mist.

Only Jodi's vibrant emerald eyes are not downcast now. Each person's hands are clasped in front of them, as if in prayer. Jodi smiles. Her eyes fixed on mine—she beckons me forward with the wave of her hand and a velvet-soft whisper.

"Come, Gille," she says, "daylight's burning."

**

Spellbound, I raise my foot to step across the high threshold.

"Stop! Don't do it Gille!" Albert grabs my shoulders from behind and yanks me away. The barn door slams closed. My arms flail for balance as we tumble backward across the walkway. There is the whoosh of escaping air from Einstein as he falls to the ground at the foot of the last Hawthorn with me across his belly.

I struggle to my feet and fling the barn door open again. It is cold and dark inside. I reach around the door jamb where I had seen Sam flick the lights on before. I push the only switch there. The dull yellow light of a single corded bulb dangling from a rafter casts deep blue-gray shadows behind bales of straw and bags of fertilizer and into the corners of the otherwise empty barn.

110

I stand frozen in the doorway, my hands gripping the jam on either side.

"What the hell, Albert!" I say.

Albert takes me by the arm with some urgency. "We must leave this place," he says, "you are in danger here. Follow me—Hurry, Gille!" Tugging me behind, Albert leans forward and quickly shuffles away.

As we scurry up the pathway in the moonlight between the Hawthorns and Mexican Rose Buds their blooms shower the ground, their arms suddenly bare.

11

The Dixie Diner

My eyes pop open to the pumping of brakes and the reflection of flashing red lights off the rear-view mirror. Instinctively, my arms shoot out to keep my face from smashing against the dash. The Chevy slides to a stop on the loose gravel shoulder of the road.

A Texas state-trooper is getting out of his patrol car ten yards behind us.

"Where the hell did he come from?" says Lightfoot.

"Where are we?" I ask.

"You're one sound sleeper, Mister Barker. We just drove through Wichita Falls and you didn't twitch a muscle."

"How big is Wichita Falls?"

"I rest my case," says Lightfoot.

The trooper walks toward our car, roadside gravel crunching under his spit-shined leather boots with each stride. He approaches Jeff's window, his right thumb hooked through a belt loop, fingers dangling over the handle of a holstered Colt 45. He leans forward until the hard brim of his Stetson clicks against the window. According to the tag pinned to his shirt he is Trooper Marcum. I'm guessing he's a Johnny Bill or Billy Bob. I will go with Billy Bob.

Billy Bob stands back and motions for Jeff to roll down the window.

"It's broken," Jeff says, mouthing the words to Billy Bob through the closed window. He wildly spins the window crank and

112

the mechanism clicks and squawks as the gears slip and the glass pops and shimmies on its track but doesn't budge more than an inch.

Jeff cracks my kneecap with the hard edge of the half-full can of beer he had been holding between his legs. I grab the can and stick it between my feet on the floorboard.

"I'll need your license and registration, sir," says Billy Bob.

Billy Bob's Texas drawl is tinged with the same croak as the sadistic deep-south prison captain's I remember from the movie 'Cool Hand Luke'.

"Sure thing, officer," Jeff says. He fishes through a stack of rubbish in the glove box — half-books of matches, gas receipts from two years back, sunglasses with bent rims and missing lenses. He pulls out a beat-up envelope with 'auto papers' scrawled across the front, and along with his driver's license, stuffs the envelope into Billy Bob's hand through the slit above the window glass.

"You know you were flying back there, Mister Lightfoot? Where the hell did you get a name like Lightfoot driving like that, son?"

Billy Bob gives Jeff a toothy grin that shows off a fancy gold cap on an upper canine.

Jeff ignores Billy Bob's trooper humor.

"Didn't seem like I was going all that fast, sir," says Lightfoot. He turns the lights on and off and on again, pointing at the always dark speedometer on the Chevy dash. "My dash lights went out on me about an hour ago. I guess I misjudged my speed, sir."

"Uh huh."

Billy Bob had heard more dash light alibis than he could count.

"Okay, Mister Lightfoot, here's the deal," says Billy Bob through Jeff's window, "I don't need the paperwork, so I'm going to cut you a break, provided you convince me you can follow the rules of the road on your way out of Texas. You *are* on your way out of Texas — right?"

"Yes sir, you can count on it. My goal is to get across that state line a–s–a–p," Jeff says.

Billy Bob slips Jeff's papers back through the slit in the window.

"Make no mistake, son," says Billy Bob, "if we cross paths again, there will be hell for you to pay."

"Yes sir. I understand," Jeff says, "and thank you, sir."

Jeff turns on the ignition. The motor races as he pushes the accelerator toward the floor and pops the transmission into first gear.

"Could you hand me that beer please, Mister Barker?" He says, pointing at the can sitting wedged between my feet.

**

Not a car in sight. The white center stripe on the blacktop road stretches endlessly past the headlight high beams into the pitch-black Texas night. I am soon asleep, hypnotized by the engine's steady drone.

A voice from the back seat breaks the engine's spell. "You know those boys are going to catch up to us sooner or later," the voice says.

"What?" Looking in the rearview mirror, I see the outline of his familiar form. "Albert? Is that you?"

"Now, who else would it be?" says Einstein. "What I said was, I think those men looking for Lightfoot will be catching up soon."

"I heard you the first time," I say.

"Are you talking to me, Mister Barker?" I hear Lightfoot say.

I turn my head slightly and see Jeff sipping a Blue Hawaiian cocktail through twin orange and white striped straws stuck in a foot tall glass the shape of a giant tulip. Pineapple slices and cherries speared on plastic toothpicks float on top of the drink's blue waters in the shade of a gaily painted paper umbrella.

Three dark-skinned boys, maybe six inches tall, balance tiny surfboards on their heads and dance across the dashboard. Foaming white waves crash on the sand behind them from the hood's deep blueberry sea. Lovers walk hand in hand to the water's edge.

Two sail boats tack in unison with the wind across the bay. A native girl with wings like an angel's, dressed in a skirt of palm strands, kneels before me with an offering of seared fresh Ahi on a platter of richly carved teak.

Hundreds of roadside palms wave in a tropical breeze. As the trade winds escalate, Jeff Lightfoot's classic flattop Chevrolet takes flight across the Pacific to the driveway of my Maui home, four thousand miles from Wichita Falls. My most trusted companion, a black Labrador who calls himself Domino, greets me with uncontrollable abandon at the front door. I reward him with a neck massage and a Texas bone. "That's my good boy," I say to Domino. He is pleased.

I have not been home for three years and more. I hear the crash of waves and feel the trade wind's refreshing breeze flush against my cheek.

Or is the window rolled down?

**

Tired and with the gas gauge bumping empty again, Jeff pulls into the parking lot of one of those giant trucker's rest stops along the freeway, this one just outside of Dallas.

It is the dead of night. A hundred eight-wheeler trucks and RV's are in the lot and at least forty Harley Hogs sit in a row, kickstand to kickstand, near the diner door. Traffic was light on the road. Where did all these people come from? How and when did they get to here?

After filling up and checking the oil, Jeff parks the car at the end of the row of Harleys. He crawls into the back seat and covers himself with a blanket he had stashed in the trunk. "Never know when one of these things will come in handy do you," he says.

"I'm going to get a sandwich," I say. "You want anything?"

"No thanks. Just wake me when you're ready to go."

**

I scoot onto a booth seat next to one of six big plate-glass windows that line the front of the truck stop's Dixie Diner. Gazing at me through that window, like an unattended child, Albert sits in the front passenger seat of the Chevy with his arm resting on the car's window frame. When our eyes meet, he smiles and waves his pipe. He sucks on the pipe and a cloud of smoke curls out the open window.

Across the room, three of the dozen clocks hanging at intervals of two feet or so across the wall behind the Dixie Diner's service counter let me know that, although it is only one-thirty in the morning here in Dallas, it is seven-thirty in London and a half hour since the noon whistle blew in Bangkok.

Truckers in baseball caps and tourists sporting shiny cowboy boots sit elbow to elbow on stools at the service counter with L.A. Hell's Angels in full leathers and a couple of real cowboys in wrangler's garb, their well-worn Stetsons pulled down on their ears.

Exhaled cigarette smoke hangs from the ceiling like a bank of smog. I feel the haze, bearing every disease known to man, drifting down to coat each of us with the flotsam of a hundred other souls.

A single swipe across the tabletop leaves a baby-poop brown skid mark on my paper napkin. Certain my hands need cleansing, I peer through the haze in search of a toilet.

**

There is no shortage of fellow weary travelers looking only for a break from the glare of approaching headlights and the monotony of the endless blacktop road. Men yawn and children rub sleepy eyes — bikers brace leather-jacketed elbows against countertops and sip from bottomless cups of coffee.

A gum-popping waitress walks from table to table, coffee cups looped through the fingers of one hand and a steaming pot held high in the other, hovering precariously above diner's heads. A second waitress joins in and they effortlessly rotate through the narrow aisles, pausing at seemingly random tables to drop cups and fill them to the brim with steaming coffee that pours like black molasses.

Endless waitress chatter with early morning regulars cuts through the din, broken into bits and pieces by the clatter of plates against Formica tabletops and the murmur of a dozen tired conversations.

Ready to order, sweetheart?

What'll it be Jake? Uh huh. How's Ginger? Haven't seen her in a coon's age.

Oh, that's right, I've never seen her. Harvey there told me she was out turning tricks at Stella's again last Saturday night—better check her ankle bindings are good and tight when you get home hon'.

How's it hanging Harvey? Yeah, right—in your dreams, you will.

You think maybe I could get your order sometime before the sun comes up, Karl?

Garland, you old fart. You're getting better looking every day, I swear. ——No, of course not. I wouldn't lie to you, hon'.

Having some hash browns with your ketchup tonight, Dale?

**

Another waitress appears at my table. She is pretty and younger and seemingly not as hardened to her circumstance as the two waitresses I had been watching make their rounds. Her name is Darlene.

"Coffee, Mister Barker?" Darlene asks.

"Lemonade, please," I say.

Darlene grabs a pitcher from the waitress station that is next to my booth. She pours lemonade into a plastic glass full of crushed ice and sets it in front of me.

"You called me Mister Barker," I say.

"And?"

"I'm wondering how you know my name?"

"I know your name for the same reasons you must know mine, Mister Barker," Darlene says. The mischievous flicker of a knowing smile briefly crosses her lips. She hands me a menu and says she will be back to take my order 'soon'.

117

**

'I know your name for the same reasons you must know mine.'

Darlene was right. Thinking nothing of it, I had known her name the moment I saw her approaching my table. I think I know what is going on here. As my alien mentor, Zargon Ron, told me when we first met in 1962, those of us selected to retain memory of alien encounters were also given the ability to recognize each other when we meet. Darlene, like me, must be one of that select group of earthlings chosen to retain memory of their encounters with our alien creators from planet Zargon. There can be no other explanation.

But, although our shared recognition has proved true in this case, I am having doubts about the reliability of the process. In my life I have only been aware of contact with four people who shared my knowledge of our Zargonian creators—yet, just today, three people I did not know have called me by name.

Maybe, although I *can* recognize those who have experienced alien encounters like my own, it is more of an on-again-off-again thing in my case, like the flaw in the selective omniscience Zargon Ron stuck me with. Once again, Ron's level of competence comes to question. Had my Zargon pal fumbled the ball?

Now I must wonder if there are more of us with memory of alien encounters than I had been led to believe, many more than I would have dreamed. What about that old jailbird in Winslow, and even Sergeant Tom? What about Belinda? How did she find me anyway? Is Shell-Station Sam one of us? Maybe an even better question—is he one of them?

**

"Could I take your order now, Mister Barker?" asks Darlene.

Before answering, my mind asks Darlene's, *'Have you spoken to any of our Zargon friends lately?'*

'Really wouldn't mind chatting, but I'm a little pressed for time, Mister Barker,' she replies in kind.

"Oh, sure thing," I say.

I order the Dixie Truck Stop Special—a Texas Burger with all the trimmings, a side of fries, and all the pink lemonade I can drink for 'four dollars and ninety-five cents, tax included.'

Darlene comes back with my order and a wooden box carousel thing that looks like a crafter's county-fair project tacked together with nails here and there. The carousel is stacked with bottles of ketchup and mustard and salt and pepper shakers and Texas Pete hot sauce.

"There you go," she says.

She tears a sheet from her guest-check pad and spears it on a six-penny nail stuck to the center of the condiment carousel.

"Enjoy your burger, Gille," she says while flickering that mischievous smile of hers at me again.

That settles it! This girl has met an alien or two. Not only does Darlene know my name, but she also knows it is pronounced Jill, not gill, like the respiratory organ of a fish. I am impressed.

**

The burger is huge and glistens with globules of cholesterol that soak the white-bread bun and ooze from under two slices of warm American cheese. A mound of crinkly cut French fries fills out the plate and spills onto the table. I did not order cheese. I lift the cheese from the burger and put it to the side. I pile on the lettuce, the slices of tomato and sweet onion, the mustard, and a few splashes of Texas Pete.

There are a dozen televisions mounted to beam supports throughout the restaurant, so no diner need be deprived of a moment's viewing. Television sound that would be rendered indecipherable by the rattling of plates and the din of conversations anyway is muted. Dialogue scrolls across the bottom of the screen for the viewer's pleasure.

A preacher named Sharky is on all those screens now. Sharky is in the process of prying the last dollars from the pockets of eighteen thousand believers who have come all number of miles to see 'the blessed one' on his pulpit. They have come to be saved by the hand of God, a God who has, according to Sharky, personally entrusted him with His power to heal.

A proposal from preacher Sharky scrolls across the top of the television screen. Send the reverend ten dollars and another five to cover shipping and he will slice a square from one of his wine-red neckties, anoint it with sacred waters, and have it in the mail to you first thing Monday morning.

But the sin of envy, not sacred neckties, is the topic of the tie-salesman-reverend's message tonight.

"As it is written in the bible," according to Sharky, King Saul despised David because David was better at murdering the men, women, and children who crossed his path than was Saul.

"Saul was envious of David," says Sharky. "Why had not his God given King Saul the talent to kill tens of thousands as he had given it to David?"

I am confused. Is Sharky saying his God oversees the murdering game? Wouldn't that be the devil's call?

The television camera pans across the eighteen thousand human beings stacked into the auditorium as they applaud Sharky like drugged loons. It is evident they do not share my concern.

Ushers in ill-fitting uniforms cruise the isles of the auditorium with silver buckets. Men, women, and children empty their pockets into those buckets as their offering to God through His self-appointed representative. Allowing that some of these people are simply hedging their bets, it remains a mystery why anyone would believe that handing this man a fist full of dollars is a good idea.

There are amens all around. Overcome with ecstasy during the grand finale, people drop to the floor at random like dramatic rag dolls and a choir of two-hundred strong bursts into song. Sharky, his fancy teeth sparkling white in the spotlight's glare, waves and makes his rock star exit.

**

I glance out the truck-stop window. Albert is leaning out the Chevy window tapping the face of his watch with his index finger.

I nod to indicate that, yes, I agree, we should be leaving — just a few minutes more.

Jeff, fresh from his nap, slides onto the plastic booth bench facing me. "How about one of those fries?" he says.

I push my plate, still half covered with crinkly-cut fries, across the table.

Lightfoot pops the top on a can of soda and pours it in a glass of ice he confiscated from the waitress station. He squeezes a trail of ketchup across the fries and a mound of mustard onto the rim of the plate. He dips a fry in the mustard and takes a bite from the end as if he is a professional French fry taster, a French fry connoisseur.

Lightfoot points at my fork and knife. "Do you mind?"

"Help yourself," I say.

Jeff unfolds a paper napkin across his lap. He cuts the cheese slices on my plate into inch squares with great precision. He places one square on top of a ketchup-soaked fry and dips it in mustard. Five minutes later, after repeating this process until my plate is clean, he dabs at the corners of his lips with his napkin.

"Tasty," he says.

I pull the guest check from the nail on the carousel and dig through my pockets for my money clip. Wanting to ask her again about her Zargonian connection, I scan the room for Darlene, but she is nowhere in sight. I toss her tip on the table.

I pop a few toothpicks from a metal dispenser on the checkout counter and stick them in my pocket while waiting for the cashier.

I notice the appreciation shown the diner's patrons by the cashier. Her enthusiasm to please is apparent in her smile. I can imagine how hard it is to hold onto that attitude while enduring the incessant small-talk chatter you get at the checkout counter in a joint like this.

Wait a minute! I know this cashier! I know her well!

She is Adel, a dwarf I met twenty years ago at Billy Bones' Midget Bar on downtown Chicago's Wabash Avenue.

As have many of us, I have learned not to take such coincidences too seriously. Otherwise, I might be led to suspect there is something going on in this world that I do not fully understand.

"Thank you, Jed," Adel says to the old bow-legged cowboy trucker in line in front of me, handing him his change. "Come back soon now," she says.

"I'll be back tomorrow, just like always — that soon enough for you, dearie?" the old grouch of a trucker says while tipping the brim of his Stetson and popping a toothpick into the corner of his mouth.

"Adel?" I say.

"Yes?" Adel looks up and sees me there for the first time. She adjusts her wire-rimmed glasses.

"Gille? Gille Barker! Well, I'll be damned. That *is* you isn't it?"

"It's me all right."

**

When my fiancée, Jodi Jones, disappeared twenty years ago, Adel and eight more of our friends, all dwarfs we had met at Billy Bones' Chicago Midget Bar, piled into Billy's silver Eldorado, and drove the two hundred miles to Mason City.

The Cadillac, its giant fins stretched behind, was a ghost ship without passengers to onlookers as it sailed south from Chicago down Route 66, dodging fender-benders and jackknifed semi-trucks that littered the highway in an early winter storm. Only the bill of Billy's blue baseball cap, barely visible behind the wheel, betrayed their presence.

They stayed at the Holiday Inn in Lincoln through the New Year, and along with police and scores of volunteers, they plodded along the banks of Salt Creek and through snow-covered fields in the search for Jodi Jones.

When Billy Bones and his midget entourage returned to Chicago, Adel stayed on. She stayed on until the 21st of January when another blizzard hit, suspending the search. Helping her up the Amtrak steps for her return to the Windy City that evening was the last time I saw Adel.

**

I ask Adel how she happened to end up working behind the counter of a Dixie Truck Stop in Dallas, Texas.

122

"Why, honey, I am a Dallas girl through and through, born and raised. Didn't you know that?"

"I thought you were from Chicago. Texas dwarfs? The thought never entered my mind," I say.

"You're still a wise-guy aren't you, Gille. Let me tell you, honey, there are midgets all over Texas, whether the rest of the Texans care to admit it or not.

"As a matter of fact, there are midget cowboys hanging all over my family tree, and you can take that literally, my friend. Hell, my Great Uncle Jake got himself hung from one, an old Elm on the east side of Waco, back in 1860 something, but he didn't weigh enough to stretch his neck and slipped the knot once the crowd thinned out. A few stragglers gave chase until they lost interest—never did catch him. Old Jake got the blame for every cow that went missing in the county for a year after, so I've been told. What do you think of that, mister smart guy?"

Adel slaps me on the arm and laughs.

"No, honey, I'm a Dallas girl all right. Didn't get out of Texas 'till I was almost seventeen—went all the way up to Chicago in a Greyhound bus to audition for 'The Wizard of Oz'. Didn't I tell you that story?"

"This is the first I've heard of it."

"Well, that's what got me to Chicago. They were doing the Wizard at the Shubert — going to take it on the road for a couple of years after that. They gave me a part straight away. Damned lucky to get it too.

"Any dwarf who thought there might be a snowball's chance in hell of getting one of those parts was lined up at the audition hall door — must have been a thousand of us. Never saw so damn many midgets. You know, unless you want to work the freak shows or the carnival circuit, it's not easy finding work when you're not much taller than a yardstick."

**

Adel was right about that. Even on the planet Zargon, where the Zargonian civilization had reached the intelligence level of today's 'human beings' more than seven billion years before the earth existed, where it had been billions of years since the last war or so much as a disagreement among neighbors, where discrimination by color or sex or ethnicity was unheard of and all Zargonians had been considered as equals for billions of years — where scientific advancement had, long ago, made a Zargonian's life expectancy indefinite as long as extreme trauma was avoided — even on that highly evolved planet, a civilization so far advanced it created our world out of boredom and a wish to fill their living room viewing platforms with interesting fare, even on Zargon one thread of discrimination remains — almost without exception, a tall Zargonian can count on receiving priority over his height-challenged counterpart, and that includes the securing of a decent dinner reservation. Even on Zargon, 'short' remains no picnic.

Improvement of circumstance in an earth-bound midgets future would seem bleak indeed.

**

In all the hours of idle Midget Bar chit-chat I had been exposed to during my Chicago days, not once had Adel's 'Wizard' connection been mentioned. How had a world-class spieler like her kept that out of those rambling conversations she so often instigated at the back round table in Billy Bones' Bar?

My question to Adel had evidently been lost in her showbiz tale, so I ask again.

"What *did* bring you back to Dallas, Adel?"

Adel flags down a manager to watch the register and jumps down from her perch on a stool behind the cashier stand. She takes my hand and leads me to a table.

"Have a seat, Gille," she says. "Let me see now – where was I?"

"I think you were about to tell me what brought you back to Dallas."

"Oh yeah. It all started about three years ago with an early morning call from Uncle Bobby, my mother's brother. Bobby called to tell me mom had been shot. I didn't know it then, but I would be flying back to Dallas for good that day."

**

124

Adel's mother, 'The Amazing Tiny Tina', worked the Texas side show circuit for years as the world's 'one and only' sword-swallowing dwarf during the freak-show carnival hay-days of the forties.

The Amazing Tina was awakened that night before Bobby's call by noises from her living room. Creeping down the stairs, she saw a man's figure in the shadows rifling through her side-board drawers. She crawled into the kitchen, climbed onto the counter, and slipped the butcher knife from its rack next to the cutting board. She crouched on the countertop beside the kitchen door and watched the pony-tailed burglar slip past her, not more than a foot away.

"You know, Gille, we midgets have an advantage when it comes to hide and seek," Adel says.

"There is always that," I say.

The burglar sat his pistol on the kitchen table. He opened the refrigerator door, took the cap off a fresh bottle of milk, and tipped the bottle up to his mouth.

"Took a drink straight from the bottle," Adel says. "Now, that's just rude, wouldn't you say?"

"I would say," I say.

Head back, the burglar's mouth was still on the bottle when the Amazing Tina leaped from the counter onto his back, her butcher knife flailing. Tina wrapped the burglar's ponytail around her free hand as if it were a rodeo bull-rider's cinch rope. She dug her heels into his sides.

The milk bottle crashed to the floor as the burglar bucked and screamed.

**

Adel said her mother sliced the blade of the butcher knife across the burglar's face six or seven times before he could flip her onto the tile floor and that, as Tina was struggling to her feet, the burglar grabbed his pistol from the kitchen table and shot her. After the third shot, the burglar dropped his gun to the floor and darted out the back door holding a bloodied kitchen towel to his face.

Though hard of hearing, Tina's eighty-three year old neighbor, Mister Molina, heard shots and was calling 911 before the third shot rang out. He grabbed an old double barrel he kept loaded next to his bed and hobbled toward Tina's house. As he crossed the alley, he saw the burglar's dark figure staggering away toward the freeway. He shouldered his shotgun and fired both barrels.

Mister Molina said he heard the burglar 'let out a yelp or two' as 'I powdered his ass pretty good', but he was too far away for the shots to bring him down. 'I couldn't chase after the little bastard,' the old man said.

**

"Anyway, Mom's doing well, and that's my Dallas story," says Adel. "You couldn't *drag* me back to Chicago now."

"I'm happy things have worked out for you, Adel," I say.

"Yes, I think they have, but enough about that," Adel says. "I'm out of here in half an hour; how about you stick around, Gille? We can hash over some old times over a cocktail."

I can think of nothing I would rather not do. Adel was a great friend, but our time together was long ago, and any talk of the memories we share could only depress both of us.

"Afraid we have to be on our way, Adel," I say. "We will be coming back through Dallas in about a week. How about I look you up then?"

"I look forward to it, Gille," Adel says.

She doesn't believe we will see each other again any more than I do, and like me she is good with that.

"Here, let me give you my number," she says, "you call any time you get through this way."

**

Jeff starts the Chevy and backs out of the Dixie Truck Stop stall.

I am lost in thoughts of Chicago and Adel and Jodi and the time we had together, almost twenty years ago now, in Billy Bones' Midget Bar. Jodi and I are sitting with our friends at the big round table in the back of the room next to the jukebox. Adel

126

is singing that song from the Wizard she sang for us then without a mention of her life story; the story she told me only today.

It was that song, running through my head now, that Adel had sung hundreds of times on the stages of the Shubert and the Orpheum and almost any other theater between New York and San Francisco that might be remembered from those days. Maybe you heard her there.

**

Ha Ha Ha, Ho Ho Ho and a couple of tra la la's
That's how we laugh the day away in the Merry Ole Land of Oz!

12

The Doodle

Jeff's shake of my leg rouses me. "We're here, Mister Barker," he says, "rise and shine."

The Chevy tires thump, thump, thump against the loose plank floor of an old wooden bridge deck; its rusty iron frame creaking with the strain. A cloud of dust swirls behind us as we shoot off the end of the bridge and land on the narrow dirt road that is the lane to the home of Ms. Hillary Boudreaux.

I look back toward the bridge at ancient Cypress trees that line the muddy banks of a lazy bayou stream. On either side of the lane majestic Oaks hung with Pele's mossy hair glisten with morning dew. The Boudreaux home sits ahead on a slight, distant knoll.

Jeff's description had led me to imagine the Boudreaux home as a slat-shingle shack with a front porch threatening to collapse into a pig wallow. It is none of that.

Between freshly whitewashed fences, the lane wends through lush green pastures like those on thoroughbred breeder farms of Kentucky. There is a spotless white barn and corral across the lane from the main house. Three smart-looking stallions rear their heads in unison to peer at us over the corral's wood railing.

Six white fluted columns support the veranda roof that extends across the front of the classic two story plantation-style main house. Jeff pulls the Chevy to a stop by the entry steps on the cobble-stone drive. Violet shadows cast by Oak branches crisscross the sap-green lawn and turn to deep cobalt as they climb the three steps to the veranda.

It is the morning of the third day on the road from northern Arizona's Navajo County to the lowland bayous of Southern Louisiana. I look at my watch. It is a quarter till nine on the twenty-first of December. I note the time because it is when I first consider that Lightfoot's professed goal of recovering Gene Cardenas's briefcase may have never been more than a ploy, that his true quest was for the hand of the wily Waynette Boudreaux.

I put myself in this fix—a fine example of my long-held suspicion that 'no good deed shall go unpunished' is a thought worth keeping in mind.

To hell with the whole mess.

At this point, what do I care? Other than fulfilling my natural writer's curiosities, whether we do or do not find the briefcase or Lightfoot does or does not rekindle his long-lost love with Ms. Waynette Boudreaux is of no consequence to me.

As Lightfoot's real reason for this road trip becomes less certain, my mission grows ever more primal and clear. Staying beyond the reach of Gene Cardenas and his sociopath sidekick is my primary goal.

**

There is a loud 'Ding' when Jeff lifts the big brass-ring mounted at his eye level in the center of Hillary Boudreaux's entry door and a 'Dong' as he drops the ring back in place.

A beautiful young mulatto, her flesh the color of brown sugar, swings the door open. Aptly dressed in simple leather flops and a long gray skirt, a lacey white blouse neatly tucked, she shows no outward sign of greeting other than standing aside to allow Jeff's entry and closing the door behind him.

Einstein taps my shoulder. "This must be the place," he says.

"Jesus, Albert, you scared the hell out of me. Yes, it must be," I say, but I'm not thinking of this place now.

I drag out Belinda's phone and call her.

"Are you safe?" she asks. I can barely understand her through the static of her phone's reception.

I tell her yes, I am safe, and I believe that could be so. If Cardenas had been following us, wouldn't we have lost him on our detour to Sam's station? If somehow our stop at Sam's hadn't thrown him off our trail, wouldn't he have betrayed his presence at the Dixie Diner?

"We've been on the road over two days. I don't see how he could find us now," I say. "I mean, what would make him think to look in a Louisiana bayou?"

"I don't know," Belinda says. "I just have this strange feeling—no reason for it really."

I know what she means; I don't mention it, but I have had the uneasy feeling Cardenas and Richard are not far behind ever since we left Winslow.

In fact, they are only hours behind. They know where we are at this moment. Our problem now is not the tracker they stuck under Jeff's Chevy—it was scraped loose on our first trip down the icy rutted lane to Cousin Luke's pig farm. It lays there, still forwarding its signal from under a drift of snow.

**

Picking up the tracker signal after their Winslow traffic stop by Officer Mendoza, Gene and Richard arrived at Luke's lane just as Aunt Wanda's old Ford pickup full of slop barrels popped up over the crest of the hill, turned south, and slid onto the blacktop road in front of them.

"There they go," said Richard. "They must have changed cars."

"I can't see a damn thing. Are you sure that's them?"

"No, but who else would be out here this time of night in this weather?"

Gene and Richard followed Aunt Wanda and her pickup full of slop barrels for seven miles down route eighty-seven until she pulled up the drive to her farm. They watched from the highway as she backed the truck into her garage. They heard the pickup door slam shut; only one door, and watched Wanda run across the drive and into the house as new snow mixed with sleet began to fall.

"Damn it, Richard! Where the hell are they?"

"Guess that wasn't them after all."

"No shit, Dick Tracy."

"Dick Tracy?"

"Yeah, Dick Tracy, you know, that detective in the newspaper comics on Sundays who had a habit of stating the obvious. 'No shit, Dick Tracy.'"

"What?"

"Jesus, Richard. For instance, I was in the fourth grade when a friend told me some sixth grade bullies took the lunch money his mother gave him that morning, and I suggested he might be in for an ass-whipping when he got home. His reply was a 'No shit, Dick Tracy'."

"I don't get it."

"Never mind, Richard," said Gene, "just get us back to where we saw that truck in the first place."

**

It was nearly a half hour drive on the icy highway back to the crest above Cousin Luke's farm. The tracker signal beeped strong as they turned down the lane.

"They must be here," Richard said.

"Douse the lights."

Lights out, Richard slid the Jaguar down the icy lane.

The house was dark. The tracker beep was strong.

"No car," Richard said. "I don't get it."

"That makes two of us. You look in that shed back there." Gene nodded toward an old weather-worn garage behind the pigpen.

The storm was a full-blown blizzard now. Huddled in their shelter, even the pigs had gone quiet.

"Just what are you going to be doing while I'm out there with those damn pigs?" Richard asked Gene.

"I'll be in the house looking for my briefcase—you know, the one that was swiped from under your nose."

The two sociopaths glared at one another for the few moments it took Richard to consider his options.

"Well, since you put it that way, all right then," Richard said.

He turned and waded into the snow toward the pigpens.

Gene plodded through knee-high drifts to the porch. He stood behind the door jam, pistol drawn, and pushed the door open. He clicked the kitchen light on. Blizzard wind whistled through cracks in the old wood-slat siding. Sleet pelted the windowpanes.

Gene climbed the rickety, narrow stairs to the second floor and searched the bedrooms there. He pulled the attic trapdoor open and a rope ladder dropped down. He climbed the ladder and was greeted only by the cooing of nested pigeons and the whistling wind.

Not finding his briefcase, Gene climbed back down the stairs and sat on a chair at the kitchen table. Idly flicking a scrap pad with his finger, he noticed the doodled words Lightfoot left behind on the top page——Thibodaux—Waynette Boudreaux—Louisiana.

The porch screen door slammed shut behind Richard. He stomped the snow from his shoes on the rickety porch floor and opened the kitchen door.

Gene slipped the piece of scratch paper into his coat pocket. "Find anything?" he asked Richard.

"They're not out there, that's for sure – no car, no nothing."

"Let's go pay the old lady in that pick-up a visit," said Gene.

**

The tires lost traction and spun harmlessly against the ice the moment Richard started up the lane's steep grade. Unfamiliar with driving on snow-packed roads, he held the accelerator near the floor while the Jaguar made the inevitable sideways slide into a drainage ditch.

"Damn it, Richard," Gene's voice exhibited his exasperation.

"What was I supposed to do? Jesus, it's not my fault."

"I know, I know. Sorry; this whole business has me on edge. It's those British fucks who made this piece of shit car that are at fault," Gene said.

"So, what's the plan? How about we call a tow?"

"Can't do that—cops would get wind of it," Gene said. "Wasn't there a tractor back there?"

"Two of them; there's a brand-new John Deere in the barn."

"John Deere, you say. What the hell do you know about tractors?"

"I know a lot about tractors," Richard said, "grew up on a farm, you know."

"I had no idea. I would have guessed you were a Jersey City boy."

"I know more about tractors than Jaguars, that's for sure."

"I should hope so," Gene said. "Can that John Deere get us out of this ditch?"

"You bet."

Buried to the axles, the Jaguar doors made angel wings in the snow when Gene and Richard force them open. Trying to stand, they both tumbled and slid down the steep, rutted lane. Back on his feet, Gene slipped again and fell nose down on the ice, skidding to the base of the hill on the side of his face.

After Richard helped Gene to his feet, they plodded through the drifting snow to the barn. Richard slid the barn door open and climbed into the John Deere cab. He ducked down toward the cab floor, out of Gene's sight. Gene could hear him fiddling with something–cables, buttons, levers–no telling what.

Gene's fingers were numb. He clicked his heels and rubbed his gloved hands together. He held his palms over his ears. He stomped his feet against the barn's dirt floor.

Finally, the grinding of the John Deere starter broke the silence. A puff of blue-gray smoke shot from the exhaust and the John Deere burped and popped and broke into a rumbling purr.

Richard found a heavy tow chain in a toolbox mounted on the back of the John Deere. Faint dawn light broke on the horizon against the dark and stormy sky as they rode the tractor from the barn.

Richard wrapped the chain around the Jaguar's frame, and with Gene in the driver seat, pulled the car out of the ditch and up the lane to the highway. It was seven-thirty, more than two hours since they drove down the lane.

Back at Aunt Wanda's front door, Gene rang the doorbell.

Richard pounded on the door sill. "Hello, anybody home? Hello?" He shouted. Fingers tingling with frost, his feet felt like someone had stuffed ice chips into the toes of his leather wing-tips.

**

Wanda opened the door until the safety lock chain stretched tight. Something was fishy about the two men she saw there.

"Morning boys, what brings you out in this weather?" She said.

Gene held a Navajo County sheriff's badge up to the crack in the door.

"Sheriff Glen Conway, mam." Gene pointed his thumb over his shoulder. "That's Deputy Smith. We'd like a minute of your time, mam."

Wanda looked past Gene and Richard to the Jaguar. She had never heard of a county sheriff driving a Jaguar, especially not a sheriff from dirt-poor Navajo County. "I'm a little busy right now," she said.

Richard kicked the door, snapping the safety chain. The door flew open, knocking Wanda to her back on the floor.

"What the hell," said Aunt Wanda, struggling to her feet.

Gene slapped Wanda square on her already bloodied nose with the back of his hand, sending her back-peddling across the room and over the top of a lounge chair.

Gene helped Wanda up from the floor and guided her to the sofa. He wiggled her nose between his fingers.

"Broken," he said, "give it a month – should be good as new." He yanked a cloth from under a flowerpot on the table at the end of the sofa, sending the pot crashing to the floor, and handed it to Wanda.

Wiping blood from under her nose with the cloth, Wanda asked Gene what he wanted from her.

"Like I said, mam, just a minute of your time, that's all."

"Well, get on with it then, mister," Wanda said.

"No need to be rude, mam. Just answer my questions and it shouldn't be necessary for Deputy Smith to burn your house down, understand?"

Wanda, holding the bloody cloth to her nose, shook her head. She understood.

"That's good," said Gene. "Now tell me, where is Jeff Lightfoot?"

"Last I saw him he was over at his Cousin Luke's."

Whap! Richard backhanded Wanda, ripping a deep gash across her cheek with his diamond pinky ring.

"You see what you did there?" Gene said. "You upset Deputy Smith. I did not ask you where you last *saw* Lightfoot, I asked you where Lightfoot *is*. That *was* my question, right?"

Wanda shook her head. Yes, that was the question.

"Let's try again," said Gene. "Where is Lightfoot?"

"He said something about looking for a briefcase. He asked me if I knew where his Cousin Luke was, and I told him I thought Luke went down by Pine with his Dad. You could probably find them in one of the usual watering holes if you were to drive down there. I don't know which one, but they shouldn't be that hard to find. That is all I know, I swear."

Richard cocked his fist back to give Wanda another smack. Gene stopped him with a motion of his hand.

"Thank you, mam," Gene said. "We'll be leaving now. I hope you understand the importance of keeping this little visit of ours between us. I'd hate to have to drive all the way back to this hell hole someday just to settle a grievance with an old pig farmer like yourself—you get my drift, mam?"

Wanda shook her head. "Yes, you've never been here as far as I know," she said.

"That's good—very good. Been a pleasure chatting with you, mam. Don't bother getting up now, we'll show ourselves to the door."

Richard and Gene walked out onto the porch. The storm had subsided for now.

"I can get her to talk, Gene," Richard said.

"No, you can't."

"I can."

"Trust me, that woman doesn't know where Lightfoot is."

"She knows more than she puts on."

"Get in the car Richie."

Richard drove the Jaguar up the lane to the highway. Gene dug the piece of scratch paper he found on Luke's kitchen table out of his pocket and again read the words Lightfoot doodled there that morning again —— Boudreaux — Louisiana — Thibodaux —Waynette. Gene had never heard of a Thibodaux.

"Turn right," Gene said.

"That'll take us back to Winslow. Pine is south of here, you know," Richard said, "If Lightfoot is in Pine, we need to take a left.

"Lightfoot is not in Pine."

"What?"

"Damn it, Richard. You heard me. Just, for once, do what I ask without all the God-damn conversation."

Gene folded Lightfoot's doodle paper in half and put it in his shirt pocket.

Both men upset, the short-tempered killers drove down the icy blacktop road toward Winslow for a quarter mile before Cardenas broke their silence.

"Sorry about that, Richie," he said. "It's just that I think I know where we can find Lightfoot."

**

Cardenas looked at his watch as his Jaguar rumbled across the tracks where I had been sitting with Lightfoot and Albert just two and a half hours before. They drove through the Winslow intersection where Jackson Browne saw a girl in a flatbed Ford and up the ramp to La Posada's parking lot.

"Drive around back to the railroad station," Gene said.

"We going somewhere, boss?"

"Just do it, Richard."

Richard parked the car in front of the station door.

In the waiting room of the deserted station, Cardenas found a single pay phone hanging next to the door. He dialed information.

An operator answered.

"Information for Thibodaux, Louisiana, please."

"Yes sir?"

"Looking for Boudreaux, Waynette Boudreaux."

136

"I show no listing for a Waynette; I have a Hillary Boudreaux."

"Yeah, that's it," said Cardenas. "Could you connect me please?"

"That will be eighty-five cents, sir."

Gene dug four quarters from his pocket and inserted them in the coin slot.

He heard the phone ringing on the other end of the line—one, two, three times.

"Hillary Boudreaux residence, Jana speaking."

"Could I speak to Waynette, please?" Gene asked.

"Ms. Waynette isn't here, sir."

"Would you know where I might find Ms. Waynette?"

"Couldn't say."

'Does she mean couldn't say, or wouldn't say?'

Gene asked to speak to 'the lady of the house' and was left hanging on the line while Jana, who had instructions not to bother Hillary with calls from strangers, pretended to search for Mrs. Boudreaux.

"Mrs. Boudreaux is unavailable, sir," Jana said on her return.

Cardenas asked Jana if she knew Jeff Lightfoot and she said yes, she knew a Jeff Lightfoot, but had not seen him for some time.

An operator broke onto the line with a request for fifty cents.

Cardenas hung up the phone.

13

Life According to Hillary

Soon after entering the home of Hillary Boudreaux, Lightfoot is back on the porch motioning for me to join him.

I step out of the car onto the cobblestone drive. On my feet for the first time since Dallas, I take a moment—rocking from side to side on the knobby driveway stones that feel like a fine masseuse's kneading through my sneaker soles. Time in prison has made me more appreciative of the simpler pleasures.

Grown impatient, Jeff walks out to meet me at the edge of the veranda.

"Come on, Mister Barker," he says, "you're not going to believe this."

That may be true, but since Lightfoot is prone to preface his comments with the phrase, it is no guarantee.

Jeff leads me into the foyer. The windows are shuttered, the drapes tightly closed. An ornate faux-candelabra chandelier cluttered with cut glass dangles hangs high above a round mahogany table with huge bear-claw paws. The chandelier's flickering electric candles dimly light an open stairway that curves up the wall into the darkness of a second story balcony.

The foyer is damp and cold. Our steps echo hollow against white plaster walls as we walk down a granite tile hall passed two sets of closed double pocket doors. The glow of a fireplace flame shimmers through another doorway, open toward the end of the hall.

Walking through that doorway, a massive stone-faced fireplace on the opposite wall first catches my eye. Set back from the fireplace, matching loveseats face each other across an extraordinary mahogany coffee table five feet square. In the center of the table a crystal urn holding a bouquet of white lilies sparkles red and gold in the otherwise darkened room's firelight.

A boy, maybe ten, maybe twelve, chubby cheeked and pug-nosed, sits between the coffee table and the hearth, facing the fire. He is wedged into a red metal toy, a Ford pickup truck, its front bumper not four feet from the fire. The truck has pedals like those on a tricycle beneath its hood.

The boy's Davie Crocket coonskin cap is on sideways, its coonskin tail dangling down over his right ear. He pays no attention to our arrival. He has a stack of New Orleans Times-Picayune newspaper pages squashed into tight spheres like paper snowballs piled on his lap. He throws one of the balls hard into the fire. Sparks fly across the hearth and sizzle on the hardwood floor. He throws another. A flame burst shoots up the chimney as the ball thwacks against the smoldering logs.

Its back toward the door, an antique sofa with wide rolled arms faces the hearth. The back of her head silhouetted against the firelight, an elderly woman with frizzy silver hair sits on the sofa's center cushion, gazing into the flames. Not having yet looked away from the fire, the old lady motions toward Jeff and me with a subtle flick of her hand above her shoulder.

"Come—sit," she says.

We approach the old lady.

"Mrs. Boudreaux," Jeff begins, "this is my friend—"

"Gille Barker," Hillary says, interrupting Jeff in mid-sentence. She turns slightly to face me. "It's a pleasure to meet you, Mister Barker." She shakes my hand. Her flesh has the feel of fine silk, something I have found common among those knocking on the reaper's door.

What is going on here? Another total stranger knows my name. Maybe Lightfoot had told her before he came to get me from the car.

"It's nice to meet you, Mrs. Boudreaux," I say.

"Yes, yes—well, you can't be sure of that," she says.

I smile, knowingly, although she gives no indication how her comment should be taken.

Jeff and I sit on the love seats, him on the one to Mrs. Boudreaux's left and me on the one to her right. The beautiful mulatto girl who had greeted Jeff at the entry door sets a fancy silver tray filled with servings of cheeses and crackers, cookies, and carafes of juice on the coffee table.

Thank you, Jana," Hillary says. "That will be all for now, dear."

I turn toward this Jana to thank her, but, as if an apparition, she has disappeared.

**

The pug-nosed boy pushes hard on the toy truck's pedals and the back wheels spin black rubber skids onto the hardwood floor. The truck lurches forward, crashing with a thud into the granite ledge of the fireplace. Amber sparks spike onto the hearth as the boy pitches another newspaper ball into the fire.

"That's John-John, Johnny Ray's boy," Hillary says, giving no indication his action had been anything out of the ordinary. "You remember Johnny Ray, don't you, Jeff?"

A twinkle in Hillary's eye betrays her pleasure in asking the question, already knowing her son's threat of feeding Jeff to the alligators has likely kept Johnny Ray's presence simmering on a back burner in Lightfoot's mind.

"Yes mam, I sure do," Lightfoot says. "How's old Johnny Ray doing these days?"

Hillary Boudreaux's spine straightens – her boney shoulders square. She drops the woolen shawl draped across her back down off her shoulders and rests her hands in her lap. Her ingenuous expression never changes as she tells us the fate dealt to her son, Johnny Ray Boudreaux.

**

"Johnny Ray was sent to burn in hell a little more than three years ago," Hillary says.

She tells us Johnny's long-suffering wife, Emma, shot him in the back of the head with his ten-gauge shotgun.

140

"Yeah, Johnny Ray beat poor Emma silly for the last time that day.

"He told Emma the next time she opened her yap he was going to stand her on that fancy-assed footstool her daddy's momma gave her last Christmas and hang her from the old oak tree in their back yard."

"That's rough stuff, for sure, but why didn't she just leave Johnny Ray?" Jeff says.

"Besides interrupting me, you don't know crap from shinola. Just thinking about what all Johnny Ray put that poor girl through makes me want to throw up." Hillary says. "I don't know what happened to that boy, but whatever it was sure turned him into one bad seed."

Neither Lightfoot nor I have any argument to offer on that point.

"Johnny Ray deserved what he got, you know," she says, "but if I had been in Emma's shoes, I would have cut off his little pecker instead — of course that would have made him mad as hell and she would have had to shoot him anyway.

"Old Judge Parker gave poor Emma twenty years in the prison over to Shreveport for blowing Johnny Ray's head off. Let me tell you, she didn't deserve one day of it.

"Parker must have been ninety then, and, hell, he wasn't the sharpest knife in the drawer even when he was a young stud, so I've been told.

"My Aunt Rita dated the judge back in the old days. Rita said he was dull as dirt, but she gave him a pass on that because he was hung like Mister Ed." Suppressing a snicker, Hillary grabs her cane and raps the tip against the hardwood floor.

An unexpected cackle rattles up from her chest as her attempt to quell a vision of old Judge Parker standing in front of the fireplace with a giant circumcised boner peeking out from between the folds of his neatly pleated black robe fails.

"This is probably more information than you boys want to know, but I know for a fact that old fart's penis was clipped too. Aunt Rita told me so, and I'll tell you what, that's coming straight from the horse's mouth, so to speak,"

This is funny stuff to Hillary. Her cackle turns into an uncontrollable cough. She takes a swig from her glass of Southern Comfort and looks back toward the fire through watery eyes. The judge and his penis have all but faded from her view.

"Let's see now, where was I?"

"Horse's mouth," I say, reluctantly, not really wanting to risk bringing the Judge's penis back into the conversation.

"Oh yeah, that's right. Well, anyway you look at it though, Parker had no business sending that girl to jail for doing what just had to be done, and I told him so.

"I swear, I would have liked to slap some sense into his pointy bald head and would have too if the bailiff hadn't hauled me out of there. It gets me riled every time I think about it."

I follow Hillary's eyes to an eight-by-ten-inch photo in a fancy gilded frame sitting at one end of the fireplace mantel. The picture is of a young couple and a little boy propped up on his unhinged father's knee.

I recognize the boy as the squeaky-clean version of the kid sitting in the toy truck in front of me, frozen in the picture for that brief period before he became a household terrorist. In the picture, Emma stands, bent down close behind the seated father, Johnny Ray, her face close to his, her hands resting on his shoulders. Pasted smiles all around fail to hide the undertow between this young couple that would soon lead to Johnny Ray's demise.

How strange it seems to see this picture of Hillary Boudreaux's first son and his soon-to-be killer spouse and their son, his genes scrambled with madness through no fault of his own, prominently displayed above the fire, a memento, a constant reminder of that razor slice of time. But I have yet to witness anything that does not seem peculiar about Hillary Boudreaux. Whatever her reason for the display of that frozen moment on her sitting room mantel, it would be of no surprise to me.

"Anyway, Johnny Ray got what he had coming," says Hillary Boudreaux. "Hell, he was a nasty bully even when he was little John-John's age, and it was straight downhill from there. If any man ever needed to be gone, he was up toward the top of the list,

I suppose — especially after the booze and barroom whores got a hold on him."

Hillary raises her hand and motions toward the silver serving tray.

Furiously pedaling his toy truck, Johnny Ray Junior interrupts Hillary's thoughts as he smashes into the fireplace hearth and recoils like a shot back to the coffee table. Spinning the pedals like a child possessed, he races around the loveseat where Lightfoot is sitting and out the door. The echoes recede with each thud as Junior repeatedly crashes his truck against the hallway wall until a final rattling crash and a slamming of the front door indicate that Johnny Ray has left the building.

Maybe Junior had heard enough about dear old dad.

**

"Try one of those ice box cookies, boys," Hillary says, "Jana and I made them fresh from scratch this morning."

Jeff and I are quick to pick up cookies at Hillary's offer that seemed more of a command. Sipping her Southern Comfort and fresh squeezed orange juice, she watches intently until we take our first bites.

"You have to admit those are some darn good cookies," she says.

"Delicious," I say, and they are.

Jeff nods in agreement. "Yes — delicious, mam," he says.

"When Waynette was little, she loved to 'help' me bake those icebox cookies, that and make egg noodles. I'll never forget that first time. Waynette was five or six years old then. While the cookies cooked, we rolled egg noodle dough and cut it into wide strips. Then, after I took the last batch of cookies from the oven, Waynette boiled the noodles. That was her favorite part — the dropping just so of those strips of doe, one by one, into that boiling water. Just watching her made my day. Now those were some good noodles too, son."

"I bet," says one of us.

"Yes. Well now, Jeff, I'm sure you didn't drive all the way down to Thibodaux, Louisiana, just to shoot the breeze with this old woman and spend a day drinking whiskey and sampling cookies. I suppose you're here about Waynette."

"Yes, mam, I am."

"People change, Jeff. It's been five years now since we last saw you down here. When you left, I swear, I sure thought that was the last I'd be seeing of you, and Waynette felt the same. Wasn't any excuse for what Johnny Ray did to you and his own sister though. Johnny knew how crazy Waynette was for you, but he just couldn't get the thought of his sister banging an Indian boy from cropping up in his head."

I look at Jeff. Apparently, he is not surprised or offended by the old bigot's remarks. He shrugs his shoulders and takes another cookie from the platter.

Hillary sips from her drink and gazes into the fire, her thoughts having momentarily wandered to there.

"As far as Johnny Ray was concerned, you might as well have been black or one of those Jew boys," Hillary continues.

Not that he takes her comment as the insult Hillary meant it to be, but Jeff is beginning to show some sign of agitation. He grabs another cookie and sticks it in his shirt pocket.

Off on another tangent, Hillary Boudreaux pulls a second cane, shiny and black, from under the sofa and draws our attention to its delicately carved ivory swan's-head handle.

"I love swans, don't you?" Hillary says.

We nod. What is not to like?

"This one was made for me by Jana's Uncle. He carved all sorts of things out of tusks from elephants he killed down in Africa. Some folks don't like that much, killing elephants you know, but hell, the way I look at it, the elephant this swan's head came from was dead anyway, you know what I mean? And I didn't kill the damn thing, you get what I'm saying?"

Jeff and I both nod—yes, her point is clear.

"Not much more to say about that," Hillary says.

Rendered speechless by Hillary's wrong-headed narration, we watch in silence as she pushes herself up from the sofa with the cane. She shuffles to the fireplace and prods the smoldering logs with a brass poker until they glow bright and their flames leap up the flue. She shuffles back to the sofa and, cradled in both hands, lifts her glass of Southern Comfort for another sip as her mind wanders back to her late son, Johnny Ray, and her daughter, Waynette Boudreaux.

**

"Must have been two years after Johnny Ray ran you off before Waynette and I found out what he had done. Probably never would have known if the liquor hadn't loosened his tongue. It was on Waynette's twenty sixth birthday that he spilled the beans, just a month before Emma shot him, it was.

"Keeping that fine secret must have been driving Johnny Ray crazier than he already was—pulling off a plan like that is just the sort of thing he would have been itching to brag about. And how those halfwits who helped him kept their mouths shut is beyond me.

"Of course, you probably shouldn't have been getting your ashes hauled by some big-city whore the night before your wedding, but that wasn't through any fault of your own, as far as I can see.

"Anybody with a little common sense knows a man isn't capable of resisting any sort of temptation starting with Adam back in the garden with Eve. For Christ's sake, all you need do is check out the bible to see how long you boys have been out of control. No offense intended to you, Mister Barker."

"No need for an exemption here, Mrs. Boudreaux," I reply.

Hillary scoots to the sofa's end cushion and reaches for a half-full liter of whiskey sitting on an end table. Her hand firmly around its neck, she holds the bottle out in front of her. She points at the label.

"You know, my great grandmother almost married the man who concocted this stuff. Heron was his name, Martin Heron if I remember right. Yeah that was it—Marty.

"Marty worked his way down the Mississippi all the way from Saint Louis to New Orleans – back in eighteen seventy something, it was. He got a job tending bar over there in the French Quarter—on Saint Pete Street. I sometimes remember the

145

name of the place, but it's lost for now; something Lafitte, I believe."

Hillary pours about a shot of the whiskey over the remaining ice and orange juice in her glass and gently pushes the ice up and down with her finger. She takes a sip and smacks her lips with exaggerated pleasure. "You know, you can't go stirring Southern Comfort like you would the common stuff, and never, ever, shake it. Saps the flavor right out of it, but you boys probably knew that."

I shrug and Jeff shakes his head. No, we did not know that.

"It's true," says Hillary. "You see, back then, back in Marty Heron's day, those mountain boys from Kentucky and Tennessee shipped some damn rough shine down the Mississippi to New Orleans. They left it up to the bar owners down here to make the stuff taste decent enough to drink and not blind too many folks in the bargain."

Hillary pauses for a sip of her favorite whiskey and smacks her lips again.

"They hired all sorts of fancy 'mixologists' to do the job, but young Marty was the one who came up with the cream of the crop, and this is it," Hillary says, tapping the label on her bottle of Southern Comfort.

"Orange and vanilla and a touch of cinnamon and who-knows-what, that was Marty's secret, and of course the alcohol. Great Grandma Pearl's boyfriend came up with the recipe for Southern Comfort, the best damn whiskey a man can buy at any price, the only whiskey fit for sipping, near perfect in every way but for one thing—rough it up and all you're left with is another lousy bottle of whiskey. Ain't that something?"

Jeff and I shake our heads. Yes, that is something all right.

The wacky Hillary Boudreaux is as nutty as a Southern Comfort fruitcake. For the moment, the road map of wrinkles that had covered her jowls are stretched smooth by her strange ear to ear smile. The fireplace flames snap, crackle, and dance in the piercing black pupils of Hillary's eyes, now as unnerving as Lightfoot had advertised.

"Marty spent quite a lot of time down here in Thibodaux chasing after Great Grandma Pearl, so they say. He stayed right here on this property when he was in town, they say. Of course, that was in the old house before it burned down to nothing but a pile of charcoal and some ivory piano keys. Guess another one of those elephants paid the price for that."

Still holding the bottle of Southern Comfort in her fist, Hillary leans forward on the sofa cushion.

"Care for a taste, Mister Barker?"

"No, thank you."

"Jeff?"

"Thank you, mam, don't mind if I do."

"You're welcome son." Ice crackles as Hillary gently pours a couple of ounces of Southern Comfort into Jeff's glass. She hands him her spoon.

How, and when, is Jeff going to get the subject of this conversation back to the problem at hand? Where can we find Waynette Boudreaux? Just as I am feeling my suspicion finding Waynette may not have been our priority after all, Jeff decides to pop the question.

"Mrs. Boudreaux, about —"

"Waynette? Yes, of course. Sorry son. I didn't mean to ramble on so. It's just that I don't get much company these days. Jana is here and John-John has me on my toes some, but they're not really company now, are they. It can get a little tedious around here with the same old faces day in and day out."

"Some might prefer it that way," I say.

"I suppose so. Anyway, Waynette left home the day after Johnny Ray got stupid-drunk and told her what he had done. You know, he put dope in your drink that night — I don't remember the name of it."

"I suspected as much," says Lightfoot.

"Well, that's what he did. Hell, you never had a chance."

The slight curl of a smile flickers across Hillary's lips. Her son may have been a sociopath, but he had one-upped the Indian boy.

147

"Anyway, I didn't see Waynette again until she came home for Johnny Ray's funeral. I was kind of surprised to see her, but then again, even though he was a bastard, well maybe not a real bastard, but I can't be for sure one way or the other about that, he was still her big brother, or at least half brother. I guess her coming back for Johnny Ray suggests blood really *is* thicker than water, as they say."

Jeff shakes his head. "Yes, blood is thicker than water," he agrees.

"We had some words after the funeral. That's when I found out Waynette had it in the back of her head that I knew what Johnny Ray was up to all along.

"She thought I was in on the whole thing, drugs and all. She reasoned Johnny Ray didn't have the brains to come up with such a scheme. I must say, it is a stretch for me to believe it myself. But I swear to you now, just as I swore to Waynette then, I had nothing to do with it, Jeff, nothing at all."

Once again, Hillary's thoughts become lost in the fireplace embers. Regaining her composure, she blinks back a tear. For a moment it appears the old woman may have a heart, but that moment is fleeting.

"I was happy for Waynette and looking forward to the wedding," says Hillary, "even if she *was* about to marry an Indian.

"Now, I am not prejudice against Indians or anything like it, you know, so don't get me wrong, but even you would have to admit it might have been a little dicey for us down here in bayou country, especially if you two started filling the neighborhood up with a team of little half-breeds. Anyway, those things tend to work themselves out—one way or another. You know what I mean? Hell, you and Waynette weren't planning on living around here anyway."

"No mam," Jeff says. He gulps down his double Southern Comfort, not shaken or stirred, the finest whiskey on the planet.

"That's the way I looked at it, you know, but Waynette, she couldn't bring herself to see it that way. I haven't seen her since— been three years now.

"Oh, she calls—Christmas, maybe Thanksgiving—and we talk some, but when we do it's like we're two strangers with nothing in common, like one of us had dialed a wrong number and decided to have a conversation with whoever we found on the other end of the line just the same."

Hillary sits quietly, her eyes cast down toward the glass cradled in her hands, her mind tripping through fond memories of Waynette Boudreaux.

**

Hillary leans hard on the ivory swan's-head handle of her cane and pushes up from the sofa's deep cushion. She walks across the room to a buffet cabinet that had been all but concealed in the shadows. She opens the center drawer and sorts through a pile of papers.

"Oh yes, here it is." She studies what is written on a cocktail napkin as she returns to the sofa.

"Waynette moved over to New Orleans two days after Johnny Ray told her what he had done to you," Hillary says to Jeff. "She and her friend, Betty Lou, just packed up and left. You remember Betty Lou Riggins don't you, Jeff? She was Waynette's bride's maid to be."

"Yes, I remember Betty Lou," Jeff says.

"I thought so. Pretty girl that Betty Lou—not the kind of girl a man like you would likely forget.

"Anyway, Betty Lou and Waynette piled most all their stuff into Betty Lou's old station wagon and moved to New Orleans, just like that, didn't even bother to say goodbye. I got worried and called the sheriff after I hadn't seen hide or hair of her for a few days. Then, not long after that, Betty Lou's momma called and told me where those two had gone. I should have known.

"Waynette and Betty Lou have been as close as twins since they were old enough to crawl on these old wooden floors— couldn't pry them apart with a crowbar. Now here they are off living together in the French Quarter, no less. I swear, I just don't know—" Hillary Boudreaux's voice trails away. She points at the smudged blue ink scribbles across the cocktail napkin in her hand.

"920 Chartres Street, that's the address. As far as I know, they're still living there." She hands the napkin to Jeff.

"Thank you, mam," Jeff says. He slides the paper napkin into his back pocket as if it is destined to be one of those notes forgotten until after it has been shredded in the wash.

Something is queer about that. There should be nothing more precious to Lightfoot than the address written on that napkin, but he barely glanced at it. It occurs to me that, just maybe, he already had the address of Waynette Boudreaux.

Is it possible he knew where Waynette was before our conversation at the Winslow railroad crossing, even before this cross-country chase began? Has this been an elaborate charade, and, if so, why did he feel the need for me to be in this picture?

I hear a voice

"You don't know?" The voice inquires.

My eyes are drawn to the darkest corner of the room where I see the glow of burning tobacco in Einstein's pipe.

I shrug. "I don't have a clue, Albert," I say.

"You surprise me, Gille," says Einstein, "The answer is so simple even you should have stumbled across it by now."

I had not, but Albert was right. I should have.

**

"Thank you, mam," Jeff says again.

"Oh, don't you bother thanking me just yet. As I said, five years can bring down some powerful changes on a person, some folks more than others. Waynette never was one to let grass grow between her toes, you know. Now, you boys better be moving on. It's a fair drive to New Orleans, and I'm afraid our visit has tired me some."

Mrs. Boudreaux picks up a small bell from the table next to her sofa. "Jana? Jana?" she calls.

"Ting-a-ling," goes the bell, and, like magic, Jana appears next to Hillary Boudreaux's chair.

"Yes, mam?" she says.

Where did she come from? I look at Jeff. Where the hell had Jana been before she was summoned by Mrs. Boudreaux?

Jeff gives me his shoulder shrug, indicating that he was wondering the same thing and that my guess was as good as his. Lack of sleep and Southern Comfort has addled Jeff's mind anyway. He could care less if Jana had been sitting by the fire all along or just now dropped in through the ceiling. He empties the last drops of whiskey from his glass and crunches an ice cube between his teeth.

"Please show these gentlemen to the door, Jana."

"Yes, mam."

After we exchange pleasantries with Mrs. Boudreaux, Jana leads us down the hall to the front entry where Johnny Ray Junior's toy pickup truck lays on its side next to the doorway. Jana gives the truck a kick, sending it screeching across the marble floor into the wall at the bottom of the stairs.

"That Johnny Ray," Jana says. "He could sure use a switching now and then."

Jana follows us across the porch to the veranda steps. Einstein impatiently waits on the back seat next to the driver's side open window of the Chevrolet. Paying us no mind, Johnny Ray Junior kneels in tall grass across the drive next to a stand of cattails and marsh grass, stalking Snowy Egrets with his bow and arrow.

**

Hillary Boudreaux had bought the boy a toy bow and quiver of arrows tipped by rubber suction cups, one of the many gifts she had showered on Johnny Ray when he first came to live with her after his mother went to prison. It was Hillary's hope 'things' would help to erase images held in Johnny Ray's mind of mother blowing pieces of daddy's brain all over their bedroom wall.

Other than the bow and arrows, Johnny Ray was not interested. But he did love his bow and rubber tipped arrows, and spent hours stalking imaginary prey across the Boudreaux plantation.

Hillary, happy that John-John had found something of interest that occupied his time, hired Louisiana's top archery instructor to teach the boy. He began by outfitting Johnny Ray with the best gear Hillary's money could buy — and then he taught the enthusiastic Johnny Ray to be the finest of young archers in all of Louisiana.

**

"Johnny Ray! John-John!" Jana stands at the top of the veranda steps with her hands on her hips, calling out his name. Johnny Ray pops up from his lair in the cattails, his coonskin cap askew.

"Get over here right now, Johnny Ray. Your grandma will skin us both she catches you stalking those Egrets again. You remember what the sheriff told you last time he was out here, don't you, Johnny Ray?"

14

Johnny Ray Goes Hunting

Our tracks remain fresh there on the bridge when Richard Gleason cruises Gene Cardenas's Jaguar across the bayou into the canopy of ancient Oaks that shade Hillary Boudreaux's dirt lane.

As they approach the house an archer clutching his bow darts across the corner of Richard's eye and into an open barn door.

"Did you see that?" Richard says to Gene.

"See what?"

"Never mind."

"What the hell do you mean, 'never mind'? Damn it, Richard, I hate it when you say that."

"Say what?"

"Never mind."

"Never mind what?

"Jesus," Gene mutters.

**

Johnny Ray is stalking three egrets in the pasture when he first hears the Jaguar's purr. Looking up, he sees dust trails and then the rapid approach of Gene Cardenas' black sedan. He has never seen two strange cars come up that lane on the same day before.

Heart racing, Johnny Ray runs across the pasture to the corral and through the open barn door. He latches the door behind him and watches through a crack between wooden door slats as the car speeds past the barn toward the house.

Two men in the car — that fat-ass sheriff has sent his deputies to haul me off to that orphanage up by Baton Rouge.

Jana had warned him this day would come.

**

"You heard the sheriff. Better leave those birds be, Johnny Ray," Jana first scolded John-John weeks ago. "Just keep on doing what you're doing, and Sheriff Bogart will be more than happy to lock you up with all the other little outlaws they keep in that orphanage up there by Baton Rouge.

"Don't you worry though. Me and Grandma Hillary, we'll come see you every month or two, when the weather's fit — of course, that's if I can learn to drive and get your grandma's old station wagon running again.

"If we do happen up Baton Rouge way I'll pack you one of those banana sandwiches with lots of that butter and sugar you think so much of. Maybe I can get Grandma Hillary to buy a bag of those ripple potato chips to go with that banana sandwich. How does that sound, Johnny Ray?"

That car doesn't look like any sheriff's car I've ever seen. Maybe those guys are here to steal Grandma's jewelry and whatever else she keeps in that safe she thinks is such a big secret. Nah, that can't be it. It's that damn sheriff.

**

Sheriff Bogart's illusory taunt kicks Johnny Ray's imagination into overdrive.

'The laws the law, Johnny Ray. I'm afraid your egret-hunting days are over.'

The sheriff's deputies strap Johnny Ray to a post in front of a stack of hay bales in the barn. A deputy with slick black hair and a dimpled chin picks up Johnny Ray's bow and shoots two fresh muskmelons from the top of his head before a miss that plants a steel tipped arrow in the forehead of poor Johnny Ray.

Convulsed with laughter, the sheriff's deputies fall to their backs and roll from side to side on the barn's dirt floor.

Sipping a Southern Comfort and orange juice, Grandma Boudreaux watches the proceedings from an old wooden rocker suspended below the barn rafters above Johnny Ray.

'This is a sad day, John-John,' Grandma Hillary says from her perch in Johnny Ray's head, 'but, looking on the bright side, at least Jana and I won't have to be packing sandwiches up to that orphanage in Baton Rouge. Heh, heh.'

**

"Nice layout — these folks must be loaded," Richard says.

"We're not here to rob the place, Richard. We get the information we need, and we're gone."

"Uh huh," Richard says.

Alerted by the sound of the approaching car, Jana watches from behind the Venetian blinds as the Jaguar enters the circular cobblestone drive and stops in front of the veranda steps. She pries the crack in the blinds wider. A man in the car takes something from the seat and slides it inside his jacket.

It might have been a billfold, or a pack of cigarettes, but Jana knows better. Jana is descended from a long line of witches and seers and casters of spells — she knows it was a twenty-two-caliber automatic pistol Richard stuffed into his coat pocket in her mind's eye.

**

Jana is the daughter of the most powerful of all New Orleans' voodoo practitioners, the Spirit Saint Priest Oswan.

Oswan was the mind behind the greatest New Orleans voodoo merchandising plan ever—buy a spell and get one of equal or lesser value free. The sales bonanza that followed made Oswan the wealthiest voodoo shaman in all of Louisiana.

Oswan's fortunes took a downward spiral when his right-hand man shot him full of lead in a dispute over the affections of Jana's mother, the beautiful young Priestess, Lady Bianca, a dispute that sent Oswan on his way to his next life as a goat on the isle of Mykonos in the middle of the Aegean Sea.

Oswan had only himself to blame. Although he had been proud of his role as a black shaman, all Oswan truly desired was to escape the bonds of racial inequality and return to earth as a white man of respect in *any* profession. As he lay in a puddle of his own blood in the middle of the French Quarter's Decatur

Street, he saw the end was near and called on his loyal Chow dog, Shorty, to deliver this last request to God.

But Oswan had forgotten to pick up Shorty's favorite jerky treats from the store that day—and the three days before that. Shorty was not pleased with Oswan. Shorty was in a funk.

And in his funk, Shorty, short of breath from his arduous journey to the gates of the Promised Land, told God that, as a human being, Oswan felt he had failed Him, the Almighty One. Shorty told God that Oswan deemed it only fair he be returned to earth in his next life as a farm animal to serve his penance.

And so it was that, when he arose in his spirit form to meet his maker, Oswan was told he would be returning to earth as a breeding heifer on Donovan's Brahman cattle ranch up by Shreveport.

Oswan was dumbstruck.

"There must be some mistake," Oswan finally came to say to God.

Though God's reply was serene, as God's replies tend to be, it was loaded with the danger that only the timber of His voice can imply.

"Do you have something against Donovan, Oswan?" The Almighty One inquired.

God leaned back on his throne and twiddled his thumbs, first one way and then the other, awaiting Oswan's answer.

"I don't even *know* Donovan," Oswan said. Unnerved, he hoped his distress wasn't revealed in his reply.

God told Oswan there could not have been a mistake, whether Oswan did or didn't know Donovan.

"You see, Oswan," God said, "God doesn't make mistakes—there are no mistakes in *God's* deck of cards."

However, God said, in consideration of Oswan's many years of service, He, "with God's infinite benevolence," would allow Oswan to spend his next life as a Billy goat in a pasture on the isle of Mykonos in the middle of the picturesque Aegean Sea.

Oswan was truly relieved. Images of his next life stuck in a yolk at the mercy of the bulls in the breeder's barn on Donovan's farm had been disturbing at the least.

"Thank you, Almighty One," said Oswan. "You certainly have a knack for making punishment sound like a good thing, don't you?"

"I'll assume that to be a rhetorical question," God replied. "Next time you pass through I suggest you make your requests in person, Oswan."

"I will keep that in mind, Almighty One."

**

Jana, daughter of Oswan, a man who learned the hard way when he placed his trust in man's best friend, is always on guard. Unaware of how or why, Jana was born with a faculty for danger – she can taste it–she can smell it in the air.

Jana hurries to the sitting room where Hillary Boudreaux remains slouched forward on the sofa, as she had been since shortly after we left her. A dribble of drool dangles from the corner of her lip. An empty highball glass hangs from her fingers.

Jana touches Hillary on the shoulder. "Ms. Hillary!" She says. She shakes Hillary's arm and her glass clangs to the floor.

"Ms. Hillary?" Jana presses her fingertips against Hillary's neck and confirms a pulse. She shakes Hillary's arm again. "Ms. Hillary!" Jana says.

The old woman's head snaps back. An eye pops open and then the other. The room comes in and out of focus as Hillary swivels her head from side to side. She finds her glasses on her lap and plops them on her nose. Standing in front of her, Jana is only a blur in her Southern Comfort haze.

"Jana?" The old woman lifts her glasses from her nose with her fingers and rubs her eyes. "What is it, Jana?" She asks.

"Two men in the drive, mam—I don't like the looks of them, Ms. Hillary."

"What do you mean?"

"Don't like the looks of them, mam."

"Isn't that what you just said?"

The knocker dings and dongs and bangs against the front door.

"What should I do, mam?"

157

"Just ignore them," says Hillary. "I'm tired. Whoever they are, they'll go away."

Richard bangs the knocker against the door again. The sound echoes down the hall. Gene peaks through a side window into the entry. He sees Johnny Ray's pedal truck lying on its side next to the stairs.

"Anybody home in there?" Gene pushes down on the latch and the door that, in her haste, Jana had neglected to lock swings open.

Gene hears the murmur of Jana and Hillary's muted conversation. He sees the dance of the sitting room firelight on the floor at the end of the hall. Before Jana can move, Gene is standing in the doorway, staring at the back of Hillary Boudreaux's head silhouetted against the firelight.

"Mrs. Boudreaux, I presume?" Gene says.

"Yes?" Hillary says. She doesn't turn to greet him.

"I have a couple of questions, if I may, mam–won't take but a moment of your time."

"You from the sheriff's office? Suppose Bogart sent you out here about Johnny Ray. Is that what this is about? Them Egrets again? Well, he ain't killed a one, far as I know. So much fuss over some silly birds—I don't suppose the sheriff could rustle up any real lawbreakers for you boys to chase down, but that's not your fault now, is it. Well, come on in here then. Let's get this business over."

Now standing in front of Hillary, Gene flashes a badge.

"I'm Marshal Claypool, mam." Gene nods toward Richard. "That's my partner, Marshal Smith, and we don't know any Sheriff Bogart–or a Johnny Ray."

"Well, that's a relief, I guess. What can I do for you, Marshal?"

"We are Federal Agents, mam—been chasing two fugitives cross country for days now. Seems the trail has brought us to your front door. Like I said, won't take but a minute of your time and we'll be on our way."

"Well now, that sounds fine because I just happen to have a minute to spare – seems my time's not near so valuable these days as it once was anyway. Care for a drink, Marshal?

Hillary points toward the few cookies remaining on the coffee table from our visit.

"How about one of those wonderful cookies? Jana and I made them fresh this morning."

Gene passes on the cookies. "Wouldn't mind a drink though," he says.

"Name your poison, Marshal. We have juice and sodas; there's Coca-Cola, of course. And I have red wine, or Southern Comfort, if that's more to your liking."

"Southern Comfort with a splash of cola, if you don't mind," Gene says.

"Southern Comfort and coke, you say? You ever drink any Southern Comfort, Marshal Claypool?"

"I've tasted the stuff, but to tell the truth I'm not much of a whiskey man."

"That's obvious, Marshal," says Hillary. If you *were* a whiskey man, you'd know Southern Comfort's not your nasty-bite, wash-tub kind of whiskey. It has a smooth sweetness to it. Ain't no need for soda to be involved at all——tastes good over ice, or just neat for that matter. I do like it with a dash of fresh-squeezed orange juice on occasion. Sometimes I take it with ice and a splash of water."

"Ice and water will do fine then, mam. I appreciate your recommendation."

Hillary turns her head slightly toward Richard, who has remained behind her at the entry, his arms crossed like a sentry at the door. "How about you, Marshal Smith?"

"I'll have the same," says Richard.

"Jana, would you get these boys some Comfort and water, please?"

**

Jana serves Gene and Richard their drinks. She sets a fresh Southern Comfort on Mrs. Boudreaux's napkin.

"Thank you, Jana," Hillary says, dismissing Jana from the room with little fanfare.

Though Hillary and Jana often perform their master and servant routine for guests, Jana is more like a live-in granddaughter there to keep grandma out of one of the homes paid handsomely to store old-folks while they await the grim reaper's call.

"Yes, mam, I'll be in the kitchen," Jana says.

Jana walks around Richard and out the door. She sees Johnny Ray crouched above her head on the stairway landing across the entry hall, peering between the banisters into the sitting room below. Jana motions for him to follow her. Johnny Ray shakes his head—he is not going anywhere.

**

Grandma Hillary and Jana, though unaware, were often prime players in Johnny Ray's fantasy plays, him the Indian brave mounting his attack on the old white woman and her mulatto slave while they hopped pieces across their checkerboard, or he was Johnny Ray, the G-man, sent to stop the two lady terrorists in the sitting room before they could poison the water supply and knock off most of the population on the west side of the Mississippi. But those were games, and Johnny Ray is aware that what is happening now is real.

**

"Well now, Marshal Claypool, how can I help you?" Hillary asks Cardenas.

"Do you know a Jeff Lightfoot, mam?"

"I know the name — haven't heard it in five years or more though. He was my daughter's fiancé for a couple of months back then. Real nice boy too."

"He's a Hopi Indian boy you know; grew up on one of those reservations up in Arizona. Can you imagine that? Making clay pots and trinkets for a living and sleeping in one of those teepee things—can you imagine?"

"I don't believe they have teepees anymore, mam."

"You don't say. Well, I'm sorry to hear that, Marshal."

160

Losing patience, Cardenas looks up from his pad. "Have you seen Jeff Lightfoot lately, Mrs. Boudreaux?"

"No sir. Why do you ask?"

"I know Lightfoot was here today, mam."

"I tell you, I haven't seen the boy. That means I have not seen him. Why would I lie about it? Why would he be coming around here anyway?"

Cardenas motions toward Richard. "Get the girl," he says.

"We've been on the road a long time, Mrs. Boudreaux," Gene says. "You need to tell me where Lightfoot is and tell me now."

"Your guess would be as good as mine," Hillary says.

Richard shoves Jana, hands strapped behind her back, into the room. Jana stumbles, falling first to her knees before tumbling forward on her face to the hardwood floor.

Richard jerks Jana to her feet and shoves her down on the sofa next to Hillary Boudreaux.

"Oh, dear," Hillary says. She takes the cocktail napkin from the bottom of her glass of whiskey and dabs a trickle of blood from Jana's nose.

Hillary gazes up at Cardenas, now towering over her, not more than a foot away. She sees the malice in his eyes. She could count the hairs in his flared nostrils if sober and time allowed.

"You're no Federal Marshal, are you, Mister Claypool," she says.

"No mam, I'm not," is Cardenas's reply.

Clutching stair bannisters in his clinched fists, Johnny Ray has been watching Cardenas browbeat his grandmother from the landing. He is shaken by Richard's unexpected slap of Jana across the cheek with the back of his hand.

"Stop–Stop this now!" Hillary says. "Jeffery was on his way to New Orleans when he left here. Now, please go. Please go."

"Thank you, mam." Cardenas sits on the sofa, next to Hillary. "Was he alone?"

Her hand trembling, Hillary reaches across Cardenas for a cigarette on the end table. He waits patiently as the old woman lights the cigarette, inhales, reaches back across him, and places the cigarette on the holder of a sterling silver ashtray. She clutches her glass in both hands and lifts it to her lips for a sip of Southern Comfort. She drops her hands to her lap, still clutching the glass.

"A gentleman was with him," she says, "from Hawaii I think he said. A writer, or artist–maybe both, I don't recall. Pleasant enough fellow, I must say. Not much of a drinker though. Had me puzzled, you know what I mean?"

"No, I don't know what you mean, lady."

"A writer who doesn't know his whiskey? Now, that sounds fishy to me. Don't get me wrong, I'm sure there *is* a writer out there somewhere who doesn't drink liquor, it's just that I never ran across one. And how would some artsy-craftsy guy from Hawaii get mixed up with a homeless boy fresh off an Arizona Indian reservation in the first place? Tell me that."

Gene raps Hillary on the shoulder with her cane. "I'm not telling *you* anything. Can't anybody get to the point these days without a long-winded conversation? Just answer my questions. Do you understand?"

A lump pops up from Hillary's collarbone–though Gene's strike was only meant to gain the old woman's attention, it hurt like hell just the same.

"Yes, I understand," Hillary says.

"Now, what was this other man's name?"

"Gille something."

"Gille Barker," Jana chimes in.

"Very good, ladies — now tell me, how long ago did they leave?"

"Close to three hours now, sir," Jana says.

Gene asks Hillary where Lightfoot is most likely to go, once he's in New Orleans. When she hesitates, he pops her again with the handle end of her cane. Streams of pain shoot to her fingers. Tears flood her eyes.

Johnny Ray has seen enough. They have hurt his grandmother and Jana, his best friends, his only friends. Now *he* is the hunter, the boy-man archer from hell.

Johnny Ray creeps down the steps and slithers across the floor to the sitting room door like the Indian warriors he had emulated so many times before while stalking egrets through the cattails. He squats on one knee at the doorway and pulls an arrow from his quiver. He readies his bow and adjusts his coonskin cap just so, its tail hanging down his spine.

"You're not going to hurt those boys if you find them, are you?" Hillary asks Cardenas.

He threatens her with another smack from the raised swan's head cane.

"Nine-twenty Chartres Street, that's where they should be," Hillary blurts out.

"Now, why would they be there?"

"Because that is where my daughter, Waynette, lives– Lightfoot is looking for Waynette. That's all I know."

"That wasn't hard now, was it?" Cardenas drops the cane to the floor in front of Hillary. "We'll be leaving you ladies now," he says. "We appreciate your cooperation."

"Yeah," mimics Richard, "we appreciate your cooperation." He reaches to draw his pistol.

Johnny Ray pulls back on the string of his bow with all the skill of the best twelve-year-old sharpshooter in Louisiana that he is and lets a steel-tipped arrow fly.

**

Now, you ladies sit where you are until you hear our car leave the drive and no one gets hurt.

Maybe that was what Richard was going to say after he pulled the pistol Jana had known was there from inside his jacket. Maybe he had meant to give that warning before sliding his gun back in its holster, bowing politely, and exiting the room.

**

With pistol drawn, Richard turns toward the door in time for his mind to register the figure of Johnny Ray crouched there. He hears the twang of the bow's string. He is aware of the whistle of the arrow speeding across the room. He feels the thump as the arrow pierces his Adam's apple, its tip passing through the back of his neck.

Richard's pistol falls to the floor; his hands, now twitching, spastic hands, now grabbing at the arrow's shaft. Blood gurgles up his throat. He watches that blood stream from his mouth and drip to the floor, not fully aware it is his own. He falls to his knees in a white haze.

With an exhaled gasp, Hillary Boudreaux clasps a hand to her chest and slumps to her side.

Gene ducks behind the sofa as a second arrow speeds across the room toward him and clatters against the fireplace mantel. He picks up Richard's pistol, crouches, and scans the room down the pistol barrel. A figure darts across the doorway. Gene fires twice into the hallway wall. He hears the front door crash against the wall when Johnny Ray flings it open.

**

Johnny Ray, his coonskin hat tail streaming behind him, runs across the drive and through the corral to the barn. He climbs the ladder to the loft. He peers out toward the house from one side of the hayloft door. He watches Gene struggle to carry Richard across the porch to the Jaguar, sighting the pistol first one way and then the other.

Gene drops Richard's listless body, hands still clutched at the shaft of the arrow, to the edge of the front seat. As Gene lifts his legs into the car, Richard falls sideways across the seat, the tip of the arrow slicing across the seatback leather.

Gravel flies as Cardenas speeds the Jaguar down Hillary's lane. Richard gurgles and gasps for his last breath. His life drains onto the Jaguar seat and drips to the floor. Gene glances out the passenger window only to see Johnny Ray, not ten yards away, racing toward him through the tall pasture grass at the side of the road.

Johnny Ray kneels and pulls an arrow from the quiver strapped to his back. His eyes focus on his prey. He draws back on the bowstring. He takes dead aim.

15

The Napoleon House

Without conversation, we cruise down Louisiana Route 1 from outside Thibodaux to Raceland with Dylan's 'Knockin' on Heaven's Door' blaring on the radio.

We catch Route 90 north-east through now familiar bayou country to Westwego and Tim's Texaco gas station, only a dozen miles from New Orleans.

While Lightfoot primes the Chevy with gas and oil, I rummage through a rack of pamphlets advertising everything from swamp tours to alligator wrestling — 'free pool at Randy's Roadhouse Bar' until the end of the month and swamp-buggy rides for ten dollars a head are now available at Jan's Bait Shop. I pay a buck fifty for a map of New Orleans, 'half price' according to a sun-faded sign stuck to the side of the rack.

Back in the car, Jeff cranks the ignition.

"Where to, chief?" he says.

My finger traces a line on the unfolded map. "Straight ahead, my man — Airline Highway to Huey P. Long Bridge and we'll be downtown before you know it."

**

It is unseasonably warm for late December, and although barely past noon, the French Quarter is abuzz. Moments after turning onto Bourbon Street we are greeted by the clamor of revelers and the sweet jangle of jazzy blues spilling into the street through open doors of bars that line the way.

Crowds have disappeared and music faded by the time we have cruised the thirteen blocks to the Quarter's north-east boundary and turned onto tree-lined Esplanade Avenue. Ahead, the three-story house where, years ago, I kept a second story flat while teaching the art of two-dimensional design to a curious mix of debutantes and serious art students at Tulane's Sophie Newcomb College comes into view. A roadside plaque on the front lawn catches my eye.

"Pull over, Jeff," I say.

"What's up?"

"Stop here, please," I say.

Jeff pulls the car to the curb and follows me toward a plaque mounted on a concrete lectern planted neatly amid a row of magnolias. I cup my hands to my eyes against the sun's glare like a horse's blinders to make out the inscription:

2306 Esplanade Avenue
Home of French Impressionist, Edgar Degas
Summer, 1872

"Well, how about that?" I say.

"How about what, Mister Barker?"

"I lived in that house for two years — the house Edgar Degas stayed in a hundred years before, according to this plaque."

We get back into the car. Lightfoot, contemplating my connection to someone named Degas and oblivious to his surroundings, pulls the Chevy back into the unusually light traffic of Esplanade, almost striking the only car in sight.

I fasten my seat belt.

"Degas: I know that name," says Lightfoot. "He was an artist — a French guy, right?"

"Right on both counts. You've done yourself proud, my boy," I say.

"Well, he must be one famous dude for sure if I've heard of him."

"Oh, don't sell yourself short, Jeff;" I say, "I'm beginning to think you might be a little smarter than you look."

166

"There's always that possibility," Jeff says. "Anyway, enlighten me. Tell me about this Degas."

"I'm no authority on the man. I did know he spent some time here in the French Quarter but had no idea exactly where. I guess the historical society types hadn't smelled that out yet either back when I was living here."

"What brought Degas to New Orleans?"

"There are differing opinions on that. Some think he came to visit his brother, René, and then, with no forethought, was smitten by the beauty of René's wife, Estelle, who just happened to be his cousin."

"Smitten with his cousin, you say. His cousin was his brother's wife? No—now that's just not right," Lightfoot says.

"That's the way the artsy history crowd would have it, but I think it's more likely Degas was in love with Estelle long before he came to New Orleans.

"Of course, we will never know the truth of it, but I think my version is more plausible. Not only that, when you add my theory of sibling betrayal to the mix, you have it all — famous and beautiful people, an illicit love affair, incest, a conspiracy of the heart in one of the world's most romantic cities — now that sounds like the makings of a best seller if I ever heard one."

"I think you might have something there, Mister Barker."

"For sure, and the plot thickens. After months of painting whatever caught his eye, most notably Cousin Estelle, rumors began to fly. According to the wags of New Orleans's high society, something other than paint was being spread by Monsieur Degas behind those studio walls."

"Sounds like a big foul ball on the brush man!" Jeff says. "So, what happened?"

"You mean between Edgar and Cousin Estelle?"

"Is there someone else were talking about?"

"Well, not long after the rumors began, Degas skipped town. Some said the heat and humidity got to him, others thought his funds ran dry, but gossip among those who believed they were in the know was that René caught wind of Edgar's affair with Estelle and sent his brother packing. Whatever the case, Degas beat it back to France and never returned."

"Like you say, that's some story. You should write *that* book, Mister Barker."

"Maybe I should—but knowing the *real* reason Degas left town, I would feel like a hypocrite spreading that delicious fraud."

"Fraud? The *real* reason?" Jeff looks at me, puzzled. "What are you talking about, Mister Barker?

"My guess is the cockroaches ran Degas off."

"What?"

You heard me. Degas might have lived in that house a hundred years before me, but I bet the roaches I met when I lived there had ancestors who were well acquainted with Edgar Degas."

Jeff laughs. "That's a good one, Gille," he says. "You really had me going."

"I'm not kidding. Roaches with any self-respect stay out of sight a good part of the day, you know, waiting for the cover of dark, but not in that house. In that house I could count on wrestling fliers the size of wrens for my bacon and eggs at the breakfast table."

"No way."

"Yes way, and you can believe me when I tell you I seldom had breakfast before ten, so it wasn't like those roaches were stragglers from the night before.

"Yes, it is true — the pitter patter of their spiny-clawed feet across the counters in pursuit of errant crumbs could be heard any time of night or day. Their rummaging through my food supplies was more insistent than that of a couple of long lost relatives of mine who showed up uninvited for a weekend stay last summer."

"*Now* you're getting silly."

"I kid you not. But the *real* trouble didn't begin until I fumigated my apartment with roach spray. Nose clipped shut and goggle eyed, I listened with satisfaction through that night as roaches plopped on their backs to the linoleum floor.

"I was scooping up still writhing roaches the next morning when the doorbell rang. It would not stop ringing, so I took a moment to squint through the spy hole in my door and saw five strangers standing in the hall, their noses as big as tennis balls in the fish-eye lens. They looked funny that way, but mad as hell."

"What did they want?"

"I was about to tell you."

"Please do."

"Where was I?"

"Five mad, but funny-looking strangers at the door."

"Uh huh. I soon found out they were my neighbors, and they *were* mad as hell. There was Mister Florendo and his wife whose name, in the four years as her neighbor, I never came to know—they lived across the hall, and Angelique and Willie from the apartments on either side of mine. Then there was Loraine Florea, a retired schoolteacher, who, at four foot ten, weighed in at one-eighty or so and blocked out the light when she waddled down the halls. Loraine had lived in the apartment that was below mine for so long most of the tenants thought she owned the place, and maybe she did.

"Anyway, they all stood there, arms folded across their chests, looking like they suspected me of stealing social security checks from their mail.

"I opened the door. 'Yes?' I said. 'Can I help you folks?'

"And Loraine said, 'good morning, *Mister* Barker', all surly-like, you know? Well, being new to the building and not especially the neighborly type anyway, I just said good morning back to her in the same manner, and that was when she went into a tizzy.

"She waved a couple dozen sheets of paper in front of my face and stabbed at the top sheet with one of her stubby fingers.

"'Did you bother to read your tenant's manual, *Mister* Barker?' she said.

"I told her, yes, I had looked through it, but that was the wrong answer. 'You must have missed page three then,' she said."

Jeff laughs. "I think I would have been slamming the door on her about then," he says.

"She *was* beginning to get on my nerves, but I just said, 'to tell you the truth, mam, I haven't had the time to read the particulars.'"

"Oh boy."

"Oh boy is right. 'You better take the time, Mister Barker,' she said. 'You better take the time,' and I told her I would get right on that project after lunch. Well, that was *not* what Loraine wanted to hear.

"She ripped that page three from its staples and held it up in front of my face for me to see, and while punching her finger at lines of print halfway down the page, she recited the house rules I had broken from memory. 'No fumigation, Mister Barker. No spraying for bugs, Mister Barker. You see that Mister Barker?' There it was all right, in black and white and underlined in red so even a fool like me couldn't miss it."

Jeff is all smiles. "Hah, she had you — not much you could argue with there. So, what did you have to say for yourself?"

"I told her I was sorry, but old Loraine was just getting warmed up. Purple veins popped through the rose blush painted on her cheeks. 'That spray chases those damned roaches right over to our apartments–makes us mad as hell. Don't you know that Mister Barker?' she said.

"'I *do* know that *now*,' I told her. 'I assure you, it won't happen again,' I said.

"'All right then. Have a good day, Mister Barker.' That's what she said, and I said, 'you too, mam,' and closed the door."

"That's some story," says Jeff.

"Well, it's all true," I say. "And that, my friend, is why I suggest roaches should receive credit for saving a marriage and chasing the great Edgar Degas' sorry ass back to France."

**

It is midafternoon now as Jeff turns the Chevy back down into the French Quarter on Royal Street. On my direction, he crosses over to Chartres Street near the purported address of Miss Waynette Boudreaux.

"There it is, that's nine-twenty Chartres, right there," I say, pointing at the address placard on a building.

"You're one hell of a navigator, Gille," Jeff says.

"That I am. And there's a parking spot." I point at the empty space directly in front of nine-twenty that must be the only open parking space on Chartres Street.

170

The two-story building is much the same as those adjacent to it, all faced with soft clay bricks that appear to have been randomly stacked row on row with little use of mortar or level. A weathered second floor veranda ten-feet wide with a precarious looking black metal railing juts out over the sidewalk. Two towel-draped beach loungers sit in the middle of the veranda's wood slat floor.

An ornate wrought iron gate guards a tunnel-like entry cut through the front of the building. I guess the tunnel at twelve feet from end to end and the same from side to side. On the other side of the tunnel is a garden courtyard of palms and in that courtyard is a fountain statue of a concrete cherub with spreading wings and a mound of curly hair. Water spouts in an admirable arc from the cherub's tiny pecker into a concrete bucket the size of a washtub.

Jeff scans the tenant names below each of a dozen buzzers mounted to the wall outside the gate.

"W. Boudreaux; there she is." Jeff pushes the buzzer above Waynette's name. He pushes the buzzer again, and again, and an elderly black lady holding a bristle floor broom upside down peers at us from around the corner of the entry tunnel's inner wall. She steps to the center of the entry, six feet from the gate, and faces us, one hand now on her hip.

"Maybe you could help us, mam" Jeff says to the woman. "We're looking for Waynette Boudreaux"

"Unless you've been ringing the wrong buzzer, I know *who* you're looking for, mister," the woman says. "Ms. Boudreaux's not home; ain't never home till after six during the week."

"Thank you, mam," says Jeff.

"No need to be pushing that buzzer no more," the old woman says.

"Let's get a drink," Jeff says to me.

**

We walk four blocks down Chartres to the Napoleon House, a favorite haunt of mine during my Tulane University days. Most of the ancient black and white marble floor tile in the Napoleon House are chipped or broken. A dozen old tables with spindly mahogany chairs, stained black with age, are scattered about the barroom floor. The high, ornately-embossed tin-tile ceiling is coated dingy yellow-gray with decades of exhaled tar and nicotine.

In one corner of the room is an old eight-stool bar, richly carved with images of sea urchins and ancient mariners. Glass-pained French doors open onto a courtyard at one end of the bar. Spider webs glimmer in light filtering through a window at the top of the courtyard's spiral stair that now leads to nowhere.

The Napoleon House has not changed since I last walked out the door twenty years ago — it is as if I never left.

**

Jeff pulls a chair back from a table near the second of four sets of open French doors to the sidewalk. Across the street artists line the cobblestone walks of famous Jackson Square to display their wares. Not even this has changed.

"How about here?" Jeff says.

"Perfect," is my reply. And, to me, it is.

A waiter approaches us outfitted in the standard Napoleon House attire of old, ill-fitted white dress shirt, slick black pants, and poorly knotted bow tie. A tag pinned to his shirt informs us that he, like the brother of Edgar Degas, is René.

I order a red wine. Jeff asks René for a 'New Orleans kind of drink'. Curious as to the result of that request, I watch the bartender pull out a foot tall tulip-shaped glass and build Lightfoot's cocktail with a scoop of shaved ice, about four shots of dark rum, a splash of orange juice, and a dash of grenadine.

Through the open doorway, we watch the Jackson Square artists hawk their wares — a bright rendition of the Louisiana Bayous, a painting of New Orleans' Saint Louis Cathedral that appears to have been painted with cake icing, paintings of roosters with brightly colored feathers — paintings with subjects of every kind done with every level of competency.

A gaggle of blue-haired garden-club matrons on a day tour of the city disgorge from a Greyhound bus. They scatter like frightened sparrows among the artist's displays. They chirp and chatter and point at one painting and then another and offer unsolicited critiques in exaggerated voices. Then, as if a blue-

172

haired-matron hunter had fired a shotgun blast into the flock, as quickly as they had come, they are gone.

Only pockets of besotted tourists taking a break from their Bourbon Street revelry are left cruising Jackson Square. Sale prospects are bleak, but there is always the lingering hope one of them will part with a few bucks if the colors are judged compatible with the fabric on a living room sofa back in Peoria or Weiser, Idaho, not that there is anything wrong with that.

**

It is twilight now and even the most optimistic of street artists are packing away their easels on Jackson Square. I am half-way through my second wine and Jeff is sucking the bottom out of his third stemmed bucket of rum.

The Napoleon House glows with the mellow light of late afternoon. Seats fill with a smattering of tourists and the regular crowd of bar flies in search of happy hour freebies, some of whom I am sure I recognize from my previous life here.

Jeff, slouched in his chair, watches through glazed eyes as the streets empty and the garden club lady's tour bus crosses Lake Pontchartrain on its way to Baton Rouge. Artists continue packing their wares – hangers-on straggle away into dusk.

Jeff has been quiet since shortly after I ordered his second drink. That was some time ago. Sugary alcoholic cocktails and lack of sleep have taken their toll.

I am startled, along with most everyone else in the Napoleon House, when Jeff jumps up, sending his chair screeching across the tile floor behind him. He points toward two women standing near the crosswalk across the street at the corner of Jackson Square.

"That's her. That's Waynette," Jeff says.

"Waynette! — Waynette!" he calls out, waving his hand above his head as he stumbles off the curb into the street and back up onto the curb next to the woman across the way.

The woman, backward leaning in a defensive stance, is looking directly at Jeff with no glimmer of recognition.

I sip at my wine and signal René for another. From a block away, the sweet smell of Café du Monde's famous fresh beignets wafts through the open Napoleon House doors. I do love this place.

The woman takes a step away from Jeff, clutching her purse with both hands. She says something to Jeff, and he makes an apparently unacceptable reply. The woman abruptly turns her back on him and quickly walks away.

Lightfoot returns to our table. He rocks back on his chair and clasps his hands behind his head, looking back toward the sidewalks of Jackson Square.

"Well, Mister Lightfoot," I say, "I hope that went better than it seemed."

I am certain I have not called Jeff 'Mister Lightfoot' before. I feel warm as the chandelier's golden glow. An affected grin is locked to the corners of my lips. I am closing in on limbo land. I am a mellow fellow. I think I take another sip from my glass of wine.

"That wasn't Waynette," Jeff says.

"Obviously."

Jeff is in the late stages of going haywire. Alcohol abuse and sleep deprivation have taken their toll. His mind U-turns back to Thibodaux then bounces around Jackson Square and settles on Hillary Boudreaux.

**

"Old Hillary Boudreaux — I bet she *was* in cahoots with Johnny Ray. You met her; what do you think, Mister Barker?"

At that moment it dawns on me Jeff has become more than an acquaintance; he is the best friend I have this side of Winslow Prison.

"I don't know, my friend," I say, still locked by drink to my Cheshire cat-like grin, "but I don't think I would trust her far from my line of sight."

"Exactly," Jeff says. "The old woman is crazy all right, but she's no dummy. I can see her and her nitwit son plotting to get rid of me, but to do that to her only daughter, that seems low."

"Well, to what lengths do you think a woman like Hillary would go to protect her own?" I say, my uncontrollable grin now as wide as the Mississippi. "Maybe the old woman thought she

174

was doing Waynette a favor. You know, saving her from the life of an Indian squaw, a life in a one room wigwam filled with squalling little half breeds—no electricity, no plumbing, beating her laundry clean on a rock down by the river."

I am witty but fading. My eyes are as narrow as two of Sam Gillette's soda dispenser coin slots.

"You *are* a funny guy, Mister Barker, but, you know, you might have something there. That's the way she would think. I knew the old woman was nutty from the first time Waynette introduced me to her down by the bayou bridge, you know – the one we crossed to get to her house?"

"I know the one you mean," I say, only vaguely aware we are in conversation.

"Anyway, she was wearing one of those floppy, wide-brim straw hats, just standing there strangling an old bamboo fishing pole with the line dangling in the water.

"I stuck out my hand and told Hillary I was pleased to meet her, but she didn't seem to hear, didn't acknowledge me at all. She just stared at the red and white bobber tied to her fishing line. That bobber sat there in the water twenty feet away, still as could be–not a ripple.

"I wasn't paying much attention, just standing there feeling awkward, when she yanked that pole up in the air and the hook came flying out of the water, up over her head, and then whipped back to catch in the brim of her hat. Old Hillary just fished the hook out of her hat and looked at it, like it was the first fish hook she had ever seen. 'Damn it, he got away,' she said."

I chuckle, the absent grin of my lips still locked in place, and sip from my red wine. "That's funny all right," I say.

"Try to pay attention Gille" Lightfoot says.

"I am all ears," I say.

"Oh yeah, I can see that. Anyway, she looked at that hook for a minute or two, reached in her basket, pulled out the nothing held between her fingers, and baited her hook with whatever she thought she saw there. When she had the hook set to her liking, she whipped the pole back and forth until it whistled and cast the line back into the bayou. Then, after the bobber floated around for a while, maybe five minutes, she yanked the line out and the hook stuck in that old straw hat, same as it did before."

"You're kidding," I say.

"Not at all. 'Damn it, he got away,' she said."

Jeff has the old woman's voice down to a tee.

"Then she did it again — pried the hook loose from her hat, dug into the bait basket, baited her hook with the nothing she found there, and threw it right back into the water – no worm, no fly, no bait of any kind.

"Waynette didn't seem to notice her mother was loony tunes. She just pulled me over by that old Oak tree; you probably saw the one I'm talking about."

I shrug my shoulders. "Seen one Oak tree, seen them all," I say, tipping my glass toward Jeff in an unreciprocated toast to that.

"Anyway, she hiked up her dress and ——"

"Thank you, Mister Lightfoot," I say. "That was truly a delightful story."

"I'm just saying, crazy like that *has* to be in the genes. I should have made a run for it right then — not because old Hillary was a loon, but because of how much I could already see of her in Waynette. That was what should have scared the bejesus out of me.

"Hell, it was obvious the butter was already in the pan. They had the same voice, the same spooky eyes; you know, the kind we talked about before that look straight at you, blank as hell, and then dart away. I'm telling you, that can get under a man's skin after a while."

"Well, my dear boy, it might have been advisable to take those things into consideration," I say in my best imitation of Truman Capote on bourbon and cocaine.

"Yeah and there's that Betty Lou – you know, the one Mrs. Boudreaux said moved with Waynette to New Orleans. Now that girl seemed to be a little strange to me right from the get-go, like she maybe was not the kind that favored men, you know what I mean?"

"Oh yes, I know what you mean. You think Waynette might have switched teams; maybe taken up a new sport all together, but what is your point?"

Jeff says he is not sure *what* he is thinking, or what he is saying, or even if he has a point.

I tell him that, if he is faulting himself for Waynette's switch to the other side of the rainbow, he should get that thought out of his mind because, if it is so, then she had those tendencies long before he came on the scene.

"It's always been a wonder to me why any woman would put up with living the straight life with a man in the first place," I continue. "I doubt if many would admit it, but most women would likely opt for the gay life and keep a man locked away in a cage in case of the need for sperm or torment or just, now and then, to relieve the pleasantries of a perfectly fine day, if given a choice.

"Of course," I say, "it is probably best not to get involved with crazy people, no matter their sexual preference."

Was I being serious? I do not know. Jeff studies my face in search of a trace of irony. Finding none, he raises his glass to mine.

"Here's to the loons," he says. "Hell, I love her just the same."

I have my doubts.

We lift our glasses again in a toast to Waynette and Mrs. Boudreaux and all the rest of us who can't seem to keep two oars in the water for a full twenty-four-hour day.

"Yes, Jeff, here's to the loons" I say. "And may we always remember, it's only a matter of time and degree."

I sip from my fourth glass of red wine and try to focus on the dinner menu René has dropped on our table. My cheeks are flush, the tips of my ears are warming.

"Hillary is probably sitting back, right where we left her," Jeff says, "cackling away, addled on her precious Southern Comfort, watching that brat, Johnny Ray, crash his pickup truck into the wall and throw paper baseballs into the fire. 'I told you so, I told you so, people change you know, cackle, cackle.' I can hear her now."

Jeff crosses his arms on the table and lays his head on top of them. He falls into a restive sleep, obviously punctuated by visions of the cackling Hillary Boudreaux. I see her too.

After a few minutes Jeff's head pops up from the table. He is starving and so am I. On René's recommendation, we order bowls of Louisiana gumbo chock full of giant shrimp parts, sliced okra, green peppers and all sorts of claws and things I'm not sure of and don't want to know. There is a basket of fresh breads to soak up the last gumbo gravy with sweeps across the bottoms of our bowls until the only remains are a few dry crab claws and empty mussel shells.

I am refreshed. I feel as though the gumbo has restored my blood alcohol content to an acceptable level. And the effect on Lightfoot appears even more remarkable. It seems his bowl of gumbo has returned him to a state approaching sobriety.

"Now that's what I call good gumbo," Jeff says.

He leans back in his chair and wipes greasy gumbo gravy from his chin. He holds his hand above his head, signaling René to bring him another Keystone, and then, resting his hand on my shoulder —— "and a glass of your fine red house wine for my friend," he says.

16

Thespians

A waitress approaches our table. She drops a coaster from her tray to the table in front of Lightfoot. "You are the Keystone?" she asks.

"Yes, that would be me," Jeff says. He turns toward the waitress and is for once, if momentarily, struck speechless.

"And that would make you the Cabernet," the waitress says to me.

"That I am, my dear—my veins run red with Cabernet." Embarrassed by my atypical attempt at a witty reply, I quickly avert my attention to the woodgrain of the tabletop.

"You're Gille Barker aren't you," the most beautiful waitress in all New Orleans says to me.

How can she know that?

"Yes, I am," I say, "and you are —?"

"Cynthia, Cynthia Canales," she says while offering her hand.

"Have we met, Cynthia?" I say, now holding her outstretched hand in mine.

"I recognized you from your photograph," Cynthia says.

"Photograph?"

"Why, Mister Barker, your picture was everywhere there for a while. People Magazine, The National Enquirer—a person couldn't go to the grocery store without seeing your face on one of those rags in the checkout line. I told Mister Sheehan I thought you were here, and he said that couldn't be because you were locked up in Arizona."

"Interesting," I say, "but I don't believe I know a Mister Sheehan." I tell her this even though I have the feeling I do know him, that this scene has played out before.

"He's sitting right over there," Cynthia says. She nods toward a table across the room where a Richard Burton type of handsome middle-aged man with long, curly-gray hair sits in animated conversation. "He'd love to meet you. May I call him over? Would you mind?"

I tell Cynthia that I would not mind in the slightest. I say that, as a matter of fact, I would like very much to meet her Mister Sheehan. There was no option for my reply. Even at this early stage in our acquaintance, it wasn't in me to say no to Cynthia Canales. Besides, I knew that was what I was going to say before she asked the question I had somehow known she was going to ask.

**

Now at Sheehan's table, Cynthia bends down to relay my invitation. He stands and looks my way, adjusting his wire rimmed glasses up off the end of his nose. A smile creeps across his face. He nods and I acknowledge with a slight bow.

Cynthia leads him to our table and introduces us.

"So, you're Gille Barker, you say," Ed Sheehan says, as I stand to accept his offered hand.

"I *have* said that on occasion, and yes I am," is my wine-induced attempt at a droll reply.

Sheehan remains skeptical.

"I heard Gille Barker was stuck in a cage over in Arizona," Ed says, "but I must say you *do* look a good deal like the man."

"Oh, he's Gille Barker all right," Jeff pipes in. "And I'm Jeff Lightfoot—pleased to meet you, sir." Jeff shakes Sheehan's hand. "And you're right about him being in the slammer. I picked Mister Barker up at the Winslow Prison gates when they turned him loose a couple of days ago."

"It's a pleasure to meet you son." Sheehan points at Jeff's pack of cigarettes on our table. "Think I could borrow one of those?"

"Sure thing," Lightfoot says.

Ed takes a cigarette from the pack and patiently waits while Jeff fishes his lighter from his pocket and coaxes it into sparking fire.

"Thank you, Jeffrey. I try not to make a habit of begging strangers for cigarettes, but my lady friend won't allow me to carry the things. She says they stink, even when unlit, and fill her clothes with such a god-awful odor her dry cleaner can't dismiss it. And then there's the cancer thing, of course. Women—we are at their mercy, it would seem. Don't you agree?"

"Sure do, but I have no complaints I care to mention," Lightfoot says.

Sheehan turns his attention back to me. "Well, it's a pleasure to meet you, Mister Barker," he says.

"Gille, please call me Gille," I say. "Pull up a chair and join us."

"I'd like that very much, but I'm with a table of fellow thespians and misfits who hold me in such high regard as to be deeply disappointed if I didn't return. Besides, given the current circumstance, I'm certain at least one of them could barely find a toilet without my direction."

Sheehan points toward a slick-domed man sitting at his table.

"Unfortunately, Freddie, the Uncle Fester look-alike in the corner there, has a prostate the size of a honey dew melon. Through no fault of his own, he may be inclined to dribble on his chair if I do not return."

Ed's raspy baritone is directed as much to the other Napoleon House patrons as to us and is greeted with sniggers of laughter from his table of friends, including Freddie

"But, if you're game," he continues, "we would be honored to have you join us for a round or two."

Jeff, enrapt by the charms of Cynthia Canales, is quick to recognize the intrinsic value of Ed's invitation.

"Sounds good to me," he says.

181

The Making of a Ham

Ed Sheehan was a toddler when he first worked the southern circuit stages in his parent's vaudeville act. Double-takes and blank-stares in response to his father's tired jokes were audience favorites from the beginning.

Though Ed would never be more famous than he was then, the stage has been his life, the only life he has ever wanted or known, and he became good at the acting part—it was the *business* of acting he never got the hang of.

As he grew into leading roles, the adulation of the New Orleans theater crowd became almost as intoxicating as the liquor that was his true addiction and remains so today.

As youth faded, so did his career. Not an overnight affair, Ed barely noticed things were going haywire until the stage disappeared from all but his own mind's eye.

Once the toast of the New Orleans stage, Ed held on to his illusions for a decade hustling a smattering of theater junkies and late-night bar crawlers for pocket change in French Quarter backwater dives.

That chapter of Ed's life ended on a Friday night, when he disappointed a young male admirer who had taken him home expecting more of him than a display of his oratorical prowess.

Ed woke around noon on Saturday, bruised and beaten, prone on a metal cot suspended by chains anchored to the drunk-tank wall of city jail. A miserably long weekend stretched into Tuesday before his wife, Margo, could get him out.

They did not speak during the half hour ride home, nor had they yet when Margo sat the bruised and still bloodied Ed down at the kitchen table and poured him a cup of coffee.

Planting an elbow on the table, Ed braced the side of his head on his hand. He scooped a mound of sugar onto a spoon and held the spoon above his cup. Tilting the spoon slightly, he watched the

182

sugar granules fall into the coffee. Silently, he counted the granules as they fell.

"Would you like some breakfast, dear?" It was clear in Margo's voice that Ed was rapidly approaching his rope's end.

'Why is she upset with me?' Ed's oblivious mind asked him. *'My life is the one that's in the crapper.'*

But, what Ed said to Margo out loud was, "Yes woman, eggs over easy and a fine portion of bacon, if you please — and make it snappy."

Make it snappy was the end of a gag-line from Ed's vaudeville days, but Margo had no familiarity with vaudeville.

She plopped a plate down in front of Ed and cracked an egg on the edge. Shell shards floated along on the uncooked yolk as it oozed across the plate. Ed, the side of his head still planted on his hand, watched patiently as Margo carefully placed a slice of raw bacon across the egg yolk.

"Is that bacon *snappy* enough for you, mister big shot actor?" she said.

Ed lifted his head from his hand, picked up a knife and fork, carved a square from the raw bacon, and took a bite. He sprinkled the raw egg with salt and pepper and a dash of Louisiana hot sauce. With his knife, he coaxed the yolk, dripping with the clear egg white slime littered with shards of shell, onto a spoon and let the yolk slide onto his tongue. As a man savoring a raw oyster, he swished the yolk from side to side and swallowed.

Ed wiped his lips and deposited shards of eggshell from the tip of his tongue onto a dishcloth. He carefully spread the cloth across his lap and carved another square from the raw bacon strip.

Margo stood over him, hands on hips, silently watching his performance. A vein threatened to pop from her forehead.

"Excellent bacon, my dear," Ed said.

"And now you have it, folks," said Margo, as if announcing the grandest of final acts under a circus big top, "Mister Ed Sheehan—the most perfect of assholes."

**

Ed's next memory was waking flat on his back, spread-eagled on the sofa. A corner streetlight cast night shadows across the room.

He strained to see the wall clock in the kitchen—it was nine-thirty, eleven hours since he polished off his bacon and eggs.

"Margo?" Ed stumbled across the room to the bottom of the stairs. "Margo?" he called out again, climbing the steps.

Not finding Margo in the bedroom, Ed pulled out her dresser drawer. It was empty. He threw the closet door open. Metal hangers hung bare in an unruly row. Margo's two fine-leather suitcases, the only survivors of BJ's Pawn Shop over in Metairie — they were gone.

He looked down from the bedroom window to the spot where their beat-up ten-year-old Studebaker Lark usually squatted in the rutted dirt drive. The car was gone too.

Sitting on the edge of the bed, Ed stared through bare winter limbs of maple trees at the blank row of tenement windows of long time, but never known, neighbors across the way. He stared but was unseeing–unaware. He was going to throw up.

Ed twisted the shower tap to cold. He let water spray his face and roll down his chest. He turned the tap until steam coated the bathroom mirrors. He washed. He toweled dry and sprinkled himself with cologne from a bottle he found two weeks ago on a Canal Street bench. He found a barely used razor in the medicine cabinet. He lathered his face with a bar of soap. Each swath of the razor blade revealed more confirmation of the toll exacted on him, by age of course, but more so by neglect. Ed considered his eyes in the mirror's reflection.

He wept.

Margo would not be back. Ed knew that. It seemed he had, at last, lost everything, but there is always that last bit of self-respect to stamp out before scraping bottom. It would take more than losing Margo and all his worldly possessions to bring Ed Sheehan to his knees.

Ed was back on a bar stool before the next noon whistle and would have continued his fight with the bottle until the mortician's wagon plucked him from a gutter if Madeline Meacham had not come along. Oh yes, there is no doubt Madeline and six months lodging in the finest rehabilitation center her money could buy saved Ed Sheehan.

Now Ed is a teacher of his trade and a master of self-promotion, things that might have made him a rock star in his salad days. And now, just steps from the Napoleon House front door, in a store-front space across the street from New Orleans' famous Jackson Square, he is the director of The Ed Sheehan Theater. He is, once again, the man of the hour. He is the handsome elder statesman with a ready-made cast of aspiring actors and theater groupies willing to pay for a piece of his wisdom and the right to assuage their loneliness with his powerful light.

**

"Here we go," Ed says.

Legs screeching, Ed drags our chairs across the marble tile floor and seats me and Jeff at his table.

In address to us and his friends, Sheehan, still standing, says that it is so good Jeff and I could join in celebration of the final rehearsal before the opening of their new play, 'Dante's Harbor.'

There is a smattering of applause. Ed taps the side of his glass with the desired effect of alerting everyone in the Napoleon House that he is about to speak.

"My dear friends, let me introduce you to the marvelous artist and writer, Mister Gille Barker and his traveling companion, Jeffrey Lightfoot, who have graciously accepted my offer to share cocktail's in our company on this special occasion."

Ed is in one of his infamous oratorical moods and just warming up when his fellow thespians and knowing Napoleon House regulars sitting at surrounding tables recognize the warning signs and cut him short with a salute and their glasses held high.

"Here, here!" They cheer in near unison.

Freddie, with his honeydew prostate and a left eye that points toward the chandelier above my shoulder while his right stares at my nose, stands and reaches his hand across the table. "It's a pleasure to meet you, Mister Barker. I am Freddie Fender, and I enjoy your work immensely."

"Why thank you Freddie," I say, while seeing images of Freddie in my head, first thumbing through my latest novel and then attempting to concentrate his gaze on my most recent painting, his eyes darting around the room like runaway pinballs.

Freddie casts an eye in Jeff's direction and shakes his hand. "Freddie Fender," he says.

"Nice to meet you, Mister Fender."

"Freddie's my right-hand man," Ed says, as Freddie returns to his seat. He counts Freddie's attributes on his fingers. "Freddie built our beautiful new stage singlehanded. He designed the sets and divined the wardrobes from thin air. I could go on in dear Freddie's praise, but time is of the essence, so let's have a toast for Freddie."

There is loud applause and hurrahs for Freddie until he is forced to stand again and give an unaccustomed bow.

Sheehan continues with introductions to the other members of his curious entourage. Next to me are the beautiful Jennie Fullerton and her husband, Bill. Bill dives from oil rigs to the bottom of the Gulf of Mexico and works down there in a rubberized canvas suit with a sixty-pound metal bowl on his head, the only thing that keeps his brain from exploding through the top of his skull on a daily basis.

Jennie is one of New Orleans' finest actors. I remember her from my previous stent in the city. Early in her career, work with Lee Strasberg in New York put her in the rare company of James Dean and Al Pacino, Dustin Hoffman and Marilyn Monroe. She worked with Dennis Hopper there. A role in Hopper's 'Easy Rider' movie was in the works until a car crash cost Jennie a leg two weeks before filming was to begin.

**

Across the table from Jennie, actor and writer, Donny Dragon, exhibits little interest in the proceedings. He leans back against the wall and exhales a perfect smoke ring that smells like Jamaican rum and bubblegum into our space from a loosely rolled brown cigarette.

Donny first met Ed Sheehan while making the rounds of the Decatur Street dives in search of a one-night stand. Instead, he ended up staggering home at daybreak with Ed in tow. They talked, but Donny mostly listened while the silver-tongued actor jabbered on about the theater, asserting the virtues of 'Dante's Harbor' along the way. 'Dante's Harbor' was the title Ed gave a play he had worked on for three years but never finished, long before entering his extended alcoholic haze.

Donny perked up when Ed outlined the story of 'Dante's Harbor'. After Ed showed him pages, Donny was intrigued. He asked Ed' permission to take the script and see if he could help finish what Ed had begun.

And so it was that six years ago, with Ed's blessing, Donny completed a rewrite of 'Dante's Harbor'. Donny had written a half dozen plays and four novels before 'Dante's Harbor', all of which have never seen the light of day. They remain neatly bundled and locked away in an old cedar chest where 'Dante's Harbor' would likely be languishing if not for Madeline Meacham.

**

"And last but far from least — this is Madeline," Ed continues in his introductions.

Always on stage, he bows to the seated Madeline Meacham and kisses her hand.

"Without Madeline, none of us would be here tonight. There would be no Sheehan Theater, no 'Dante's Harbor'. For that matter, there would probably be no Ed Sheehan."

That brought a satiric smattering of applause from a bearded stranger at an adjacent table.

Ed, looking down at Madeline and still holding her hand, makes a theatrical pause to acknowledge the knowing nods of his audience.

Thank you my dear," Ed finally says, having milked all of the moment.

Even Donny Dragon cracks a knowing smile and joins in the appreciative applause.

**

Madeline has the look of elegance gone slightly awry that often plagues the chronically well-to-do. Her face is long, horsy narrow, and as white as the napkin under her stemmed glass of whiskey sour. The bone lines above her sunken cheeks are high and sharp and painted robin-breast red, like those of a sophisticated circus clown. A long string of pearls the size of Chinese marbles dangles from her ostrich-like neck. The scent of money oozes from her pores.

Madeline was the wife of Fargo Meacham, a New Orleans real estate mogul, until a sultry summer day little more than three years ago when, while sitting on their courtyard balcony, Fargo stopped swatting mosquitoes the size of house flies and blew his brains out with his pearl-handled Colt 45.

Ed and Madeline first met while sitting at this same Napoleon House table more than twenty years ago, when Ed's star was at its brightest. Fargo and Madeline were among the New Orleans theater's most generous patrons then, and Ed was one of their favorite performers.

When, years later, Ed hit the skids and was sleeping in doorways or bunked up at Father Duncan's Saint Theresa's shelter, it was the Father who, in passing, happened to mention to Madeline that the once celebrated actor was spending his days standing in the church soup kitchen line and drawing straws for a cot at night.

Newly widowed, bored, and with more cash than she could ever spend, Ed Sheehan was just the project Madeline needed.

She picked Ed up from the gutter and sent him to the finest of rehabilitation centers to hobnob with the rich and famous. Six months later Ed walked out a new man, a man with a plan, a man with the powerful Madeline Meacham in his corner.

**

At some point in the hours of alcohol infused conversation that follow, I am made aware that, not only is Cynthia our waitress, but she is also a prime player in Sheehan's production of 'Dante's Harbor'.

Cynthia has joined us. Once again our waiter, René leans back against the bar, arms crossed, with an empty serving tray held dangling from one hand. It is late. Other than René, the bartender, and our table of eccentrics, the Napoleon House is deserted.

René looks at his watch. It is a quarter till one, time for last call.

Ed whispers to Madeline. She smiles. The hot embers from a cigarette he holds behind his back inch precariously close to his fingers. Smoke curls lazily toward the ceiling. Freddie Fender's head has not moved from the tabletop for two rounds.

I have been seriously overserved.

More than an hour has passed since Jennie, grown tired of rambling bar chatter, slipped out through the French doors to the Napoleon House courtyard. Eyes closed, she rests curled in a hammock-chair swing hanging from the ceiling that is two stories above near the top of a winding stairs to nowhere. Her prosthetic leg hangs over the side of the hammock, its shiny plastic heel scraping the rough brick floor in concert with the chair's pendulum-like motion.

Motionless, Jennie's husband, Bill, sits glassy-eyed at the table, as do I, withdrawn from conversation.

Jeff has an arm draped behind Cynthia. She sips on a tall glass of fruits and rum and nods her head in abstract agreement with whatever the smitten Lightfoot might be saying.

Just as it seems last call has brought the night to a merciful end, Donny Dragon rises from his chair on a second wind and suggests we continue the night's festivities at his place.

He has a wonderful Judy Garland album we should all hear: *Dear Mister Gable, Sweet Sixteen, You Can't Have Everything, Embraceable You———*."

"Well now, Mister Dragon," Ed says, "that's a fine offer I think none of us should refuse. I can only suppose you have refreshments at your abode?"

"Your assumption would be correct, Mister Sheehan. And what I may not have is readily available on our way."

Ed surveys our table. "All of those in favor of adjourning our meeting and regrouping at the Dragon residence signify by a show of hands," he says.

Freddie's head thumps against the table as Ed drags his arm out from under it and hoists his hand skyward.

"That makes it unanimous, says Ed."

"Not quite." Madeline pushes her chair back from the table. She bends to kiss Ed on the cheek. "I'm afraid it's past my bedtime, and I have an early morning."

"Pleased to have met you, Ms. Meacham," I say.

"Oh, the pleasure was mine, Mister Barker."

"Maybe Jennie and I should call it a night too," Bill says. "Could we catch a ride, Madeline?"

"Of course."

Bill wakes Jennie and they follow Madeline to her limousine, now waiting at the curb.

The rest of us bob and weave our way up the mostly deserted Chartres Street to Conti. We stock up on chips and dips, six-packs of beer, and pints of whiskey at the corner grocery there before following Donny across the street and up three flights of rickety wooden stairs.

Donny unlocks his apartment door and pushes it open. The safety chain catches and then the door is slammed shut.

There is the sound of a dead bolt latching and a voice from the other side of the door.

"Go away," the voice says.

Donny taps on the door. "Ronnie?"

There is no answer. He taps again. "Open the door, Ronnie. I am sorry. Please open the door."

"Go away," Ronnie sobs. "You promised."

"I know. I'm late. I'm sorry. I will make it up to you. Opening night is tomorrow, you know — we will have dinner at Antoine's. How does that sound?"

Ronnie makes no reply.

"I have Ed and Cynthia with me," Donny continues. "Freddie's here. And, you know that writer, Gille Barker? He is here too. He wants to meet you, Ronnie," Donny lies. "Open the door, please."

**

It strikes me odd when I hear myself referred to as 'that writer'. Before my stint at Winslow Prison, I was Gille Barker, 'you know, that artist guy — owns the bar down on Keawakapu Beach.' I had written nothing longer than a theme paper before Winslow, and probably never would have if any other distraction to relieve the tedium of prison's endless days had come to mind.

Two years after my incarceration my first novel was published. Three weeks later my agent called. As if in passing, he mentioned the book had shown up on a New York Times list, but he gave me no indication that anything was out of the ordinary. It seems strange now that, while I whiled away the hours in the anonymity of my eight by ten concrete box, outside my prison cell I had become something of a celebrity to those few who consider novels, or those who write them, of interest.

And the novel, also unbeknownst to me, had already developed a cult-like following among the hard-core believers in alien encounters of any kind. In fact, a fan club, reputed to number more than ten thousand of those believers, claimed to have infiltrated forty-two of the United States—including Hawaii. Yes!

The club's President was a Green Valley, Illinois farmer's wife named Peggy Snoot. Peggy became the lonesome widow Snoot when her husband, in a moment of distraction, was attacked by an ancient piece of farm machinery. She organized my club of fans and named it 'Friends of Dargo' after the home galaxy of my alien mentor and occasional cellmate, Zargon Ron, for the same reason I had written the novel in the first place—to further deceive the mind's misconception of the passage of time.

**

"Gille Barker?" Ronnie asks through the door. "Gille Barker is with you?"

"Yeah, Gille Barker is here. I told him all about you, Ronnie. He wants to meet you. Please open the door."

Ronnie could not care less about meeting Gille Barker. He has never heard of a Gille Barker.

The dead bolt clicks. Ronnie pulls the door open and stands in front of us, his hands on his hips, a flowery silk robe cinched around his tiny waist by a tasseled velvet belt that was obviously once a drapery tie.

"I'm still mad at you, Donny," he says, "and who the hell is Gille Barker?"

Donny ignores the question. He hugs Ronnie and kisses him on the lips. "Oh, you sweet boy," Donny says. "You are going to be so happy you opened that door."

Donny stands aside, motioning toward the rest of us patiently waiting in the doorway to enter.

"See, look what I brought you," he says.

**

"Mister Barker." Jeff is shaking my arm. "Wake up, Mister Barker."

I am sprawled across the sofa, my neck bent at an impossible angle, my head wedged against a sofa armrest. I am wearing Ronnie's now wine-stained flowery silk robe.

I turn on my side and struggle to a sitting position. Sharp pains shoot across the cheeks of my ass. I fall back on my side.

I rub my fingers across my butt and feel what seem to be shards of glass sticking, randomly spaced, across both buns. I look around the room. A naked Ronnie and Donny are curled up close on a lounger, partially covered by a silky bed sheet. Cynthia is asleep on a shag throw rug in front of the sofa, her cheek resting on a matching pillow to Ronnie and Donny's bed sheet.

Chin stuck to his chest, Ed Sheehan is propped to a sitting position against the front of a blue velvet chair. He is stripped down to striped boxer shorts and shiny-black socks. His pants and shirt are neatly folded across the arm of the chair. A half full glass of red wine rests against his crotch between his outstretched legs.

Freddie Fender is passed out too. Other than rainbow-striped socks, he is naked, spread-eagled on his back across the kitchen table. His legs are bent at the knees, hanging over the side of the table toward the floor. Like a prospector's divining rod, a purple-gray semi-woody the circumference and length of three and a half D batteries precariously stacked end on end points from Freddie's crotch in the general direction of a cabinet above the kitchen sink.

In the living room, a large puddle of wine jogs my memory of the night before when Ronnie poured a gallon of Red Ripple on the old hardwood floor and belly danced his way through Judy Garland's rendition of *The Boy Next Door*. It's all coming back to me, including Ronnie's dedication of his performance to me with a kiss on my cheek and the lei of dead flowers I'm removing from around my neck.

I am remembering Ronnie's dance finale now, his naked backslide through the puddle of wine, his obscene gestures to the beat of Betty Garland's *Embraceable You*. Looking around me then, I could not help but notice Ronnie's rather spectacular performance was receiving no more attention than an old black and white Jeff Chandler movie playing silently on the screen of a television left on across the room.

**

I roll off the sofa to the floor on my hands and knees, almost landing on Cynthia. I leverage my body to a standing position and walk around the puddle of wine remaining on the dance floor to a full-length mirror mounted on the inside of the front door. I lift the bottom of Ronnie's silk robe that I am wearing for reasons I do not want to know to get a good look at my sore ass. A half dozen wine-soaked wood splinters stick out of my butt cheeks like porcupine quills.

Until now, my mind had blanked out my acceptance of Ronnie's dare to join him in a dance that climaxed with a slide through the puddle of ripple.

"Oh Jeez," I say, attracting Lightfoot's attention.

I see his amused expression as he watches me examining my buns in the front door mirror's reflection.

"Want me to yank those splinters out of your heinie for you, Mister Barker?" he asks.

"I'll handle it, thank you."

"You're one swell dancer, Mister Barker — get that wine slide perfected and maybe we can get you on the Tonight Show. What do you think, Mister Barker? Might be a big payday in it for you."

"Shut the hell up and help me find my pants."

Jeff retrieves my clothes from the kitchen floor. He picks up a brown paper bag tied closed with butcher's twine from the coffee table. I had first noticed he had the bag with him yesterday but, though curious, had not asked about it.

"What's in the bag?" I ask. Jeff does not seem to hear and does not reply.

**

In the bathroom, I find the tweezers Ronnie used last night to pluck ninety percent of the hair from his eyebrows in a few moments of depression. Using a hand mirror as my guide, I pull the splinters from my butt cheeks. I shower and dry. I search a bathroom cabinet for medical supplies. White foam froths as I dab my backside with cotton balls soaked in found hydrogen peroxide.

Ed's eyes flutter open to see me, now fully dressed, hobbling behind Jeff as we creep toward the stairway. With some effort, he briefly raises a hand and points in the general direction of the door.

"Exit, stage left," Ed says.

The latch clicks as I pull the door closed behind us.

17

Darla's

The rumble of thunder races us down the rickety stairs from the loft of Donny Dragon. Lightfoot opens the door at the bottom of the steps. A gust snatches the handle from his grip sending the door crashing against the outside brick wall.

Windbreaker pulled over my head, I follow close behind Lightfoot as he dashes out into the sudden squall. Clothes drenching sheets of freezing rain sting our faces until we find cover in the alcove to a building at the corner of Conti and Bourbon Streets, a half block from Dragon's door.

**

"A few years back my cousin lived right here in the Quarter — played football for Tulane." Jeff rocks from foot to foot and exhales warm air onto the palms of his cupped hands. "You went to Tulane, right, Mister Barker?"

"Sure did," I say.

"Billy Lightfoot is his name. Maybe you heard of him."

"Afraid not," I say, "besides the fact I'm no football fan, my guess is Cousin Billy was still in diapers when I was at Tulane.

"What made football pop into your head now anyway?" I ask.

"I don't think it was the football so much as the weather in this town that made me think of Billy and a story he once told me," Lightfoot says. "So, you're sure you never heard of Billy Lightfoot?"

"No, I think not, but like I say, I'm not a big football fan."

"Yeah, right. Anyway, the story Billy told was about an old Ford convertible some Tulane booster-club bigshot gave him. The guy bought the car new for his daughter a few years before he gave it to Billy, and, according to Billy, it had seen better days.

"Billy said the top had rips he patched, but that didn't solve the problem because the latches were broken, and he couldn't keep the top up anyway. He said, unless he had a passenger with him to do the job, he had to hold the top closed with one hand and steer with the other to stay dry when it rained."

"That could be inconvenient," I say.

"For sure, especially since the thing was a stick shift," Lightfoot says, "and, like I said, Billy lived in the Quarter so there was no place to park except out on the street. Of course, the top would stay up when the car was parked and out of the wind, but there was always a gap between the top and the window trim because he couldn't fasten it shut. Billy said that, when it rained, which seemed like three or four times a week, the water would be ankle deep on the floorboard when he left for morning classes."

"Sounds like Billy might be prone to exaggeration."

"Billy said he drilled holes in the floorboards so the water could drain — that's what he told me."

"Uh huh," I say.

We exchange skeptical smiles.

"That's right," Lightfoot continues, trying unsuccessfully to keep a straight face. "Billy told me drilling those holes solved the drainage problem, but, even so, his ass was usually soaked by the time he got out to Tulane.

"He said he carried towels and baby powder with him to keep the butt itch at bay. He said he still ended up with a nasty rash every now and then. Funny, huh, Mister Barker?"

"What time is it?" I ask.

Jeff looks at his bare wrist. "Damn it!"

He thrusts his hands into his pockets.

"Damn, my Zippo's gone too — must have left them at Dragon's place."

196

Jeff pulls his jacket over his head and dashes for Dragon's stairway door that had slammed closed after our exit. Unable to open the locked door, he dashes back to the alcove.

"Jeez, that was one perfectly good watch too — cost me a hundred bucks. I don't suppose we'll be running into any of that crowd again."

"Probably not in this lifetime," I say.

Jeff turns toward the glass-pained alcove door. He cups his hands at the corners of his eyes to peer inside.

"Looks like a hotel lobby," Jeff says.

I do not bother to point out the 'Welcome to the Saint Ann/Marie Antoinette Hotel' brass placard mounted on the wall next to the door.

"Could be," I say.

"There's a clock," Lightfoot says. "It's a quarter till ten, if you're still interested. I see a couple of chairs. Maybe we could hang out in there till this storm blows through."

I pull the door open. Lightfoot steps across the threshold ahead of me, shaking like a wet mutt, splashing rainwater to puddle on the slate tile floor.

A lone clerk with long black dreadlocks streaked with strands of strawberry sits on a stool behind the front desk, her chubby fingers stuck in a bag of barbecue chips. She shows no interest in us, not questioning why we are there.

Across the back of the lobby, French doors stand open to a cobblestone courtyard. There is a small swimming pool and garden of magnolia and Louisiana iris and two more sets of open doors toward the back of the courtyard. Painted above those doors on an unassuming wooden sign is a half-full martini glass garnished with two olives on a stick.

"Is that a bar back there?" Jeff asks the desk clerk, pointing at the sign.

"Now what would give you an idea like that, Mister Sherlock Holmes?" she says, showing Jeff the slightest of smiles.

She points toward a hallway with the pinkie of her chip-eating hand. "You boys can get back there around that way if you want to stay out of the rain. Darla's back there someplace—don't know if she's open though."

"Thank you," Jeff says.

"Uh huh, you're welcome, honey."

**

Although the courtyard French doors to Darla's stand open, the room is dark and deserted. The wind has subsided to an occasional gust that splashes rain onto the bar's hardwood floor.

The only interior illumination in this cozy hideaway is the glow from a green rope-light strung around a back-bar mirror, maybe ten feet wide and four feet high. Seven black-leather stools are upside down across the bar top.

A woman I guess to be forty or so sticks her head out from behind the side of an open storage room door at the end of the back-bar. She looks like she just stepped off a time machine from 1962, her long blonde hair permed curly and stiff as starched stacked straw.

"I thought I heard somebody out here," the woman says. "You boys lost?"

"Not if this is a bar and it's open for business," Jeff says.

"Well, as you can see, this *is* a bar, son," she says, "and I say it's open. Grab a couple of those stools off the bar and take a seat. I'll be right with you."

The woman steps out of the storage room and plops her clipboard onto the bar. There is a flash of lightning and the clap of thunder.

"Holy shit — coming down in buckets out there now ain't it," the woman says.

"Sure is," I say.

"What'll it be then, boys?"

"Bloody Mary for me, please," Jeff says. "I like it hot with a salty rim. He sets the paper bag he has been carrying for the last two days on the bar in front of him.

"Well, son, you've made a wise decision."

"How's that?" Jeff says.

"Hate to brag, but I just happen to make a Bloody Mary that's famous around these parts — hell, folks from New York City to

198

Singapore have asked for my recipe, and I can heat that puppy up till it sets your tongue on fire."

She turns her attention to me. "How about you, mister? What'll you have?"

"Ginger ale, please."

"You do look a tad under the weather, honey. Think you might have been over-pored somewhere along the line?"

"That's a possibility," I say.

"I guarantee there ain't anything better for a hangover than a Darla's Mary, but if you don't feel you're up to a proven remedy I can give you one of those ginger ales with a splash of bitters. Some folks say that combination does the trick.

"I should warn you though, I've tried that concoction with no noticeable effect other than a severe case of the dry heaves. Come to think of it, maybe I shouldn't blame that on the bitters *or* the ginger ale — I'll leave it up to you to name your poison."

"Now, after that pitch, I would feel like a fool if I didn't go for a Darla's Mary," I say, "but hold the salt and take it easy on the hot sauce, please."

"Congratulations, honey," she says, "you are on your way to recovery."

Darla grabs a couple of what she says are called hurricane glasses, "but don't ask me why", from a rack full of all sorts of fancy glassware hung upside down above the bar top.

"I get the feeling we've met," Darla says to me while casually poring unmeasured double vodka shots into our glasses.

"I don't think so," I say.

Jeff chimes in. "He was in the news a while back—Gille Barker?"

"You're *the* Gille Barker—that writer guy?"

"I guess I am," I say.

"Well I'll be damn. I have a book of yours here someplace. Think I could get you to put your John Henry to it for me?"

"It would be my pleasure."

"Oh, great; I'll get it soon as I have you fixed up here.

"Funny, huh, Mister Barker," Darla says.

"What's funny?"

"They toss you in jail, you write a book, your hard-luck story becomes a headline on all the checkout-lane rags, and wham-o— your books are selling like hot cakes. Now, I doubt if you enjoyed your time in the slammer, especially since you shouldn't have been there in the first place, but some folks would say prison might have been a lucky break for you — just saying."

"I'd bet all my royalty checks against our bar tab none of those 'folks' you are talking about spent any time in Winslow Prison. Maybe ten or fifteen years down the road I'll see it in a different light."

"Well, you're one hell of a writer, Mister Barker, jailbird or not, I'll give you that."

Darla dips celery sticks into our drinks and floats some Aquavit on top. She places the hurricane glasses on our coasters as if they are filled with liquid treasures.

"There you go boys," Darla says. "Now excuse me while I see if I can find that book. I hope nobody stole the damn thing."

Darla rummages through a line of books, some new, some dog-eared, a few ripped and probably missing pages, all on a shelf across the far wall of the bar.

"I try to keep a few books around, you know," Darla says. "Some people like to thumb through them to pass the time. Tourists take them out by the pool. It gives them an excuse to come back – that's the way I look at it.

"Here it is — afraid I wasn't going to find it. One of my regulars borrowed it a couple of weeks ago and I didn't remember her bringing it back."

Darla opens the front cover and flips through to the title page. She hands me a pen.

"Could you make that 'to Darla Duvall, my favorite bartender'?"

"Sure thing — that might even be true."

"Yeah, I guess you haven't had contact with many bartenders lately," Darla says.

"Not many," I say. "There *was* a bartender doing five-to-ten two cells down from me though."

Darla only smiles at my reply. She picks my book up and inspects my signature. "Now I'll have to read this thing again," she says. "That'll cost me a half dozen night's sleep for sure. Well, thank you anyway, Mister Barker."

"Please call me Gille. And thank you Darla for making my day."

A sudden gust knocks Jeff's glass crashing to the floor. A solid sheet of rain blows sideways through the open door.

"Jesus Christ!" Darla starts out from behind the bar.

"I'll get it," Jeff says. He pulls the doors shut and latches the safety catches. He helps Darla mop up the mess with old bar rags.

"Why thank you, dear," Darla says. She makes Jeff another Bloody Mary 'on the house'.

**

My bones ache. My head throbs. I try to speak, and words roil up from my belly in tongue. I lift my glass to my lips and set it back down on the bar in slow motion, unscathed.

Carrying a rocks glass full of shaved ice and tequila, Einstein sits down on the stool to my side. He sets an uncorked bottle of gold Patron on the bar next to his glass. He squeezes a wedge of lime across his drink and gently plunges his index finger down into the shaved ice twice. I am surprised, but not because I'm unfamiliar with the routine. Hillary Boudreaux had explained the process to me and Lightfoot only hours ago.

"You must be gentle with good liquor," Albert says. "A heavy-handed stir can knock the edge right off a cocktail."

"Well now, that's interesting. Hillary Boudreaux gave me the same advice only yesterday, but old Hillary was in la-la land, so I considered her theory suspect."

"Son," Einstein says, "trust me, the woman knew what she was talking about."

There is no scientific explanation offered by Albert as to why a vigorous stir would "knock the edge right off a good cocktail." When I quiz him further, Einstein makes it clear that this theory was provided to him by a most reliable source — his daddy told him it was so.

I am not well. Darla's Bloody Mary is not providing the curative powers I had hoped for.

"You look a little under the weather, Gille," Albert says. "You know, partying all night at your age might not be the best idea."

"Jesus, Albert, how old do you think I am?" I ask.

"I was only voicing my opinion," Einstein says. He leans against the backrest of his stool. He sips at his top-shelf tequila. He puffs rings of deadly carcinogens from his pipe into my atmosphere.

"Albert?" I say.

"What?" Jeff answers. "What did you say?"

"Why are you here, Albert?" I ask.

"Mister Barker." Jeff shakes my shoulder. "Mister Barker," he says again.

I try to lift my glass, but it weighs fifty pounds — maybe more.

"I should find Mister Barker a place to rest," Jeff says to Darla. "He's had a couple of hard days. I guess it's caught up with him."

"Spring chicken?" I inquire. "What the hell's this about a spring chicken?"

No one hears my nonsensical query.

"They have a special on some of the rooms here," Darla says to Jeff. "I could check on that for you, if you'd like."

"That would be great," Jeff says.

Darla waits patiently while the front desk phone rings a half dozen times.

"Oh, there you are," Darla says into the phone, "didn't wake you, did I? ——— Uh huh, I don't doubt that, but it is way more information than I want to know. — Never you mind. I have a man here in need of a room. Is that special still on? ——— Okay, I will send him over.

"Josie says if you're interested you should come to the front desk now; there are only a couple of the special price rooms left."

"I'm on my way," Jeff says.

I am precariously slouched forward on my stool. Darla helps Jeff move me to a booth at the back corner of the bar.

My balance is suspect. Queasy, I ask Jeff if there is a restroom nearby. I feel that my lips are moving but there is no recognition or reply.

Jeff crosses my arms on the table in front of me for a cushion and rests my head on them.

"You just relax, Mister Barker," he says, "I'll take care of everything."

18

Boys and Bayous

Cardenas is speeding away down Hillary Boudreaux's lane when Johnny Ray pops up from tall grass at the roadside. He catches the glint of the arrow's silver tip as Johnny Ray turns it loose from his bow. Frantically stabbing at the window closer, Cardenas watches the arrow strike the rising window glass and drop to the side of the road.

Not quite under control, the Jaguar flies up the bayou grade and smacks down on the bridge, narrowly missing the wood-plank runway. Sparks fly as the passenger side of the Jaguar scrapes against the metal railing until the car sails off the rumbling wooden slats and slams back to earth on the loose gravel road.

Pumping the brakes, Cardenas coaxes the Jaguar to a sliding stop just short of a roadside drainage ditch.

It is eerie quiet. A cloud of trailing gravel dust settles into the weeds. Gene takes a moment to soak in the calm before putting the Jaguar in reverse. He turns to look out the rear window as he backs away from the ditch.

'There's that damn kid again!' Says 'Karl', Cardenas's mulish doppelganger, who, though silent recently, has been the longtime voice of unsolicited opinions from his lair in one of the darker recesses of Gene's mind.

Halfway across the bridge, Johnny Ray kneels and sends another arrow into flight that ricochets off the rear window as the

Jaguar speeds away. Now at the end of Hillary Boudreaux's gravel lane, Cardenas turns right on the blacktop road that leads to Thibodeaux.

Every quarter mile or so rutted dirt trails shoot off the blacktop and snake into the bayous. Cardenas drives until he comes to one that looks least traveled and is barely distinct from the overgrowth of swamp weeds and brush. He eases the Jaguar off the blacktop. Forty yards from the road the trail turns to sludge and soon dead ends at the edge of a bog.

Cardenas turns off the ignition and wrestles Richard's body out of the car. He skins Richard's Rolex from his wrist and his fancy red-ruby insignia ring from his pinky finger. He takes the diamond stud earring from Richard's left ear. Cardenas puts the Rolex on his wrist and stuffs everything else in the glove box.

**

"What was the story on Richard' and that earring?" Karl asks Gene.

"How would I know?"

"Just asking—did he have a pair and lose one? And why did he wear the thing on his left ear? Was it like a woman wearing a flower in her hair—right side, spoken for, left side, fair game? Was Richard gay, Gene?"

"What do you care?"

"We had seen him with women, hadn't we, Gene? Come to think of it, I'm not sure."

"Now that you mention it, no, I never did," says Gene.

"The man did like his leather jackets and fancy shoes–boots made of alligator hide, shoes with buckles and shoes with brightly colored laces—shoes, I bet he had forty pair. He did walk a little funny.

"Not that there's anything wrong with that."

**

Gene takes off his socks and puts his shoes back on his now bare feet. He rolls his pants up above his knees and lays his jacket across the seat. He grabs Richard by the ankles and drags his limp body across a slush of swamp weeds into the peat bog until he can drag him no more. Finding his blank stare disconcerting, Gene closes Richard's eyes before covering him with a layer of swamp gumbo and leaves.

**

Gene sloshes back to the car through the sucking mud of the bog. Sitting on the edge of the passenger seat, he cleans the black mud gunk from his shoes with sticks and fern leaves. He rinses his feet in a puddle close to the car and throws the shoes into the back seat.

Gene guides the Jaguar in reverse as it slips and slides to the highway. Scrub trees and weeds block his view as he backs onto the blacktop road. Startled by the blare of a horn, Gene slams on the brakes. A pickup truck swerves to miss him, whisking by inches from the Jaguar's back bumper.

A red haired, Alfalfa-looking kid is riding shotgun in the pickup. He shoots Gene with a finger pistol and a menacing stare. "Watch where you're going, asshole!" he yells.

Now, back on the blacktop to Thibodeaux, Gene watches in disbelief as the pickup, maybe a quarter of a mile ahead, makes a U-turn to face him. Three boys standing in the bed of the truck yell and make obscene gestures as the truck races toward him head on, engine screaming.

Gene swerves off the road as the pickup speeds by. A concrete culvert looms only feet ahead. He cranks the steering wheel and skids back across the black top, coming to rest in the weeds of the siding with the Jaguar's nose against a barbed wire fence.

From half the length of a football field away, the pickup truck has turned around again. Barreling toward the Jaguar, the band of juvenile nitwits standing in the bed of the truck bang their fists on the top of the cab and scream threats into the wind.

Gene grabs Richard's pistol from the front seat. He takes aim at the pickup windshield.

"Jesus Christ, the fucker has a gun!" Alfalfa yells.

The boys standing in the bed of the pickup crash against the back of the cab as the driver hits the brakes and slides the truck to a stop so close to the Jaguar he later claims he could pick out the color of Gene's steely gray eye sighting down the pistol barrel.

206

The pickup jumps as the kid driver grinds the gears into reverse and slams the accelerator to the floor. The truck screams down the highway in reverse for fifty yards before coming to a stop. Cardenas hears the boys' muffled voices yelling final threats as the driver turns the truck around and races away.

He shuffles through Richard's stuff searching for his cigarettes and lighter. He shakes the few cigarettes from the pack that are not blood-splotched onto the seat.

Popping the Jaguar's console door open, Cardenas grabs a Louisiana map and his ever-present bottle of Pepto Bismol. He shakes the bottle and takes a swig. Forgetting his shoes are in the back seat, he steps onto a roadside patch of cockleburs. Orange-gray dusk settles on Route 308 while he gingerly extracts a dozen spiny burs from the soles of his feet.

It is quiet now but for the occasional croak of a frog and a lone blackbird's caw. An early evening mist settles low across the bayou.

Gene spreads the Louisiana map across the hood of his car. He lights one of Richard's cigarettes and inhales. He coughs. The ground spins at his feet. He braces himself against the fender.

Jesus, how did I ever smoke these things?

He flips the cigarette into the road.

Gene leans against the door of the Jaguar and looks at his face in the side mirror. He brushes his hair back with his fingers. He looks up and down the deserted blacktop road.

Which way? Best I put some distance between me and Thibodaux in case that old lady does something crazy, like call the cops. And that truckload of kids —

Gene runs his finger across the road map, down route 308 to 90 and on up to 310 until he stops at the first town in reasonable size print.

La Place — the name sounds familiar — must be a decent motel there, someplace to get a burger and a few hours rest before deciding what to do about Lightfoot.

**

Now nine-thirty and more than twenty-four hours since his last meal, McDonalds golden arches on the outskirts of La Place is a welcome sight to Gene Cardenas. He picks up a Big Mac and fries and a chocolate shake. Nibbling on a fry at the pick-up lane exit, he sees the lights of a motel across the street. After renting a room, he parks in the shadows of the motel's solitary back lot. Grabbing his duffel from the trunk, he walks around the side of the building and up a flight of stairs.

Once in the room, Cardenas pulls a table next to the bed and unwraps his meal. He clicks the television on and lays on the bed, his back propped up on pillows against the headboard. He flips through the channels until he comes to an old movie about an FBI agent who commits murders and then frames 'likely' suspects to display his uncanny powers of investigation.

Head throbbing, Cardenas pulls back the bed covers and crawls between the sheets. His back aches from dragging Richard through the bog. He knew that, somehow, Richard would make him pay for that. Smiling at that thought, Gene closes his eyes and drifts into sleep only to be greeted by yet another round of Karl's disparaging remarks.

**

"What are we doing in this hell hole?" Karl wants to know. *"I can't believe this. How could you let an Indian kid cause us so much grief? We are gangsters, professional gangsters, for Christ's sake. And that damn writer guy. A writer! That's even worse than an Indian getting the best of us. How embarrassing are you intending to let this get for us, Gene?"*

In no mood for more of Karl's criticism, Cardenas rolls to his side and crooks his arm across his eyes against the slight light filtering into the room through the window shades. But Karl will not shut up.

"We should pack it in and forget the whole damn thing. We don't need this aggravation—chasing these two assholes half-way across the country, Richard dead, our car beat to hell, three or four days wasted already. And what about all that blood? How are you going to clean up that mess? Don't expect me to pitch in, Gene."

Cardenas rolls to his back and plumps two pillows under his head. Idly flipping through channels, he comes across an old western movie starring a scrappy Alan Ladd as the most reluctant of sharp-shooting gunslingers in the old west.

"I heard they stood Alan Ladd on an orange crate so he wouldn't have to swing up hill to smack the bad guys around," Karl says. *"I wonder if there was any truth to that."*

Gene clicks the television off and rolls back onto his side. He drifts into sleep.

**

It is dusk on the Hopi Indian Reservation of Arizona's northern plains. A blazing red sunset splits a deep blue sky from the desert floor and red-rock mountains.

A score of surly Indian braves, their faces streaked with red and black paint, pound on Tom-Toms of deer skin stretched across shaped wooden frames like tambourines. The braves chant to one of their many all-knowing gods. They make threatening gestures and strut their stuff around a bonfire shooting flames fifteen feet into the night sky.

One of the most menacing of those Indian braves dances close to Gene. He shows his teeth, all rotting with decay except for one upper incisor, ill-fitted with a shiny gold cap that previously adorned a tooth in a white man's head, a head now eight feet in the air, stuck on the pointy end of a spear next to the fire.

The Indian brave scowls. He sticks out a tongue split serpent-like and licks close at Gene's face. He yelps to the moon.

Gene goes rigid under the sheets as the savage steps back and smiles, his teeth now somehow shiny and porcelain in the firelight, but still sporting the golden cap pried from the white man's skull, and now Gene recognizes the savage is Jeff Lightfoot.

"Your sorry ass is mine, mister gangster man," the savage Lightfoot growls.

Gene pops upright on the bed.

He looks at the bedside clock. It is eight-thirty—can that be? Gene pulls the drapes open and morning light floods the room.

Gene studies his face in the bathroom mirror. He looks like shit. He hasn't shaved in three days or showered in four. He slides his tongue across the fuzzy surface of his teeth.

Gene soaks a hand towel with hot water and lathers it with motel bar soap. He scrubs his teeth with the towel and gargles tap water. He showers.

It's nine-fifteen when Gene pulls out of the parking lot and turns right on route ten toward Metairie and on to New Orleans.

**

He had considered turning left and heading back to Flagstaff.

"Let Lightfoot have the damn briefcase, Gene. We don't need the aggravation," Karl argued as they neared the intersection,

"But, what about the principal of the thing? What about Richard?"

"The importance of principals is highly exaggerated, Gene," Karl said, *"and as for Richard, the boy killed him, not Lightfoot — we can let that slide on a technicality."*

"Someone has to pay —Lightfoot has to pay." Gene's decision was final.

**

Cardenas spots an empty carwash on an access road and turns into what is Metairie. After taking the cash and identification cards from Richard's wallet, he throws the wallet in a dumpster. He buys a hand-full of quarters for the coin drop, points the wash wand at the bloodstained seat of the Jaguar, and pushes the wash button. The car's interior almost disappears in an ocean of suds. After rinsing the interior, Gene cleans the exterior of the Jaguar, blasting mud and debris from the fender wells. The Jaguar passes his cursory inspection—no evidence of Richard demise is visible to the naked eye.

Gene's backside is soaked by the time he drives the half block to a Walmart store. He buys clothes and towels. He buys a razor, toothbrush and paste, and deodorant.

Cardenas drives down a side road to a city park's nearly deserted aquatic center parking lot. He buys a day pass and helps himself to the locker room, He showers again and shaves his beard off for the first time in fifteen years. He coats the pits of his arms with Old Spice. He puts on his Walmart duds — khaki pants and an imitation-silk Hawaiian shirt covered with brightly printed palm trees and sandy beaches.

Cardenas rubs his chin, surveying the unfamiliar face he sees in a locker-room mirror. Even Richard would not have been able to pick him out of a line up if it were not for his own Rolex now strapped to Gene's wrist.

**

While driving from Metairie into the city, Gene drifts again to the barren high desert of Jeff Lightfoot's Hopi ancestors.

He is the lone passenger on a stagecoach racing across the desert. He levels his revolver at Jeff Lightfoot, now an Indian warrior, galloping bareback alongside the stagecoach on a brown and white pinto with Gene's stolen satchel lashed to the pinto's back. Lightfoot holds a long-blade clinched between his teeth and a cocked-at-the-ready Winchester rifle in one hand.

Cardenas takes aim at the savage redskin warrior, Lightfoot. He squeezes the trigger. He fires again and again, to no avail, until the revolver clicks on empty. Reaching for more ammo, for the first time he sees the word "BLANKS" scrawled across one end of the cartridge box. He hurls his revolver at Lightfoot. The gun arches high and twists slowly through the air before falling to the ground, woefully short of the Pinto's pounding hooves.

Lightfoot, his Pinto now in full gallop, pulls the long blade from between his teeth and flings it toward Cardenas. In terror, Gene watches the blade tumble end over end toward his chest. He ducks behind the steering wheel and the Jaguar's tires catch the edge of the gravel apron, throwing the car into a skid through brush at the side of the road. With Gene holding firmly to the steering wheel, the Jaguar rights itself and climbs back onto the highway.

Gene shakes his head and slaps his cheeks. He rolls down the windows. He twists the radio volume to high.

It is not yet noon when Cardenas reaches the city. Turning off Canal into the French Quarter on Bourbon, he once again feels the familiar adrenaline rush of the hunt coursing through his veins, a feeling he had sorely missed.

"Now, where is that Lightfoot fellow?"

19

The Reunion

It's homecoming weekend at Thibodaux's Nicholls State University. Walking alone across the quad, Waynette Boudreaux hears a familiar voice.

"Waynette? the voice calls out.

"Jeff?" The rush at hearing Lightfoot's voice is dashed when Waynette turns only to see Jeff's cousin Danny, Nicholls State's football coach, bounding down the steps of Polk's Hall toward her.

"Danny, what a pleasant surprise," Waynette says in a vain effort to hide her disappointment.

They exchange the quick embrace and pleasantries common to unexpected encounters by old friends.

"What's it been, five years?" Waynette says.

"Five and then some," says Danny.

"Time flies," says Waynette.

"You're disappointed."

"Disappointed? Why would you say that?"

"I read minds, Waynette. And, of course, I did hear you call out Jeff's name."

"Now I'm embarrassed," says Waynette. "I never could tell your voices apart."

"Nothing to be embarrassed about. Our mothers never could tell us apart over a phone. Speaking of phones, Jeff just called a few days ago."

"I haven't heard from him since he left Thibodaux."

"Believe me, that I know," says Danny. "Waynette this and Waynette that—I think the only reason he calls me is to see if I've heard from Ms. Waynette Boudreaux. Of course, the answer is always no, but that doesn't stop him from asking."

"He could have called *me*. I would gladly have given him the lowdown," Waynette says in a flip reply.

"Don't you get it Waynette?" says Danny. "Jeff knows he screwed up. I think, in his mind, calling you would only add an insult to the damage he had done."

"*Really*—and that makes sense to you?"

"I didn't say it made sense, Waynette, I just think that's the way Jeff looks at it."

Danny digs a business card from his wallet and hands it to Waynette.

"Rio's Pool Service? What's this?" Waynette asks.

"Other side, Waynette. Jeff's number is on the back of the card."

Danny points at his watch. "I have to run."

Jogging away toward the stadium, he shouts back over his shoulder. "Give him a call, Waynette. What could it hurt?"

**

At half past two that night, thunder amid the chatter of a sudden shower on the veranda outside her old sorority house bedroom window wakes Waynette. Now restless and unable to get Danny's suggestion off her mind, Waynette turns on the bedside lamp and dials Lightfoot's number.

Jeff has just completed his first slide through the wine puddle on Donny Dragon's living room floor when he hears the muffled chime of his phone. He traces the sound to the sofa and finds a leg of his pants hanging out from under a cushion. He tugs at the pants cuff and his phone tumbles to the floor.

At the fourth ring, Waynette is about to hang up when she hears Judy Garland singing a song about lonely nights through the receiver.

"Hello?" Waynette waits for an answer. "Hello? Jeff?"

Lightfoot is leery of answering — *has Cardenas tracked me down? How could he have this number? But it's a woman's voice, a familiar voice.*

"Who is this?" Jeff asks warily.

"It's Waynette."

"Waynette? How did you know I was here?"

"How did I know you were where?"

Jeff hops to the bathroom while buttoning his trousers and zipping his fly and closes the door behind him.

"Here," he says, "in New Orleans — where are you?"

"I'm in Thibodeaux for homecoming. I ran into Danny and he gave me this number. How are you answering your phone if you're in New Orleans?"

"It's a cell phone, Waynette."

"A cell phone? What are you doing in New Orleans?"

"Looking for you, Waynette—just looking for you."

Lines like that come to Jeff naturally. He has the gift.

"Looking for me? But why now?" asks Waynette.

Jeff tells Waynette about his Flagstaff run-in with Cardenas and Richard and the briefcase mix-up—the same story he had told me. He tells her about our search for the briefcase at Cousin Luke's farm and our conversation while waiting at the railroad crossing that put us on the road to New Orleans.

"That must have been *some* conversation," says Waynette.

"It was," says Jeff, "I was telling Mister Barker about what happened that night before our wedding and how sorry I was for the way things turned out for us."

"Oh Jeff, I'm sorry too."

"I told Mister Barker how much I missed you and how I often wondered if there was a chance of us getting together again someday."

"And what did he say?"

"He said 'someday' won't show up on its own. He said the only way to find out was to come down here and ask, and that's why I'm here looking for you."

"I love you Jeff. I've never quit loving you." Tears well up in Waynette's eyes. "I should never have let you go."

"I love you too," Jeff says. "When will you be back in New Orleans?"

"I should be home before noon."

"See you at noon then?" Jeff says.

"Oh, yes."

They babble on until, finally, there is a silence on the line as even Waynette can think of nothing more to say. Jeff had crossed that threshold long ago.

Waynette breaks the silence.

"Jeff? Jeff? Are you still there?"

"Yes, I'm here."

"Jesus, Jeff, what about those men? They think you have their bag."

"I do have it, Waynette," Lightfoot says. "I've had it all along."

20

920 Chartres

"Darla called about a room?" says Jeff to Josie, the Saint Marie Hotel's dread-locked desk clerk.

"Uh huh," says Josie, glancing up from a magazine spread across the check-in counter, "— the sixty-five-dollar special, right?"

"Unless you have something better to offer."

"Nothing at that price, but there's a great suite above the bar for one-twenty-five. Now that's a steal—big balcony over the courtyard too, deluxe all the way."

Lightfoot drags a fist-sized roll of hundred-dollar bills from his pocket and peels off a couple for Josie.

"Let's go with that one," he says

Josie pulls a key down from a rack of keys on the wall behind her and hands it to Jeff.

"Suite two fourteen," she says.

**

Upon opening the door to suite two fourteen, Jeff is hit by a rush of hot air from a space heater left on high. He turns the heater to low and opens the double French doors to the balcony. Back in the parlor, he finds a television behind the doors of an antique armoire. Dropping onto a plush velvet sofa, Lightfoot idly clicks through channels; Days of Our Lives – As the World Turns —

Lightfoot is startled awake by the clatter of the remote as it drops from his hand to the hardwood floor.

After a quick shower, Jeff steps onto the balcony. He looks down over the wrought iron railing at the fountain and the pool and the gardens in the courtyard of the Saint Marie–he loves this place. He loves New Orleans.

The rain has stopped. Lightfoot quickly ducks back into the room when he sees Donny Dragon step out into the courtyard from Darla's bar. His mind races.

What is Dragon doing here? How long have I been asleep? Did Dragon bring my watch?

What exactly went on last night? Not wanting to deal with Dragon straightaway, Jeff ducks behind a corner of the balcony. He peers down through a sheer curtain as Donny, standing in the doorway to Darla's bar, surveys the now blue sky.

"I don't believe it, not a cloud in sight," Donny exclaims. "Road trip everyone — let's go someplace special!"

Other voices spill from the bar, the deep baritone of Ed Sheehan above the din. Then he hears the unmistakable voice of Cynthia Canales suggest a caravan by trolley to the Audubon zoo.

Jeff closes the balcony doors. He finds a pen and a pad of stationary in the drawer of a writing desk. He sets the butcher-twined paper bag he has been carrying the last couple of days on an antique coffee table in the parlor. He writes a note and slides it under the bag before leaving the room.

It is twelve thirty when Jeff glances at the lobby wall-clock at the bottom of the stairs. Supposedly he has been waiting five years for this second chance with Waynette and he is already a half hour late. He runs out the lobby door and turns toward Chartres Street and the apartment of Waynette Boudreaux.

**

Keeping an eye out for Lightfoot's Chevrolet, Gene Cardenas is slowly cruising up Chartres Street when he sees the Chevy parked against the curb a half block ahead. He pulls the Jaguar into a rare parking space close by. He checks for the time on his newly acquired Rolex—it is twelve thirty-five. He gets out of his car and stands in the shade of a storefront canopy directly across the street from Waynette's entry gate.

Just settling in for a long wait, Cardenas is caught off guard when Jeff runs into sight from around the corner of Dumaine Street, a half block away. Jeff sees him standing there but doesn't recognize him. Clean shaven and in his Hawaiian get up, Cardenas looks more like a Waikiki tourist than the drug-dealing sociopath that Lightfoot knows.

Turning his back toward Jeff, Cardenas pretends to peruse bobble head dolls and tee shirts in a tourist trap store window that acts as a mirror for Lightfoot's reflection.

In his window-mirror, he watches Jeff unfasten the bungee cord from the Chevy trunk, reach in, and toss an assortment of rusty tools and a blanket aside. Cardenas is stunned when Lightfoot pulls his missing bag from the trunk and sets it on the curb.

"Our briefcase!" says Karl, now on full alert in the head of Gene Cardenas. *"The kid had it in his trunk all along!"*

Cardenas pulls his pistol from its shoulder holster and holds it down close at his side. He steps into the street and quickly jumps back to the curb, narrowly missed by an irate cab driver. The cabbie leans on his horn.

"Watch your step, old man," the peachy-faced cabbie yells.

A Greyhound bus full of Japanese tourists follows close behind the cab, blocking Gene's view of Lightfoot.

The street clears in time for Cardenas to see the gate to 920 Chartres clang closed behind Lightfoot, the briefcase in his hand.

Having buzzed Lightfoot in, Waynette is outside her apartment door watching him climb the stairs. She hugs Jeff as he reaches the landing, almost knocking him back down the steps.

Inside her apartment, Waynette pulls Jeff down next to her on the sofa. She tells him how much she has missed him, how she could not sleep last night thinking about him. He counters with an apology for being late and one of his standard "I missed you too" replies.

Then Waynette asks the question Jeff had anticipated and prepared for with an honest answer so outrageous that it would be left alone.

"By the way, where were you when I called last night?" she says. "Did I miss something?"

"Not really. While looking for you, we ran into some friendly gays and theater types who turned out to be fans of Mister Barker's. Anyway, they invited us to a party—you know how those things go. One of them got naked and did a belly dance while Mister Barker scooted around on the floor in a puddle of Ripple—not much to report other than that."

"How interesting. They're all friendly, aren't they?"

"What?"

"Gays—you said the gays were friendly. All gays are friendly, aren't they?"

"Maybe so. I couldn't say," Lightfoot says. "Growing up on the reservation there was only one I knew of and he was certainly friendly enough. For the most part I suppose they're a friendly lot, but I'm no expert."

Betty Lou Riggins walks into the room, a terrycloth robe cinched at her waist, her damp hair stacked high, loosely wrapped in a bath towel. "Oh, excuse me. I didn't know we had a guest, *Mister* Lightfoot," she lies, with no effort at concealing her contempt.

"Hello Betty Lou," Jeff says, his cheerful reply only fueling Betty Lou's ire.

**

The last time Jeff spoke to Betty Lou was at the party after his and Waynette's wedding rehearsal five years ago, moments before Betty Lou made her opinion of him clear to everyone in that crowded room.

Betty Lou, standing next to him, turned away from Jeff then after what he thought was a pleasant enough conversation and raised her glass of wine in salute toward Waynette.

"And now, before I leave, a toast to my dearest friend, Waynette Boudreaux, who is about to make the worst mistake of her life," said Betty Lou.

The room went silent. Tears welled in Betty Lou's eyes

"Marry this *man* you barely know," she continued, now sniveling and motioning her outstretched finger in Jeff's face without turning back his way. "Why would you do that, Waynette? An *Indian*, for Christ sake! What could you be thinking?"

It was deadly quiet then as Betty Lou ran out of the room, but the party resumed as if her rant never happened once she slammed the door behind her.

One thing remained stuck in Lightfoot's mind though, and it was not that most of Thibodeaux was obviously in agreement with Betty Lou's assessment that troubled him. What disturbed Jeff was that it seemed Betty Lou had more skin in the game than he realized.

**

Her move to New Orleans with Waynette was meant to be a new beginning after the bachelor party fiasco brought an end to Jeff and Waynette's wedding plans. And everything was going as Betty Lou had hoped until this morning, when she answered Waynette's excited call from her old sorority house bedroom in Thibodeaux.

"Hello?"

"Hello? Betty Lou?"

"Yes."

"It's Waynette."

"Yeah, I know, Jesus. Hold on a minute." Betty Lou looked at the clock. It was after four o'clock on Sunday morning. Betty Lou had been in bed barely an hour and a half. She reached for the glass of water she kept on her bedside table.

"This better be good," said Betty Lou.

"You won't believe what happened."

"You didn't get laid, did you? Homecomings can be the damnedest things. Tell me you didn't. Tell me all about it, but not right now —— wasn't Johnny Wayne, was it? I always thought you two would make a great pair. Well, maybe not great, but a definite step up from your usual suspects. Besides, 'Johnny Wayne and Waynette' has a nice ring to it."

"No, I didn't get laid by Johnny Wayne or anyone else. Are you sitting down?"

"Jesus, Waynette, why would I be sitting down? It's past four in the morning; I'm flat on my back and alone, as far as I know.

221

Wait a minute while I make sure – nothing under the covers, all clear in the closet – I am alone all right. Now, if you did not get laid, please get to the point, for Christ's sake."

"I talked to Jeff Lightfoot."

Waynette listened to the silence and the crackle of the phone. "Betty Lou? Betty Lou?"

"I heard you, Waynette. I heard you just fine."

**

"Damn!" Jeff jumps up and walks to the front window. He pulls back a corner of the drape. The man he saw earlier is still across the street, leaning against a car fender.

"I knew there was something about that guy," Jeff says. "He's Cardenas all right. The son-of-a-bitch shaved his beard. Where did he come up with that costume? How the hell did he find me?"

Waynette comes to Jeff's side and peers down at Cardenas. "You're talking about the guy in the Hawaiian shirt?"

"Yeah."

"Jesus, Jeff, why don't you just take the briefcase down there and give it to him?"

Jeff takes Waynette by the hand and leads her to the sofa. He puts the briefcase on the floor in front of them and sits next to her.

"Please listen to me, Waynette," Lightfoot begins. "Like I said, I came by this briefcase by accident, but I can't give it back. It is full of hundred-dollar bills, Waynette. Whether I took his money by accident or on purpose is unimportant to that guy. I have his money now, and what might be even more important to him, I know how he came to get it. He is an extremely dangerous man, Waynette.

"He doesn't look all that dangerous to me."

"The man is a killer, Waynette. That is what he does. And I've been told by reliable sources he's not only good at it, he enjoys the work."

Sitting at the kitchen table, Betty Lou slaps her hand down on the tabletop.

"God damn you, Lightfoot!" Betty Lou says. "I had a feeling you'd get me killed someday, you son-of-a-bitch!"

222

Betty Lou lights another cigarette and stomps out of the room.

Waynette, contemplating the severity of the situation, doesn't seem fazed.

"What are we going to do?" she asks Jeff.

"Let me think." Jeff paces. He grabs the briefcase from the floor and sets it on the coffee table. He spreads the handles, pulls out a handful of hundred-dollar bills banded in batches of ten thousand dollars each and drops them to the table. He shuffles through the rest of the bundles of cash—seven hundred and fifty thousand dollars when he first counted it back in Winslow.

Jeff goes back to the window and looks down at Cardenas.

"He's just standing there. Is that gate the only way in?" Jeff asks.

"I think so," Waynette says. "And we have security. We should be safe here."

"Are you kidding? I saw your 'security'. A seventy-year-old rent-a-cop isn't going to stop Cardenas. The only things holding him back now are daylight and that piece of crap buzzer lock on the gate. It won't take him five seconds to kick that gate in once the sun goes down. How about us getting out of here? Where are the fire exits?"

"There aren't any I know of."

"What? Now that's just not right," Jeff says.

Betty Lou strolls back across the living room to the kitchen. She pours a cup of coffee and sits at the kitchen table. Waynette joins her.

"What should I do?" Waynette asks her friend.

**

Last night's phone call from Waynette is still bouncing around in Betty Lou's head

"I talked to Jeff Lightfoot," Waynette had said.

"I heard you the first time," Betty Lou had replied.

Waynette told Betty Lou she had run into Danny Lightfoot, and that Danny had given her Jeff's number.

"So, I finally worked up the nerve to call him, Betty Lou, and guess what — he still loves me."

Betty Lou was awake after that and finding what she was hearing from her usually level-headed best friend hard to comprehend.

Damn it, girl, don't you remember what that asshole did? Nobody forced him to screw that cheap little whore the night before your wedding; what kind of man does a thing like that? Now, there is no excuse for that kind of behavior. And you caught the little prick red handed, so to speak — saw him with your own eyes. For Christ's sake, Waynette, wake up!"

That was what Betty Lou wanted to say.

"How the hell do you know you'll still even like the guy?" Betty Lou did say. "It's been five years, five *long* years, I might add. He might be bald as a cucumber. He might weigh three hundred pounds. For all you know, he is a serial killer these days. Hell, girl, he might be all those things. And you can bet he's lying about *something* — did you even take that possibility into consideration?"

"He's here; he's in New Orleans. I have to see him, I have to; you know I do," Waynette said.

"Yes, I know, I know, but don't expect me to like it," was Betty Lou's resigned reply.

**

It is after one o'clock when two boys, one bouncing a basketball, open the gate to 920 Chartres and close it behind them. Cardenas walks across the street, jiggles the gate and checks the lock. An old woman wheeling a long-handled straw broom appears in the light at the far end of the entry tunnel shadow.

A big-bottomed black man with no shoulders, cropped gray hair, and a white mustache waddles into the entryway and stands next to the old woman. He has a badge pinned to the chest of the rumpled security cop uniform that hangs like a damp paper bag on his frame. He has a glass of sweet tea in one hand and the thumb of the other hand hooked through the loop next to a nightstick dangling from his belt.

"Something I can help you with, mister?" he asks Cardenas.

"I'm looking for 820 Chartres," Gene lies.

The watchman unhooks his thumb from his trousers, raises his hand, and points in the general direction of downtown. "This here is 920, sir — 820 would be a block that way," he says.

"Thank you," Gene says.

With little interest, the old guard watches until Cardenas turns and walks back to his car.

Lightfoot shouldn't be long, Gene thinks to himself. *He didn't recognize me. I will just wait him out — at least until the sun goes down.*

Reclining the passenger seat of the Jaguar, Cardenas leans back against the headrest and twists the radio dial.

"What's he doing now?" Waynette asks.

Jeff peeks through the lace of the window curtain. "He's just sitting in his car."

The sound of a trumpet's mellow jazz wafts through the apartment's open window from the Jaguar radio below. A delivery truck in reverse beeps its warning from a block away.

"I think I know his plan," Jeff says. "He'll be coming after us tonight."

"What?"

"We have to go now, before he makes his move, before dark."

21

The Promise

Einstein slides up next to me in the corner booth of Darla's Lounge. "Gille," he says, shaking my arm, "wake up, Gille,".

He flicks my ear with his index finger.

I raise my hand in protest and mutter a mild obscenity.

"Well, look who's alive," says Albert.

Still unaware of my surroundings, I lift my head from the tabletop. Although at first only a blur, my eyes discern Einstein's unruly mane.

"Go away, Albert."

"That's the spirit," Albert says. He pats my back.

"Where's your friend?" he asks.

"Lightfoot?"

"Well, since I'm not aware of others—yes, that would be the one."

"Don't have a clue. I just woke up, you know.

"Just regained consciousness would be more accurate."

"What time is it? I ask.

"Middle of the afternoon. I don't know the precise time of day, if that's what you're asking.

"Whatever. Please don't give me a hard time, Albert.

"*Hard* time, now there's a slice for you, my friend."

"What the hell are you talking about, Albert?"

"You brought it up."

"You mean 'time'?"

"Bingo!" Einstein says.

"No bingo here, Albert. I'm not interested in your hard or any other kind of time baloney right now," I say, "and what exactly do 'slices' have to do with time anyway?"

"Well, if you consider my thoughts on *time* to be baloney, I'm not sure I want to take the *time* to explain that to you at this *time*."

"Jesus, Albert, could you give it a rest? How about we save this conversation for later, okay?"

"Any *time* it suits you is a fine *time* for me," he says.

**

Einstein's wry grin only adds to my exasperation with his 'time' word games. My hangover symptoms intensify. Elbows propped against the tabletop, I cradle my face in my hands and massage my temples. I signal Darla for attention and ask her to bring me a soda water with bitters.

"Well, I'll be damn," Darla says, "soda with bitters coming up, Mister Van Winkle."

As Darla walks the soda to my table, I notice something I don't know how I missed before. Her hands, like my alien friend Zargon Ron's hands, have only four fingers, all thin and of an equal length that I would guess to be five inches or more, and one of those fingers opposes the others in the same manner as my thumb or yours.

And another thing — when I first saw Darla I attributed her chartreuse appearance to the rope of green light close to her around the back-bar mirror. Now, away from that light, I see I was mistaken, and that Darla's complexion is every bit as pasty green as that of my Zargonian friend.

My curiosity about Darla and her shared characteristics with Zargon Ron is more than I can bear. While trying to regain my awareness with sips of soda water and bitters, I motion her to my table. I ask if she would mind my asking a personal question, and she says she would not mind at all.

"Well this might sound a little strange," I say, "but I have a friend from the planet Zargon in the galaxy of Dargo — Ron is his name. I don't know his last name, or even if Zargonians have last names, but I have to wonder if you might know him."

227

Lightly tapping the tip of her extra-long fore-finger against her chin, Darla makes a show of pondering the question.

"Why yes, I do know a Ron from planet Zargon—the Great Zargonie, I call him." Darla says. "He gets a kick out of that name. Kind of a funny looking fellow with his big forehead and no ears and no hair anywhere, not so much as a sprout. Now that freaked me out when he first took his pants down, but I got to where I kind of liked him that way. He and I had quite a thing going too when we were both stationed in the home office on Zargon. Of course, that was a couple of light years ago, and I was much younger then."

"I was only asking," I say.

"Yeah, now that I think about it, that Zargon Ron was one funny guy back when we were an item," Darla continues. "He could do things with a ripe tomato you would not believe. The stories I could tell if I had a mind to. And, of course, there is his banana stunt—that's a classic—a real crowd pleaser."

"All right, all right, I'm sorry I asked," I say, hoping to escape her sarcasm barrage, but Darla shows no mercy.

"I'd love to show you how that tomato trick works," Darla says, "but I don's know where I could find a Billy goat on such short notice. What do you think, mister writer-man? Should I see if I can round one up for us."

"That is a kind offer," I say. "Maybe next time I'm in town we —"

Darla interrupts. "I found the best way to arouse Ronnie was to rub his tummy real slow in a clockwise motion," she says. "Let me tell you, it didn't take any time at all once I got the timing down right.

"And he knows how to please a girl, believe you me. One thing I did learn though—never rub that tummy of his any direction but clockwise. It makes him taste sour as a persimmon. I found that out the hard way."

"You don't say."

"I *do* say. Now, would that be the Zargon Ron you are talking about, Mister Barker?"

"I wouldn't discount the possibility," I say.

228

Since Darla and I conversed only by telepathic means, apart from Einstein who seemed slightly amused by our banter, the few other patrons in the bar were unaware of our conversation.

**

I am sipping at my soda and bitters, trying to tune out Einstein as he prattles on about the ridicule a genius who hasn't yet made his mark must endure in his youth when revelers suddenly break the silence of the courtyard. Their laughter and incoherent jabber intensify as they approach Darla's bar.

"Damn, it's wet out there," says Ed Sheehan, the first of the revelers to burst through Darla's French doors.

Without so much as a 'see you later', Einstein grabs his bottle of tequila and strolls away down the hall.

Shaking the rain from his hat and stomping his soaked shoes on the entry's Oriental rug, Ed spots me sitting in my corner booth, still wide-eyed with the surprise of seeing him standing there.

"Gille! I thought you might be here," he exclaims. "It's Gille everyone," he calls out over his shoulder —"didn't I tell you the weather might well have run him to cover?"

Squeezing past Sheehan, Donny Dragon prances to my table and plants a kiss on my cheek. The urbane persona he displayed on our first encounter at the Napoleon House has dissolved in early-morning cocktails.

"Over here everyone," Donny says, "it's Gille!" He plops down on the bench seat and scoots up against me, soaking my side with his rain-drenched costume. His forwardness is leading me to question my recall of last night's goings-on.

"What's with the getup?" I ask.

"It's a dress-up day, silly boy. Don't I remind you of Danny Kaye?"

"Danny Kaye?"

Donny stands and does a passable pirouette to show off his orange and red diamond-patterned court jester's tights trimmed in gold sparkles. He takes a bow and tips his three-pointed red velvet hat with Tinker Belle tassel. He plops back down next to me. He lifts his legs straight out in front of him. He waggles his feet and golden bells on the toes of his sequined slippers jingle-jangle.

"Where is that beautiful Jeffrey Lightfoot?" Donny asks. "I love that man. He is so m–a–n–l–y. You know what I mean, Gille?"

"I'm not sure," I say, with some relief Donny's interest in me was not that of my first suspicion.

"Indians, you know," Donny says, "all that ruddy flesh and raven hair, and those eyes—those eyes are to die for. Is it getting warm in here?"

Donny makes a show of fanning his face with a bar napkin.

Ronnie, dressed in leotards of a similar design to Donny's, sulks at a corner table across the room.

Clad in fancy suspenders and bright red pedal-pusher shorts, Freddie Fender has his slick-bald dome covered by a matching baseball cap, its bill cocked to the side.

Warm and fresh and showing no sign of having just come in from a rain, the beautiful Cynthia Canales slips into my booth. She scoots around to my side and rests her hand on my thigh. I am clear of eye now. I think I might order a cocktail.

"Good afternoon, Gille Barker," Cynthia purrs. "I was afraid we had lost you."

"Fat chance of that, my dear," I manage to reply.

Ed Sheehan, dressed in fine black tails with green-glitter lapels and pocket flaps, stands with drink in hand at the side of my booth. He sports a Mad Hatter's top hat covered in matching green sequins. I notice my reflection in the bar mirror and see that I sport that same Mad Hatter's hat and am wearing those same fine tails. I am quite handsome, for my age.

We are midway through a first round of cocktails when the skies clear and the rains stop. The courtyard cobblestones steam in the heat of the afternoon sun.

"Oh, look." Donny points at the bright light from the newly exposed sun outside the French doors. He bounds up from our table and into the courtyard. He surveys the blue sky. "I don't believe it — barely a cloud in sight. We should do something. We should go someplace special," Donny says.

Ed is warming up on one of his potentially long-winded dissertations – this one on love and friendship, and the exorbitant price of fine chocolate, when, to everyone's delight, Cynthia intervenes.

"I know!" says Cynthia. "Let's catch the trolley! Let's go to the zoo!" Her excitement is contagious.

"What a grand idea," Ed says. He raises his hand. "All in favor — let me see a show of hands."

All hands shoot up in agreement, including my own. To everyone's delight, I order a round of drinks for the road.

I ask Darla if she has any idea where Lightfoot might have gone.

"He went to the front desk to get you bad boys a room," Darla says, "but he should have been back by now."

"I will go see what's keeping Lightfoot," I announce.

"Hurry back, Gille," Cynthia says. "We need to get this show on the road."

At the front desk, I ask Josie if she has seen Jeff.

"Sure have," Josie says. "He rented two-fourteen, that suite just above Darla's with the balcony." She points back toward the balcony above the bar and hands me a key.

"I don't think he's up there though," she says. "He was out on the balcony about the time those other folks showed up, but I thought I saw him shoot through the lobby after that."

I thank Josie and take the stairs to the room. There is no Jeff, but I see the paper bag he has been carrying the last couple of days sitting on the coffee table. There is a note written on hotel stationary propped against the side of the bag.

For you Gille. Thanks for everything, my friend — Jeff, the note says.

I open the paper bag. There are five ten-thousand dollar bundles of hundred-dollar bills stacked inside — fifty thousand dollars. I sit on the corner of the sofa and read the note again. I'm stunned. I close and rewrap the bag and stuff it in my carry bag.

I use the stairs back down to the lobby and cross the courtyard to Darla's.

Cynthia is waiting at the door. "What, no Lightfoot?" she says to me.

I tell Cynthia I did not find Jeff, and that I left a note to let him know where we were going in case he returns.

"All right, everyone," Cynthia says, "shall we go?"

A bright call of 'Aloha' from Darla causes me to look back as we spill out the barroom door. Smiling, Darla stands in the doorway waving a four-digit shaka farewell that I return in standard kind.

**

We parade through the Saint Marie lobby, down the half block to Bourbon Street and turn toward Canal. All doors are open. The mellow tones of a honky-tonk sax reach out to the sidewalk from Bourbon Street's House of Blues and pull us inside.

Though the place is packed, I spot three empty stools at a prime high-topped table, where a couple is sitting alone next to the dance floor. Leading Cynthia by the hand, I wend my way through the crowd to the table.

I ask the couple if the seats are taken.

The man is ugly-big and obviously not sociably inclined. Thick strands of barbed wire tattooed around his stump of a neck drip blood-red ink. It is no wonder there are empty stools at his table.

Normally his snarly 'help yourself, pal' reply would have given me pause, but, this time, I hold my ground. I blame excessive alcohol consumption and my wish to impress Cynthia Canales in equal parts for clouding my judgment.

"Thank you, *pal*," I say, and I don't stop there.

"Name's Gille Barker," I say, continuing to run my mouth despite knowing I should hold my tongue.

I offer the angry man my hand.

He hesitates a moment before accepting my offer. The bones in my knuckles audibly grind in his grasp.

"Billy Bones," he sneers.

"Billy Bones, you say. Well now, that's a coincidence," I say, enduring my pain without a grimace. "I have a friend named Billy Bones. He is an old, gray-haired midget—not much to look at, but quite the dance man. I don't suppose you two are related – cousins, maybe?"

Cynthia, having not yet taken leave of her senses, grabs my arm and yanks me away from Billy Bones's grasp. I swap sneers with the old body builder as Cynthia pulls me toward the crowded dance floor and the band cruises into some rocking blues.

Ed Sheehan takes my place at the table. He had not witnessed my exchange with Billy Bones, not that it would have mattered if he had — Ed would chitchat with the devil himself if the opportunity came to hand.

Ed smiles and thrusts his hand out toward the surly muscle man, much as I had done before. "Ed Sheehan," he says.

"Billy Bones," the man says, ignoring Ed's outstretched hand.

Hand still extended, Ed turns his attention toward the lady sitting next to Bones. "And you would be —?" he says.

The woman cautiously smiles and leans away from Billy Bones, as if simply shaking Ed's hand might earn her a slap to the side of the head.

"Louise," she says. Her voice is deep with a chain smoker's rasp.

"It's nice to make your acquaintance, Louise," Ed says with a slight bow and an intonation on 'Louise' that is so erotic as to bring a blush to Louise's pasty cheeks.

Ed turns his attention back to Billy Bones.

"May I ask you a question, sir?" Ed asks.

Billy Bones' eyes narrow to a menacing glare now. He nods as if to say— *ask your question, if you dare.*

With no more encouragement from Bones than that intimation, Ed continues. "You look familiar, Mister Bones —— have we met?" He asks.

Ed takes a deep drag from his cigarette and exhales a cloud of smoke that smacks Billy Bones between the eyes. Unfazed, Bones studies Ed Sheehan's face. Something about that face had seemed familiar to Bones from the moment Ed approached the table.

"Could be," Bones says, "—— Bourbon House, The Abbey Lounge maybe?"

Mention of those two favorite haunts from his alcohol induced blackout days transports Ed Sheehan back to the night before his first encounter with this Billy Bones. It was in Ed's darkest times, before his reformation, before his rescue by Ms. Madeline Meacham.

**

On that night, now coming to his memory, Ed awoke from a drunken stupor unsteadily perched on a stool in The Abbey, a seedy Decatur Street dive bar of last resort. Before he had passed out, a fellow bar fly and frequent drinking companion Ed only knew as Dion was sitting on the stool next to him. Now there was no one to either side and only an empty glass in front of him. Ed surveyed the dark, almost empty room. He called out to the bartender for another drink and was told he had had enough.

Ed thanked the bartender for being a prick and warily rose to a standing position from his bar stool. He scraped the few dollars and coins lying on the bar in front of him into his pocket and staggered out the open doorway into dawn's first light.

After stumbling blindly for several blocks, Ed turned on Saint Peter Street, toward Bourbon. He thrust his hands in his pockets in search of an elusive cigarette butt and pulled out the unexpected wad of dollar bills from the bar.

Holding on to a storefront balcony post and lowering himself to a seated position on the curb, Ed spread the bills out across the street gutter in front of him — a five, seven ones, and a twenty-dollar bill.

'Thirty-two dollars – Jesus – that's more than I had when I went out yesterday morning. I think that was yesterday.'

Ed struggled to gather his thoughts.

'I must have picked up Dion's money from the bar–but he wasn't there when I left, was he? Maybe he was in the toilet. Thirty-two bucks–I better get it back to him before he throws one of his damn hissy fits.'

Having decided to take the money back to Dion, Ed grabbed the awning post and pulled himself upright. He stuttered a first step in what he assumed was the direction of The Abbey.

**

In the bar, Ed's drinking pal, Dion, had returned to his stool and discovered his money was gone.

"That motherfucking Ed took my money!" said Dion.

"Ed, you son of a bitch!"

Dion raged on to Charlie, the bartender, and an inattentive audience composed of the night's other two remaining bar flies.

"Every dollar, Charlie — that damn Ed took my last nickel. I kid you not, Charlie. I'm serious, man. I will have to pay you tomorrow. Wait till I get my mitts on that hack of a ham ——."

**

After that first step, Ed stumbled sideways and braced himself against the building. His glassy gaze wandered across the street and through the wrought-iron gates to Jackson Square where the bigger than life statue of Andrew Jackson came to life, pulled back on the reins, and reared his trusty steed, Sam Patch, on his back legs. Andrew stared into Ed's eyes and doffed his cavalry hat, holding it high above his head. And he spoke to Ed Sheehan right then and there.

'Don't worry about Dion,' the 7th President of the United States said to Ed, *'you can give him the money next time you see him. Give it back now and he will only fritter it away on more booze and a five-dollar blow-job from that poor excuse for a whore who has been panhandling drinks from him all night. You will be doing Dion a favor if you keep his cash. Take care of yourself. Put some food in your belly. Clean yourself up, get a shave, take a shower, and buy some decent deodorant. Buy the deodorant first, Ed. Do it now — Spread your wings, Ed Sheehan. Spread your wings.'*

Sam Patch nodded in agreement with his master and let loose a final blast of air between his fluttering bronze lips before the statue fell silent.

The small Jackson Square fountain gurgled and then roared like Niagara Falls. Ed covered his ears, but the roar would not stop. He fell to his knees, still covering his ears. Finally, the roar faded, and a halo of light appeared to him as it rose from behind the majestic spires of Saint Louis Cathedral — the light of God it was for sure.

Ed squinted up into God's light there and asked The Almighty One this question:

"What the hell do you want of me now, God? Can't you see I'm a little under the weather?"

To Ed's alarm, the light brightened and spread across the sky and a bright ball of flame rose above the tallest of the Cathedral spires, and then Ed heard clearly the booming monotone voice of Him.

'Andrew knows of what he speaks,' God said. *'Get your shit together, Edward Sheehan — time's-a-wasting, my son, and the cotton is tall.'*

Then a dark bank of storm clouds smothered that flame in the sky, and a light drizzle turned quickly to hard rain. Ed leaned back and dropped to a sitting position against the building's soft brick wall under the cover of an overhead balcony. A blank gaze of understanding fixed Ed's eyes on the stream of rainwater picking up gum wrappers and paper cups as it flowed toward the gutter drain.

Dog-tired, Ed felt suddenly queasy. The milk in his scotch that started this bender was the closest he had come to food since yesterday morning—or was that the day before? He closed his eyes.

**

When Ed awoke, the sun was high. Waves of humidity rose from the rain-soaked pavement. Ed stood and stuck his hands down to the seams of his pockets. The wad of dollar bills wasn't imagined, it was still there.

A tourist couple, probably newlyweds, held hands and gave Ed a wide berth as they walked around him.

"Pardon me, sir, would you have the time?" Ed asked the young man.

Although Ed's unkempt appearance was disconcerting, his Shakespearean baritone and subtle bow persuaded the man to pause and glance at his watch.

"Quarter past eleven," the man said, as he and his lady quickly moved by.

Ed had been passed out on the street for five hours.

"Thank you, sire, for your kindness," Ed said. He doffed his stylishly tattered Panama and embellished a deep bow to their backsides, nearly fainting as blood rushed to his head.

Unsteady but game, Ed was now ready to take the advice offered by none other than God and Andrew Jackson. He walked across the corner to Liz's grocery and bought a pint of chocolate milk and a stick of deodorant.

He bought a pack of cigarettes on discount for twenty-five cents, even though he seldom smoked. He splurged. Made in a part of France where the citizenry never learned how to make anything well that was not bottled and corked, the cigarettes were stylishly brown, the kind that come in a flat box and burn like damp rope, but Ed did not mind.

Ed drank the chocolate milk while waiting in the checkout line and tossed the empty bottle in a trashcan just past the register.

"Thank you, Mister Sheehan — you have a good day," Liz said, handing him his change. Ed took a half dollar from the change. He flipped it in front of Liz and she snagged it from the air.

"Thank *you*, Elizabeth, and the very same wish for your day," said Ed.

He stopped at his old friend Jerry's barbershop for a trim and a hot straight-razor shave. Already in improved spirits, by the time Jerry was finished with him he was feeling like a new man.

Ed rose from the chair and grandly handed his old barber friend a generous tip.

"It's good to have you back, Mister Sheehan," the barber said.

"It is good to *be* back, my friend," Ed replied over his shoulder on his way out the door.

237

Just like old times. Now to get a shower and something to wear that does not smell like dirty feet.

**

Ed walked up Royal Street the five blocks to his friend Dottie's bungalow. Dottie Delcambre was her name. Dottie had supplied wardrobes for the finest New Orleans theater productions of Ed Sheehan's hay days. Dottie was still the one called by theaters when they needed someone who knew her business.

It had been a while since Ed had talked to Dottie, but he was sure she would help him out. If he could borrow something fashionable from Dottie's wardrobe and get cleaned up, as President Jackson had suggested, maybe he could get back in the game.

A De Niro movie was set to begin filming in New Orleans in the spring. Auditions were next week, and Ed just knew he had a chance for a part. Bobby would help him. They did that movie together — well, yeah, Bobby was the star and Ed had only a few lines.

But we were great friends, weren't we, Bobby?

A chance — that is all I need. Is that too much to ask from an old friend down on his luck?

Bobby will remember me.

Let me see, what was the name of that movie? 'Mean Streets' – that was it. It is all coming back to me now — seems like a lifetime ago. Bobby will give me a hand, once he knows I need one, I know he will, even if he can be a bit of a dick.

Ed tripped Dottie's doorbell, waited, and tripped it again. He pushed on the door latch and the door opened.

"Dottie," he called out, "Dottie, it's Ed, Ed Sheehan."

He walked in.

Something was not right. The silence was eerie, the air sticky and still. From the kitchen the familiar meow of Matilda, Dottie's senile Cheshire cat, broke the silence. Dottie's prized antique

238

clock chimed in the noon hour as Ed moved through the dark living room.

"Dottie?" After the clock's twelfth chime, the house fell silent again except for the tick and tock of each pendulum swing and then a Matilda meow.

"It's Uncle Ed, Matilda. I'm coming, Matilda." Ed walked to the kitchen doorway, picking up the cat's milk bowl in the hall on the way. "I have your bowl. Milk is on its way, Matilda."

"Oh shit!" Ed dropped Matilda's bowl crashing to the floor.

Dottie lay at his feet in the middle of the kitchen, eyes bugging from their sockets, a scream stretched frozen on her face. Other than the dress hiked high above her breasts, Dottie was naked, her legs spread wide and disjointed, like a chicken's splayed wishbone.

Ed sensed a figure behind him in time to see a man run out of the kitchen pantry and bolt for the back door.

Ed dove toward the figure and wrapped his arms around one of the man's ankles.

("Merely a reflex action," he would later reply to a police captain lauding him for his courage. "I'm not really that stupid when I have time to think," Ed said.)

The man was huge and barrel chested with arms the size of a lumberjack's. There were even muscles flexing in the ankle Ed held tight in his grasp. But Ed could not let go. The man busted Ed's ribs and pummeled his kidneys with blow after blow to his back until Ed's grip finally failed. The man kicked Ed in the chest and then grabbed him by the hair. He turned Ed's face toward his and Ed saw a giant fist draw back like a piston to smash his nose toward his brainpan. It was in that moment that he saw the man's face — the face he now remembers.

Billy Bones! It was the face of Billy Bones!

**

Ed's stomach churns as he glares into the dead eyes of that face, the face of Billy Bones, now sitting across the table from him in the House of Blues. Unsteady, he grasps the edge of the table to hold his balance.

239

"Excuse me," Ed says in the general direction of Billy Bones and Louise. He turns and hurries into the crowd of revelers. A dancer's wild gyrations knocks Ed's Mad Hatter hat to the floor as he pushes his way across the dance floor to the toilet. He bends over the crapper, braces against the wall, and heaves.

Ed leans over the restroom sink and splashes his face with cold water. Wiping his face dry with a paper towel, he searches his reflection in the sink mirror for the telltale scars left there by Billy Bones. The violated and bloodied Dottie Delcambre appears behind his mirrored reflection, her lifeless eyes staring into his from the void.

Ed walks back into the toilet stall and pulls the door closed. He props his foot on the toilet seat and rolls up his trouser leg to reveal a derringer–the derringer he has holstered there ever since that afternoon Billy Bones killed Dottie Delcambre.

**

On that day of Dottie's murder, after Billy Bones had knocked him senseless, Ed pulled himself to his feet, staggered across the kitchen, and grabbed Dottie's derringer from its hiding place in an old cookie jar covered with ceramic grapes. Ed had known Dottie kept the derringer there since she pulled it from the jar and showed it to him years ago, two days after a burglar shimmied in her second-story bedroom window and stole most of her jewelry and a drawing by Pierre Bonnard while she was entertaining guests downstairs.

"I'll be ready next time thieves come a knocking," Dottie said to Ed that day, waving her shiny new derringer above his head.

Dottie's derringer in his hand, Ed had stumbled after her killer the few steps to the kitchen porch door before blacking out. When he regained consciousness, he stuck the derringer in his pocket and called the police.

'You get yourself a gun, Mister Sheehan.' That was the advice given him at Dottie's wake by the same police captain who commended him on his courage in the tackling of Billy Bones. *'Learn how to use the damn thing. Keep it with you. When you*

shower, set it on a shelf where you can get to it easy; tie it to your leg or strap it to your side, slide it under your pillow at night–that will help keep the demons at bay—trust me on this, Mister Sheehan. Get a gun.'

Ed, already with Dottie's derringer in his pocket, listened intently as the police captain gave him that advice.

As Ed stood by Dottie's coffin, the stifling odor of a hundred flower bouquets filling the air, he promised Dottie he would someday even the score with her killer, though he wasn't so sure he would have the stomach for the job if the chance came to hand.

Leaving that question to be answered, Ed learned how to use Dottie's derringer. He bought the ankle holster and strapped the pistol to his leg every morning before he walked out the door. He would at least have the tool necessary for the job if the opportunity came.

**

Ed takes the derringer from its holster and sticks it in the pocket of his sequined tails. Looking in the House of Blues toilet mirror, he wets his comb and carefully runs it straight back through his long, gray hair.

"Mister Sheehan!" Cynthia calls out to Ed as he passes next to us on the dance floor. He does not hear. Dancers jostle Ed from side to side as he walks back toward Billy Bones' table. He takes no notice. His senses are focused on the face of Billy Bones, the man who murdered Dottie Delcambre.

His gaze now somewhere off in the space between Billy Bones and Louise, Ed leans forward and plants his arms against the top of the table. An inattentive smile crosses his face. The band kicks into overdrive, masking the drone of Billy Bones voice as he berates Louise for some unknown transgression — flirting with the man at the next table, holding her glass wrong, showing too much cleavage between her sagging breasts, having shit for brains.

Ed leans back from the table and pulls the derringer from his pocket. He holds it down at his side. With one easy motion, he tips his head back and throws down the last of his Dewar's and water.

Feigned smile intact, Ed bows slightly toward Louise while moving to the side of Billy Bones. He sticks the end of the derringer's barrel against the space above Billy Bones' third rib and whispers in his ear.

"Here's a little something from Dottie Delcambre, Mister Billy Bones," Ed says.

Bones swivels his head toward Ed and his scowl quickly turns to a look of bewildered recognition. Finally, his eyes betray his minds acceptance that the final shit is about to hit the fan.

"It's you!" says Billy Bones.

Other than a faint 'Argh' as the first bullet strikes, those were the last words of the notorious Billy Bones.

The band's horns blare and a bluesman blasts fine raspy tones straight from his soul as Ed sends another bullet into the torso of Billy Bones. The two shots are no more noticeable than distant pops of a cap gun.

A wisp of smoke curls toward the ceiling from Bones' shirt and mingles with the haze from a hundred cigarettes as Billy's last sip of whiskey gurgles back out over his lower lip and barely beats his head to the tabletop.

If Louise finds any of this disconcerting, she gives no indication.

No one hears the clatter of the derringer when Ed drops it to the floor on his way out of the House of Blues.

Only Cynthia Canales notices Ed leave. She picks his hat up from the dance floor and grabs me by the hand. She motions for the others to follow as she pulls me across the room and onto Bourbon Street. We all run after Ed, who is, by then, a quarter block away.

We are in sight of Canal Street when we catch up with Ed. Even dressed, as am I, in ridiculous black tails with pockets trimmed in garish glitter that sparkles in the afternoon sun, Ed exudes a powerful presence. He acknowledges his pleasure at our arrival without breaking stride.

Cynthia hands Ed his Mad Hatter's hat retrieved from the dance floor of the House of Blues. He stops for a moment to consider his full reflection in a jazz club's darkened window. He adjusts the brim of his absurd hat just so, jauntily cocked to one side of his brow—it is perfect. His chin is high, his face radiant with the foremost of promises fulfilled.

With Cynthia holding Ed's hand and mine her's, we three continue in silence toward the intersection of Bourbon Street and Canal and on to St. Charles to catch the next trolley to the Audubon Zoo. Donny and Ronnie, the court jesters in their harlequin leotards and tasseled hats, follow close behind us arm in arm with Freddie Fender.

**

An eye for an eye. It is said to be the way of things in a book of fables written by a committee formed of the few literate individuals on this earth long after the time of the subject at hand—the story of the beginnings of time as we are told to accept it to be some two thousand plus years ago, only a few million off the mark if you do not count the billions of years before we came on the scene. Who can care about any of that?

What does it have to do with the reality of things? Maybe everything — maybe nothing at all.

In any case, an eye for an eye is an acceptable policy to me. I was not yet aware Ed Sheehan had taken this policy literally when he snuffed the last life's breath from Billy Bones, one of the planet's more despicable persons, but I have no quarrel with his deed. Einstein made his opinion on the matter clear when he said to me much later —

"Fuck Billy Bones and zee horse he road in on."

22

The Saint Charles Trolley

Twilight nears as Lightfoot prepares for his escape from Gene Cardenas. Disguised as housekeepers at his request, Waynette and a skittish Betty Lou sit side-by-side on the couch, dowdy as any Decatur Street bag ladies.

Betty Lou lights one cigarette with another and stubs out the flaming butt of a third cigarette on the ashtray. Jeff, at the window watching Cardenas in his car below, asks her for the time.

Betty Lou glances at her watch.

"Two fifteen, Jerk-O," she says.

Cardenas is slouched in the front passenger seat, but the sun's reflection off the windshield makes it impossible for Jeff to see if he is awake.

He has been sitting like that for two hours. Is he awake? Where is Richard? If Richard is in New Orleans, wouldn't he be with Cardenas now? Of course he would.

**

"It's time, ladies," Jeff says. He takes another look at the mound of bundled dollars on the coffee table. "I'm going to need another bag," he says.

Waynette pulls a backpack from behind the couch and tosses it to Jeff.

"That's perfect – thank you, my dear," Jeff says.

Noticing Betty Lou sitting there, nerves a-jangle, chain smoking cigarettes, Jeff attempts to lighten the mood.

"I must say, Betty Lou, you have done a bang-up job on that costume," he says. "all you need is one of those old grocery carts full of rags to push around town.

Betty Lou smiles and takes a final drag on the cigarette held between her fingers before stubbing it out along with the one that was burning in the ashtray.

"Why thank you, you are too kind," she says.

Jeff takes four of the ten-thousand-dollar bundles of hundred-dollar bills and stuffs them in Waynette's carry bag.

His plan is simple. First, Waynette and Betty Lou walk out the front gate. Since Cardenas has never seen either Waynette or Betty Lou, their appearance as two cleaning ladies leaving an apartment building in the late afternoon should raise no suspicion.

"I will leave when I'm sure you two are safely away," Jeff says.

"And then what?" Waynette asks.

"And then, nothing. That's it – that is the plan. In a couple of weeks, when it looks like the heat's off, I will call you," Jeff says, "and we will be on our way."

Jeff unzips the backpack and begins to load it with the bundles of bills.

"We'll be on our way to what–to where?" Waynette asks.

"I don't know. We have a bag full of hundred-dollar bills here, Waynette — we should be able to figure something out."

The backpack is full. Jeff pries the sides together with his fingers to zip it closed. One of the ten-thousand-dollar bundles falls to the floor under the coffee table. Jeff scoops it up and sticks it in with the other four already in Waynette's bag.

"I can't do this," Waynette says.

"It's the only way," says Jeff. "Cardenas won't follow you. You will be safe."

"Jesus, Jeff, that's not the problem. I can't just leave everything behind, run away — always knowing that man is out there looking for us. I can't do it. I won't do it."

In exasperation, Jeff sits next to Waynette on the arm of the sofa. Whatever his priorities were when he and I began this trip from the Winslow railroad crossing, Waynette Boudreaux is not one of them now. He is relieved that his plan requires they go their separate ways.

That thought first surfaced in the middle of last night's phone call when the voice of Waynette that had seemed so precious to him as heard through the filter of his memories unexpectedly morphed into her nutty mother's same shrill twang.

Now wondering why he stuck that last ten-grand in Waynette's bag instead of his own, Jeff lights his last cigarette and watches the black sulfur smoke from the match curl away. He twists the empty cigarette pack and throws it and the match book into the ashtray on the coffee table.

Jeff puts his arm around Waynette and holds her close.

"I understand, sweetheart," he says. "We can talk about this later, but the most important thing is to get you and Betty Lou safely out of here now."

Jeff kisses Waynette and tells her he loves her, which he supposes he does, in some way. It makes no difference —. 'I love you,' is all he can think to say.

Holding Waynette there in front of him, her eyes rimmed with tears, for a moment Lightfoot feels sorry, but sorry for what, he has no clue.

"You and Betty Lou have to leave now," Jeff says, "and you can't come back here."

"But where will we go? What about my clothes?"

"You have fifty thousand dollars in your bag, Waynette. Go shopping. Go to the Bahamas. You always wanted to see Ireland — check out the Tullamore Dew. How about Mexico? Take Betty Lou to Aruba. For Christ's sake, Waynette, use your imagination!"

Though Lightfoot instantly regrets betraying his irritation, he feels no need to amend his reply.

**

The front gate creaks open and then slams closed with no noticeable disturbance of Cardenas from his reclined position. Jeff watches from the window until Waynette, her bag full of cash flung over a shoulder and Betty Lou ambling close by her side, disappears around the corner.

246

Jeff straps on his backpack. He peers down at Cardenas, still slouched, apparently sleeping, on the passenger seat of the Jaguar.

Jeff walks down the narrow wooden steps and across the courtyard. He slings the gate open. The clang of the gate against the brick wall rouses Cardenas. Jeff, running hard, is already out of sight around the corner of Dumaine Street before Cardenas can fumble out of his car.

The security gate is ajar. Cardenas searches through the names on the line of mailboxes at the entrance.

Boudreaux–there it is–W. Boudreaux, 202.

Cardenas sprints up the stairs. He pulls his pistol from its shoulder holster. He twists the doorknob and throws the unlocked door open, scanning the room down the barrel of his gun. He sees his briefcase on the table in front of the sofa.

Setting his pistol on the table, Cardenas thumbs through the empty briefcase compartments. Contemplating his next move, he pulls Richard's last cigarette from his shirt pocket, sits on the sofa, and absently taps the end of the cigarette against the tabletop.

There is a book of matches next to an ashtray on the table. On the matchbook cover is a martini glass and "Darla's Lounge" printed in fancy script. He flips the matchbook over and studies the message there– *'The French Quarter's Best Kept Secret, Darla's Lounge, On the Courtyard of the St. Ann/Marie Antoinette Hotel, 717 Rue Conti'*. A map inside the cover marks the hotel's location.

**

A scowling old woman sporting a long handled broom in one hand and dustpan in the other pops into Cardenas' view at the open apartment doorway.

"What are you doing in here, mister?" the woman says to Cardenas. He recognizes her as the same old woman he encountered at the front gate earlier in the day.

Cardenas sticks the matchbook in his pocket and stands easy next to the coffee table. He smiles. He raises his hand in greeting.

"I'm Gene," he says, "an old friend of Waynette's mother. Remember? We talked at the gate earlier today. And you are — —?"

The old woman sees Cardenas's pistol sitting on the coffee table. She drops her broom and turns to run. She screams but only a high-pitched squeal escapes her lips that sets the African Greys in the courtyard below screeching their parrot replies.

"Aye, Aye, Aye – Hello — Is that you, Jane? – Never mind – Never mind."

Gene grabs the old woman's arm. He smashes the butt of his gun against the side of her face, knocking her to the walkway floor.

"Hello – Risky business—risky business," one of the African Greys says while the other launches a screech and whistle.

Gene takes the old cleaning lady by the ankles and drags her back into Waynette's apartment. He stuffs a dust rag from her pocket in her mouth and ties her wrists together around the leg of a heat radiator.

**

Lightfoot is halfway across Canal Street, with the Saint Charles trolley-stop in sight, when he hears his name called out above the traffic din and downtown hubbub. He sees Donny Dragon, conspicuous in his court jester's attire and Tinker Bell hat, jumping up and down on the trolley-stop bench amid the waiting crowd, arms waving wildly above his head like a drowning man about to go down for the final count.

"Jeffrey! – Sweetheart! – Over here! – Over here!" Donny calls out.

**

Cardenas runs down the steps and out the front gate of 920 Chartres. He fumbles for his car keys.

There is a screech of metal against metal as he pulls away from the curb and scrapes the side of the Jaguar across the bumper of an old Dodge Dart.

He cuts across Ursuline Avenue to Royal and picks up speed, now rocketing toward Canal past Toulouse and St. Louis Streets. Realizing he has missed the turn onto Rue Conti, Cardenas skids the Jaguar to a stop, barely missing an old street vendor wheeling his hot dog wagon off the curb. The vendor slams his fist down on the hood of the Jaguar.

"Watch where you're going, bitch," the old hot dog man says to Gene Cardenas.

"Shut the fuck up, dog man" says Cardenas.

He backs the car around the corner onto Conti and parks in a yellow zone next to the corner. He runs across the street into the lobby of the Saint Ann/Marie Antoinette Hotel. Across the courtyard, he sees Darla's bar sign, the same tilted martini as is on the book of matches in his pocket.

**

We members of Ed Sheehan's entourage have barely arrived at the trolley stop when Einstein shows up. He squeezes in next to me on the trolley-stop bench. Wearing white tennis shorts, a V-neck sweater trimmed with red and navy stripes, and matching navy-blue tennis shoes with red laces, he makes no explanation for his attire. Instead, he launches into another of his unsolicited recitations—this one on the speed of a New Orleans streetcar as it relates to that of a city bus, and, with barely a pause for breath, on to how a person might keep an intergalactic wormhole open long enough to pass through, maybe into 'a parallel universe, not unlike our own'.

I change the subject. I ask Einstein his opinion on why the people at the Mars Candy Company felt the necessity to raise the price of my favorite snicker bars a nickel simply because of a tenth of a cent rise in the cost of a pound of cacao somewhere in South America.

Albert is about to reply when we are startled to attention by Donny Dragon's bouncing up and down on the bench boards and his sudden lilting soprano screeching of Lightfoot's name.

"Jeffrey! — Jeffrey Lightfoot! — Over here!" Dragon screams out, waving both arms above his head until Jeff sees him and waves back.

I turn to ask Einstein what he thought the odds were that finding us was Jeff's plan only to find an empty bench seat next to me where Albert had been.

The traffic light changes and Lightfoot, forty pounds of dough strapped to his back, plods across Canal Street. Winded, he staggers to the trolley stop bench and plops down next to me.

249

I ask him where he has been, how he had found us, and by the way, what the hell is he carrying in that bulging bag strapped to his back. He tells me it doesn't really matter where he has been or how he found us.

"And the bag is stuffed with hundred-dollar bills, not that it's any of your business," says Lightfoot.

"That's a lot of hundred-dollar bills," I say.

"About six thousand of them."

I have little reason to doubt his word since he had left me a paper sack full of hundred-dollar bills only hours ago.

**

A freshly painted red streetcar screeches into the trolley-stop. We pile on—Ed and I in our sequined tails and Mad Hatter hats, Donny and Ronnie in their court jester tights and Tinker Bell hats, Freddie Fender and Lightfoot, a Hopi Indian cab driver from the outback of Arizona, who just happens to have over six hundred thousand dollars strapped to his back in a canvas bag.

Cynthia looks spectacular in her sharply pleated pink skirt and fresh white blouse, and very much out of place in our company. Last to the trolley, she runs to grab my outstretched hand and I pull her onto the streetcar steps to the enthusiastic cheers of our entourage as the trolley rolls away from the Canal Street Station.

Cynthia and I find an empty wooden bench halfway to the back of the trolley. There is a boy wearing a coonskin cap sitting on the bench ahead of us facing the front of the trolley, as are we. He has a bow and a quiver of silver-tipped arrows slung across his shoulder.

Wearing a bright African-print sarong and matching bandanna, a young mulatto woman sits motionless next to the boy.

Thinking I recognize her, "Jana?" I say.

The woman turns toward me. She is Jana. Her face shows the barest hint of recognition. In a tone that betrays no surprise or special welcome, she says, "Afternoon, Mister Gille."

Jana has a strip of white tape strapped across the bridge of her nose. Heavy bruising is visible around her eyes despite the camouflage afforded by stylish dark glasses.

250

"Please forgive me for my boldness, Jana" I say, "but what happened to you?"

"Nothing to forgive you for, Mister Gille," Jana says. "Wasn't more than ten minutes after you and Mister Jeff left that two men broke in on me and Ms. Hillary. They forced Ms. Hillary to tell them about Mister Jeff, about him being at the house. She would never have told them anything if one of the men had not hit me.

"I guess all that carrying on was just too much for Ms. Hillary," Jana continues. "Weren't nothing I could do — poor thing was dead just like that." Jana startles me with a loud snap of her fingers to emphasize the suddenness of Hillary Boudreaux's demise.

"Jesus, Jana, we should never have been there in the first place," is all I can think to say.

"Well, even if that be so, it is on Mister Jeff, not you, Mister Barker," Jana says.

"Oh, how awful," Cynthia says.

"Yes, it was, mam," Jana says, "but Johnny Ray made those men pay for what they did. He shot the one that broke my nose with one of his arrows — shot that man right through the neck, Johnny Ray did."

Jana's pride in the prowess of her often-maligned ward, Johnny Ray, is apparent in the serenity of her fleeting smile.

"Now that was something to see, Mister Gille," Jana says. "The man was still bleeding like a stuck pig when his friend dragged him outside and loaded him in their car — was no reason for the bother – that man dead for sure."

Jana tells me all this with no more emotion than if she were describing that weekend's weather.

Though raptly intent on Jana's every word, Cynthia holds her curiosity in check.

I have no idea what I should say to Jana. Further questions on the subject seem inappropriate. Sorry had fallen woefully short of the mark. I change the subject.

"What brings you and Johnny Ray to New Orleans?" I ask.

With no answer to my query, Jana, first daughter of the Spirit Saint Priest Oswan, most powerful of all voodoo priests in the Louisiana bayous, turns away.

A peculiar cooling breeze bearing the scent of clove and cinnamon swirls through the open trolley door.

From over my shoulder, Donny Dragon points out the homes of this and that New Orleans high-society-type like a tour bus narrator as we click and clack down the tracks between the rows of antebellum mansions with their fluted columns and neatly manicured lawns. We pass under moss covered Maples that line Saint Charles Avenue from Poydras to our trolley stop across from the wide-open spaces of Audubon Park.

As our trolley pulls away, Donny Dragon blows kisses to a neatly attired small girl and boy looking back at us from the trolley's rear window. Eerily expressionless, they each raise a hand in farewell.

Jana, with Johnny Ray at her side, is already situated on the bench of a roadside picnic table when we cross the street from the trolley stop, her gaze fixed away from us on the nearly deserted park lawns. A wicker basket sits on the table near Johnny Ray filled with pears and potato chips and butter and banana sandwiches on sugared sweetbread.

As I step over the curb into Audubon Park, I turn at the sound of screeching brakes behind me and see a black Jaguar sliding to a stop across the street. A man wearing a Hawaiian shirt and carrying what looks like a pistol in his hand jumps from the car.

Jeff, walking next to me, hitches his bag full of hundred dollar bills high on his back and starts running across the park. I have never seen anyone run faster.

I first realize the man in the Hawaiian shirt is Gene Cardenas when he rushes past us, pushing Ronnie aside and knocking a squealing Donny Dragon to his knees on the sidewalk.

Cardenas stops, levels his pistol at Lightfoot, now some thirty yards away, and squeezes the trigger. Jeff tumbles forward to the ground like a man struck by lightning. He does not move.

Is he dead? The screams of Cynthia and Donny Dragon echoing across Audubon Park indicate he is. Cardenas gingerly approaches Jeff's prone body, pistol held down at his side.

Jeff jumps to his feet and races toward a hedgerow, and there is a ka-thunk and a ka-thunk when two bullets plow harmlessly into Lightfoot's backpack full of hundred-dollar bills.

Jeff leaps over the hedge and sprints across the lawn of one of the mansions that line the park like upper-crust track homes for New Orleans' haut-monde. He dives through a set of closed French doors. A house alarm, loud as a hurricane warning-siren, has barely begun to shriek across Audubon Park before sirens of a dozen police cars, racing to what the cops think is the rescue of an upper-crust citizen's possessions, add to the commotion.

From across the street, curious Tulane students and their professors pour out of Gibson and Dinwiddie Halls. They line the sidewalks, some jeering and others cheering, as Cardenas runs back to his car with his pistol flailing the air.

Cardenas trips across the center curbing and falls, bashing the side of his head against the door of the Jaguar to a smattering of applause from the student critics. The pistol flies from his hand and lands out of his reach under the car. Cardenas opens the car door and crawls in. Tires smoke black rubber as the Jaguar squeals away with three squad cars in close pursuit.

**

As the siren shrieks fade down Saint Charles Avenue and students drift back toward Dinwiddie Hall, Cynthia takes my hand and motions for the others to follow. She tugs me across Audubon Park to where Jeff had disappeared into the row of mansions and spreads a brightly colored quilt on the grass next to the hedgerow.

We watch the mansion doors for signs of Jeff. We nibble at sliced cheeses and wheat crackers and black and white cookies filled with cream. We watch police search the mansions and surrounding grounds. Donny tosses a found frisbee toward Ronnie that skids off his forehead into a thorn bush. Freddie Fender sits cross-legged on the grass. He mumbles insults at cards in games of solitaire.

Jana, the voodoo priestess, and her charge, Johnny Ray Boudreaux, have moved to folding chairs. Like royalty, they sit at a classy wooden card table, not fifteen feet from us, nursing milk from crystal glasses while sampling fancy finger sandwiches with sweet pickles from hand-painted china plates trimmed in gold leaf.

A firefighter's cry from inside the mansion nearest us draws our attention.

"There's blood on the kitchen door jamb here," he calls out.

Three cops run to the firefighter's cry with guns drawn. There are shouts and replies and sounds of hurried footsteps muffled by mansion walls as cops scurry here and there across hardwood floors.

Two officers full of purpose, rookies I would judge from their youthful appearance and neatly pressed trousers, approach us with note pads drawn. They ask our names and where we live and what brings us to New Orleans and what did we see? Can we describe the shooter? Did we know the man who was shot?

We all have variations of the same reply. *It happened so fast, officer—I am afraid I didn't see much of anything, really.*

One of the rookies is about to give me a third degree that could easily put me on a bus back to Winslow State Prison for any number of parole violations when his captain motions for him to come back to the mansion. Within minutes the search for Jeff is over. The cops file back to their squad cars and speed away in all directions with suddenly more pressing business in mind.

"God, I didn't think they would ever leave," Donny says. "What do you suppose that was about, Gille? Why was that man shooting at Jeffrey?"

I shake my head. "I have no idea," I say.

At the sound of an approaching trolley, I turn in time to see Jana and Johnny Ray standing, hand in hand, waiting next to the tracks. I wave a farewell to them as they board the trolley, but they give no sign they have seen me.

With some fanfare, Donny opens a bag of goodies he picked up at a liquor store while we were waiting at the Canal Street trolley stop. In the bag are plastic wine glasses for all and three bottles of a reasonable Cabernet.

At last triumphant at solitaire and returned to good spirits, Freddie opens the bottles and pours each of us three fingers of wine. We click our glasses in a lighthearted toast to Jeff Lightfoot, to life and new friends, and to John Audubon, himself the illegitimate son of a Creole servant and her master.

We relax into spirited conversation there and have other, more liberal, pours.

**

The sun tops the park's oldest Oak trees on its descent to the western horizon. At Cynthia's call, we rise as one from our afternoon idle, we Mad Hatters and acrobats and Bourbon House avengers, and follow her lead down a cobblestone path to the Audubon Zoo.

23

Pink Flamingos

Of the twenty pink flamingos standing sentinel at the Audubon Zoo, only one acknowledges our approach to the ticket master's kiosk. With subtle nod and side-eyed glance, he shifts his stance from one leg to two before joining the others in silent disregard, shin deep among the display of tropical plants in their fresh-water pool.

I lean in and place a stack of crumpled bills on the kiosk counter. Without looking up, the old ticket master says, "I have bad news and good news folks–what's your pleasure?"

A familiar thatch of unruly gray hair sticks out from the sides of the ticket master's blue-striped cap. A curly-cue pipe I recognize rests in an ashtray on the kiosk counter near his elbow.

For the moment, I feign a lack of recognition. "Personally, I prefer the good," is all I say.

"The good it is then," he says, but makes no further reply. He shuffles through a sheaf of papers as if in search of a document of utmost importance.

"What are you doing here, Albert?" I finally ask.

"I work here, buddy-boy," he says.

"Buddy-boy?" I say.

Sensing an impasse in the making, Cynthia nudges me aside and leans in against the ticket master's kiosk counter.

"Why don't we begin with the bad news, sir?" she asks Albert. "Could we do that?" she says.

Albert looks up and a beam of light breaks through the clouds as his eyes are struck with Cynthia's radiant smile. His chalky complexion warms in the glow. His face, a topical map of wrinkles and ridges before, turns smooth as burnished silk.

Albert points over his shoulder at a clock hanging on the wall behind him. "The bad news is the park closes at four, my dear, and as you see it's a quarter till four now."

"Oh my," Cynthia says. "We've come so far. And the good news?"

"The good news? Yes, of course. The good news is that I have been made ticket master for the day."

"I suppose congratulations are in order," Cynthia says, "but why exactly is that good news for us, sir?"

"It's good news for you because I've decided the zoo should remain open until dusk today for you and your friends." Albert motions for me to take my wad of dollar bills off the counter. "My treat," he says.

"Oh, thank you, mister ticket master" Cynthia says.

"Yes, thank you, Albert," I say.

"Think nothing of it, my dear" Albert says, pointedly acknowledging only Cynthia with his reply.

**

"Wait," Einstein calls out to us as we turn toward the zoo's gated entry. He pulls down a wooden shade, steps out, and locks the kiosk door. He follows us into the zoo and chains the double gates closed behind us.

As the final few stragglers are escorted to the exits, the sky turns cerulean and a late afternoon breeze hurries the last strands of threatening clouds toward Westwego.

Workers busily close concession stands. A man in coveralls drives a small red tractor across our path pulling a wagon heaped with pungent fresh dung and straw. A midget clown passes by — he turns back toward Cynthia. He hands her his clutch of a dozen yellow and red and blue helium-filled balloons.

"These were meant for you, my dear," the midget clown says.

"Why thank you, mister clown," Cynthia says.

The clown tips his purple derby and a single yellow daisy sprouts upright from a toupee of plastic grass on the crown of his head.

"The pleasure is mine, my dear," the clown says.

Cynthia shares the balloons with Donny and Ronnie as the three climb a walking bridge across a water-filled moat into the land of tigers and lions and a pair of famous Audubon gorillas named Edward and Eloise. Freddie Fender, leaned forward in his urgent quest, paddles past them in search of a toilet.

**

Ed motions toward chairs at a roundtable near the edge of the flamingo pool. "Shall we sit," he says, "or would you gentlemen rather traipse along with the children?"

I shake my head. Events of the day have left me with a lack of interest in shagging after reptiles or gorillas. I plop down on the nearest chair. Ed drags a chair maybe ten feet from the table where I'm sitting to the edge of the flamingo pool and sits facing the water. He pulls a crumpled bag of pumpkin seeds from his pocket and casts a few onto the water.

Einstein joins me at the table. He takes a pipe from his pocket and fills the bowl with clippings of Prince Albert tobacco.

"Got a match?" he asks.

I take a book of matches from my Mad Hatter's hatband, strike one, and cup my hands to hold the flame. Albert inhales in short draws until the tobacco glows red in the pipe bowl. Exhaled smoke drifts across the tabletops toward the nearby concession stand sign advertising Coney dogs, and a larger sign warning that there will be a two-hundred-dollar fine waiting for anyone caught smoking in the zoo.

"I love hot dogs," Einstein says. "A steamy-hot Coney dog with onions and mustard — when the weather's cool, like it is today—you can't beat that. Care for a Coney dog, Gille?"

"I couldn't say no to a Coney dog," I answer.

"I'd like one of those dogs while you're at it, please," Ed says, casting more seeds into the pool. "Extra mustard and onion would be nice, and maybe a bag of chips–the barbecue-flavored kind–and a Coke."

"Anything else you can think of?" Einstein says. "I hear this is lobster night at Antoine's. I could skip on down there and pick one of those bad boys up for you if you'd like."

"Oh, no thanks, Albert, no need to go out of your way, but it is kind of you to ask," Ed says.

Apparently, kibitzing with one of the world's most famous men, dead or alive, leaves no impression on Ed, or maybe he thinks he is talking to an Einstein pretender.

**

Albert sets a tray stacked high with Coney dogs and bags of chips of various flavors on our table. He pulls three cans of soda and a handful of mustard packets from his jacket.

"There you go," Albert says, "caught the girl just as she was putting her dogs away for the night."

Ed pops the top on a soda. He squeezes a double trail of mustard down the center of his Coney dog, takes a bite, and sucks for air.

"Damn that's hot, but undoubtedly as good a dog as any I've had. Thank you, Albert."

"You're entirely welcome, Mister Sheehan," Einstein says.

Ed turns back toward the flamingos, throws a few pumpkin seeds into the air, and watches them drift down toward the water.

"What do you know about flamingos, Albert?" Ed asks.

"There's a sign there that says you shouldn't feed them — that's about all I know," Einstein says. "They seem harmless enough though, and I do like pink."

"Not exactly an expert when it comes to color are you, Albert. Granted there are pink flamingos, but these are coral," Ed says. "I suppose you know why they are that color."

Einstein thinks for a moment. "No, I can't say that I do."

"You are *the* Albert Einstein, right?" Ed says.

Ed does know an Einstein when he sees one after all.

Albert nods his head. "Yes, that I am."

"I suppose even an Einstein can't know everything," Ed says. "Anyway, it's what these flamingos eat that makes them that color.

259

They are born gray, but they eat things rich in something called carotene, like these pumpkin seeds, for instance." He casts another handful into the pond.

"Carotene, you say," Einstein says.

"Yeah, carotene — same stuff that makes carrots orange, so I've been told."

"I *have* heard that about carrots," Albert says.

Sheehan arches an eyebrow at Albert's comment before continuing. "Anyway, whatever it is, there's enough of it in their diet to turn them from gray to shades of coral. The males are more colorful but it's that carotene that makes all of them more pleasant to the eye."

"Good grief, Albert — it seems we have a nature guide among us," I say.

Einstein smiles and nods in agreement.

"Another thing about flamingos," Ed continues, ignoring my impudence, "unlike most of our feathered friends, flamingo lay only one egg each year and that egg is white as a chicken's. Did you know that?"

"No, I can't say that I did," says Albert. His interest is flagging.

"And a flamingo has only one mate—monogamous, that's what flamingos are. How about that, Mister Einstein?"

"I'm guessing that's a hard cross to bear," says Albert.

**

Ed motions his hand in the general direction of the flamingo pool. "You know what they call a group of flamingos like we have here?" he asks.

"A flock?" says Einstein, now resigned to his fate.

"A colony — that's a colony of flamingo's right there."

"Hmm," Albert says.

"I tell you, Albert, the more you learn about flamingos, the more you realize what an amazingly varied bird they are," Ed says. "Some are coral, like these. Others are almost a crimson color, but there are white and black, and even blue flamingos — and all sizes too.

"I'd say these flamingos are of a medium size. Some are no taller than a kindergarten kid — others, like the ones down in Brazil, I've been told, stand as tall as a man of six feet, maybe more."

"You don't say."

"Of course, flamingos have those skinny-assed legs and long necks, and they *are* birds, you know, so their bones are hollow.

"How much do you think a flamingo might weigh, Albert?"

"I have no idea."

"Take a guess."

"One of the big ones?"

"Sure. How much would you say a flamingo six feet tall from down in Brazil weighs? Just take a guess."

Einstein parodies contemplation. "I'll say thirty pounds."

"The biggest flamingos weigh no more than nine — five or six for these we have here."

"That's hard to believe."

"Well, it's true, whether you believe it or not."

"Oh, I don't doubt it. I'm sure you know what you're talking about, Mister Sheehan."

"There's another little piece of flamingo trivia you might find interesting," Ed says.

"I'm listening," Albert claims while exhibiting far more interest in the last bite of his Coney dog.

"A flamingo won't look you in the eye," Ed says. "He might acknowledge you with a blink or a nod, but he will never face you straight on and look you in the eye. My first wife got that way. I didn't understand what was up until I caught her fucking Benny Dunlap, our next door neighbor. I could never trust a flamingo."

Overdosed on Coney dogs and flamingos, I feel the need for a nap. I lean forward, my elbows against the tabletop, my head cradled in my hands. In that suspended state, I fix my empty gaze on a flamingo not more than a dozen feet from my table, daring him to look into my eyes.

Ed Sheehan casts his last seeds onto the pond. He could well be as mad as the hatter of his disguise. For that matter, so could I.

**

"Enough of my flamingo talk," Ed says to Albert. "What about you?"

"What do you mean, what about me?" Einstein says.

"Well, your thoughts on time travel for one thing. From the little I have read, I gather you have some strong opinions on that. It's all so damn puzzling to me — time travel, and spacetime too, I believe that's what you call it."

"Is there a question there, Mister Sheehan?"

"Well, the way I get it, you believe time doesn't exist–or that space and time are one and the same, and all things that happen, whether in what most of us call the past or think of as the future, are just there, frozen in space the same as now is now. In other words, my lunch date a week ago Saturday at Brennan's as well as the day of my eventual demise are out there, stacked in space like so many slices in a really big loaf of bread."

"It would seem you are suggesting I believe the future is among those 'slices' to which you refer and our 'now' just hasn't arrived at that inevitable point yet," Einstein says.

"Yes, that would be part of it — that's the impression I have been given."

"Uh huh." Albert puffs on his pipe and leans back on his chair. He clasps his hands behind his head and closes his eyes.

"And, if that is the way of things," Ed says, "if that is the way of it, I could travel back to one of those space slices—or, for that matter, forward into a future slice — if I knew the mumbo-jumbo to the routine. What is your thought on that, Mister Einstein? Is travel to another time possible? Could Madeline and I pop back to Brennan's a week ago Saturday for a second go at that Praline Anglaise Bread Pudding special of the day?"

Einstein taps the tobacco ash from his pipe onto the table and whisks it away with the back of his hand. He pushes his chair back and stands next to the table. He looks down at Ed and slowly claps his hands in applause.

He turns toward me and shakes my hand.

"Gille; it's been a pleasure," Albert says.

He turns his attention back toward Ed and smiles.

262

"You know, Mister Sheehan, I believe you are far more intelligent than you look," Einstein says.

He places his hand on Ed's shoulder.

"As to your question, Ed, take this thought into consideration as we fly through the Universe on a twirling speck of dust at the edge of the Milky Way. Here we are, in front of this colony of beautiful flamingos, you and I and Gille, in this place we all know as New Orleans. Just how do you think three paths as disparate as ours came to cross at *this* here and now?"

Ed calls after Einstein, who has turned and is walking away. "At this here and now? What the hell is that supposed to mean, Albert? What does that *mean* to *me*, Professor Einstein?"

Einstein gives no reply. He does not look back. He hoists a hand to the side of his head in a sign of farewell as he walks away through the closed zoo gate into Audubon Park.

Ed shrugs his shoulders and returns his attention to the flamingos.

Freddie Fender appears from around the corner of the concession stand. He drags a chair next to Ed's.

"Well now, this is a pleasant surprise." Ed pats Freddie on the back. He looks at his watch. It has been almost an hour since Freddie left us in search of a toilet.

"I thought the gators got you, my friend," Ed says.

"Jesus, you're not far from right. I've been all over this damned zoo," says Freddie. "I went over to those arrow-shaped signs by the bridge there." He points toward the arched cobblestone moat bridge that leads to the 'Wild Kingdom'.

"In case you can't read it from here, 'restrooms' is painted on that top arrow, so I took that path. The building wasn't far, but the door to the men's room was locked, so now I was in real trouble, what with the anticipation and all. You know how that works."

"I certainly do, my friend," Ed says. "Reminds me of the time I was stuck in the elevator at the top of Chicago's Sears Tower, world's tallest building at the time, as I recall — restrooms almost within smelling distance, and ——"

Cutting Ed short, Freddie says, "So I tried the women's toilet door."

"Locked, I suppose," says Ed.

"Tight as a drum. Could I have a swig of that soda?"

"Sure thing–help yourself."

Freddie takes a deep draw through the straw of Ed's soda.

"Then I came to 'Swampland'," Freddie continues, "and it must have been feeding time because there were a dozen gators, all of them twelve or fifteen feet long, maybe more, standing around right up next to the pathway.

"You should see the teeth on those things, Ed — scary as hell. I did see a building with toilet doors on the side twenty paces past those gators, and wouldn't you know it, one of the doors was ajar."

"So?"

"So, nothing. I hiked down another path past some elephants and a couple of white tigers and a cage full of screaming monkeys that scared the hell out of me. Finally, I came to some bushes next to a big Oak tree and ducked in there." Freddie leans back in his chair. "Now that's what relief is all about, my friends," he says.

"Don't take this wrong, Freddie," I say, "I'm delighted your venture into the Wild Kingdom had a swell ending. It made for a fascinating story too, it really did, but I have to ask — why didn't you use the toilet over there?"

I nod toward the concession stand.

"Over there?" Freddie attempts to follow my nod.

"By the sign," I say.

"What sign?"

"That sign." I point to a restroom sign hanging next to the menu on the corner of the concession stand where Einstein purchased our Coney dogs, not fifteen feet behind me.

Freddie smacks his forehead with his palm. "You've got to be kidding."

"I don't think so," I say, "and it seems drinking that extra-large soda has given me good reason for further investigation." I scoot my chair away from the table, stand, and stretch my legs.

"Now, if you will excuse me, gentlemen," I say.

24

The Turquoise Room

Against the resistance of its automatic closer, I tug the restroom door open. Other than the slightest light flickering between blades of an exhaust fan high in the corner of a far wall, the room is dark. Ominous shadows cast across the room as the fan blades slowly whirl one way and then the other at the whim of a fickle evening breeze.

Bracing the door open with my heel, I find the light switch and click it—first up and then down, and again, but there is no light. The door slams closed behind me as I step into the darkness. I lean against the wall and wait while my eyes dial in the faintest of forms.

It seems I am not alone. I hear the quick shuffling of leather soled shoes at the far end of the room and a rodent's scuttle across the slick tile floor. Rats carry on in agitated conversation from inside the cinderblock walls. I struggle to calm my senses.

My eyes adjust somewhat to the dark. Toilet stalls line the wall against which I lean and stretch away into the darkness. I count their reflections in the row of sink mirrors mounted to the wall across the way until those mirrors fade in the distant veil.

Facing the wall of mirrors, I feel my way along the bank of toilet stalls. A stall door swings open at my slightest lean. I stumble backward inside, quickly regain my balance, and latch the door behind me.

In the stall there is an antique canopy bed visible in light like that of a quarter moon. I take off my shoes and climb onto the bed. In a sitting position, my legs stretched out in front of me, I rest my back on pillows stacked against the headboard. Next to me is a bedside table and brass lamp with a shade of leaded ruby and emerald cuts of glass. An ancient wardrobe floats suspended above the stall's white porcelain commode.

A cushy lounge chair, its wide arms covered in a fabric of red-wine velvet, sits at the foot of the bed. And in that chair is Albert Einstein. He draws on his pipe — his eyes nearly sparkle in the amber glow.

I ask Albert what he is doing here.

"I should be asking you that question — this *is* my room," says Einstein.

"What?"

"This is *my* room, Gille."

Mystified by Einstein's claim, I make no reply. Instead, I scoot down from the headboard until I am flat on the canopy bed, my head resting on a single pillow. I am tired. Gazing up past the quarter moon and beyond the thousands of stars, I drift into the bed canopy's black velvet void.

**

I awake to an insistent rapping at the stall door.

"Mister Barker? — Are you in there, Mister Barker?" The voice from the other side, though muffled, is menacing; I think I have heard the voice before. Is it the voice of Gene Cardenas? How did he find me here?

"What do you want?" I ask.

In a futile effort to alter this reality, I pull the bed covers over my head.

"Mister Barker?"

"I can't help you," I shout to the voice from the other side of the restroom door, "I don't have your money."

The knocking becomes more insistent.

Einstein walks to the side of the bed and rests his hand on mine. I pull the covers from my face and look up at him.

"Have I gone mad, Albert?" I ask.

266

I interpret his sympathetic smile indicates he believes that may be true.

"What should I do, Albert?" I ask the old dead theorist, certain in my belief he will have the answer to my plea.

"What should I do?" I say.

Albert pats my hand. "No one knows the future, Gille," he says. "I suggest you find a safe place — a place out of harm's way."

"What?" The gears whir in my brain.

"Damn it, Albert," I say, "is that the best advice you have to offer?"

"The truth is you should pay no attention to me, son," Einstein says, "I deal in theory and have no idea what is *really* going on."

**

The door rattles as the intruder bangs his fist against its frame. Eyes wide open, I spring upright in my bed.

"Mister Barker? Are you in there, Mister Barker?" comes the query again.

"Yes, yes," I reply, "a moment, please."

I survey my surroundings, and for that moment am puzzled by what I see.

My thoughts are interrupted by the voice calling out to me from outside what I now realize is my La Posada hotel room door.

"The front desk tried to call you, Mister Barker, but there was no answer," the voice says.

A glance toward my nightstand verifies that the red message light is blinking on the bedside phone.

"Is there a problem?" I ask.

"No problem, Mister Barker; it's just that no one has heard from you since you checked in. When you didn't answer our calls, Anna asked that I look in on you, sir"

I open the door slightly.

"Please tell Anna I'm fine," I say to the young messenger boy standing there, "and that I'm sorry for your trouble."

"Yes sir— anything I can do for you, Mister Barker?"

"Could you tell me what time the restaurant closes?"

"They accept orders until nine, sir. It is just past seven now. Thank you," I say.

Still tired, I return to bed and fall back against my pillow. My eyes close.

**

I brush my fingers across the satin sheets. I grasp a canopy post and shake it—it is real. Unsteady, I stand. I touch the velvet cover of the armchair on which Einstein sits again at the end of my bed. I rest my hand on Einstein's shoulder. Paying me no attention, he blows doughnut-sized smoke rings across the foot of the bed. I smell the tobacco. The man is real—he is sitting in that chair at my side.

"You look a little peeked, Gille," Einstein says.

"I look a little peeked, you say. Jesus, Albert, tell me what's happening here?"

"Why would you think I know?"

"Because you're Albert Einstein?

"I'm afraid my being Albert Einstein carries little weight in this case. However, due to the circumstance of my 'situation', there are a few things I know that might interest you."

"And what 'situation' is that, Albert?" I ask.

"You do realize you're talking to a man considered dead in your space and time, don't you, Gille?"

"Of course," I say, and it is true that I do, although that realization had slipped my mind.

"Please continue, Albert," I say.

"Well, to begin with, I can travel through time with no more effort than a snap of my fingers," Einstein says, snapping his fingers close by the tip of my nose, "and I believe that you, along with many others of your circumstance, can do the same.

"What the hell are you talking about, Albert?" I say. "I think I would know it if I were spending weekends zipping through spacetime."

"You would have no idea. One slice of time is no more real than the next."

"That doesn't seem possible."

"Well, trust me, that's the way it is. Listen, son," Einstein says, "I know time travel is possible for me. I know there are parallel Universes because I have been to a few, and though this is true, I have no way of knowing which universe we are in now— am I in yours? —are you in mine? —is there a difference? I have no idea. I *do* know dreams are the reality from time to time. There is no changing of that, no matter the universe we are in."

"But what is the *secret,* Albert?" I ask. "What is this – this *life* – all about?

"*Secret*? Don't you get it, my boy? It is as obvious as that artfully crafted nose on your face. In a Universe where no two people even live in the same reality, how can there be a *secret.* What you believe is what it is, that is the whole ball game, Gille — it is all in your head.

"What?"

"It's all a mirage, a magical sham — you make your reality up as you go, my friend — hocus-pocus is what life is about."

I sit in silence, contemplating the old time-traveler's eyes, but there is no hint of the sarcasm I expect to see.

I am half listening as Albert drones on about spacetime tricksters and black hole hoaxers until his words become indecipherable and his image dissolves like a fading hologram into nothingness.

**

In bed, my head is spinning. I open my eyes and look at the clock; it is five minutes after eight.

I look around the room. My carry bag sits on the floor under the window, the same carry bag in which I had stuffed the paper sack full of hundred-dollar bills Lightfoot left for me in our room at New Orleans' Saint Ann/Marie Antoinette Hotel.

I open the carry bag. I sort through socks and undergarments and a souvenir French Quarter T-shirt with skeletons playing trombones silk-screened across its back, and there, sitting on the bottom of the bag, is a brown paper sack tied closed with butcher's twine.

I walk to the bathroom and splash my face with cold water. I turn the shower knobs open. I brush my teeth, gargle, and brush again. I adjust the shower until steam curls over the top of the enclosure door.

Hot water and lather cascade down my body and swirl into the drain. I am still tired. How can that be? What were those pills Lightfoot gave me? I turn the hot water off and stick my head under the icy cold shower spray.

As I dry, I hear a noise. Thinking Einstein may have returned, I call his name, but there is no answer. I open the bathroom door slightly and peek into the room.

"Albert?" I inquire.

Again, there is no reply. I see that the chair he was sitting on at the foot of my bed has been moved back to its original position against the wall.

Within moments I am dressed and on my way to La Posada's Turquoise Dining Room.

**

As I approach the Turquoise Room, muffled voices and laughter filter into the hallway from the Martini Lounge. Anna Towahongva stands next to the host-station dais awaiting my arrival. Anna's resemblance to Cynthia Canales is striking. How curious that had escaped my notice before.

"It's so good to see you, Mister Barker," Anna says. "I didn't want to disturb you but became anxious when you didn't answer my call."

"Thank you for your concern, Anna."

"You're welcome. One for dinner?"

"Yes, please."

There are only four couples scattered among the tables in the grand dining hall of the Turquoise Room. A beautiful lady with long auburn hair sits alone at a corner table against the back wall. She is looking out a table-side window toward La Posada's rail station, not more than fifteen yards away across the veranda. A single light above the station entry sways in the gathering breeze. Small pellets of sleet, the beginnings of a high-desert winter storm, bounce on the flagstone walkway to the station.

"How about there?" I say to Anna, pointing toward a booth three tables from the woman with the auburn hair.

Anna leads me across the room and waits while I slide to the center of the horseshoe-shaped booth, my back against the wall. My time in the prison cafeteria surrounded by murderers and rapists and plainly ill-tempered souls who, at least in my imaginings, would stab me in the heart for my cup of syrupy mixed fruit, even if they hated mixed fruit of any kind, had made it important to sit with my back to a wall whenever possible. It remains so to this day.

Anna hands me a menu and moves aside. A girl steps forward and pours me a glass of iced water.

"This is Gwen; she will be your server tonight," Anna says.

"Good evening, Mister Barker," Gwen says, as Anna walks away.

Gwen has a mouth full of braces that sparkle like fine silver. She looks at her watch. "Not to rush you, sir," she says, "but your order should be in the kitchen by nine. Would you like a few minutes?"

"What time is it, Gwen?"

"It's a quarter till. We have time. Could I get you something from the bar?"

I ask Gwen for a Budweiser.

I stare at the fancy script on the double-faced menu. 'Churro Lamb — Braised Duck and Sausage — Wild Turkey Pâté — Halibut Fillet 'flown in fresh from Ninilchik, Alaska this morning'. Those items and a dozen more meld together in my mind. It is as if I have forgotten how to process a restaurant menu.

And it just so happens a highly entertaining resident of Ninilchik considers my Maui Outrigger bar his home on his frequent trips to Hawaii — I am familiar with Ninilchik. There is no way to get a Halibut from Alaska's Kenai Peninsula to the La Posada kitchen in Winslow, Arizona without at least three stops along the way. Fresh halibut indeed. I close the menu and set it on the corner of the table.

Gwen brings a basket of fresh breads and whipped butter to the table. She sets my bottle of beer and a frosty glass on coasters in front of me.

"May I have your order now, sir?"

"All I really want is one of your beef burgers, but they don't seem to be on the menu."

"Oh, I'm sure I can take care of that, Mister Barker. I'll just give the chef's arm a little twist. What would you like on that, sir?"

"Your goat cheese with all the trimmings–and a slice of dill pickle on the side, please."

"Sure thing."

"Oh, and a glass of Cabernet when you bring the sandwich, please."

"Yes sir. You should try that warm bread while you wait, Mister Barker. There's white and pumpernickel – my favorite. My sister-in-law bakes it fresh every morning."

"I'll do that. Thank you, Gwen."

**

I splash Tabasco and Worcestershire on my burger. I pile Romaine lettuce and sliced tomatoes and Kula onions on top. I spread a tablespoon of Dijon across the bun. Some say the proper method for applying Dijon is directly on the burger, but I disagree. I push down on the sandwich with my fingers until the juices from the sauces mingle with those of the burger and drizzle to the plate.

So much for Halibut flown fresh from Ninilchik this morning or Wild Turkey Pâté with cherries and hazelnuts.

While enjoying my sandwich, I can not help but observe Gwen at the waiter station, only a few steps to my side, sorting through her mug of tips. She throws the coins in a plastic jar and twirls the lid closed. She straightens and counts a wad of bills and sticks them in her purse. From her unguarded expression, I would guess the tip total was not as much as hoped for but better than it had seemed. She looks past me and across the nearly empty room. I guess Gwen to be at least seventeen, and this is the weekend. I know what she is thinking — *finish your damned sandwich, Barker, so I can get out of here.*

Gwen sees me looking toward her and feigns a hard but pleasant smile. I feign one of my best back her way.

A young couple is sitting at a table in the center of the room, their chairs close, side by side. They smile secret smiles. They

272

touch. They talk and laugh in confidential ways. Newlyweds on honeymoon? That could be. Lovers on careless holiday? More likely so.

My eyes come to rest on the profile of the lady with auburn hair sitting alone at her window table, her finger looped through the handle of a steaming cup. Her gaze through the window is seemingly fixed on the entry to the rail station, as it had been when I first entered the room. The icy rain has turned to snow. Flakes hit the window at her side, streaking the panes with rivers of melted light.

The woman looks so familiar. She could be an actress I had seen on stage or someone I met on the beaches of Keawakapu on the island of Maui that is still my home. Maybe she is the pretty tomboy with flaming red hair I had a crush on until she wiped out my prized collection of Milky Ways in a single afternoon recess on the playground of Mason City Eastside Elementary.

So long ago — what was that girl's name?
**

The lady with auburn hair gently places her cup back on its saucer. She turns toward me. Her eyes meet mine. They are the color of translucent emeralds. I am embarrassed, like a stalker caught at his stalking. I turn away. My elbow slides across the table knocking my napkin to the floor. I reach under the table to retrieve the napkin.

When I sit back up, the lady is standing in front of me. She is tall and slender and beautiful, even more beautiful than she had seemed from afar. Her smile – Jesus, that smile. I *do* know her!

"Could I have your autograph, Mister Barker?" she says.

"Belinda?"

Startled, I jump up to greet her, knocking my glass of Cabernet crashing to the floor.

I wipe traces of the spill from the plastic bench seat of my booth with a napkin while Gwen and her busboy mop up the spilled wine and shards of glass. After apologies to everyone — Gwen, the busboy, Belinda, the secretive lovers sitting four tables away — I ask Belinda to join me.

She slides into the booth beside me. I take her hand in mine.

"It's so good to see you, Gille," Belinda says. "I swear, you haven't changed since that night I took you home with me from Claire's. You were such a beautiful boy then."

"Well, I wouldn't go that far," I manage to say.

"You *do* remember that night, don't you, Gille?"

"I could never forget that night."

"What has it been, twenty years?"

I nod yes while thinking it might have been twenty years, or yesterday, or not have been at all in this space of time. A dream can be the reality and reality the dream — that I know.

Belinda brushes her fingers through my now graying hair.

She rests her cheek against my shoulder.

"Care for a cocktail?" I say.

The End

G. Rodgers Brinner

George Brinner

In 2015, thirty some years after the over-night delay that resulted in my extended stay on the island of Maui, I, along with Jodi (Georgette Kaapo'okalani), my life partner for the last twenty of those years, packed our bags and moved to the middle of the Arizona desert. That is only relevant here because, though this work is fiction, that history and Jodi's death six months after our move to the mainland led to my writing of 'Einstein in Flamingoland'.

Other locations of note in 'Einstein' are Winslow, Arizona's La Posada Hotel and the French Quarter that was my home while a student at New Orleans' Tulane University.

A prequel to this surreal world of Gille Barker moves to Chicago and Indianapolis and the farm town of Mason City, Illinois, my hometown. At this writing, it is in progress.

Paintings by George Brinner
www.brinnerart.com

George Brinner's paintings are in private and public collections across the USA, Europe, and Japan. They are included in the public collections of the Houston Museum of Art, Tulane University, The Blaffer Foundation Collection, and the Hawaii State Foundation for Culture and the Arts. Jury selections of note include The Illinois Artist's Exhibition at the Chicago Art Institute and three Indiana Artist's Annual Exhibitions. Over the years, more than twenty pieces have been accepted by jury to the prestigious Annual Art Maui Exhibitions. Mister Brinner was one of only four painters selected for both the first and second editions of Hawaii's Schaefer Portrait Challenge and one of the eleven artists selected for inclusion in the singular 'Witness to Time' exhibition in recognition of the art of Edward Bailey and the Bailey House Museum

Keawakapu Beach IV   34"x 60" Oil on Canvas

"Watson Lake"   34"x 60" Oil on Canvas

"The Blue Milk Bucket"   38"x 49" Oil on Hardboard
www.brinnerart.com

"Tsunami"
48"x 30" Oil on Canvas

www.brinnerart.com

"Grand Canyon Bend"48"x 60" Oil on Canvas

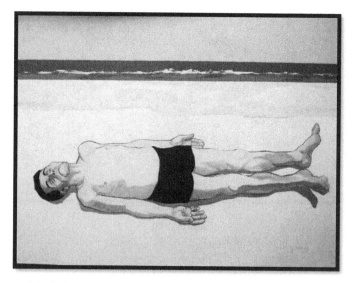

"Ralph on Keawakapu" Oil on Canvas 36"x 48"
www.brinnerart.com

"Red Rock Canyon" Oil on Canvas 34"x 60"

"Options" Oil on Canvas 48"x 60"
www.brinnerart.com

"The Aloha Shirt" Oil on Canvas 36"x 18"